DOWN ISLAND

DOWN ISLAND

A Novel of the Caribbean

Mark R. Hill

iUniverse, Inc.
New York Lincoln Shanghai

Down Island
A Novel of the Caribbean

iUniverse books may be ordered through booksellers or by contacting:

iUniverse
2021 Pine Lake Road, Suite 100
Lincoln, NE 68512
www.iuniverse.com
1-800-Authors (1-800-288-4677)

This is a work of fiction. All of the characters, names, incidents, organizations and dialogue in this novel are either the products of the author's imagination or are used fictitiously.

ISBN-13: 978-0-595-38402-0 (pbk)
ISBN-13: 978-0-595-82810-4 (cloth)
ISBN-13: 978-0-595-82776-3 (ebk)
ISBN-10: 0-595-38402-1 (pbk)
ISBN-10: 0-595-82810-8 (cloth)
ISBN-10: 0-595-82776-4 (ebk)

Printed in the United States of America

"Fifteen men on the Dead Man's Chest—

Yo-ho-ho, and a bottle of rum!"

—Robert Louis Stevenson

For Patricia,

my first mate.

British Virgin Islands

Payback's Path

0   1   2   3   4   5
Nautical Miles

Anegada

Necker Island
Prickly Pear Island
Mosquito Island
Virgin Gorda
Seal Dogs
George Bog
West Dog
Scrub Island
Marina Cove
Great Camanoe
Guana
Beef Island
Tortola
Jost Van Dyke
Little Tobago
Tobago
Great Thatch
St. Thomas
St. John
Peter Island
Norman Island
Dead Chest
Salt Island
Cooper Island
Ginger Island
Fallen Jerusalem

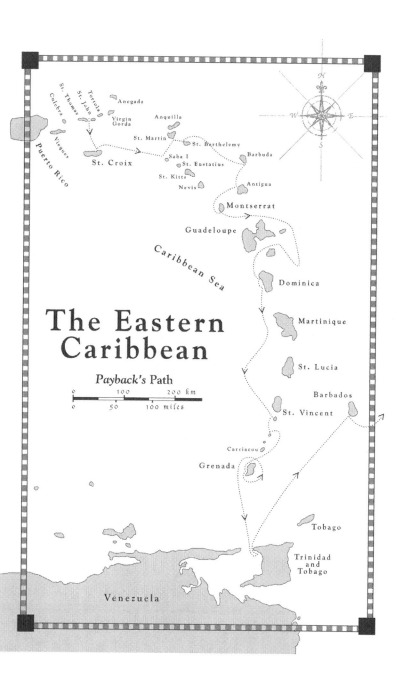

The Eastern Caribbean

Payback's Path

CHAPTER 1

▼

TRINIDAD

Cassie MacDuff Spencer suddenly woke up with a cold rifle muzzle under her chin. A young, white man dragged her topside just in time for her to see two solidly built, Hispanic men holding her friend, Leo, and walking him to the transom of the *Moby Dick*. Leo had a jagged head wound and was bleeding all over the pristine deck.

"Hey, Hunter. You only find one *chica* down there?" asked one of the Latinos.

"Stop!" she screamed. "Just leave him alone and take what you want."

"We're already taking what we want," laughed Hunter as he gestured with the rifle. "Your grandpa here never even heard us coming up astern."

As Cassie struggled to break lose of Hunter's grip, Leo appeared to summon up a final spasm of effort. He broke free of the two men holding him, lowered his head like an angry rhino, and charged toward Hunter. Still holding Cassie, Hunter reached down with his free hand and instantly came up with a boot knife. He deftly moved sideways and slashed Leo's throat when the heavy man thundered by.

Cassie screamed. Leo's momentum kept him moving. His lifeblood jetted across the teak deck. Leo hit the gunwale and toppled overboard.

Cassie sobbed as Leo's body drifted away. "Why? Why? He was only a sweet, old man who couldn't hurt anybody."

"Maybe he was, and maybe he wasn't, but slicing him made damn sure. Dead men tell no tales," Hunter recited, almost singing the last part melodramatically.

The two crewmen watched to be sure Leo was dead. Then the taller one went back aboard the smaller motorboat tied alongside *Moby Dick*. The shorter one advanced toward her. Cassie knew she was next and quickly suppressed her grief and surprise. She knew she had to save her own life now. Cassie pasted a smile on her face as she turned toward the men.

"Okay, guys. Take it easy, now. He was a nice old fellow and paid me real well, but I don't totally know him. Look, I was just hired from the escort service in Vegas to ride this boat with him for a couple of weeks and keep him happy." Cassie smiled and flipped her hair while she lied to them. Her stomach churned when she thought about how savagely these men had murdered Leo, and she firmly braced one arm against her stomach to keep herself from throwing up. But she knew that if she didn't keep her cool and contain her fear, there was an awfully good chance she'd end up like Leo. Or worse.

"Who are you guys, anyway?" She tried to say this as nonchalantly as possible, as if they were just drunk patrons asking for her number back in Vegas.

The crewman started toward her again, and maneuvered to corner her.

"Hold it, Garcia. Y'all leave her alone a minute while I think this over," said the thin white man as he ran his eyes up and down Cassie's body.

"It is your call, *Señor* Hunter. We have our own women," Garcia said with a shrug and went over to help untie the speedboat.

"Who are we? Madame, I must tell you we are honest-to-god pirates, and you are our captive," the man said with an exaggerated flourish of an imaginary hat. "I am Captain Hunter Lamar Schoenholz, and I'd like to introduce you to Mr. Garcia and to Mr. Sanchez, over there on the other boat."

Sanchez rolled his eyes at Hunter's continued playacting. He advanced the throttle on the motor launch and took off to take up a position ahead of the trawler. Garcia tied Cassie's hands behind her back and shoved her into a seat in the galley. He went up to the bridge to pilot *Moby Dick*. Hunter stayed behind, leaned his AK-47 against a bulkhead, and fixed himself a rum and Coke from Leo's bar.

"So, what other presents did your old man leave us?"

"I don't know. Take a look. It's all yours now." She knew she had to play for time and stay alive. "Come on, you don't have to keep me tied up. I'm no threat to you guys. Hell, where am I going to go? Anyway, I'm from Vegas, and I've seen this kind of shit before. I don't care whether you're pirates or drug smugglers or whatever.

"Listen, I've been paid for two weeks, and there's only one week left. Then I've got to get back, though, or the boss will miss me, and you sure don't want that guy mad at you. You know, maybe I could cook and clean and keep you guys company. It'll be good cover for you to have me on the boat. Besides, I know how to run all the equipment on the *Moby Dick*."

Hunter stroked his chin and appeared to consider her plea. "You're probably blowing smoke up my ass, bitch. On the other hand, a babe on the bow in a bikini will make us look like an innocent owner and his trophy wife. We'll just be cruisin' along north with our two handsome deck hands. Okay, but now we gotta get serious."

Hunter reached out, grabbed Cassie, and roughly threw her on the table. He retied her hands under the table between the supports. Hunter took the still-bloody, double-edged knife and slowly waved it near her eyes.

"Please, please, please," Cassie begged as she felt her self-control slipping away.

"Tell me your name, whore. I want to know before I cut your tongue out."

"Cassie. Cassie Spencer." She immediately regretted that she told him her real name.

"I like using a knife, Miss Cassie. I really like it. A knife is so much more up close and personal. Any faggot can kill someone from a hundred yards away with a rifle. Only a real man has the balls to get in your face and kill you with a knife," Hunter said while he bent down, pulled up her t-shirt, and pressed the point of the Gerber survival knife to her belly button. A drop of blood arose from her navel.

"Please! I'll do anything you want." Cassie flinched, but stopped herself from striking out at him. She knew this wasn't the time.

"Damn straight, you will. Listen up, you stupid split-tail. If you are a very good girl, we may take you north with us." He took the knife away from her navel and slid the point slowly downward. It created a thin red line but surprisingly little blood. "But, if you ever, ever cross me, we're going to strap you down, and all three of us are going to pork you at the same time. We're going to make you watertight. After we have our fun, I'm going to take this knife and slowly skin you alive and throw you to the sharks. You got that straight?"

Cassie quickly nodded and Hunter stood up. He wiped off the knife on the seat, slipped it back into its black sheath, and closed the thumb-snap. She let him lead her below and tie her up. She didn't beg anymore. As she walked, Cassie furtively looked around for anything she could turn into a weapon of her own.

CHAPTER 2

▼

NORMAN ISLAND

Doug Thompson drained the bottle of Blackbeard Ale then raised his voice over the din, "Yeah, we get some wild people here. Norman Island is way out on the southern edge of these islands, and it's uninhabited after the two bars close at night. You ever notice people get a little crazy at geographic far ends? Consider Key West, San Francisco, or the tip of Cape Cod. Maybe that's it. Or maybe the oddballs simply wash up there then can't go any farther."

Doug's brother, Nate, nursed his Red Stripe and watched the girl in the blue bikini hop up on the bar. With a nervous look in her eyes, she stretched out on her back as if on an Aztec sacrificial altar. The bartender took a frayed piece of halyard and loosely tied the girl's wrists around the support pole.

In spite of tonight's Caribbean heat, the bartender wore a black bandanna, patterned with white skulls and crossbones, tied tightly around his head while he worked. With a practiced ease he reached under the bar of the "Willy T," placed a lime slice on one of the girl's tanned thighs and sprinkled a pinch of margarita salt on the other.

The bartender then warned her to hold still as he poured brown tequila into her quivering navel. He shook up a can of whipped cream, carefully slid it under the top of her suit, and filled her cups with foam. At the urging of her waiting new husband, the girl unhooked the blue halter, slowly removing it to allow the bartender to complete the job while not exposing her nipples. A pair of maraschino cherries completed the buffet.

"Want me to do the bottom, too?"

Doug thought the faux pirate spoke in a surprisingly jaded tone regarding such a task.

"No way! That's good enough, man."

Doug smiled when the girl's eager husband licked off the "body shot" ingredients in the proper order—finishing with the cherries for dessert. Over the years, Doug realized he'd witnessed this tableau played out a dozen times before on the *William Thornton*, or "Willy T," an old steel-hulled schooner now permanently anchored in the harbor and functioning as Norman Island's infamous floating restaurant and bar. *William Thornton* was named for a colonial resident of the British Virgin Islands, or BVI, who'd submitted the winning architectural design for the U.S. Capitol building.

The honeymooners bounced off to rejoin their cheering new friends.

✳   ✳   ✳   ✳

"Goddamn it!" Nate said, and interrupted Doug's reverie. "I was hoping she'd take her bottom off, too."

"Hey, haven't you been the only disbeliever in the family since you were five years old?"

"Yeah, but 'goddamn' is an expression everybody uses. Anyway, being an atheist is a damn sight more honest than being a wussy agnostic like you, Doug."

Doug leaned back and gave a knowing smile. "I know, I know. I'm just jerking your rusty chain, bro'."

"In fact, old Reverend Dad might be the only guy I don't recall using a few good 'goddamns,'" Nate continued. "You pretend to be the calm and moderate grown-up now, but I remember some fire in you as a kid. Look at you now, Mr. Solid Citizen, taking his well-earned early retirement. This sailing stuff must be good for you, though. You've lost some weight, but added some muscle."

"Yeah, but you're still the tall, skinny one the girls love. I don't see any gray in that brownish-red mop on your head, either." Doug thought back on how his younger brother had always been the wild one. Nate was the black sheep in the family, both then and now. Nate had rejected every norm and every rule; yet, somehow, he could always be counted on when it really mattered. Now middle-aged, both brothers had grown up to believe a man had to live by his promises. *Strip away all crap modern society wants you to believe in, and you find keeping your word is one of the few rocks left to stand on*, thought Doug. His brother was a good man to have by one's side in times of trouble. Not that there was any trouble looming here in the islands. In fact, the fun had just started.

"Well, Nate, I guess going naked was beyond the young woman's current adventure limit. We all have our limits. I've seen some wild things in this floating bar, though. You should see me dancing the 'jump-up' here after midnight."

"Yeah, right! What a bullshitter you are! I need to buy you one of those Rasta hats with the fake dreadlocks so you fit right in then," laughed Nate.

"Hey, Bomba's and Foxy's get way out of control at certain times, too. I'll take you to those bars when we get to the west side of Tortola or over to Jost Van Dyke. You know, Nate, since you're currently the one and only honored guest on my sailboat, I'll treat you to a tour of all the best sights in the BVI. Anywhere you want to go. Here or down island."

"So what kind of wild crap have you seen right here at the Willy T, bro'?"

Doug smiled and said, "How about a daughter hearing girls get a free t-shirt for jumping off the second deck naked, convincing her mother to do it with her? They held hands and jumped off together just so the daughter could score an extra t-shirt for her admiring pizza-faced boyfriend. Or the time I saw a sixty-two-year-old lady getting naked up on the bar? Or some 'chick' getting a body shot revealing she was a 'he'? Friggin' in the riggin', dude. You see it all here. And eventually, every cruising sailor shows up. I've even met guys here who were sailing around the world alone. Man, that takes balls! Oh, and the sixty-two-year-old looked damned good, by the way."

"Plastic surgery can accomplish miracles, I guess."

"Those people have adventure boundaries way beyond mine, Nate. I'm just here to sail the mighty *Payback* and enjoy my early retirement." Doug raised his nose in the air and pronounced, "As the noble Plutarch once said, 'Moderation is best' and 'to avoid all extremes.'"

"Who the hell is Plutarch? Another bar owner down here?"

"No," Doug chuckled. "Only a wise, old Roman telling us to choose the calm path of moderation. It's like they say, there are old sailors and bold sailors, but no old, bold sailors. We're going to be very calm and just enjoy cruising the Caribbean."

"Maybe it's time for you try something bold instead. Take some tips from the old pirates they had down here. At least before you get old, brother'."

Doug ran his fingers through his salt-and-pepper hair and sighed, "Yeah, I don't need to run into any pirates, but maybe you're right. I do need some excitement."

CHAPTER 3

▼

VENEZUELA

Tied to her berth below, Cassie struggled against the ropes until her wrists and ankles were raw. The knots were getting tighter and she was afraid her movements would attract unwanted attention. Panting, she laid back and reflected on how she'd gotten into this mess.

✳   ✳   ✳   ✳

Growing up unsupervised in San Diego's Ocean Beach neighborhood, Cassandra Spencer spent her free time surfing and hanging around at the beach. Her mother was a secretary in a bank, while her seldom-seen dad was an eight-year veteran of the police force. When she was thirteen, her family disintegrated due to her father's drinking and his sudden arrest on corruption charges. She and her mother moved to the manager's apartment of an aging motel two blocks inland. Her mom ran the place for an absentee Pakistani owner and rented out cramped, Murphy-bed studios by the day or week. The tenants were generally Mexican immigrants, sailors from the nearby San Diego Naval Training Center, and the ubiquitous druggies who plied their wares on the beach each evening.

Cassie moved out on her eighteenth birthday. She struggled to work her way through a couple of years of college until waxing restlessness and waning funding caused her to give it up and head for Las Vegas. Cassie soon landed a cocktail waitress job at the refurbished Tropic Island Casino. With her good looks and natural friendliness, she quickly learned how to work the players and dealers to increase her tips. A tall dirty-blond with azure eyes and a couple of ankle tattoos, she received and refused many offers of special gratuities for meeting customers upstairs. Casual sex didn't interest her. Smiling and teasing, she was always able to sweet-talk her way out of any kind of trouble.

By promising to kickback a certain percentage to a well-connected boss, Cassie eventually snagged the roped-off high-roller area as her exclusive territory. During her shift, she served drinks to men who sometimes cursed her, sometimes ignored her, sometimes squeezed her, and sometimes left her black $100 chips.

Cassie lived alone. She didn't have to spend much on clothes since she wore a uniform daily. She rarely used her vacation time and never ate out. Before long, Cassie managed to accumulate more than $50,000 of undeclared "extra" cash in an air duct in her apartment. She felt a little guilty that she only reported a portion of her tips to the IRS, but the other girls told her everybody did it. She finally decided the politicians would only waste it on vote-buying agricultural programs, museums dedicated to locals of dubious national importance, and various other stupid boondoggles. She'd earned the dough and wasn't giving it up.

By her late twenties, Cassie had grown bored with her life and with herself. One of her regulars, Leo, was a high roller from Houston who frequently rhapsodized about the islands and his motor boat, *Moby Dick*.

"You know the casinos call the real high-roller customers 'whales,' don't you?" asked Leo.

"Sure."

"I also realize I'm a bit overweight," said Leo. "At my age, I simply don't give a damn anymore. So *Moby Dick* is a great name for my white trawler. It's a Nordhaven 40 and can do just over eight knots. If I go slower, though, I can get over 3,500 miles of range. Have you ever been to the islands, honey?"

"No, only to Catalina," answered Cassie.

"Hell, that doesn't count. I'm talking about the Caribbean. You'd love it, Cassie. I'd be happy to take you. No strings attached. I'd just get a kick out of showing it to you. I don't have any kids or grandkids to take, and I'll be damned if I'm treating the ex-wife to any more free trips."

"Okay, Leo. Someday, I may take you up on it."

"I'm counting on it. I need to make another trip before I get too old. Right now, I'm just killing time, and time's killing me."

Leo frequently boasted about traveling through the islands on his sturdy boat. He said it was designed for safe, comfortable cruising and wasn't like the cigarette-type boats favored by the Miami posers with the gold chains and unbuttoned shirts. Leo also told her of the high returns and financial privacy he enjoyed by putting his considerable funds in offshore banks in the Caymans and Trinidad.

Cassie liked Leo a lot. He was always nice to her in a platonic way. She liked older men, but Leo was balding and almost forty years her senior. He smoked too much and got real sleepy after more than two drinks. Cassie continued to politely refuse his offers to take her cruising in the Caribbean—until the night she turned twenty-nine and realized she had no one to celebrate with.

She wondered if Leo's grandfatherly act was for real, or whether he basically wanted to jump her bones like most men seemed to want, regardless of their age. *What the heck*, Cassie thought. She hadn't been anywhere in her life, and she could probably handle Leo if he tried anything.

Cassie immediately filed to take all of her accrued vacation for a trip to the Caribbean. She spent the night of her birthday talking and drinking with Leo in his casino-provided suite until he fell asleep on the zebra-skin couch. As she left Leo passed out in his suite, she looked around at the glaring lights and savage greed of Las Vegas and said to herself, "To hell with this." She returned to her apartment and packed up her bags and her money, which, by Leo's accounts, might have a bit more flexibility and secrecy if stored in the offshore banks he mentioned so often. By the end of the week, she was on *Moby Dick* sailing southeast out of Texas, heading for the islands.

$$* \qquad * \qquad * \qquad *$$

The trip with Leo opened her eyes to a whole new way of life. He taught her about boats, living on the islands, charts, fishing, and more. Cassie was surprised to find she didn't care if she ever went back. They strolled Grand Cayman's famous seven-mile beach, gambled in Aruba, shopped in Curacao, and snorkeled some world-class reefs in Bonaire. When they reached Trinidad, Cassie decided once and for all that it was time for her money and the IRS to part ways. Leo took her to his bank where Cassie deposited most of her savings in a numbered account under a fake name.

"So you're saying all I have to do is remember this number and duplicate this signature?" Cassie asked the bank officer. "No identification papers? Then I can get all my money out again?"

"Yes, madam. Some or all of it. With the interest."

"Cool."

"Cassie, I need to stay here at the bank for another half hour or so to transact some other business," Leo said. "Why don't you do some shopping and I'll meet you back on the boat?"

"Sure, Leo. Don't be too late." Cassie couldn't believe how everything had gone so well for her. If she wasn't sure how she'd feel about island life when she left Texas, it took only a few days for her to decide that she was meant for the tropical life. Spending days at a time on *Moby Dick* hadn't made her seasick at all; in fact, she grew to love the yacht's unsteady bobbing, and proudly told Leo how she'd finally gotten her "sea legs." By the time they left Trinidad, she was wondering how her relationship with Leo would eventually turn out. That night, she surprised Leo when she warmly kissed him goodnight. Before he could respond, she scampered to her cabin.

Leo took the midnight-to-six watch, piloting the boat on a long passage north. It was when *Moby Dick* was passing west of the neighboring island of Tobago that Cassie's new princess-like existence fell apart.

✳　　✳　　✳　　✳

Hunter was feeling very pleased with himself and his acting. *Maybe it wasn't acting anymore*, he thought. Things were changing for him and he was changing, too.

The fat cat was the first man he had ever killed, although he didn't want anyone else to know. Hunter figured he had earned the two beaners' respect with the murder. All they'd done was bring the faster boat alongside and jump onto *Moby Dick*. He was the one who'd hit the old boat owner with his rifle butt and cut the pig. He was an authentic blooded pirate now and had even captured a maiden on the high seas of the Spanish Main—just like in the books he'd read as a kid.

Hunter studied Cassie on the table and sipped his rum. Things were going according to plan as *Moby Dick* headed north, and Hunter felt Cassie would come to respect and like him. *It would be so much better that way*, he thought. *It wasn't any fun sticking it in a woman who lay there like dead meat.* He'd tried to screw some willing, passive girls back in Florida. Frequently, he had a problem getting and staying hard, but it was their fault. They were all druggie skanks and not good enough for him. Cassie would be different. She would be something special, something the new Hunter deserved. He knew he wouldn't have any problem with her.

He considered how far he'd come to get here. It was a long way for a poor kid who had grown up in a trailer in Fernandina Beach, Florida. His mother commuted to the Mayport Naval Station, near Jacksonville, where she was a civilian employee. His father, Lt. Colin Schoenholz, was an embezzling supply officer who had frequently beat her. He'd gotten her pregnant, but quickly took a transfer to the Great Lakes Training Center to disappear before Hunter was born. The Lieutenant sent some money back on an irregular basis so Hunter's mom gave the baby his father's surname, and hoped the bastard would return to marry her. He never did. Hunter figured that made two bastards in the family.

Hunter had grown up with a bunch of other redneck kids who made fun of what they called a stupid, kraut name. It'd been even worse being short and fatherless. He had to fight his way all through school until he finally dropped out to work on a local shrimp boat.

There was a pirate statue on the waterfront and the local high school teams were named the Pirates. From childhood, Hunter had thrived on the local pirate imagery and always dreamed of being a real buccaneer. He'd committed some petty thefts and had been arrested a couple of times in his teenage years. Once, a breaking and entering charge was dropped for lack of sufficient evidence to successfully prosecute. A rape charge was also dropped when the girl admitted there had been no actual penetration. Hunter's acquaintances had unmercifully ribbed him about that one. He told them the bitch was lying because he'd threatened to kill her if she didn't.

Hunter still didn't remember whose idea it was, but he and his Cuban crewmate eventually hatched a plan to leave town and do something on a larger scale. With the owner of the boat partying hard at the annual Fernandina shrimp festival, they calculated they wouldn't be missed for a couple of days if they simply stole his vessel. They were right. Hunter reckoned, at twenty-six, he was finally fulfilling his destiny of becoming a pirate. He wished he'd bought a black skull-and-crossbones flag to fly as they chugged past Fort Clinch, the harbor's brick Civil War fort, and into the open sea.

Hunter practiced his Spanish along the way and read every nautical "how-to" book on board. They stayed out of sight of land, refueling in ports like Gonaives, Haiti, where they could sell off some of the equipment with no questions asked. The Cuban had some friends in Colombia, and which was where they'd sold the boat to a mid-level cartel member. The shrimper would probably be repainted and turned around to head north with fake documents and a load of cocaine. The Americans would keep looking, but never find it.

The Cuban wasn't happy with the "two for me, one for you" way Hunter had split the proceeds from the sale of the shrimper, so Hunter left Colombia quickly and rode a bus east to Venezuela's Paria Peninsula. There he'd checked into a waterfront hotel where half the rooms were rented to hookers by the hour and included two clean towels at check-in. Hunter relaxed and spent time pondering what his next career move should be.

He met Sanchez and Garcia over drinks one night, and they soon became his drinking and bragging buddies. Sanchez was technically still in the Venezuelan army, but was somehow free to spend most nights with his other associates on fast boats out in the ocean passages between Venezuela and Trinidad. Garcia was some sort of liaison to the underworld in the Dominican Republic and Puerto Rico. The Latinos' English was good, if somewhat formal and without contractions. They had all conversed in English after Hunter was firmly told his Spanish made him sound like a retarded Cuban *puta*.

Hunter's half-formed plan had been to eventually return to Florida, steal another boat, and bring it south to sell to the Colombians. *If it worked once, it should work again*, he figured, and now he had the connections and navigational knowledge. The two Latinos, however, eventually convinced him a better idea was to buy drugs in South America and steal a boat to take them north so he could profit from both legs of the trip. They explained he didn't have to risk going all the way back to the States, although it would pay more. The Bahamas or Virgins paid less for the cocaine, but were safer for him than Florida. The Virgin Islands were the closest at 550 miles away.

So Hunter had reinvested his funds in kilos of coke. The seller had thrown in the shovel at Hunter's request. Then, playing the pirate again, he'd buried his treasure late at night in a couple of suitcases. Finally, he'd rented a fast launch from Sanchez's pals for a week.

Sanchez and Garcia had signed on for wages and a share of the profits. Sanchez supplied the AK-47s and the 9mm Beretta pistols from army supplies. They'd started cruising for a victim, but had to let several sailboats pass by unmolested as none of the three men knew how to sail. They'd gone out hunting nightly in the section of sea lanes bordered by Trinidad, Venezuela, and Grenada. On the third night, they spotted and hijacked *Moby Dick*.

*   *   *   *

Hunter finished his rum and his reminiscing. He went to the bridge to check on Garcia.

"We should be back in Venezuelan waters in three more hours," Garcia said.

"Good. Just leave the bitch tied up until we're done loading the boat. Don't mess with her, either. It'll be good if we can drop off the launch and turn this new boat around to get offshore before it gets light."

CHAPTER 4

▼

BIRD ISLAND

The two-boat flotilla arrived back in Venezuela and the men quickly loaded up *Moby Dick*. Hunter got his luggage, including the shovel, and checked out of the decrepit hotel. He slipped into the pre-dawn humidity and quietly dug up the suitcases.

After some consideration, Hunter came up with what he thought was a great hiding place for transporting the white powder by boat. He unstrapped the oil-drum-shaped life-raft canister and left the inflatable raft ashore. The empty container opened like a white clamshell. Hunter poured most of the coke into a triple-thick layer of garbage bags and shoved it into the empty canister. Then he crammed in plenty of anchor chain so the canister would have negative buoyancy. Finally, he took a caulk gun from the boat's tool kit and caulked the seams securely. He relocked the fiberglass drum. Using another bag, Hunter hid the remaining coke under a cabin deck board along with his operating cash.

"Hey, Garcia!"

"Yes?"

"Take that long, blue rope and run it halfway through that snap swivel on the transom rail," ordered Hunter. "Now, throw me both ends." Hunter took the doubled line and tied both ends to the canister.

"Why are you tying the drum to the boat?" asked Garcia.

"So we can tow it behind us. It should move along right under the surface when we're moving. I looped it for strength. The blue color will make it hard to see in the water. Anybody passing by will figure we're just trolling some fishing gear or maybe a water-driven generator or something."

"*Si.* Maybe."

"What do you mean, 'maybe'? It'll work great. Now stick your head under and tie this other shorter line to the rudder post."

Garcia hesitated then went under and brought the other end of the short line up to Hunter. "What is this one for?"

Hunter tied the short line to the snap fitting at the transom and beamed triumphantly. "See, now if we get stopped by some cops or the Coast Guard, all we have to do is unsnap this from the stern and stop the boat. The coke will then hang straight down from the rudder and nobody will see it there underwater. Then we can grab it and snap it up to the back of the boat again when the pigs leave. It'll work slicker than shit."

Garcia shrugged. Hunter went below to brag about his brilliance to Cassie instead. He was pleased when she appeared impressed.

Cassie seemed calmer now, and Hunter untied her after they lost sight of land. "There's nowhere for you to go and no life raft. The kayak and dinghy are chained and locked securely up on the top deck. I have the key," Hunter said and dangled the key in front of her.

"Okay, no problem. I told you I'd be fine, didn't I? Can I make you guys something to eat?" Cassie asked. She bustled around the galley and moved food to the table. Hunter noticed she used the sharp galley knives in making lunch and stepped over to grab them.

"I'll take those. You can damn well use the regular silverware from now on."

✳   ✳   ✳   ✳

"So now you can tell me where we're going, right?" Cassie asked, when she finally felt bold enough to ask Hunter a direct question about her future.

"Yeah, I guess so," he replied. "North to Tortola, up in the British Virgin Islands. We'll knock down coconuts, make piña coladas, and see all the pretty fish. You'll like it, baby."

Taking advantage of her new freedom, Cassie tried to search the boat without arousing suspicion. She'd watched enough movies to know that most seafaring boats carried items that might be useful to someone being held hostage. Plus, Leo had spent their first few days making sure Cassie got a decent introduction to the ins and outs of marine living. Unfortunately, she found Hunter had locked up the flare gun, the life jackets, and the large kitchen knives. He had even unplugged and hidden the microphone to the VHF radio.

On the second day, she discovered a lock-back jackknife, with a four-inch blade, in the toolbox and took the knife below to hide beneath her mattress. She couldn't hide anything on her person as Hunter made her constantly stay in her swimsuit—a dark-green bikini patterned with a white floral design—in case another boat was sighted and she had to play the trophy wife on the bow. Each night, he tied her to her bunk. She had to kick the bulkhead or yell in case she needed to use the toilet.

Cassie considered her options. During the day she could simply throw herself off the boat, but somebody might hear or see her. Besides, what good would it do? Their course took them far to the west of the Lesser Antilles island chain, and she never saw any land.

Even if she slipped over the rail, hugging a boat cushion, she would likely end up floating until a shark found her or exhaustion made her release the cushion. *Better to keep playing along with Hunter*, she thought. *He might get careless when they approached Tortola. Then maybe I would get an opportunity to swim ashore or run away.* All she wanted was to go back to Trinidad, recover her money, and fly far away. She wondered if she could ever return to Las Vegas since Hunter knew her name now and could contact the local mob to find her again.

During the trip from South America to the BVI, Hunter spent hours telling Cassie his embellished life story, and she smiled and humored him. Twice, when they were alone, Hunter tentatively fondled her. The first time, he softly put his hands on her thighs and buttocks while she was sleeping.

She awakened, and saw him backing off.

"What are you doing?" she demanded.

"Nothing, nothing. Sorry, you just looked so pretty there when you were sleeping."

Realizing she should be stringing him along instead of rejecting him outright, Cassie said, "Hunter, just wake me up first, will you? You kind of startled me." She lowered her head so that she was nearly looking through her bangs, and under the circumstances tried her best to put on some doe eyes.

"Yeah, no problem. I've got to check on Sanchez, anyway."

She was surprised when he meekly left. The second time he made a move, she was able to distract him by loading him up with the boat's booze and a liberal amount of his own cocaine. Cassie thought to herself what a poor drug runner Hunter must be to dip into his own stash, but she was surprised and grateful when Hunter didn't force himself on her. *He probably will next time*, she thought.

When Hunter was partying and snorting the coke, Cassie felt she had to use a little of the drug to play along and keep him going. She thought she handled it okay, but was terrified when he talked of having her smoke some crack cocaine with him after they reached their destination of Tortola and he could cook up some. A little coke was one thing, but crack was something far more addictive. She'd seen how the crackheads ended up in Ocean Beach and Vegas. Cassie thought she had to get off the damn boat before she was too far gone.

✳   ✳   ✳   ✳

More than halfway through the trip, Cassie woke up when a very strong light flashed into her cabin. It went off immediately and then flashed again. It was coming through the porthole and the overhead hatch as well. She strained against the ropes to get her head up to see what it was. Soon the flashes became weaker and faded. The next day, she asked Hunter if he had seen the flashes too.

"Sure, I saw them," he said. "I was on the helm last night because I wanted to make sure we didn't run into the tiny island we passed. It's called Bird Island, or Aves, and the Venezuelans have a lighthouse on it to push their claim to it. Usually, there's nothing there but a lot of birds and bird shit, baby. It's the only land we'll even see on this course until we sight the Virgins."

Hunter had picked Tortola for his destination because he'd heard it had plenty of rich "snotty yachties," so a young, white man in an expensive boat wouldn't stand out. Tortola provided good cover, yet the 2003 Central Intelligence Agency Fact Book (which, of all books, he'd found and read on the shrimper) still listed it as a "transshipment point for South American narcotics destined for the U.S. and Europe."

While researching further and preparing for the trip back in Venezuela, Hunter had purchased the relevant charts and studied them. Working with the BVI chart, he now plotted a course coming up through the Salt Island Passage, between Peter and Salt, since it was the most direct route from the south. With a red marker, he circled the shallow spots, but didn't worry about anything like rocks or wrecks unless the clearance depth was shown as less than eight feet. Since *Moby Dick* only had a shallow draft of four feet, nine inches, he thought the boat should be safe in anything deeper than eight feet, even with normal wave crests and troughs.

*   *   *   *

It was past sunset when they finally reached Salt Island Passage. The drag of the canister made the voyage longer than Hunter had planned. Cassie had a general idea where they were because she had sneaked quick looks at the charted positions whenever she took food up to the bridge. It looked to her like they were going to make Tortola tonight. She knew Hunter would come below soon to tie her up. Cassie had to stay free tonight and stall him until she could get away.

Cassie made her decision. She went to her cabin and checked to be sure the opened jackknife was still under the mattress. Then she combed her hair and put makeup on for the first time since the hijacking. She waited nervously. Soon she heard Hunter approaching.

"Okay, baby. It's nighty-night time again. Put your hands together so I can tie them." He sounded in a good mood for once.

"Sure, Hunter, but I was thinking…"

"I'll do all the thinking on this boat, baby. Why do you look all painted up for once?"

"You know, I was thinking we could lay off the rum and the blow tonight and maybe finish something this time. It might be fun," she said, trying to smile.

"Well, well. I knew you'd come around. I was waiting patiently. I'm going to be big in the islands, baby. I can pull this coke and boat trade over and over, and you can enjoy the ride."

"Yeah, you're definitely something, Hunter. I've never met anyone like you."

Cassie leaned on her elbow and patted the bed to entice Hunter to sit beside her. Hunter sat, but quickly rolled on top of her and started pulling Cassie's swimsuit bottom off.

"Slowly, Hunter. What's the rush?" She grabbed his hands and pulled him to her and kissed his cheek. Hunter kissed her and stroked her hair. He ran his hands over her body and kissed her on the lips. She fought the desire to bite his lip, tear it off, and spit it in his face. Cassie contained her emotions and kissed him back until he became impatient to move on to something more.

"That's it, big boy. It'll be better if you make it last." Cassie looked through the porthole and noticed it was almost dark enough. She needed to delay things a touch more so she could jump overboard without anyone seeing her. With islands close by, maybe she could swim ashore or attract another boat to pick her up. She swallowed her revulsion and stuck her tongue in Hunter's ear. His body stiffened as if hit by an electric shock. He groped under her top kneading her breasts then pinched her nipples and started twisting them back and forth.

"Ouch! Not so rough, Hunter. Keep it nice and gentle. You're trying too hard." Cassie could tell he wasn't very experienced at this. He acted tentative and unsure as he went through motions he'd likely seen in a porn video. Or worse, maybe he didn't desire her. *Damn, this had to work.*

Hunter rubbed her nipples in a gentler fashion and pushed up her top to kiss them. He began sucking on her breasts and licking her silver-dollar-sized areolas, alternating from left to right every few seconds. Hunter moved up and kissed her mouth. He stuck his tongue in and Cassie reluctantly reciprocated. He grunted, animal-like, when his right hand finally pulled the bottom of her bikini away and then found the smooth mounds of her ass. Her grunted again, louder this time, as he dragged his finger between the globes. He stopped and pulled his head back to watch her while he moved his hand to part her legs and bury it between them.

Cassie faked her pleasure and arched her hips to meet the insistent probing. She was still dry and knew he would soon notice and wonder why. *That's enough,* she thought. *It's now or never.* First, she had to get him to stop watching her so she could act. She couldn't reach under the mattress and palm the knife if he was looking at her. Cassie hoped she had the fortitude to go through with it. Once she started, she had to finish it; otherwise she was going to get brutally beaten, raped, and cut to pieces.

"Oh, it feels so good. Do you mind going down on me a little, too? I've always enjoyed that."

"Okay, baby. Then I'll get undressed, and you can do me, too."

Hunter smiled and moved his hands to cup her firm bottom. He held her steady and buried his face to apparent great effect since she purred and sighed. Cassie slowly reached under the mattress.

"Oh, yes. Yes, keep going," moaned Cassie. He was now in the perfect position, and it was time to act. Her hand quickly reached the knife, and she held it in her fist like an ice pick. She figured she could reach as far as his neck and wondered if she should stab him there, or instead, ram the knife into his ear canal. The ear would be harder to hit, and a neck wound might keep him from yelling for the crew. She decided on the neck and tensed her arm.

"Land ho!" yelled Sanchez from the bridge.

Cassie quickly hid the knife when Hunter stood up.

"Shit! Keep your motor running, baby. I'll be back in five minutes."

*   *   *   *

Hunter quickly bounded up to the bridge. "Hey, Sanchez, slow down. We're getting close to Tortola, and I want to figure out a new course to take us straight to Road Town." Hunter wanted to return to Cassie before the mood faded. He was sure he would be able to go all the way this time, with no problems. She was the special one he deserved. He just knew it.

"Okay, you see the little island to the west and those lights to the southwest?" Sanchez pointed and pulled back on the throttle while Hunter checked the GPS and marked the chart.

"Yeah, I got it. We'll clear them." Hunter could see they were now approximately a mile west of Salt Island. They had passed Peter Island and could now see some of the lights from the island's resort to the southwest. They were only a half mile east of Dead Chest Island.

Ignored by the overconfident Hunter, the chart clearly showed a hazard named Blonde Rock lurking nine feet under the surface in the middle of the passage, slightly closer to the Dead Chest/Peter Island side. Hunter hadn't red-circled it earlier. It was popular with scuba divers and was named for the light color of the fire coral covering the rock's tip.

Tonight, the wind and waves were minimal, and the trawler's keel skimmed over the east side of the rock. As the boat slowed, however, the canister wobbled and sank more than ten feet deep. One side of the securing loop of line suddenly snagged the coral on Blonde Rock and was chewed to pieces.

The canister sprang free, trailing its long blue line. The white drum bounced down the slope of the rock until it reached the ninety-foot sea bottom. Because of the flat sea bed and the unusually strong current, the round container slowly rolled and slid a mile to the east. It finally hit an obstruction, and jammed in place on the sea floor.

When the drag from the towed cargo disappeared, the boat immediately surged forward at a higher speed.

"What the hell are you doing, Sanchez? I said slow it!" shouted Hunter. He grabbed the wheel roughly away from Sanchez, causing the boat to heel steeply. When the boat crossed its own wake, the tilt worsened, and poorly-secured docking lines and boat cushions fell overboard. The boat fenders slipped over the rail and followed the other items into the turbulent water around *Moby Dick*. Hunter straightened the wheel, saw the debris, and finally stopped the engines. Garcia and Sanchez had been tossed around the interior and were loudly cursing in Spanish.

∗   ∗   ∗   ∗

When Hunter left her bed, Cassie had tucked the knife under the mattress again and adjusted her swimsuit. She jumped up and looked through the porthole toward the west. She could barely discern a dark hump of land blotting out the stars on the horizon. There were a few scattered streetlights off to the left side of the first hump of land. *There must be people on the island.* Cassie saw nothing but water and stars when she looked out the opposite starboard porthole. She had to leave immediately before they got too far away. She felt the boat slow then speed up and violently turn.

Cassie left everything and quickly staggered across the listing deck to the stern. She vaulted over the rail and into the turbulent wake. Treading water, she saw the boat slow and stop. Maybe the killers had heard or seen her. She dove below the surface and swam as far away as she could. Her lungs burning, she surfaced again to see *Moby Dick* farther away. She considered getting one of the fenders or cushions to hold on to, but they were over by the boat, and the men were scanning the water. Cassie oriented herself toward the closest dark hill of land and began swimming.

∗   ∗   ∗   ∗

"Check around and see if everything is okay," Hunter ordered after the boat had come to a full stop. Sanchez went aft, and Garcia took a flashlight forward to the bow.

"*Jesu Cristo!*" shouted Sanchez. "The stuff is gone, *hombre.*"

"What the hell are you talking about?" demanded Hunter.

"The canister is gone. The fitting is here, but no rope."

"Shit! Okay, let's start up and go looking for it," said Hunter, as he started the engine.

"Wait! Stop!" yelled Garcia. "Do not put the boat in gear yet."

"Why not?"

"Because I see all kinds of shit floating around in the water. Like the cushions, fenders, and boat hook. There are lines dangling off the boat. They could already be wrapped around the prop. If you start it up now you will suck more in and mess up the engine. Wake up!"

"Goddamn it, you're right. Get your snorkel stuff on and check," ordered Hunter.

"How come it is always me?" complained Garcia.

"Hey, *chico*," laughed Sanchez. "Because you are so big and strong. Also, the face mask doesn't fit me, because I have this pretty mustache. Shit, you should go swimming, Hunter. You are the one who yanked the wheel. Maybe you cut the ropes by running over them when you turned so tight."

"Screw you, Sanchez. The lines and dope must've been gone already when I grabbed the wheel. It must be why the boat moved faster all of a sudden.

"Hurry up, Garcia. The boat is drifting with the wind and currents and I don't want to run into anything. Right now, I wish we were some goddamn, unreliable, rag-hanging sailboat."

Garcia went over the side and confirmed his fear: there were lines wrapped around the propeller and shaft. Sanchez held the flashlight aimed at the rudder. First, Garcia threw the rest of the floating items up to Sanchez and Hunter. A seat cushion and two of the fenders were never recovered. Garcia dove several times with a knife to cut off the knotted mess. Finally, he inspected the bow and keel to be sure there was no collision damage.

"Okay, *vamos*," said Garcia when he climbed back aboard.

The crew went below to clean up. "Hey, where's the *gringa* bitch?" Sanchez suddenly shouted and got blank stares from Garcia and Hunter.

They frantically searched the boat and then called out into the darkness for Cassie.

"She is gone, man," said Garcia.

"Goddamn it, but when and why?" Hunter said.

In all the confusion regarding the boat and the canister, no one had thought to check on her. Hunter figured that was when she jumped ship. Or maybe Cassie fell overboard when he made the tight turn. She should've stayed on the bed where he left her. Hunter didn't know what happened, but he desperately needed to find out.

"Now what do we do?" asked Garcia.

"Find the coke, man," said Sanchez.

"No, it probably sank as soon as it came loose from the boat. Don't worry. It's not deep here like it was in the open Caribbean. It's less than 100 feet." Hunter showed them the chart. "Look, I've got a GPS reading marked on the chart from where I'll bet we lost the load, so we know where it is. We can come back and look for the stuff in the daylight. Later, if we have to, we can get somebody with scuba tanks to go out and find it. It's a white drum in clear water. The coke isn't going anywhere. Let's find her first."

"Why do we need the bitch? She probably fell off and drowned," Garcia said.

"Yeah, she probably did, but what if she didn't? I want her back. She might know what happened with the canister. If we don't get her, she could tell someone else where the coke is. Shit, she knows our names and could describe us and the boat to the cops if she's still alive. I don't want to end up in some rat-infested island jail for smuggling or murder. Do you?" said Hunter, showing his nervousness. He spoke quickly and out of breath, betraying his usual arrogance. "Anyway, I want her back. We have to concentrate on her first. We can afford a few days on it."

During the first night, they finally got the boat going and crisscrossed the area for hours calling for Cassie. To the crew's relief, none of the tourists aboard the chartered boats they passed seemed to care about or even notice their shouting. At dawn, they returned to the spot where the cargo was lost and ran a spiral search pattern without positive result. Then Sanchez took the dinghy and slowly circled nearby Dead Chest Island as he looked for wreckage or a body. It was a small islet, and he easily scanned the whole cay from the water. While Sanchez was gone, Hunter ran *Moby Dick* along the adjacent coasts of Peter and Salt Islands, but saw nothing unusual on their shores.

They studied the charted current and tide tables and determined to spend the next day intensively searching Ginger Island and Cooper Island. There hadn't been any wind so if Cassie had held on to something and floated all night, it was the farthest she could be by now, four or five miles to the east. They decided to start at the farthest possible point and spiral in to the starting point. If they found nothing, they'd go back and work the prior islands again; all on foot this time. It shouldn't take too long as each of these islands in question was only a couple of miles long.

The first island turned out to be a thorny problem after all. Ginger was uninhabited, with no harbor or even a place to anchor. Finally, Garcia kayaked ashore and clambered all over the rocks looking for Cassie. Cooper was easier since there was a dock for the dozen-room hideaway hotel and restaurant. There was still no sign of Cassie, though. They casually described her to everyone at the hotel bar and on the boats, but no one had seen her. They picked up a mooring buoy off the Cooper Island Beach Club for the night and Sanchez made some quick burgers for supper.

"We need to get some sleep. Tomorrow, we'll try the other direction and search Peter Island, piece by piece." Hunter looked at the nautical chart. "Then we'll land on Salt and do Dead Chest again, too."

"You better try something, boss man," said Sanchez.

"Yeah, and I do not like doing all this paddling and climbing around either," added Garcia. "Somebody is going to start asking us questions."

"Maybe she is the one who cut the ropes and stole the stuff," Sanchez said.

"How the hell could she do that? The canister would've sunk," said Hunter.

"Do not be so sure. She could have tied those missing boat fenders to it so it would float, and she swum it off somewhere. Or maybe she tied a marker buoy and a long line to it. Or maybe she contacted some friends somehow and they were following us and picked her up and snagged the coke. She was a smart bitch and was only playing you for a fool. You should not have let her run around loose like you did."

"Bite me, Sanchez. Nobody plays me for a fool. We would've seen a marker buoy if there was one. You might think you're smarter than me, but I'm still running this boat, not you. We'll find something soon." Hunter spat on the deck and stalked off to his cabin.

CHAPTER 5

▼

DEAD CHEST ISLAND

Doug woke up twice during the night and came up on deck. Tired as he was after a second day of hiking and snorkeling on Norman Island, he still felt he had to check to see if his boat was secure and some other vessel wasn't dragging its anchor, bearing down on *Payback*. It was a calm night for Norman Island. Nevertheless, every good skipper learns to ignore the usual wave slapping and creaking sounds on his boat, but wakes instantly when his unconscious mind detects something out of the normal rhythm.

He got up the first time hearing loud voices from an overloaded dinghy full of drunks, without a flashlight, looking for their newly chartered yacht.

"Is this it?" a slurred voice said.

"No. I can't even pronounce the name on this one."

"What about that one?"

"I don't know. What was the name of the one we rented, anyway?"

"Oh, man. You lost the stupid boat!"

Doug hoped they'd find their boat without waking up everybody in the harbor or getting something thrown at them. *They should carry a light,* he thought. *Some other boat might run into them.* Doug always kept oars, a flashlight, a small anchor, and some water in *Payback*'s dinghy.

The second time he arose both from the normal desire to check and from an urgent need to take a piss. Doug looked up and admired the myriad stars above the masthead light. He recognized Orion, the Big Dipper, and Polaris (also called the North Star), but that was the extent of his astronomical knowledge.

Doug reflected on sailors in the pre-electronic era and how they had to navigate using sun and star sightings taken with a sextant. *Maybe celestial navigation would be a good thing to learn someday,* he mused. *Payback* had a built-in Global Positioning System, or GPS. He'd also packed a handheld Garmin GPS for backup. Like every other male sailor in the harbor, Doug stood at the bow and pissed past the anchor roller to avoid using the noisy head below. He then jumped through the forward hatch and went back to his berth to try for some sleep.

For awhile, Doug lay awake and thought back on all the great cruises he'd enjoyed here in the British Virgin Islands since he'd done his first bareboat sailing charter. A bareboat rental meant his sailing resume was good enough to pilot the yacht himself, without a licensed captain. Doug's sobering role of skipper made him responsible for both the safety and the enjoyment of his family, but by the end of the charter, he felt like a proud Old Salt.

Doug enjoyed his first charter so much he bought a forty-six-foot Beneteau sloop through the Moorings Company's program. This allowed him to have his own sailing yacht based on the main BVI island of Tortola to take out four or five times a year using family and friends for crew. When Doug didn't need the boat, the Moorings rented it to other vacationing sailors and forwarded his contractual share of the funds.

Unless you counted the savings on his own "free" use, Doug's vessel, *Payback*, hadn't actually paid back the investment, but he wasn't in it for a profit. He felt the boat was payback for all the delayed gratification of endless school, the lean early years, and his hard work at some very boring mortgage banking jobs. It was payback for all the times he'd put the corporate mask on and played yes-man to some ignorant, self-serving bosses while still trying to keep them within the bounds of legality.

The kids and his late wife, Jeanne, also came to think of their weeks in the islands as their real life. The other school or work weeks were only necessary prerequisites to going sailing and snorkeling again.

As he was falling asleep, Doug considered what an idyllic two days this had been. He still missed Jeanne, but he hadn't had time to feel sorry for himself for awhile. Before Jeanne's sudden death from a brain aneurysm, Doug was considering either selling *Payback* or trading her in on a new charter boat at the end of the original five-year deal. With the children grown up and Jeanne gone, everything changed. For over a year, the loneliness had been almost unbearable, but Doug worked through it by focusing on what he could now do with his unasked-for new freedom. Instead of selling the boat, Doug decided to sell the big house in Long Grove, Illinois, and take early retirement.

The boatyard finally finished the improvements to *Payback* Doug had ordered, and he'd permanently moved aboard. At least he had a brother to share the good times this month. Sun and fun in the Caribbean was hard to beat. Doug felt he deserved a good time for once and trusted nothing would come along to spoil it.

*   *   *   *

On the top of the islet's southern cliff, an apparently lifeless body was stretched out in the rising sun like a salmon filet under the broiler. The green iguana nearby raised its head and looked at the woman for a full minute, and then resumed its effort to consume a flower blossom. A laughing gull swooped above. Its right eye was outlined in white on a sooty black head, and the eye was sharply focused on the floral print pattern of the topless woman's green bikini bottom.

The woman had light hair and a good figure marred only by dirt and several small cuts and insect bites. Her skin was tan, but was starting to get pink overtones. A bridled tern appeared, and the first bird objected to its encroachment by issuing its loud raucous "ha-ha-ha-ha" call. The woman moaned and moved her head, causing the iguana to run off with its strange butt-wagging gait.

Cassie slowly opened her crusted eyelids and rolled sideways. Her ankle hit a prickly pear cactus, and she sat up quickly.

"Shit!" That's all she needed—another bit of damage when she had more than her fair share lately. She plucked out the spines that, ironically, had pierced the barbed wire tattoo encircling her ankle. Her other ankle sported a tiny flower inside of a heart. Both feet had a few points of black sea urchin spines broken off and now festering under the skin. She'd hit the urchins while walking ashore at the rocky, southern bay of the island three nights ago.

Cassie remembered something she'd read regarding the use of vinegar, meat tenderizer, or even urine on such injuries to counteract the urchin spine chemicals and ease the pain. She squatted and tried to pee on her ankles but found she had little fluid in her bladder. *It must be a sign of dehydration*, she thought. Cassie wondered if her lethargic mental state was from thirst and hunger or from Hunter's cocaine and rum. *Probably from all of those reasons, and exhaustion, too*, she thought.

Cassie had no idea what the name of the stinking little island was. In fact, she'd recently referred to it as "Stinking Little Island," and now her primary concern was how the hell she could get off of it before she died of thirst. The islet was only a half mile in length and sported no trees or buildings.

During the first full day and night, she'd hid in the bushes, terrified that Hunter and his crew would find her. She'd seen Sanchez circling the island in a dinghy, but she stayed low, and he never spotted her. The following day, her second full day, she'd painfully tried to circle the island, but the shore had been too steep and rocky in places to completely circumnavigate. Switching plans, she'd climbed to the 160-foot summit and looked at the water all around, which confirmed the fact that she was on an uninhabited desert island.

"Water, water, everywhere, nor any drop to drink," she recited, as she remembered Coleridge's "Rime of the Ancient Mariner."

Cassie saw the long mountainous island across the channel to the north and figured it must be their original destination of Tortola. It was extremely frustrating to see boats out in the channel and other islands all around, including one with buildings that looked less than a mile away. Lights shone from there each night. Cassie cursed her luck in originally swimming to Stinking Little Island instead of the inhabited Big Island next door. When she'd jumped off of Hunter's boat during all the confusion, it had been dark, and her point of view made it look like there was only one island to the southwest, not two. *Maybe it was for the best*, Cassie thought, since she barely made it there. She was probably not a strong enough swimmer to have made it all the way from the boat to Big Island in one swim.

Cassie still wasn't sure what caused the excitement and yelling on the boat. She'd felt the boat first slow, and then speed up and turn sharply before stopping, but she hadn't felt the boat shudder or stop as if it had hit anything. Whatever it was, it had finally presented a great opportunity for her to slip over the side with land in sight. *Maybe it wasn't so great after all*, she thought. She had been so worried about either Hunter or crack use killing her slowly. Now she worried she had simply changed the method of her death.

After climbing the hill yesterday, she'd waved and yelled at passing boats with no positive result. Only one catamaran, flying the French tricolor, had come close enough to see her on the small western beach. A man even hoisted his beer in a sociable salute before turning back to his companions. Later, on the top of the cliff, she'd jumped up and down and even took off her bikini top and waved it for what felt like hours. No one appeared to notice her, and the top had finally slipped from her weakened grasp in a gust of wind and blown off the edge of the cliff into the sea. Cassie had burst into tears and eventually collapsed in exhaustion.

Cassie told herself today she couldn't afford the moisture for any more tears. She yelled into the wind, "I'm going to get the hell out of here!" She stopped abruptly. Simply talking hurt after all the yelling yesterday.

✳   ✳   ✳   ✳

The island birds came to life early and called to each other on the rocky slopes of The Bight, the main harbor on Norman Island. The sky lightened quickly at this latitude. Navigation was possible even before six o'clock if you were confident as to the location of the rocks and reefs. Doug was secure in his local knowledge, but there was no rush this morning. There were very few lighthouses or lighted buoys of any kind outside of U.S. waters. The native or naturalized BVI "Belongers" might zoom around in unlit motorboats at night, but no one else in his right mind did.

Doug scrambled some eggs, but found both he and Nate more thirsty than hungry. Glasses of water, orange juice, diet Dr. Pepper, and traditional vodka and tomato juice Bloodies were consumed—in that order. They sat in the cockpit and watched as the sun finally rose above the ridgeline and brightened the water.

Pelicans worked the shallows. A magnificent frigatebird patrolled overhead. Nate laughed when he noticed naked crewmembers of both sexes swimming and then using the handheld showers while standing on the open-swim platforms of several of the European boats.

"Sure don't see them on Lake Michigan."

"Too darn cold there," Doug replied.

"None of them this morning was worth seeing anyway. Maybe tomorrow."

"Yeah, maybe over at the fancy resort at Peter Island."

"Jesus! Look at all the boats over in the harbor now. It's getting crowded. I think too many people have discovered your favorite island, Doug."

"That's for damn sure. When I first started coming here, there was nothing on the island but feral goats and cattle. There were no mooring buoys in the harbor so only a dozen boats had room to anchor on the few shallow spots, and they all partied at the Willy T. You could snorkel around the place and see conch and turtles and even an octopus."

"Too many goddamned people in the world," Nate said and took another swig of water. "There's your real underlying problem. I guess we all want to be the last son-of-a-bitch to find someplace great and then keep the knowledge from others.

"Sorry for the rant. I get going sometimes. Anyway, I definitely do appreciate you letting one more jerk come and see your special islands. Thanks, Doug. I mean it."

"You're welcome, Nate. You know, I should have been a travel guide or charter captain or something. I get a real kick out of sailing around and showing people these great islands and seeing the looks on their faces."

"Maybe you could still be a charter captain."

"Probably not. I could study and pass the Coast Guard exam, but then I'd need a new wife or partner to help me with the cooking and the boat. I miss Jeanne. She could've handled it. Also, I bet I'd get sick of wearing a groove in the water sailing around and around the BVI taking tourists on the same seven-day itinerary and listening to them all bitch about the heat or the waves. You've got to be able to handle the heat to climb that old goat path to the top of Norman like we did yesterday."

"It figures you used that route, since you're an old goat yourself. You could join that herd I saw on the airport grounds when I flew in," said Nate.

"Those were sheep. I noticed them when I picked you up."

"No, Doug. They were skinny and shorthaired. I know what sheep look like."

"Caribbean sheep aren't all fluffy and shit. It's too hot. The way you can tell is the tail on a sheep points down while a goat's tail curves up."

"Man, everything is different down here."

"It's a different world, bro'."

"Hey, Doug. Were there actually pirates here in the BVI?"

"Oh, absolutely! They used Norman Island all the time. They hid their ships here and posted a lookout on the top of the hill. I think the only spot they liked better was Soper's Hole on the west end of Tortola because it has four exits. Great Thatch and Little Thatch islands are over in the same area and, you see, 'Thatch' is actually a corruption of 'Teach' which was Blackbeard's real name, Edward Teach.

"Did you also know Black Sam Bellamy had a fort on a little island east of where the airport is now? Henry Morgan, John Hawkins, and Francis Drake all sailed here. In fact, the stretch of water we sailed over yesterday to get to Norman is called Sir Francis Drake Channel. All of the famous pirates hid here around 300 years ago."

"As usual, you are a veritable font of useless knowledge," said Nate.

"Hey, you wouldn't think it was so useless if you found some treasure here, brother. You know, Norman was also known as Treasure Island. The first reason is because of the treasure caves we'll snorkel into this afternoon. A $450,000 treasure was found there in 1750. More was dug up in 1907. The second reason is Robert Louis Stevenson's uncle sailed around here and told his nephew of the island. Stevenson later used some of the features in *Treasure Island.*

"That hill we climbed is named Spy Glass Hill, and it's the tallest point on the island, just like in the story. The book even has a reference to Dead Chest, which actually is a small island right off Peter Island. Blackbeard supposedly left fifteen mutinous men marooned on Dead Chest Island with one cutlass and a bottle of rum to fight over."

"You're kidding! The 'Dead Man's Chest' is a real island?"

"No shit, bro'," said Doug.

"Yo-ho-ho, and a bottle of rum!" sang Nate, waving an imaginary sword.

"Exactly!"

Doug took the dishes down to the galley. "Okay, are you about ready to go?"

"Aye, aye, Captain Bligh!" said Nate with an exaggerated, British-style open-palm salute.

"Okay, prepare to cast off. Go up on the bow and untie one end of our mooring bridle. Then, when I say 'Cast off,' let your end go and pull in on the other end so it slips through the loop of the buoy pendant and coil the mooring line on the foredeck. Then point at the buoy when I motor past since I can't see it from here, and I don't want to run over it. It could burn out the engine if we got the pendant line tangled around our propeller. I'll mind the dinghy painter, this towing line from the bow of the dinghy to *Payback*, so it doesn't get sucked under, either."

"Got it," said Nate in an impatient tone of voice.

"Sorry, Nate. I keep forgetting you were a Navy man. You probably know all this stuff already."

"No, seriously. Go ahead and tell me exactly what you want me to do so there's no misunderstanding. I'm just not awake yet. Sure, I know this part, but not the actual sailing. We didn't have sails on my sub. No windows or screens on the hatches, either."

Doug smiled. "Okay, but from now on I'll only fill you in on the sailing and surface navigation."

After *Payback* rounded Water Point, Doug reduced speed and turned east into the wind. He set the autopilot to maintain the course for Peter Island.

✳   ✳   ✳   ✳

Cassie slowly worked her way back to the rocky southern bay below. The leeward side to the west had a nice sandy beach. It was easy on her feet, but the rocky bay was still the closest point to Big Island in case she had to try to swim for it. Small sharp rocks and thorns tortured her bare feet, and the hot sun continued to stress her skin on the way to the bay.

As she climbed down, she noticed a large, muddy puddle on a ledge under the cliffs. Could it possibly be rainwater? Cassie lay flat on the mud and slid toward the center to the water's edge. She tried a sip and immediately spit it out. Too much mud, sand, bird droppings, bugs, and God knows what else. It didn't taste salty, but there was too much sediment for her to swallow.

Cassie walked over to the line of rocks and flotsam at the shore, looking for anything she could use to make a fire. She discovered some dry driftwood, but no way to get it started. Even if she was some kind of super Girl Scout, she didn't think she would find the right kind of rocks here to make sparks. She picked up a couple anyway and smashed them together, but they only produced a dull sound and hurt her hands. She tried rubbing sticks together over some coconut husk fiber, but only succeeded in making herself more exhausted. She looked for some glass, but found nothing shaped properly convex to serve as a magnifying glass. Cassie sighed and gave up on the signal fire idea.

There was nothing with which she could make a raft. There weren't even any coconut trees on Stinking Little Island—only scrub and cactus. She knew red cactus buds were edible, but didn't see any ripe ones. The sea grape bushes had some fruit on them, and Leo had told her they were edible. He'd also warned her regarding the poisonous manchineel tree, though, and she wasn't sure she could tell the difference. The manchineel tree also produces small fruit that taste great, but can cause death within hours. He'd told her the tree is so poisonous that a light touch, or even breathing smoke from burning its leaves, was damaging. She decided she better not eat anything unless she knew exactly what it was. Maybe she could spear some fish later or catch lizards or find some bird eggs.

There was plenty of Styrofoam, pieces of net, and all types of plastic garbage. Cassie found a half full water bottle without a cap. She took a cautious sip. It was hot and salty, and she spit it out. She emptied the bottle onto the sand. Saltwater would only make her die of thirst more quickly.

If only she could squeeze some fresh water from the mud puddle. Finally, she had an epiphany and emptied out the saltwater bottle. She then took it to the ocean and rinsed it. Cassie walked along the shore and collected another bottle the waves had deposited. She took both empty bottles back to the mud puddle and took her bikini bottom off.

Working slowly, Cassie took her swimsuit and skimmed water and mud from the top of the puddle with the first bottle, and slowly poured it through the green fabric. She squeezed the suit and let the resulting liquid drip through the suit and caught it in the second bottle. She cautiously took a sip. It still tasted awful but it was fresh water, and not simply mud anymore, so she made a face and swallowed. She repeated this until there wasn't enough to scoop up anymore.

Cassie cleaned her suit in the ocean and put it back on. She sat at the edge of the water looking across to Big Island. Maybe she could actually swim it. She knew she was only going to get weaker, so today might be her best and only chance. Or maybe she'd simply be killing herself.

Maybe Hunter will find me. I could tell him I fell overboard by accident. Just suck up to the freak, and tell him what he wants to hear. Or maybe I could find something shiny and signal a boat or the people on shore. As Cassie sat and considered her limited options, she was so still the tiny crabs came out of their holes and started toward her, apparently hoping she might already be dead.

When she stood up, the crabs scampered sideways back into their holes again. Cassie walked slowly into the water trying to avoid the sea urchins and sharp coral. She started swimming when she was waist deep. Her knee scraped on something. Soon she was in deep water out in the cut between the two islands. The water felt colder. Whitecaps on the yard-high waves slapped her face.

Cassie thought she was doing well, using an energy-saving sidestroke, but then she noticed the rocks off the southwest end of her departure beach appeared to be getting closer, while Big Island looked farther away. Realizing that a strong tidal current was sweeping her into the open Caribbean Sea, she switched to an overhand stroke and redoubled her efforts.

It still wasn't helping. She screamed and started kicking furiously. On the edge of exhaustion, she came to her senses in time to change direction to swim with the current and head toward the outermost rock. Her arms and legs were becoming sluggish. She wasn't sure she was going to make it now. Cassie became almost resigned. It was sad to think no one would ever know what happened to her after the sharks cleaned up any remains.

Her foot scraped against something sharp, and she looked up to see the wave-splashed rock only a few feet away on her left as she drifted past. With a final burst of speed, Cassie reached the rock and desperately hung on to the leeward side. She got one leg up on it and was able to sit on a small ledge.

Cassie almost passed out and fell into the sea, but finally recovered after several minutes of panting and shaking. Half swimming and half wading, it took thirty more minutes to work her way from one rock to another until she made it back to the edge of the same exposed bay where she'd first landed three nights before. She staggered along the shore, went up the trail a little, and collapsed in the brown mud she had filtered earlier.

CHAPTER 6

▼

PETER ISLAND

"Okay, Nate, we were in a hurry the first day, but now watch how I hoist the sails, and then you can do it next time."

"Yeah, unless I'm too drunk," Nate laughed. "Seriously, though, I want you to teach me all this sailing shit. I always wanted to learn, and this will be my one good opportunity. Plus, I can impress the hell out of girls, and maybe even my kids. If I don't learn to do it right, I could get myself hurt so go ahead and teach away, Skipper."

"I changed the autopilot course to head straight into the wind. Go ahead now and hoist the mainsail. Use the winch after you feel some resistance."

"Don't we have wenches to crank the winches?"

"You wish! Anyway, stop when you get near the top of the mast. Then loosen the mainsheet and coil and stow the halyard," Doug continued. "Hey, have you ever heard the expression 'three sheets to the wind'?"

"Sure, I've even been three sheets to the wind myself," chuckled Nate.

"Literally, it means all three of these control lines, or sheets, have come loose and are flying in the wind over the side of the boat—the main sheet and the two jib sheets. So then both sails are flapping freely and we're totally out of control. Lots of modern expressions have nautical origins."

"Thank you, Captain Hornblower."

Doug reset the course for Peter Island and unfurled the jib. Now at full sail on a starboard beam reach, *Payback* was moving perpendicular to the wind with the breeze coming in directly from the right side of the boat. *Payback* heeled over to port and accelerated to eight knots while she towed her dinghy through a clear blue wake.

"We're really moving now, Nate."

"Yeah, this is great! Just by using the wind, and some surprising knowledge on your part, this big mother is scooting through the waves without any motor."

"Surprising knowledge, huh? What I especially like is it's so quiet, and you don't smell all the fuel and exhaust like you would on a motor boat. We can feel virtuous in being oh so clean and green. Plus the sails keep the boat heeled, or tilted, to one side so it doesn't feel like you are rocking side to side as much as you would on a stinkpot motorboat. A planing-hull speedboat is even worse. It feels like you're on a stone being skipped across the water. A sailboat has that solid feel of a positive connection with the water.

"Almost anybody can drive a stinkpot, but it takes some skill to go sailing. There's simply something classy about it. Not that I'm biased or anything," Doug said with a smile

"You know, you're right. It's so peaceful. I can feel my stress level dropping already," Nate admitted and opened a Blackbeard Ale for each of them. "I suppose it could get boring if we were slowly drifting along, though. What's the top speed on this baby?"

"The theoretical hull speed in flat water is 8.4 knots. Beyond hull speed, all the wind or motor force you apply won't make any difference since you are basically trying to push the whole ocean out of your way. It has something to do with hull shape, displacement, boat length, bow wake wavelengths, and other scientific stuff way beyond my pay grade."

"I suppose motor yachts are a lot faster," said Nate.

"Sure, some are, but the particularly fast ones usually can't carry enough fuel to go very far without having to stop and fill up again. A lot of stinkpotters who want to go long distances, or cross oceans, buy a full displacement-hull trawler instead of a planing-hull speedboat. The trawlers don't go much faster than we do, and sometimes they're even slower if they want to economize on fuel. Trawlers are also favored by so-called retired sailors who get too old or lazy to mess with sails.

"Now, on this boat, we could sail around the world if we had enough food and guts to do it. But remember: don't wave at the stinkpots first. No matter how many millions their putt-putt boats cost, you are now on a sailboat, and therefore, morally and socially superior. By the way, Commodore Vanderbilt supposedly once said, 'One can play cards with anyone, but one only goes sailing with gentlemen,'" laughed Doug, putting his nose way up in the air. "You probably think I'm nuts telling you all this shit."

"As your brother, I already know you're nuts. So this is the relaxing part now," Nate said, and then slipped into his Colonel Klink voice that he knew grated on Doug nerves. "Ve haf der sails up und trimmed, und Herr Otto Mattick, our self-steering German crewmember, iss on duty at der helm zo ve manly sailors can simply sit, trink and bullshit. Vat vould ve talk about: sex, religion, or politiks? As for sex, I'm in favor of it, but haven't gotten any lately since the separation. You've probably forgotten how; given your advanced age, you old fart."

"Very funny," responded Doug with a grin. "I believe, at forty-six, I am only two years older than you and obviously in better shape." Doug paused and looked down at the deck, "I don't know. I guess the body has been ready for quite awhile, but it's only recently I've felt I might be ready for somebody new."

"Heck, you never know who you might meet here."

When they rounded the western tip of Peter Island, Doug tightened up the sheets and turned to tack to the northeast. They passed Little Harbour and continued toward Great Harbour. The brothers decided to stop and have lunch at the Callaloo restaurant in Buttonwood Bay.

"So what improvements did you make to *Payback* now that you're keeping her for yourself instead of renting her out?" Nate asked, while he stuffed another conch fritter in his mouth.

"Oh, I had to upgrade her to change over from chartering to more of a cruising boat. I had the yard put in a freshwater maker, a carbon fiber mast and boom, a special radar reflector/repeater, and even a set of yacht-saver bags. I had them change the backstays to a single adjustable model like they use for racing. Then I had some of the excess water tanks converted to fuel tanks. We don't need as much water storage now since we can make reverse osmosis water from the sea, and the extra fuel capacity will give us more range."

"What are yacht-savers?"

"Inflatable lifting bags inside the cabins we could supposedly blow up if the boat was sinking. They come with compressed air cylinders. Using them, the boat would still float, even if it was filled with water. It would give us time to find and fix the damage, and sail to a safe harbor. Although, the boat would still be slow and half full of water. I've never tested them. It's a one-time deal."

"Knock on wood and hope we never need half that shit Captain Steuben," said Nate.

"The radar gadget isn't technically legal, but it'll make us look the size of a tanker on a radar screen. This way some freighter won't ignore us on a dark night. We have a fiberglass hull and carbon fiber spars now so we'd be almost invisible on radar otherwise. I also added more storage, a couple of complete scuba outfits, new bottom paint, and some cosmetic crap. Cost me a bunch! It's like the old joke where a boat is like a woman—it's not the hull that's expensive, it's all the paint and rigging."

"Yeah, I've heard all your lame-ass jokes. A boat is a hole in the water into which you pour money. Sailing is the fine art of getting sick and wet while slowly going nowhere at great expense. Or, sailing is like standing in a cold shower and tearing up hundred dollar bills."

"Stop already, you're making me feel poor, and it's only our third day," groaned Doug.

The brothers finished their lunch and spent the afternoon snorkeling around the rocky shore of the bay. The fish were abundant, and they even saw an eagle ray with its spotted wings slowly flying through the water. Nate noticed there weren't a lot of shells in the bay. Doug promised him they would make a stop tomorrow morning at a good shelling spot.

They returned to *Payback* and used the engine alone to go around Great Harbour Point and into Sprat Bay. There were five buoys and a small marina run by the exclusive Peter Island Resort. They snagged a buoy with the boat hook and set up for the night.

"I've always wanted to come in here and have a fancy dinner. The buoys are more expensive than elsewhere, but a hell of a lot cheaper than renting one of those fancy A-frame cabins on the shore. You can use their bars and restaurants as long as you dress up a little after six o'clock. It's my treat, Nate."

"I won't argue with you. Hey, look at the size of the big yacht with the blue hull!" Nate said and pointed at a 90-foot immaculate motor yacht tied to the pier. "Wow, the crew members even have uniforms. Now there's a real gold-plated gin-palace. Caviar and champagne served by hot and cold running waitresses."

"Yeah, what a life. You know, the British don't consider any motor vessel to be a proper yacht, no matter how big it is. It has to be a sailing vessel to qualify for the term. On, the other hand, Americans tend to think of a huge boat like the blue one there when they hear the word yacht. By definition, though, a yacht is simply a pleasure craft more than thirty feet in length."

"Relax, Doug. I know you're very proud of your little toy, and I like it, too."

Doug looked at the other vessels around the harbor and noted a nice, white trawler named *Moby Dick*. The home port, lettered in gold on the stern, read Houston, Texas. There was a big American flag on the stern jack staff, but Doug wondered why it wasn't also flying a small, British courtesy flag, called the red ensign, on the starboard shroud like all the other boats. Foreign vessels are supposed to fly the proper host country's flag up there, right after they clear into the country. If *Moby Dick* hadn't bothered to check in with customs yet, then they should still be flying a yellow quarantine flag until they did. *Forget it*, he thought, *it's their problem*. He and Nate went below, showered, and dressed to go ashore.

✳   ✳   ✳   ✳

Hunter sat at the Peter Island Resort's main bar since the casual beach bar had closed at sundown. He drank Jack Daniels and ate their complimentary mixed nuts from a carved wooden bowl. He was alone, because neither Garcia nor Sanchez had the required long pants and collared shirt to meet the resort's evening dress code. Over by the pool, a guitarist performed his repertoire of Jimmy Buffett songs to the applause of the dozen well-heeled guests. The bartender sang along softly. Hunter caught something regarding knowing where to go when the volcano blows.

"Hey, bud. I want another Jack black and some more of these nuts," interrupted Hunter.

The bartender stopped singing and said, "Yes, sir," with a tight, neutral expression.

Hunter wasn't in a Jimmy Buffett mood. He was angry and had been angry for three days. It had been going so well, and now somebody had screwed the pooch. How the hell had this happened, and how could he get it back on track? *Find Cassie*, he thought, *and then I'll find the dope*. As he learned in childhood, if he didn't give up, he'd eventually come out on top.

Today, they'd circled Peter Island and landed in some likely spots, but found nothing. They used a story involving Cassie being off by herself kayaking on their non-existent, second kayak. They said they were trying to catch up with her to move on, but no one had seen any such woman.

Hunter gobbled another handful of nuts. He decided to search Salt Island first tomorrow. If nothing turned up they'd go on in to Tortola and ask around. He would also hire a diver there to help recover the coke. Hunter figured he had to give the greasers a rest and keep them happy somehow.

He finished his drink and walked out of the bar past the gift shop. Two men passed him coming into the restaurant and bar area. One of them was solid-looking with some gray hair. The other was tall and lanky with sandy hair.

"Good evening," Doug said while passing.

Hunter only grunted at the strangers and walked on to his boat.

"Did you have a good time with all the rich *gringos?*" Sanchez challenged when Hunter stepped aboard.

"Shut up and get your swimsuit on."

"Why? It is dark now," said Sanchez.

"Because I want you to quietly swim over to one of these other boats, and steal their little British maritime flag for us so it looks like we're legal and all. See, like the one over there, the one named *Payback*," Hunter pointed. "It's your turn to do some swimming."

"Okay, today you are still boss man, but you better come up with the coke or some extra money to pay me soon, or you are not going to be giving orders to anybody," warned Sanchez.

Garcia laughed.

"You stay out of it, Garcia, or I'll find you something to do, too."

"*Sí, sí, El Jefe*," said Garcia in a sarcastic voice.

"We'll find the bitch and the stuff tomorrow," Hunter assured them and tried to believe it.

CHAPTER 7

▼

SALT ISLAND

Cassie awoke very early in the morning and found she'd rolled over into the mud during the night. Where the mud had coated her abused skin it felt cooler, and she had far fewer mosquito and no-see-um bites than she'd suffered during the prior nights. Cassie completed the job, as she redid the portions rain or motion had removed and fully coated herself in the brown goo.

The mud puddle had some new water in it, either due to water table seepage or some blessed rain that occurred while she slept. Cassie crawled over to her bottles and took off her suit. She used the fabric again to filter a few precious ounces of liquid until the surface water was gone. Then Cassie came up with a new idea and placed a ball of wet sand and mud in the swimsuit. She twisted and wrung the suit until she got a few more ounces of water dripping into one of the bottles. Cassie drank quickly and rested until she felt slightly refreshed.

She now knew she was stuck on the island and would need more water to keep going. Cassie patrolled the shore and picked up all the shells, pieces of plastic, or glass having a concave surface. She washed them in the ocean, dried them, and then set them up on a large rock above the high tide line.

Cassie was delighted to find a plastic bag. She dug a small scrape in the earth to stretch it over. She put rocks around the edge of the bag to secure it and another rock in the middle to create a bowl shape. If the clouds would ever provide some rain, maybe she'd catch some this way. Cassie was now exhausted and fell fast asleep under a bush.

Waking from her nap later that morning, Cassie was overjoyed to feel rain on her face. She opened her mouth and relished the drops she could catch. When the rain stopped, she looked up searching the clouds for more, but it was only a localized shower passing through to the south.

A rainbow appeared briefly over Big Island. She smiled as she thought she'd gladly give up the pot of gold for a big pot roast and a six-pack of Perrier. Cassie skimmed and squeezed the new rainwater from the mud before the fluid evaporated again. She then reapplied the mud to protect her skin.

Suddenly, she remembered her rain catchers and raced over to check. Sure enough, there was almost a quart of rainwater distributed among the shells and plastic. Cassie tasted the water. Maybe it was still a touch salty since she had rinsed the shells in seawater earlier, but it was mostly fresh water without mud or bugs. She sat on a rock and happily sucked up every wonderful drop.

Cassie got up and moved to the sand beach on the western side of the island. For the first time she noticed the small metal sign on a post that read: "Reserved for Royal BVI Police Pistol Range." Cassie wondered if the police came weekly, monthly, annually, or what. Maybe she'd found the reason boats had stayed away from the place. She hoped the police would come to practice soon and find her before she died of thirst or starvation.

While she didn't know anything regarding the BVI force, she instinctively distrusted any cop, as her father had taken payoffs from criminals and lost his job. Also, Hunter had bragged about his thugs' contacts with corrupt cops in the Caribbean. But at this point, she didn't care. Anyone other than Hunter who showed up on the beach would be welcomed ashore. She'd even be happy to see old Blackbeard himself.

Cassie considered what she might say to the police versus Hunter versus an unknown and untrusted rescuer. She scooped out a hollow in the sand at the edge of the bushes and curled up in the shade.

As she lay in her little burrow, avoiding the sun, Cassie wondered if anyone would ever find out if she died on Stinking Little Island. Would there be enough bones left to determine who she was? Would they care?

As she considered what to do next, Cassie decided her best chance was to stay near the beach with the police sign and wait for someone to come. She could still make short trips to the mud puddle or her rain catchers. Somewhere she'd read a human could survive six days without any water and more than six weeks without food.

She forced herself to get up and carve big "HELP" letters in the sand. The beach was flat, and no one but an airplane pilot would have much of a chance to see her sign. Still, something was better than nothing she thought. Cassie sighed and curled up in the shade of what she imagined would be her sandy grave.

✳   ✳   ✳   ✳

"Wake up! Y'all go ahead and eat something, but then we gotta get over to Salt Island," ordered Hunter. Garcia and Sanchez moved sluggishly and eventually got *Moby Dick* underway. Rather than hoist the dinghy and kayak up to the top deck, they continued to tow them behind the boat since they weren't going far. They cruised out of Sprat Bay, turned to starboard, and left Peter Island behind as they set a course to round the north end of Dead Chest. Soon, they approached Salt Island from the northwest.

Hunter had trouble anchoring the boat in Salt Island Bay. The bay was very choppy since there was a wind from the north, which was unusual for May. He pulled up the dragging anchor once and tried again with more chain out to increase the scope, or ratio of chain length to water depth. He backed the boat hard until he was sure the hook actually bit into the turtle grass this time.

"Okay, it should hold for awhile, but I don't want to be here too long. We'll have to put a second anchor down if we end up staying here tonight. Let's get in the dinghy and get ashore. When we land, Sanchez, you go to the east, and Garcia, you go to the west. When y'all meet up on the south side of the island, come back north together to the dinghy to report."

"And what are you going to be doing while we are climbing through the cactus and sharp rocks?" asked Garcia.

"I'm going to check out this Caribbean ghost town right in front of us," replied Hunter, pointing to the ruins on the small strip of land between the beach and the two interior salt ponds. "Get going."

A concrete pier pointed back toward a white house with green shutters. The other buildings of the small settlement looked abandoned. Gardens were still laid out, but not planted. Lofty, mature coconut palms swayed their fronds far above. To the right was a small graveyard with a low fence of coral rock. Inland and behind the houses, they could see a blinding-white deposit of salt crystals in a large depression. They split up as planned, and Hunter checked the ruined houses. Afterwards, he walked up to the white house and banged on the door. After a long wait, an elderly black man opened the door.

"Good morning and God bless. Step on in. How much do you desire today?" the man said softly.

"How much what?" Hunter was surprised by the old man's educated tone.

"Sea salt, captain. Aren't you here to buy some good Salt Island sea salt? I've got five pound bags. Nice and clean."

"Oh, yeah right. I'll take three bags," Hunter said to allay suspicion. He quickly looked around the inside of the house after the old man shuffled off to get the salt. Hunter scrambled to return to the front door when he heard the man returning.

"You own this island?"

"No, the Queen, herself owns Salt Island. I pay the Governor one barrel of salt each year as rent. Same as we've done here for 200 years."

"How many people live on this island?"

"It's only me now. I moved back out here after the last caretaker died. Used to be more in the old days, but salt doesn't pay what it used to. The young folks all moved across the channel to Tortola. I only let the sea into the pond once a year now. Then I dam up the channel again, and let the water dry up. I don't like it much on Tortola, myself. It's too busy now, and there's even talk of putting in a traffic light."

"Hey, gramps? Have you seen any white girls walking around the island this week?

"I see white girls on the boats most every day, but few of them go walking around here. They tour in a regular circle, either coming east or west. They all stop at Norman, the Baths on Virgin Gorda, Marina Cay, Jost Van Dyke, and Cane Garden. Other islands, too, but those are the big tourist stops. When they come here, they mostly moor over in Lee Bay, on the west side, snorkeling over the shipwreck."

"What wreck?"

"Man, you don't know much about the BVI do you?"

"It's my first time here."

"Well, young fellow, the wreck is the Royal Mail Steamer *Rhone*. The park service has buoys all 'round the ship now, and folks go diving to see it. The big 1867 hurricane threw RMS *Rhone* onto the rocks. The water rushed in, the boiler blew up, and 125 passengers died. My people here on Salt Island saved a few, and the Queen thanked us for it. That was the old Queen, mind you—Victoria herself.

"Movie people came here once, and made a diving movie, *The Deep*. They filmed the underwater part right here, on the *Rhone*, not in Bermuda like the book reads. I told them to watch out. Salt Island Passage can be a dangerous place."

"Yeah, tell me about it. Anyway, gramps, the white chick I'm looking for is blonde, five-eight, blue eyes, nice headlights, couple of ankle tattoos, and wearing a green bikini. We were supposed to meet her over on Cooper Island, but we think she got confused."

"Cooper doesn't look anything like Salt Island, young fellow, and I didn't see any such girl carrying any lights or what all. And I'm sure not your grampa. Sounds like you're trying to humbug me. It'll be fifteen dollars for the salt, and good day to you."

"American dollars?"

"Yes, of course! Yankee dollars are all we use here. We're so close to the U.S. Virgin Islands and get so many Americans. Sweet Jesus."

Hunter briefly considered killing the old man in return for thinking he was stupid. It would be so easy, but some other boat could show up before he left, and he didn't need to attract any attention from the authorities. Hunter paid the money and went back to the pier to wait for his crew.

"It's about time you clowns made it back," said Hunter when they finally approached.

"You try climbing on the rocks next time. Look what Garcia found," said Sanchez with a smug expression.

Garcia presented a green bikini top with a white floral print. The hooks on the back were snagged on a short piece of ragged blue line.

"It is the bitch's swimsuit and a piece of the rope that was towing the coke."

"No shit, Sherlock. Where did you find it?" demanded Hunter.

"It was on the shore on the west side. There were a couple of boats near there with scuba divers swimming around."

"See, I told you she did it," crowed Sanchez.

"You don't know for sure," said Hunter. "She still could've fallen overboard if she came up on deck right as the boat tilted. Then she could've gotten tangled up and died. At least we know she had some kind of problem or she wouldn't have lost her top. She didn't take half her goddamn suit off to swim faster. So she's around here somewhere, or her body is. This is warm water and not too deep. If Cassie's dead, gas will build up in her body and it should float soon."

Hunter actually hoped she wasn't dead, and that it was all an accident. She better not have had anything to do with their recent problems. *Damn it*, he thought, *she is going to be the one. She's going to be my pirate queen, like Anne Bonny with Captain Calico Jack.*

"So, now what do we do?" Garcia asked Hunter.

"We still have to find her. If she's dead, her body might wash up on the closest edge of Salt Island, Peter Island, or even little Dead Chest. I know we've checked all those once, but we didn't walk around on Dead Chest. Tell you what, now that we know she might've had something to do with the canister, we'll get a diver down there and get it back right now. Then every day we'll return and check those three areas around where we lost her. After we look, we'll check all the boats and ask around to see who she's with if she's alive.

"Got it? So first, we get the coke back today, and then we'll land on Dead Chest tomorrow. Finally, each and every day, we check for her body and search the other boats. If she isn't dead, she'll wish she was after I find her," said Hunter for their benefit, but he recalled her moves in bed and still felt confused.

"Do we have to go to Tortola to get a professional diver?" asked Sanchez.

"Hell, no. There's two boatloads of tourist divers right here on the other side of Salt Island. Garcia saw them diving on some shipwreck already. They've probably got a couple of pros running each boat. We can deal with them quickly and in cash. They can't see *Moby Dick* from there, and we can give them fake names just in case."

The men jumped in the dinghy and went to *Moby Dick*. Hunter left Garcia on the boat to work on putting a second anchor out to secure the vessel for a longer stay. He and Sanchez grabbed the marked chart and took the dinghy around the point to Lee Bay where the scuba diving boats were. Hunter picked the biggest one and came alongside.

"Permission to come aboard?" asked Hunter when he saw the dive boat's skipper.

"What do you need?"

"We lost something overboard and I want to hire you to dive for it."

"Okay, but kill your outboard and paddle over here. I've got my assistant and a bunch of paying customers coming up from the wreck soon, and I don't need them to get a haircut from your prop."

"Oh sure, no problem," Hunter replied. He and Sanchez paddled the last few yards and tied their dinghy to the stern of the dive boat. Hunter summoned up his best "country boy on vacation" persona and launched into a performance. "Howdy. I'm Grant Michaels, and this is Ken Travis. We were taking our boat, the *Running Start*, from Peter Island over to Salt Island this morning when we lost a white canister overboard. We were wondering if you wanted to earn some quick cash picking it up for us."

"Hell, I'm always interested in quick cash. I'm the divemaster and skipper. Be glad to do business with you. Where's your boat now?"

"She's just around the point, by the Salt Island settlement. The wife wanted to buy some sea salt."

"Yeah, it's an interesting stop. Do you know exactly where you lost your item?"

"Sure do," said Hunter and showed him the chart with his GPS notations marked on the side.

"Heck, your position must've been right on top of Blonde Rock. See, if you take the ruler on the side and match your latitude reading, then read across to this longitude, your GPS fix matches the location of this underwater pinnacle here. The tip's only nine feet down, and Blonde Rock's our next stop once the customers are done looking at the *Rhone* here. How deep a draft do you have on your boat?"

"Only five feet," said Hunter, who suddenly understood what the canister and lines must have snagged on.

"Then you wouldn't have hit it in waves like the ones we have today. The water can get disturbed around the rock, though, and I can understand something falling overboard. What did you say you lost again?"

"It looks like a white oil drum. It's an old life raft canister, but we had some extra chain and life jackets and stuff in it. The drum was heavy enough to sink, I guess. It's not worth much, but I still need it to put the life raft back in when it returns from the shop."

"Yeah, those inflatable rafts have to be serviced every few years to be safe. I tell you what, Mr. Michaels, I'll only charge you $300 to go down and look since we're going over there anyway. You can ride along with us, and take your item back to Salt Island Bay in your dinghy."

"How about $200 to look, and the other $100 only if you bring it up?" said Hunter. He didn't want to appear too eager.

"Okay, you've got a deal. I'll tell my customers the diver who finds it splits the extra hundred with me so you'll have a dozen guys looking for your canister. They'll enjoy that, anyway. They get to see the fish and coral around the rock, and have a sunken treasure hunt, too. You and Mr. Travis want something to drink?"

"Right on. I will take a brewski, dude." said Sanchez, apparently trying to sound more Anglo.

The boat recovered its divers. The dripping tourists each grabbed another tank for the second dive of the trip while they moved over to the area of Blonde Rock. The divemaster introduced "Grant" and "Ken," and told them of the fifty-dollar prize to the diver who found the missing canister. The ten American men and two Japanese women were all tourists and eager to help out.

The boat anchored after reaching a good spot near both the rock and the recorded site of the loss. The divemaster gave his standard briefing regarding Blonde Rock: stay with your dive buddy, and instructions on how long you can safely stay at the various depths there. He reminded the divers the visibility was so good they could scan the bottom without having to go too deep. After the briefing, they put the ladder into the water, and the skipper led the way. Hunter, Sanchez, and the assistant divemaster waited aboard.

"Shit, that was easy. We'll have the stuff back in no time, with all these suckers looking for us," whispered Hunter to Sanchez.

After more than a half hour, the customers started coming up. They all had smiles on their faces. Unfortunately, it was only the colorful fish and coral they were pleased with. One after another nodded politely at Hunter and apologized for not seeing his lost equipment. Finally, the skipper himself surfaced and climbed aboard.

"Sorry guys, it looks like you only owe me the $200. I didn't even bother to enjoy the sights. Instead, I went straight to where I could see the bottom and did an expanded box search from there. I must have looked for more than 100 yards all around. It's pretty flat once you get away from the rock. Your white canister isn't there. We can tow your dinghy again and give you a ride back to your boat if you want."

"Shit! No thanks, bud. We'll get there on our own." Hunter grudgingly paid the man. He and Sanchez got in the dinghy to go back around the point to their hidden trawler.

"All that freaking coke gone!" said Hunter as soon as they were out of earshot of the divers. "Don't you say nothin', Sanchez. I'm not in the goddamned mood for it!"

When they told Garcia the bad news, he swore and said, "It has to be Cassie. She either has the stuff, or she knows who took it."

"Okay, maybe you're right. Let's go and search Dead Chest properly, and then look on the boats like I said. We'll get her."

*   *   *   *

Doug got up early Monday morning, and prepared *Payback* for another day of fun. He got the boat underway by himself and carefully exited Sprat Bay. Doug turned west and, in only ten minutes, had dropped the anchor in Deadman Bay. The sound of the anchor chain running out over the roller finally woke up his brother.

"Avast there, Captain Crunch. Where are we now?" asked Nate with a yawn.

"Deadman Bay. We're still on Peter Island, just around the corner from the restaurant. I want to take you over to Cabey Point to look for shells. Sometimes, especially after a storm, you can find a lot of shells there. They'll be on the beach or rolling in the surf." Doug pointed at the little beach to the west. "You want to eat something first?"

"No, I'm about to bust a gut after all the food last night."

They got in the dinghy and beached it. There were a few small shells, but not as many good ones as Doug hoped. Doug was surprised by the sight of a bull-dozer working on a new jetty being constructed out into bay.

"More damn progress! The jetty wasn't here last time. I guess all the new rock they pushed into the surf changed the currents. Now the shelling sucks."

"It's okay. I found a couple anyway."

Doug entertained Nate by telling him the names of the island birds, lizards, and cacti as they continued to look. Nate appeared surprised by all the species.

"So you've got masked boobies, brown boobies, and red-footed boobies, right? Then there's the dildo cactus and the woolly nipple cactus? Are these names for real, Doug? It sure sounds like some awful horny sailors named all this stuff."

"I wish there were more sea shells, though. You want to try somewhere else?"

"What about the island over there? It's not connected to Peter, so the resort guests won't have picked it clean of shells."

"You might be right. You're pointing at Dead Chest Island. I haven't been there for years. Jeanne and I unwisely landed on the windward shore there once. Some big waves came up and swamped our old hard-sided dinghy. We had to swim the dinghy to deeper water and bail it before we could climb in. Then, I had to row until we could dry out the outboard enough to make it start. The next time, I smartened up and came in on the leeward beach on the west side there. So you want to try landing on Dead Chest?"

"Sure, Captain Flint. It sounds cool. Let's take a sword and a bottle of rum, too. Arrgh, matey! Belay that. Shiver me timbers, and all that shit."

"Okay. You got it, Long John Silver. Truthfully, Nate, I don't have a set plan. Anywhere you want to go, just ask and we'll go there. I promise."

"I might actually hold you to your promise, brother."

"You do that. I'll even take you down island like you mentioned at the airport."

"What's so tough about going down island anyway?" asked Nate.

"It's not so tough, only different. I guess it's the whole comfort-level thing again. As you move south down the chain of islands, the conditions change. The

Bahamas and the Virgins are developed, sheltered, and fairly easy to sail. As you move south, the islands are strung out with some tough, open-ocean sailing in between. Here, the islands are dry, but they get wetter down south, and some have rain forests and waterfalls. There are volcanic hotspots, and even active volcanoes."

"Awesome. Where's the closest volcano?"

"I guess Montserrat is the closest active one. The Soufriere Hills volcano there erupted in 1995 and has been active on and off since then. Half the population left, and you can only visit the north end of the island. After Montserrat, Dominica has a boiling lake and hot waterfalls. Farther south, you find Mt. Pelée on Martinique. It blew up in 1902 and killed all 30,000 people in the town of St. Pierre, except for one drunk who was in a thick jail cell."

"See! I would've been safe," chuckled Nate.

"The next island, St. Lucia, has the Qualibou volcano with boiling mud craters you can drive right up to. Farther down island, you'll find an underwater volcano north of Grenada. It erupted twice in the '80s and still bubbles up poisonous gas occasionally. It's called 'Kick 'em Jenny.'"

"Can we check out a couple of those spots, too?"

"Sure, anyplace you want to go. Another aspect of going down island is the people are poorer and the crime rate increases in places. The islands depend more on agriculture than on tourism and wages are quite low.

"When you reach the Windward group, these so-called 'boat boys' will come to your yacht and get real insistent on helping you tie up or anchor. Then they want a tip. Others will come out in bumboats to sell you fish, vegetables, water, ice, ganja, or even play a song for you. Farther on, when you get to Trinidad, I heard the foreign business managers have to carry concealed pistols for safety. Finally, Venezuela has nests of actual pirates. Many of them are renegade soldiers, moonlighting."

"Are you yanking my chain, Captain Kidd? There aren't actually modern pirates are there?" said Nate with a raised eyebrow.

"*Au contraire, mon frère*. There are genuine pirates, and they're getting more prevalent. Piracy simply means boarding a vessel with the intent to steal, or worse. You don't need a wooden square-rigger with muzzle-loading cannons to be a pirate. Look at the sailing magazines and you'll see urgent warnings to stay away from sections of Columbia, Venezuela, the Dominican Republic, Jamaica, and big chunks of Central America. People have been robbed, stabbed, shot, raped, and had their boats stolen. Not only boats, but full-size ships carrying oil or freight. Remember the cruise ship getting shot up off Somalia recently? All the various revolutions and drug wars tend to be related somehow to some well-armed groups of pirates."

"Wow, I never realized it was so bad," admitted Nate.

"Piracy's still very rare, but it is a growing problem. It's like I used to tell our guests, sailing the ocean is a real adventure, not a sanitized 'Adventure Land' a la Disney World. The sea itself kills far more people than any modern pirates do, though. You have to be careful with your equipment and planning. The ocean neither knows nor cares you are only on vacation."

"Right, like on my sub. Everybody had to keep their shit together. If one guy screwed up, he could kill us all."

"On the other hand, life is short, and you have to get out there and have some fun. Safe can be the opposite of fun, I guess," said Doug.

"Do you have a gun onboard?"

"Yeah, I finally decided to get one. You have to have some good judgment about whether you want to actually use a weapon, though. If they have the jump on you, then it might be better to hand over some money and hope for the best. However, if you are positive they're going to kill you anyway, you might as well try to defend yourself and go down fighting.

"Anyway," Doug continued, "you can usually prevent a pirate boarding simply by displaying your weapons so they see you aren't a soft target. I'll show you the gun later."

"Yeah, I'd appreciate it," said Nate.

"You can't obsess over it. Something is going to get you someday. I know some people back home who can't imagine how we can even sleep on a boat. Others have a comfort zone letting them sleep on a docked boat or maybe a moored boat, but certainly not on an anchored boat off an uninhabited island. Others have sailed for years, but are scared to charter a bareboat and sail on the ocean. Some can handle the ocean part, but can't handle being out of sight of land.

"Actually, most people who sail can handle short inter-island hops, but are justifiably nervous regarding crossing oceans. It's about where I am, I guess. I've never gone out more than a hundred miles, but I might try someday."

"Yeah, what do you have to lose at your age? You've got one foot in the grave already," chuckled Nate.

"You're not getting any younger yourself. You might be one of these guys with a bigger comfort zone than he should have," responded Doug with a smile.

"What do you mean by that? I might be offended if I can figure it out."

"Don't strain your brain. I'm only teasing. On a serious note, I have certainly seen a plethora of idiots come here and attempt something they're not ready for. They lie on their sailing resumes and convince the rental company they know what they're doing when they damn sure don't. We call them credit-card captains. You can usually tell who they are. Sometimes they dress up like they think a skipper should, y'know. They'll have a t-shirt that says 'Captain' across the front, or a gold-braided hat, or one of those fake Greek fisherman caps.

"You see these guys anchoring right in the middle of a mooring field. At night, they piss me off royally by letting their halyards slap the mast like a schoolyard flagpole. They hit well-known reefs, or come charging into a harbor at sunset during the crowded Christmas season and still expect an open spot to magically be there for them. I even knew one overconfident doctor who ignorantly crossed international boundaries and showed up in St. Thomas thinking it was Jost Van Dyke, an island twenty miles away."

"Yeah, a lot of doctors think they're infallible gods," agreed Nate.

The brothers took the dinghy over to Dead Chest, and ran the inflatable's rigid bottom up on the sand. They jumped out quickly, and pulled the dinghy higher up the beach. Doug noticed some strange lines in the sand, but the north wind and disturbed waves had erased any pattern.

"This looks like a good spot. I'm going to do some shelling. Do you want to tie up the dinghy to something for us?"

"Aye, aye, Captain Kirk." Nate took the long dinghy painter towards a stunted sea-grape tree at the edge of the beach. As he approached the vegetation, he noticed a depression in the sand containing an extremely dirty, topless woman curled up in the fetal position. He yelled, "Doug, get over here now!"

CHAPTER 8

▼

VIRGIN GORDA

"Lady, are you okay?" asked Nate.

Cassie slowly stood up and brushed ineffectively at her thick coating of sand and mud. She struggled and croaked out a single word. "Water."

"Water? Sure, we've got water. Stay here and I'll go get it." She watched as Nate raced back to the dinghy, grabbed the water bottle, and ran up the beach. "Here, take it. It's all yours. What's your name? I'm Nate Thompson, and this is my brother, Doug."

"How's it goin' eh?" Doug deadpanned as Nate shot him a dirty look.

"How long have you been here? How did you get here?"

Cassie stared at the water bottle in her hands and ignored Nate's rapid-fire babbling, as well as Doug's weak attempt at a joke. She slowly unscrewed the top and cautiously tasted the water. *Oh, thank God,* she thought to herself. *It's so good!* It was not like the sludge on which she had been surviving. She gulped down the whole bottle and silently held it out to the newly arrived Doug. Maybe he could give her another bottle. Tears made lines in the mud as they ran down her face.

"Let's get her to the dinghy," said Doug. He took the bottle and put her arm around his neck. Nate held her waist and other arm. They walked Cassie to the water and eased her into the dinghy.

"Wait." Cassie let go of them and walked into the ocean until she was chest deep. She rinsed herself and rubbed all the mud off. She washed off her face and hair and surfaced again with her hair hanging over her forehead. Cassie flipped her blonde hair backward and stepped out of the water like a dripping, reborn Venus rising from the sea. One arm covered her breasts.

The brothers were mesmerized. Doug snapped out of his trance first, pulled the shirt off his back, and offered the garment to Cassie. Then Nate gave her his khaki cap that read "S/V *Payback*" and "Crew" on the front and "Tortola, BVI" on the back.

"Thanks," she said and tugged the t-shirt down over her wet torso. She put the cap on over her dripping hair. "I'm going to be okay now. Do you have any more water or maybe some food I could have? I feel better than I probably look, but I'd certainly appreciate some."

"Sure, we have plenty back on the boat," said Doug. Both brothers scrambled all over each other to quickly turn the dinghy's bow seaward, and push it into the turquoise water. They held it while Cassie stepped into the boat. The men pushed off and then jumped in after reaching deeper water. Cassie sat starboard on the inflated tube while Nate sat on the port side facing her. Doug perched in the stern and started the motor.

Conversation was difficult on the way to *Payback* due to the noise from outboard. It gave Cassie some time to think. She had to follow the plan she'd formulated on the island regarding how much she could tell these guys. After all, who were they, and could she trust them? She didn't want the news of her rescue to get back to Hunter in any manner. She should be cautious.

"What was the name of that stinking little island?" asked Cassie loudly.

"The one you were on?" Nate shouted back.

"Yes, and the bigger one over there," said Cassie.

"The big one's Peter Island. We just came from there. The little one's Dead Chest. You know, as in 'Fifteen men on the Dead Man's Chest,'" said Nate.

The front of the yellow shirt had embroidered green words that read: "Sunny Caribbee—Island Art and Spices—Now Two Locations—Tortola and Neptune Beach, Florida—Great Food—Great Fun." "Did you two come off a ship?"

"No, we have our own boat over there," said Nate, pointing towards the southwest. "It's called *Payback*. It's only a boat, of course, not a ship. Okay, it's actually Doug's boat, not *ours*. I'm just riding along for a while.

"Anyway, it is a sloop-rigged sailboat. You can also call it a yacht, because it's a pleasure craft over thirty feet, but it's not one of those big, fancy yachts with air conditioning and uniforms and all."

Cassie smiled at Nate's rambling chatter. *He's acting as awkward as a junior-high-school boy on his first date*, she thought. The two brothers looked fairly innocent so far. She didn't want to actually lie to them. Maybe she could convince them to let her hide with them for awhile.

She didn't want to see Hunter again and didn't want to attract any attention in case he found where she was. She figured Garcia would have a contact, or mole, in any group of local island cops. She needed more time to think this all through.

Doug piloted them to *Payback*'s stern, and the brothers helped Cassie aboard and below deck. She sat at the galley table while they scurried around to get her various drinks and some food. Cassie drank and ate greedily while she slowly answered their questions.

"Slow up on the liquids, now," admonished Doug. "Take little sips. If you get bloated, you might screw up your body temperature and pass out. How did you get marooned on Dead Chest anyway?"

"Okay, I'll only sip now. I promise. My name is Cassie MacDuff, and I'm from San Diego. A jerk named Hunter Lamar lives here now and thinks he's my new boyfriend," she said, using middle names instead of surnames. She told herself it wasn't a lie because Hunter lives on the boat, the *Moby Dick* is here in the BVI, so he lives here now, too.

Cassie continued, "We were on his motorboat, and he wanted me to do some things for him I just wasn't ready to do, so I jumped off the boat to swim ashore." Cassie looked down demurely and batted her eyelashes.

"That asshole!" interjected Nate. Both Doug and Nate tut-tutted and shook their heads like offended maiden aunts.

"He just took off without me. He knew we were close to Peter Island and probably figured I'd get a ride from there. The current was too strong, though, and I ended up on Dead Chest. I didn't even see him come looking for me." *That's technically true, too*, she thought. *It was Sanchez who was looking.*

"What kind of boat does he have?" asked Doug.

"It's a forty-foot trawler. It's his wet dream. He just loves it," said Cassie, stalling for time.

"It figures. It such a trashy boat name, yet I must've seen ten boats named *Wet Dream* out there. These young jerks think they are so damn original," said Doug. "He probably flies one of those tacky Jolly Roger flags on it, too."

"He did say he wants to buy one." She was relieved at Doug's fortunate misunderstanding of her vulgarity literally being the name of Hunter's boat. "Anyway, could I stay with you for a few days? I could cook and clean and help with the boat. Just until I'm sure he's not looking for me anymore?" She paused, took a deep breath, and gazed at the deck again. "He can be kind of rough. Please?"

"Oh, absolutely! Right, Doug?" Nate said quickly and looked over to Doug like a boy begging to keep a puppy that followed him home.

"Well, okay. But first we have to call this in on the radio and get you some medical attention."

"No, please! I can't let Hunter hear it on the radio, and I don't know what the police would do. I don't want a hassle from some island cops. It'd be a big mess, and I don't have a passport or money or any I.D. on me now. Couldn't we just finish your BVI trip, and then you guys could drop me somewhere else when I know he's gone? I'll get my stuff from him later."

"Yeah, Doug. It would basically be a he-said, she-said kind of deal."

"All right. It's your call, Cassie. However, I want you to know the BVI police are very reputable. This isn't some banana republic. I do insist we take you to a doctor and pay for it." He looked in the cruising guidebook to the BVI. "There's a hospital on Tortola and a clinic over on the island of Virgin Gorda. With this north wind today, it would actually be quicker to sail to Virgin Gorda, even though it's a little farther. It's where we planned to go next anyway."

"Thanks. That sounds great. I'll definitely pay you back later for whatever the clinic charges. Pay back, like the boat I guess," Cassie said with a smile. She thought any other island would be better than Tortola because that's where Hunter said he was going. Maybe she actually could trust these men. Cassie considered if she should stop worrying and just tell the police what happened—for Leo's sake.

She decided she would tell the brothers the whole story tonight after all—if they actually took her to a doctor. She still felt weak and needed a little more time to think on it. "It'll do Hunter some good to miss me for awhile. Say, I'm really tired now. I probably ate too much. May I use one of the showers and a bed please?"

"You bet," said Nate. He jumped up and escorted her to the port aft cabin adjacent to his own starboard cabin. Doug had the larger, forward cabin. Each cabin had its own enclosed head. Nate showed Cassie how to operate her shower and marine toilet.

"We should get there soon," Doug called down from above as he prepared to get underway.

*   *   *   *

Nate came back up and helped when they pulled up the anchor and initially headed north into the wind to set the sails. Then Doug turned to starboard and steered around the northern end of Dead Chest.

Right before the island blocked his view, Doug noticed the white trawler from the night before. It was coming around the south side of Dead Chest, rounding up into the wind and turning towards the beach he had recently left. In the few seconds before the boats were blocked from each other's view, Doug noted *Moby Dick* was finally flying the red ensign on her starboard shroud. Good. They must have finally checked in. Doug kept an eye out for any similar trawler named *Wet Dream*.

"I'm going to keep the engine on at its cruising speed of 2,200 rpm, even though there's a good wind. So we'll sail and motor at the same time. We need to make some speed and get to Virgin Gorda on this one tack.

"I hope Cassie is okay below with the bunk tilting. I guess she'd sleep on anything now after what she's been through. You know, this is pretty wild for me. It's like picking up a hitchhiker at sea. I don't ever pick up hitchhikers when I'm driving. We don't know much about our castaway. Maybe she's dangerous in some way and we shouldn't have done it. What do you think of her?"

"Dibs!" shouted Nate suddenly.

Doug asked quizzically. "What?"

"I call it. I saw her first."

Doug laughed, "I saw you staring at her tits first maybe. She's interested in food and water and rest now, anyway, not some scurvy sailors like us."

Nate smiled. "Guilty as charged. What is it with boobs anyway? We men are so damn fascinated by a couple of overgrown sweat glands. Tits are just fatty tissue hanging on female chests until they eventually sag and collapse. They aren't of much use to us. Mammary glands should be hypnotizing to infants—not to grown men."

"Ah, that explains the infantile behavior. You are my baby brother after all."

"Oh, don't give me that crap. I do it and you do it, too. Even the Pope looks at hooters. Any man, seeing a shapely woman appear, spends maybe a tenth of a second looking at her face to see if he knows her. If he recognizes her, he keeps his eyes on her face if she is within a few feet or so. If he doesn't know her, he immediately drops his eyes and checks out her fun-bags. Three seconds later, he'll scope her ass and legs. Finally, he'll go back to the face."

"And eventually he'll listen to what she's saying, right?" said Doug.

"Yeah, maybe. You know, I worry about my girls a lot. Growing up with all these goofy influences could definitely mess them up."

Doug didn't know what to say. He knew Nate constantly worried about his girls. Avoiding an awkward silence, he went up and adjusted the boom vang when it didn't technically need any tweaking. *Payback* was in the groove, charging along with no pressure on the helm one way or another.

The yacht motorsailed swiftly and easily past Salt Island, Cooper, Ginger, Round Rock, and Fallen Jerusalem. The brothers furled the jib and lowered the mainsail as they approached their destination. They headed for the entrance to the Virgin Gorda Yacht Harbour north of Spanish Town.

"Here, tie two of these fenders over each side. I'm going to call in on channel 16 and see where the harbormaster wants us. Use a clove hitch knot and don't let them dangle too low. Okay?"

"Okay, Mr. Fussy. I got your low dangle right here. Hey, Doug? Doesn't *gorda* mean fat in Spanish?"

"I think so."

"What about Tortola?"

"Tortola means turtle dove. Lots of small doves all over the place in the BVI."

Doug briefly went below to use the VHF radio. "All right, I've got our slip assignment."

"Aye, aye, Captain Morgan. So, are there actually any fat virgins on Virgin Gorda?"

"I think the name came from sailors who'd been at sea too long, somehow seeing a fat woman's silhouette in the mountain over there," said Doug, pointing north.

Cassie stuck her head up through her cabin hatch. "Who's Captain Morgan? I thought you told me his name was Doug?" She sounded worried.

"Oh, it's only my little joke. I give him various names of famous skippers so he doesn't get too damn uppity. I won't do it anymore if it bothers you."

"I can't get any respect," chuckled Doug. "This morning, I was Captain Crunch. I guess this time I'm either an old buccaneer or a bottle of spiced rum. How're you feeling, Cassie?"

"I'm better, thanks. You need me to help do anything when you dock?"

"Nah, we can handle it. Hey, see if any of our reef sandals can be adjusted to fit you. We don't have any flip-flops and the shoes sure won't work. We'll be there soon and walk you to the clinic," said Doug. "You know, I actually dislike marinas. They're noisy, and the water isn't clean like it is anchoring outside.

Docking can be tricky too if there's a big wind or current. This'll be the quickest way to get you ashore, though, so it makes sense today."

After Cassie went below to find some footwear, Nate leaned over and whispered to Doug, "Oh man, I hope she didn't hear all that about tits. Damn it."

Cassie came back up wearing Doug's sandals. "These work after I tightened the straps. Thanks. Oh, and thanks for the shirt Doug. I certainly don't make a habit of running around topless. I lost my top up on the cliff while trying to signal somebody. Thank God you guys came ashore."

"No problem. Maybe after you see the doctor we could see if there's a shop open to get you something to wear."

They kept the red buoys to starboard and followed the curve of the breakwater. *Payback* approached the slip slowly. Doug eased her in. Nate made the jump and tensioned the spring line so the boat moved closer to the pier when it slid forward. The fenders softly kissed the rough wood. Doug locked the boat, made some positioning adjustments to the docking lines, and the crew all stepped ashore on Virgin Gorda.

CHAPTER 9

▼

THE BATHS

The brothers sat outside the Virgin Gorda health clinic and waited for Cassie. As with most business in the islands, it was taking quite a while. Doug was used to "island time" and knew it was generally due to the islanders' friendly and polite nature. They socialized and didn't rush, but usually did a good job. He'd rather be on island time than have to do things "in a New York minute."

While they waited, Nate went into a nearby store and bought a copy of yesterday's *St. Thomas Daily News*. "Look at this, Doug. Those poor cheese-heads back in Milwaukee got down into the forties last night. It's the last half of May and they're still freezing their nuts off. What is it here, in the low eighties now?"

"I think so. Yep, I'm done with living up on the frozen tundra. Here, it's a little toasty three months a year, but it's perfect the other nine months. Where we came from, you get the opposite. You might get three months of decent weather and nine months of depressing, dreary crap. I sure don't get winter cabin fever living in the cabin of my boat."

Hearing Nate talk about Midwestern winters led Doug to think about how two brothers could grow up together yet turn out so completely different. Though two years younger, Nate always had the daring wildness that Doug now felt he had missed. During his teenage years, Nate got into various minor problems with the law—usually standing by some ill-chosen friend. He'd tried all the pharmaceutical experiments of those days and only dabbled in his schoolwork.

Nate hadn't gone in much for sports, even though he was tall and lanky with great running ability.

While the stocky Doug had been a shy kid, Nate's sandy hair and easy smile always attracted the girls. Unfortunately, Nate was as poor a judge of female character as he was of male. His first marriage had quickly fallen apart. Soon afterward, he'd dropped out of school and enlisted.

Surprisingly, Nate had done well in the Navy. Doug was amazed that Nate tolerated the discipline and actually volunteered for the elite Submarine Service. Doug greatly respected Nate for doing his duty under hazardous conditions, and he got a vicarious enjoyment from the stories his brother told him of playing chicken with Soviet subs and of wild nights in Pacific ports. Nate never made it to the Caribbean or even to the Atlantic side where Doug had done all of his sailing.

In spite of his history, Nate had married again. This marriage lasted long enough to produce two sweet girls. Unfortunately, Nate had let Doug know he and his second wife were now having some problems and were now in a trial separation phase, but he didn't divulge the specifics. Nate had failed at running a backyard nature franchise store, then a miniature golf course, and was now "in between" commission sales jobs. Doug knew his brother was always hurting for money so he was surprised when Nate had agreed to take a sabbatical from job-hunting to join Doug. He'd appeared eager and had even paid his own airfare to join Doug to cruise the BVI and head south, or "down island" as the locals said, to the end of the Antilles chain.

Nate was especially interested if Doug planned to go all the way to Trinidad. Doug didn't know why. Nate had only said he'd heard there was some great beer and steel-drum music there. Other than that, he didn't know much regarding the islands or sailing. It didn't matter. Doug was happy to have a new pupil.

＊　　　＊　　　＊　　　＊

Doug watched closely as Cassie walked out of the clinic. She had some salve on her face and arms. Her feet were bandaged in several places.

"What'd the doc say?" asked Nate.

"He's says I'm going to be fine. I'm supposed to avoid the direct sun for awhile, drink plenty of fluids, and get a lot of rest. I probably could've figured that myself and saved some charges on your credit card. He did give me some antibiotics and pain pills, though. I guess the sea urchin spine tips simply dissolve eventually. I was worried he was going to want to dig them out with a scalpel. Sorry about all this, Doug. I'll definitely pay you back with interest."

"Oh, don't worry. You're part of my crew for now, and I always take care of my crew. I'm just glad you're okay. Do you both want to go have lunch at the Olde Yard Inn? The food's great."

"Sure, let's go."

"Hold it guys! I appreciate the offer, but I can't go anywhere else dressed like this. I'm still wearing your sandals and shirt, the bottom of an old swimsuit, and no underwear. You two go ahead. I'll eat something on the boat and wait for you."

"Oops! Sorry, Cassie. Let's take you shopping first. We promised to check for an open store, didn't we? Maybe you could wrap a towel around you for a skirt. We don't want to offend the locals by having you run around in a swimsuit any longer. They don't appreciate visitors wearing swimsuits away from the beach. Good thing it's Monday and everything's open. I'd be happy to take a woman clothes shopping—after all this time. It'll be just like the old days with Jeanne."

"Are you divorced?"

"No, my wife died over a year ago, and my two kids are grown now."

"Oh, I'm so sorry to hear about your wife. I recently lost someone close to me, too." Cassie paused and suddenly started crying. She hugged the surprised Doug and held him tight. She sobbed and said, "It's just not fair. You work so hard to make things right, and your life is finally going so well, and then it's all taken away. It's not right! Why do so many bad things have to happen?"

Doug held her as she let it all loose. It felt good to hold a woman again. Obviously, Cassie had been through a lot lately and needed some help. He was grateful to be needed. Comforting the sobbing woman tripped the chivalry switch in Doug's brain. He became committed to her happiness even if he didn't consciously realize it. He asked softly, "Did you lose your husband or child, Cassie?"

*   *   *   *

Cassie wiped her face and slowly got under control. "No, a good friend of mine. I haven't had a husband or any kids yet." She changed her focus and asked, "How about you Nate?"

"I've got two girls staying home with their mom, in Wisconsin. We aren't divorced yet, but things are probably headed there soon. We're just separated now. Life's a bitch, isn't it? Time and age will steal everything from us eventually anyway, won't it? So, come on. Let's just go have some fun while we can. It's the only philosophy which makes any damn sense to me."

They walked south into Spanish Town and visited a couple of shops. The brothers waited outside and cooled their heels while Cassie bought clothes and shoes. She also picked up toiletries, a little makeup, and even pantyhose in case Doug decided to take her somewhere fancy. She changed into a new outfit in the dressing room and put Doug's old clothes in a bag. She signaled and Doug went inside to sign the credit-card receipt, but then got caught up in looking at a display of Cuban cigars. Cassie decided to go wait outside in the breeze with Nate.

"Wow, it's a whole new girl! Get everything you need?"

"Kind of. They didn't carry my exact size in a couple of things, but beggars can't be choosers."

"I think I'll go in and see what's keeping Doug. You want to read this paper? I caught the American news and weather already. Save the sports section for me, though."

Cassie took the paper and flipped through it. In the Caribbean news section she noticed a small article datelined Grenada, with her face staring out of a blurry photograph. She spotted Leo's name in the text. Cassie nervously looked around then read the whole text.

The paper said a fisherman had netted a body west of Grenada and brought it in to the island. Cards in his wallet identified Leo as a wealthy American investor. A receipt from a hotel in Aruba was also found. Employees there confirmed his recent stay at the hotel, and his use of the hotel safe to keep a waist-pouch money belt. They also stated a young woman, filmed by a casino security camera, had checked in with him. The article went on to note the coroner determined death was the result of a knife wound and blunt trauma to the head. The waist pouch was not found on the body, and the police now wanted the unknown woman for questioning.

Cassie quickly glanced around to see if anyone was looking before she tore out the article and stuffed it in the trash bin. Her heart pounded as she relived that terrible night. They'd been halfway between Trinidad and Grenada when it all happened. Leo, fully dressed, was piloting the boat, and had gone over the side with whatever was in his pockets. Now the police wanted her.

A new woman mysteriously appeared in Leo's life. He was carrying a lot of cash, and now it and the yacht were gone. It didn't look good. She knew he'd already deposited the money in a secret bank account in Trinidad, but she'd have a hard time proving it. Of course the police would suspect her. Cassie thought

she couldn't tell them or the brothers anything now, at least not until she talked
to a lawyer. She needed more time to think.

Nate and Doug came out of the shop with a clear bag of fat cigars. Nate put
the bag to his nose and sniffed deeply.

"Ah, so good! Hand-rolled on the smooth, brown thighs of Cuban *señoritas.*"
Cassie rolled her eyes.

"Let me have one of those bad boys," demanded Doug.

The brothers happily lit their cigars. They grabbed a waiting taxi to ride to the
restaurant for lunch. Nate and Doug puffed away with the speed and affected
seriousness of men who only smoke on special occasions, but want onlookers to
think they are sophisticated cigar aficionados.

As the taxi hesitantly moved north, hens and chicks ran across the
palm-shaded road while proud roosters perched on fence posts and loudly
claimed the world. A tethered goat nibbled the roadside grass and watched the
taxi pass with its strangely satanic, yellow eyes. Twice, the driver stopped the car
dead in the middle of the road to say hello to friends lounging on nearby porches.

Cassie sat in the front seat and watched the scenery pass on the right. The
brothers sat in the back and talked. She was silent and lost in her thoughts during
the short trip. Even so, she was surprised when the driver stopped a third time to
lean across to her window and discuss business with a fellow cab driver who also
had patient passengers in his cab. When the driver talked to his friend, he shifted
into a swift dialect of English that used words and accents nearly incomprehensi-
ble to her.

Cassie wondered what would happen if someone came around the corner and
rear-ended them. Driving on the left in standard American cars was weird
enough as it was. Why didn't they buy cars with steering wheels on the right?
Drivers would never get away with these stops in Las Vegas. If the cops didn't
move them along, the passengers, or other delayed drivers, would certainly curse
them until the air turned blue.

She wished she could simply relax like everyone else. She wished she could
close her eyes and be back on *Moby Dick* with Leo, before any of this had happened. It still seemed like a bad dream. She needed to get a new passport and
then go to Trinidad to get some of her money.

During lunch, Cassie asked the brothers various things to avoid talking about
herself. Nate told some funny stories regarding his time in the Navy so she asked
him to expand and tell her why he'd picked submarines.

"That's a good question," agreed Doug. "You know, Nate, I always wanted to ask you why you volunteered for submarines instead of an aircraft carrier or shore duty."

"I guess it was because I wanted to be essential instead of merely a cog in a big machine. On a carrier the pilots are the hot shots, but on a sub everybody is part of an elite group. I'm sure I'm being unfair to those carrier guys, but all the submariners, or 'bubbleheads' feel the same. We were all specially screened volunteers getting hazardous-duty pay, and we ate the best food the Navy had to offer. Being sealed up in a sewer pipe for months didn't bother me. I'm not claustrophobic.

"I also thought about the way the ground-pounders experienced war and I rejected it. I didn't want to walk through rice paddies or deserts all day and then see one after another of my buddies get hurt or die. On a modern submarine, everybody usually makes it out in one piece or everybody dies together. None of this shit where you get your arms and legs blown off, but keep on living. I couldn't exist like that, Doug. I couldn't be crippled and dependent on somebody. Seriously, if I get senile or screwed up and lose my independence, I want you to shoot me and end it."

"Shit, how will I know? You're screwed up already."

"You know what I mean! We treat dogs and horses more humanely than our own relatives in this society. We put animals out of their misery so they don't suffer needlessly. Don't shoot me in the head, though. I might want to get my perfect brain frozen like Ted Williams did."

"Nate, you know you only have one chance in a billion of cryogenic theories working don't you?" said Doug.

"Yeah, yeah, I know. But one in a billion is still better than zero in a billion, isn't it?"

After lunch, they grabbed another taxi south, making quicker time. A panting dog occupied a shady spot in the road and didn't move when they swung around it.

"Are you okay, Cassie?" asked Doug. "You're awfully quiet. You sure you don't want us to go try to find this Hunter guy? We could get him to give your stuff back."

"No, I don't want you to find him!" She lowered her voice and added, "Thanks, but I'm okay. I'd rather wait a few days and let everything cool off. I don't have to return to the States for awhile. I guess I'm just tired and maybe a little spacey from the pills." Cassie knew Doug and Nate would be no match for Hunter and his crew and didn't want to see them hurt. Maybe she should ask them to sneak her onto the U.S. mainland or Trinidad. She'd think about the issue tonight.

"Okay, I forgot the pills," said Doug. "No problem, Cassie. We enjoy having you with us and you're welcome to stay. I told the driver to take us all to the Baths, but I'll have him drop you off at the boat on the way. You can sleep while I take Nate to the Baths. Normally, I'd go by sea, but since we're tied up in the yacht harbor already, it'll make more sense to let you off at the marina and continue by taxi. He'll take us to the end of the road above the Baths and we'll walk down to the shore. It's not worth moving the sloop such a short distance south to the Baths."

"What baths, bro? I already took a shower this morning."

"You need a bath for your dirty mind," laughed Doug. "No, these aren't literal baths. Actually, the name comes from geology. The Baths are a formation of huge igneous boulders called batholiths."

"Watch out, Cassie. Here he goes with his Professor Emeritus of Tropical Tourism act again."

"Come on, it's really cool! The boulders are the size of houses and are all jumbled up on top of each other on the southwest shore of Virgin Gorda. It's a national park now and probably the most beautiful spot I've ever been. You squeeze through these narrow caves and climb over the boulders to get from one sandy cove to another. The waves wash up into shady pools with light coming down through the gaps in the boulders above.

"They have a bar on the beach and another bar with shops on top of the hill where the trail starts. This would be a great time to go because there aren't any cruise ships in today. Sometimes it gets so crowded you can't squeeze past all the tourist groups."

"If they have two bars, count me in," said Nate.

"I remember one time when an Italian ship's photographer insisted on taking my daughter's picture. He thought she must be part of their group and would buy the photograph from the ship's store. He didn't speak English so we finally gave up and let him take pictures of us. There were a bunch of unpurchased pictures in a ship's display case floating around out there awhile. I sure liked it better before cruise ships started coming to the BVI."

"The Baths do sound good, Doug. Maybe I'll join you after all," Cassie said. She didn't want to be separated from her rescuers right now.

"Great. You can still sleep on the boat later when I take Nate snorkeling in Savannah Bay. You know, we have to go swimming at least once today."

*   *   *   *

Doug had the taxi let them out where the road ended at the Top of The Baths restaurant. They drank piña coladas and admired the view from the deck around the fresh water pool before they started down the short trail. Doug lent Cassie some more money, and she bought a Virgin Gorda t-shirt from a woman at the shore who displayed her wares on the tree branches. Nate bought one that read: "Sail Fast—Live Slow," and another that stated: "Life's a Reach and Then You Jibe" to celebrate both his philosophy and newly acquired sailing knowledge.

Tall coconut palms shaded patches of white sand alongside turquoise shallows and giant gray boulders. A heavy swell splashed against ancient granite outpost rocks. The crew took their shoes off and walked among the boulders and through the tide pools to Devil's Bay before returning in forty-five minutes.

"Man, you were right on this one. It doesn't get any better than this. But, I feel like I've been here before and recognize some of the views, even though I know I haven't," said Nate. "It's the *déjà vu* thing."

"Yeah, they constantly use this as a backdrop for a lot of tourism and boating ads. More likely, though, you read the *Sports Illustrated* swimsuit issue showing most of the supermodels posed on these humongous rocks. The edition also covered Necker Island, Guana Island, and had a special feature on Bomba's bar."

"You're right, Doug! I remember it was the issue where they painted fake swimsuits on some of the models. You could barely tell if the suits were real or not. Those girls looked good either way, of course. And now I'm actually here! Most excellent, bro."

Doug noticed Cassie looked tired. "Everybody ready to go? We're burning daylight, and we still have another stop before sailing to our final destination today."

They walked back up the hill and caught a taxi to the yacht harbor. Cassie went below to organize her new clothes and wash her makeshift outfit from the morning. She hung the wet clothes on the boat's fence-like lifelines and went below to get some sleep.

The brothers took *Payback* out of the marina and sailed north to Savannah Bay. The bay was still on Virgin Gorda, but north of the Baths and yacht harbor areas. Doug cautiously motored through the southern gap in the reef and anchored twenty feet of water off the beach. Doug noted the same trawler he'd seen before at Peter Island and Dead Chest came into Savannah Bay soon after *Payback* did. He watched when it anchored to the north of *Payback*, deeper in the bay. He thought nothing of it. Doug and Nate went for a quick swim while Cassie slept.

CHAPTER 10

▼

SABA ROCK

That Monday, after their stop on Salt Island, Hunter didn't notice *Payback* leaving as *Moby Dick* approached Dead Chest Island. He sent his crew ashore to do an intensive walking search of the small island for Cassie. When they returned empty-handed, Hunter absolutely knew Cassie was either fish food or she'd somehow hooked up with someone else. With the search of Dead Chest, they'd now completed an intensive search of all the nearby islands on which she could've washed up. She had to be on another boat. It was time to search the harbors for her and her accomplices or rescuers, whoever they were.

Following the information gleaned from the old man on Salt Island, Hunter decided to start from Norman, then work counterclockwise around the BVI tourist track. *Moby Dick* moved southwest and slowly cruised through the harbors of Norman Island. The drug pirates questioned the staff of the Willy T and Pirates restaurants. Then Hunter quickly rechecked the Peter, Salt, and Cooper Island anchorages for any sign of her on the yachts there.

The next stop on the circuit was the Baths on Virgin Gorda. Even the crew of *Moby Dick* was impressed by the sheer physical beauty of the spot.

"*Amigos,* we should return right here to relax after this is all over," said Sanchez.

"When you're right, you're right," admitted Hunter. "Not today, though. Put us alongside the catamaran on the orange buoy."

A couple of the skippers on the moored vessels were coldly hostile when *Moby Dick* approached, and it took Hunter awhile to figure why. Apparently, there was a shortage of park-service buoys, and boats already on the buoys thought *Moby Dick* was coming to pester them regarding when they would be leaving. No independent anchoring was allowed in the park. Additionally, there were a couple of other yachts already circling outside the mooring field waiting for something to come open. When the circling boats saw *Moby Dick* approach a moored vessel, they thought *Moby Dick* was trying to jump the line so they also raced up to the targeted yacht like a sheepdogs guarding a lamb from a wolf.

"Ahoy, the trawler, we're next for this spot. We've been waiting a half hour already."

"Y'all can stop worrying. I'm just asking them a question. We're looking for my girlfriend. She swam in to the beach and was supposed to be back by now. She's not resting on your boat is she? A blond in a green bikini?"

"No, we haven't seen anybody swimming out this far."

Each intercepting skipper grudgingly backed off after Hunter painstakingly reassured him he didn't want a buoy this afternoon and was only searching for a lost crewmember.

"Goddamn tourist sailors and their precious buoys. I think I actually saw two of them using boathooks to fight over one back on Norman Island. It must be too deep to anchor at a couple of these spots. Anyway, this search is getting to be a giant pain in the ass," said Hunter. "We've got to get the hell out of here. We're starting to draw too much attention to ourselves."

Hunter turned north for the nearby marina to make his next search, even though the old man had only mentioned the Baths stop on Virgin Gorda. As they approached the entrance, they had to move to the side of the narrow channel to let a white sailboat exit past them.

"Holy shit! Boys, we've found the boat she's on," exclaimed Hunter. Garcia and Sanchez quickly moved to the port side to look.

"How do you know?" asked Garcia.

"He is right, *cabron*. Look, there is the bitch's swimsuit bottom drying on the line. It matches the top you found on Salt Island. Wake up and pay attention."

"Wake up yourself, Sanchez. I am the one who spotted the bathing suit. What have you done for us lately beside complain?"

"Both of you shut up! Stay down so she doesn't see us." Hunter continued into the harbor then used the wider area near a boatyard to turn his vessel around and follow the white sailing yacht out. Soon he could read the transom. The black letters read: "*Payback*, Long Grove, Illinois." Hunter quickly wrote the information down. He dropped back a few more yards so his following wasn't so obvious.

Sanchez went below and came back up holding the three AK-47 assault rifles they'd brought from South America.

"Jesus Christ. Put those away!" ordered Hunter. "And keep your *pistolas* hidden under your shirts, too. We aren't going to shoot them right here with everyone watching. We're only going to follow and figure out who is helping her and why. At least until it gets dark."

They followed *Payback* when the sailboat moved north and into Savannah Bay. Hunter took *Moby Dick* a little farther north, anchoring near the Giorgio's Table restaurant. He studied the sloop and watched two men get into the water to snorkel around. Hunter focused a set of binoculars on the sloop and scanned it intensely. Cassie didn't appear.

He needed more information. Who were those guys and were there more like them on board? Were they armed? Could it be a trap set by the cops? Thirty minutes later, the two snorkelers returned and got their sloop underway. Hunter vaguely recalled seeing the pair somewhere before, but couldn't place them. It made him feel uneasy, and he didn't like it.

When *Payback*'s stern turned to face Hunter, he noted the two men weren't watching him so he raised anchor and cautiously followed. He observed *Payback* make a turn to the right and exit the bay. When *Moby Dick* approached the general area where the sailboat had turned, a dark cloud blew in from the east and blotted out the sun. A gentle drizzle started, and Hunter turned on the pilothouse window wipers. He noticed the water was a uniform gray color now. The shades of blue, green, and brown had disappeared.

"Maybe we should wait here until it clears up," said Sanchez.

"No, I don't want them to get away. You go up on the bow and tell me if it looks like we're going to hit anything." Sanchez put on a yellow slicker, moved forward, and leaned over the bow pulpit.

"I can not see *mierda* with these clouds and rain."

"Just keep looking for rocks or a reef," said Hunter. "I'm pretty sure this is where they turned." He spun *Moby Dick* sharply to the right and headed offshore to directly intercept *Payback*.

"Slow down!" said Sanchez.

"Okay, okay." Hunter moved the throttle back a little more.

Suddenly, there was a crunching, scraping sound. The trawler jolted twice like going over two speed bumps, and then came to an abrupt stop. *Moby Dick* was hard aground. Hunter and Sanchez swayed forward then back when the trawler's motion stopped. Garcia fell forward and ran his nose into a bulkhead below.

"Shit fire!" said Hunter. He slammed the throttle into reverse. Clouds of sand erupted from the bottom and the keel groaned, but the boat didn't move. Hunter went to neutral then pulled the throttle hard into reverse again. This time *Moby Dick* scraped and squealed and slowly backed off the coral reef. Hunter eased off a little from the reef then turned to go farther south. He went a few yards then aimed at the open ocean again. This time, he slowed until he barely had enough speed so the boat would steer. "Why didn't you see the damn reef?"

"Hey, I told you I could not see shit," said Sanchez.

"Well, look harder. I think I see the exit this time. Garcia, is there any water in the bilge?"

"No, but it was very noisy down there. I bet you have some big gouges and lost some paint. You should go in the water and look first before reversing and knocking the boat around. You could have made it worse."

"Do not cut the corner this time or you will hit it again. Go all the way south, like they did, and then go straight out," said Sanchez.

"Oh, hell, what do you guys know? I got it off, didn't I?"

The big patch of clouds and rain soon moved off to the west. The sun shone down at a high angle again, and Hunter could now see the dark blue channel. He made a small course adjustment and ran the engine up to full speed. *Moby Dick* cleared the bay and turned to follow *Payback* before the sailboat could disappear into the sheet of rain. They were quickly catching up when a red light flashed on the control panel and a shrill alarm sounded.

"Now what?" yelled Hunter. "The red light says engine temperature."

"Stop the engine, it is overheating!" advised Sanchez.

"Okay, okay. Damn! I must've gotten sand into the water intakes when I was trying to pull us loose."

"So now what are we going to do?" asked Garcia.

"We'll have to go back to the boatyard we saw in the marina south of here and have them take a look. We can make it if we go slow and shut off the engine for a few minutes whenever we overheat."

"What about the girl and the *norteamericano* pigs?" said Sanchez.

"Now we know who she's with so we can find them again. She had to be on that sailboat. Nobody else would have only one piece of the exact same swimsuit. They looked like they were just taking a leisurely sail around the BVI like all these other white-bread dumb-shits. I wonder why we didn't see them panic when we followed them into Savannah Bay? It doesn't matter. We'll get her," said Hunter.

He paused and continued, "Wait a minute! I know where I saw those dudes before. They were going into the bar at Peter Island last night right when I was leaving. So their boat was over near where we lost the girl and the coke. She has to be with them."

Moby Dick limped into the marina and was lifted out of the water on the slings of a seventy-ton Travelift mobile boat hoist. The boatyard cleaned the strainers of sand and debris and inspected the hull. A big scrape had thinned the fiberglass, but there were no leaks. The good news was the other damage was only cosmetic. Hunter didn't bother repairing anything else since they didn't have time to spare.

While waiting, Garcia used the payphone to contact his *patron* in the Dominican Republic. He stood by the phone until he got the return call. After the call, he went back to the trawler. "Okay, I got a name and an address for us. Now we go see our local man."

Hunter dug into Cassie's abandoned luggage and pocketed her passport before he hopped into a cab with Garcia. Sanchez stayed to supervise the boat's launch. The taxi took them to a small house near the old copper mine. The house looked cheery with its pastel color paint scheme accented by flowering bougainvillea vines growing all over a white picket fence.

The fragrant fence had a "Beware of Dog" sign on it, though, and a large German Shepherd snarled at them from behind the gate. A young man with an afro who was smoking a huge blunt came out of the house and approached the gate. "Are you Hunter and Garcia?" he asked.

"Yes, you Maxwell?" asked Garcia.

"That's me, mon! Down, Gruner!" he told the barking beast. "A little bird called me about you. Where's your other buddy?"

"He's back with the boat. What just happened to your island accent, "mon"? asked Hunter.

"I turn it off and on. I kind of lost it going to school in Terre Haute, Indiana. Yassuh, don't I look exactly like Larry Bird?"

"If you say so. Can we come through the damn gate?" said Hunter.

"Yeah, she won't bite you now." Maxwell led them into the house and to a rear room bristling with sophisticated computer equipment. Machines hummed and lights blinked through the ganja haze.

"You grow up here?" asked Hunter.

"No, mon. I'm from down island, St. Vincent. But I went to college at Indiana State and got another diploma at Rose-Hulman Institute of Technology. Couldn't seem to stop. Certain mutual friends of ours made me a scholarship offer I couldn't refuse, but now I'm back in paradise where I belong. Okay, so what do you have for me to work from?"

Hunter handed over Cassie's passport picture and gave Maxwell the name and home port of the target vessel. Maxwell worked backward from the yacht's name and hacked into the U.S. Coast Guard computer data records to get an owner's name. It took him more time getting into the Illinois DMV records.

"Piece of cake," said Maxwell, taking another drag. "These were relatively easy to get into. Now the Pentagon—there's a hard one! I'm working on it in my spare time."

In another half hour, they had extra copies of Cassie's picture, copies of Doug's driver's license, plus a used Canon mini-camcorder with zoom.

"I scanned her picture and this guy's picture and description into our special little computer network. This camera will take digital stills or movies. You need to get me a good picture of the other guy and anybody else on their boat. Or you can drop a picture off with any of our other people, and they'll put it on our coded Web site. I'll ask our friends in the States to try to figure out who he is. This Doug fellow's not on any of our friends or enemies watch lists. He could be mister square citizen, or he could be a slick operator who hides his tracks, so be careful.

"I changed *Moby Dick*'s registration for you so it looks like she's owned by one of our front operations, "Kolb Enterprises." The Coast Guard records will now show the original owner, Leo, had a totally different boat. This is your new document packet. Here's a list of contact numbers for this area and down island. Anything else I can do for you fine gentlemen?"

"No, what you got was pretty damn good," Hunter admitted and paid him the substantial fee agreed. They went back to the marina where Sanchez had the motor yacht ready to go out again.

"So where do we go now, great leader?"

"Stop being such a wise guy and listen up, Sanchez. These guys must've picked up Cassie over near Peter or Salt, and now they've taken her to Virgin Gorda. So if I heard the old man right, the next probable tourist stop is Marina Cay. They were heading west towards the Marina Cay area anyway, right before we lost them in the rain. We'll start looking there. We need to get a picture of the guy with the lighter hair and see who the hell else is onboard that stupid sailboat. Let's go."

*   *   *   *

The rain started soon after *Payback* left Savannah Bay. Nate brought up the foul-weather gear. The brothers only put on their yellow jackets since it was too warm to get all bundled up in pants, sea boots, and hoods. Doug noticed *Moby Dick* had gotten underway and was following them out. It wasn't unusual in any way. Frequently, he would be on the same island circuit as another boat and see the same vessel again and again. Soon, he lost sight of the trawler behind them in the rain.

Doug judged they were now far enough offshore to avoid the reefs and the Mountain Point peninsula so he turned and headed straight north. Now *Payback* was going up the coast of Virgin Gorda. Before the turn, and before the rain closed in, an onlooker would have thought *Payback* was heading straight west for Marina Cay.

After they cleared the point, *Payback* turned to starboard to round Mosquito Island, then sailed southeast to pass Colquhoun Reef and enter North Sound, also called Gorda Sound. They doused the sails, and the rain tapered off at last.

"Where are we now?" asked Cassie from below. She came up the ladder, laid a dry boat cushion on the port cockpit bench, and demurely sat.

"You look nice in the new clothes, Cassie," said Doug. *She actually does look nice*, he thought. *Then again, she'd also looked nice earlier without clothes.* Doug watched her every move whenever he was with her now. She moved with a grace and confidence unusual in a woman her age.

"Hey, sleepyhead. You missed the swimming and a nice sail," said Nate. "I sailed us most of the way here."

"Yeah, but we got here anyway," laughed Doug. "We were at Savannah Bay before. Now, we're at the far northern end of Virgin Gorda. The reefs and the surrounding small islands of Prickly Pear and Mosquito make this into a kind of sheltered lake called Gorda Sound.

"Over there is Leverick Bay, where the road from the rest of Virgin Gorda ends." Doug pointed forward and continued, "The two fancy resorts to the east are Biras Creek and Bitter End Yacht Club. They have to bring in guests and supplies by boat. Prickly Pear, on our left, has the Sand Box bar while the rest is a nature preserve. The tiny key, that looks like a floating building, over there between Prickly Pear and Bitter End, is Saba Rock.

"There was only a dive shop on a big flat rock at Saba before, but now it has a small hotel and a great restaurant. You can walk around the whole place in three minutes. I think we'll pick up one of their moorings and eat supper there. They give you a free buoy and top off your fresh water tank if you have dinner with them so it's a fair deal. I don't know about you, but I need some shots of their tasty rum. It's been one hell of a long day."

∗   ∗   ∗   ∗

Moby Dick left the Virgin Gorda Yacht Harbour in a light rain late Monday afternoon. Running at full speed, they followed Hunter's guess and the old man's tourist circuit description, motoring west over to Marina Cay. They fruitlessly searched the harbor for *Payback* before Hunter went ashore.

The tiny islet of Marina Cay was owned by the Pusser's Company. The firm ran a store, restaurant, bar, and small hotel on the island. They had similar interests on other islands. In the store, Hunter learned "Pusser" was a corruption of the ship's job title "purser," and learned the company's original product was British Navy Rum. Now they had upscale sailing and resort clothing as well. He was also informed "cay" is pronounced "key." All this island knowledge was interesting, even to him, but he really wanted knowledge regarding the elusive sailboat. Hunter bought a couple bottles of the rum so he could make small talk with the clerk.

"No, sir," the stocky woman said, "I've not seen a sailboat named *Payback*, but I don' pay much mind to boat names anyway. Try the folks at the beach restaurant."

Hunter walked the path to the restaurant and looked at the pictures on the wall of old Tortola and Robb White and his wife in the 1930s. The captions told him how the young couple had led a pioneer/castaway existence on Marina Cay and built the small, cement house on the summit. A white man sat at a table folding napkins and watching Hunter study the display.

"Good pictures, aren't they?" said the man, folding napkins. He had a British accent. "I'm the manager here. Let me know if I can help you."

"Sure looks like things have changed around here," Hunter commented.

"Well, Robb White's house is still here up on top of the hill. You know he had to leave to be an American submarine officer in World War II. White later wrote a number of books including *Up Periscope* and *Torpedo Run*. His young wife went home to Georgia during the war. The couple drifted apart and never returned here. Later, Robb White wrote a book, *Two on the Isle*, concerning their years on this key, and it was turned into a movie, *Our Virgin Island*, with Sidney Poitier."

"You don't say."

"Now, Sidney wasn't from here. He was born and raised on Cat Island, in the Bahamas."

Hunter interrupted the talkative restaurant manager. "Never saw the movie. That's a real interesting story, though. Say, have you seen a white sailboat named *Payback* come in today? My friends are aboard, and they were supposed to meet me here."

"No, I haven't seen them, but you could try Clarence."

"Who's Clarence?"

"Oh, he tends bar up at the top of the hill in Mr. White's old house. He's got a set of binoculars, and he looks at the boats when he doesn't have any customers. Folks do a lot of crazy things on those boats."

"Ain't it the truth?" Hunter agreed and started up the path to the summit. There was a good view all around. He could even see the yachts over in Trellis Bay by the airport. A young man was wiping off the bar, built on the patio of the old house.

"Good day. What can I get you, sir?"

"Are you Clarence?"

"Yes, sir. Clarence Ledbetter at your service."

"Say, Clarence, I lost track of my friends from another boat. Have you seen a white sloop, maybe forty-five feet or so, called *Payback*?"

"Sure mon, that's a nice boat. I used to see *Payback* in here most every week."

"No shit? Did you see it come in earlier today?"

"No. I saw it reg'lar for five years, but not lately. She was one of the Moorings charter boats, but she must be phased out by now."

"What do you mean 'phased out'?" asked Hunter.

"See, those charter yachts are all privately owned, and they rent 'em to vacationers for fi' years. Den the owners trade or sell 'em, or maybe keep 'em and sail home. You must know the owner."

"Yeah, I know him. His boat's not going home, though. You can bet on that. Thanks," said Hunter. He tipped Clarence and walked back down the hill.

＊　　　＊　　　＊　　　＊

"You learn anything?" asked Sanchez.

"Yeah, I heard the stupid boat comes here all the time and this Doug guy used to rent it out to other people. We don't know why they have Cassie, but it's past time we took her back. Let's keep looking."

"Hunter, we can *not* keep asking these people so many questions," said Garcia.

"Hey, Einstein. We don't have to ask any more questions. It'll be easy now because we know what boat she's on. We only have to cruise around the tourist circle until we spot them. If they don't come here, maybe they'll still go to Jost Van Dyke like the old geezer said. We find the boat, we try not to let her see us, we snatch her, and then find out what the hell is going on."

Moby Dick motored over to nearby Beef Island. From there, they kept watch on Marina Cay using binoculars and taking a final trip in the dingy through the harbor after dark. *Payback* never showed up, so the crew of *Moby Dick* called it quits and went ashore to drink and argue at De Loose Mongoose beach bar. Hunter assured the crew they'd have better luck tomorrow.

CHAPTER 11

▼

ANEGADA

The crew of *Payback* got up late on Tuesday morning despite having gone to bed early the previous evening. They'd been tired enough to sleep right through the competing steel drum calypso bands playing late into the night from both Saba Rock and the Bitter End Yacht Club on Virgin Gorda. Southeasterly trade winds blew through the boat's open hatches, keeping the bugs away. A silvery tarpon made a loud splash nearby when it chased a school of small fish into the shallows. The late spring sun was already baking the deck and the heat finally roused the skipper.

Doug unrigged the sloop from night mode and set it up for another day of sailing. He untied the lines connecting the main halyard and the boom to the starboard grab rail. Doug had fastened the small lines to keep the boom from creaking and the halyard from slapping the side of the carbon fiber mast during the night. He put the anchor back on its roller since he no longer cared if the mooring pendant snagged it and caused a noise. Doug stowed the two hammocks he had put up for optional evening use. He pulled the dinghy in close to the stern, and then took off the extra safety line he had rigged to the mooring buoy.

A sea turtle with a shell bigger than a garbage can lid raised its head and exhaled with a hiss. It floated thirty feet off the port beam and watched the skipper perform his morning duties. In order to charge the refrigerator and batteries, Doug started up the diesel and ran it in neutral at 1,600 rpm. The startled brown Hawksbill dove and swam for shelter in the turtle grass below.

The engine vibrations finally awakened the other two members of *Payback*'s crew. In another fifteen minutes, Cassie was the first to come up and sit with Doug.

"That was the best sleep I've had for over a week. It's so peaceful here. It's like the rest of the world, with all its troubles, doesn't really exist," she said. Cassie and Doug sat silently, enjoying the morning. Conversation was unnecessary; having company was nice enough. A couple of minutes later, a yawning and tousled-hair Nate came up topside and sat with them, admiring the new day. Finally, Doug got up to grab an expanded chart of the Virgins to show them his latest plan.

"Cassie, if you like being away from it all, you're going to love today's destination."

"Where are we going now?" asked Nate.

"Over the horizon to Anegada. The boat renters call it 'the forbidden island.' I think Anegada translates, from the Spanish, as 'drowned land,'" said Doug with raised eyebrows and a smile.

"Okay, you got my attention. What's so special and forbidden about it?" asked Nate.

"Unlike the other Virgins, Anegada isn't a high, volcanic island. It's a flat piece of ancient coral hard to see until you get quite close to it. Anegada is barely above sea level. In the old days, ships had real problems seeing it at night. What's worse is the ten-mile long reef on the southeast side, which has claimed over 300 known shipwrecks. The charter companies forbid their customers from taking the rental boats there without a guide. So the place has comparatively few visitors.

"Anegada has ponds with pink flamingos, miles-long unspoiled beaches, big iguanas, and plenty of surrounding live coral. The few restaurants there won't even take credit cards. Is my valiant crew interested?"

"Getting farther away from everybody definitely interests me," said Cassie. "What can I make for breakfast?"

"Oh, you don't have to bother. We don't need much for breakfast, and I can make it," said Nate.

"No, I insist on cooking after all you guys have done for me. I saw some eggs in the galley. How about some scrambled eggs, bacon, and lightly-toasted English muffins?"

"Okay, that does sound good. I'm sold. We have to sit here for an hour anyway while we run the engine to cool the freezer and icebox. Thanks, Cassie," said Doug.

Cassie went below and started breakfast. Nate quietly asked, "What do you think of her now, Doug? Personally, I like her, but she's not telling us something. A lot of things, probably."

"Yeah, I get the same feeling. I think she's a good person, though. I'm sure she'll fill us in soon. She's had it pretty rough lately. We should give her some time, I guess."

"You're probably right. I'm just curious."

"Me, too."

"Okay, Captain Aubrey. So why did somebody name these the Virgin Islands anyway? Perhaps they found an overabundance of virtuous teenagers here?"

"Believe it or not, the current natives are pretty religious, but that's not the reason. Once again, it was Columbus who named the place. He thought there were thousands of little islets here so he named them after the story of St. Ursula and her eleven thousand virgins."

"Eleven thousand! What happened to all these saintly virgin girls?"

"Supposedly, they killed themselves rather than be captured and raped by the Huns in the fourth century. Maybe all the Huns looked like you, Nate."

"Ha, ha, you're so funny...not. You know, I didn't want to bring this up, but Mom always liked me best."

Doug laughed. It was great horsing around with his brother again. Following breakfast, Doug took them out of the sheltered harbor, let the dinghy ride farther behind, and set the sails for the trip north. A course of 005 degrees, magnetic, would take them safely toward Anegada. After a couple of hours, he handed the binoculars to Nate and had him occasionally check the horizon ahead. Cassie sat high on the windward side and was assigned to keep a lookout ahead for fish trap floats for *Payback* to avoid. The wind picked up when they got farther away from Virgin Gorda's highlands.

"Hey, I think I finally see something. Land ho! I always wanted to yell that," laughed Nate. "It looks like the tops of trees coming right out of the ocean. They're over there, a point off the starboard bow. I can't see the trunks at all yet."

"Gee, I guess you were wrong, and the earth is round after all. As we get closer you'll see the rest of the trees and some houses rise up," Doug said. He made a small course correction toward the treetops, and started keeping a closer watch on the depth sounder. After another hour, they could see the tops of some buildings and then the land itself. Doug worked *Payback* slowly past the entrance channel buoys and anchored in the inner harbor off Neptune's Treasure restaurant. He set up the boat with the hammocks and tie-downs again. To cool off, the whole crew jumped over the side and enjoyed a quick swim before lunch.

They ate lunch aboard, took the dinghy in, and docked it at the Anegada Reef Hotel. Nate bought Cassie some snorkeling gear in the small gift shop while Doug made reservations for the hotel's lobster barbecue supper. Nate secured a rusty taxi, and they piled in to bounce along the rough road to Loblolly Bay on Anegada's north side. Doug had the driver drop them at a pink-and-yellow beach establishment named Flash of Beauty.

"We can put our stuff on a beach chair and use the bar for our afternoon head-quarters," said Doug. "I arranged for the driver to pick us up again in another three hours."

  ✳   ✳   ✳   ✳

Cassie greatly enjoyed snorkeling and walking on the deserted beaches. Amazingly, there wasn't anyone on the beach for miles in either direction. *If this isn't the actual end of the earth, you could probably see it from here*, she thought. She felt well hidden and safe and was finally able to relax and enjoy her surroundings. The live coral started only a few feet off the beach, and she snorkeled with the brothers through a maze of coral heads and walls until they reached the line of breaking waves at the outer edge of the reef. Schools of brilliantly hued tang, French grunts, and long-spine squirrelfish hid under the brain and elkhorn coral as the swimmers approached.

Snorkeling back to the bar, Cassie was startled to see a small shark resting in a coral crevice. She tapped on Doug's shoulder and got him to raise his head out of the water. "Doug, look over to the right! Is that what I think it is?"

Doug lowered his mask into the water. He raised his head again and said, "It's only a nurse shark, Cassie. They're generally harmless if you don't mess with them."

"Okay, if you say so." Nevertheless, she hurried ashore and was happy to sit and drink a rum punch while the men went snorkeling again.

Only another couple of days, she thought, *and maybe I'll get over to the U.S. side, replace my passport, and go home. Maybe I should talk to a lawyer before talking to the police. First, though, I want to call a co-worker to see if anybody's asking for me at the casino in Vegas.*

After returning to the small hotel for the famous outdoor lobster dinner, they rowed to the boat and had a nightcap. Nate told her about his earlier snorkeling on Norman and Peter.

"I liked the coral off the beach here better than the other stuff Doug showed me before we picked you up. This had more colors today—more greens and pastels. The coral heads and ledges were like a puzzle maze you felt like you could get lost in."

"I agree, Nate. It was great. Say, Doug, don't these BVI restaurants ever have big docks where you can take *Payback* right up to the restaurant and simply walk in?" Cassie asked.

"Most of them don't," replied Doug. "There are only two or three such places in the BVI and even fewer down island. Docks are expensive and they get torn up during tropical storms. I like it better this way myself, because docking is a hassle with handling the lines and fenders and everything. Most places we simply anchor or tie up to a mooring ball near the restaurants and then take the dingy in and back. Almost all the establishments provide dinghy docks. Think of *Payback* as our movable house and the dinghy, or 'dink,' as our car."

"Okay then, Pops. The car's in the driveway and I'm going to bed," said Nate.

*   *   *   *

Moby Dick left the Marina Cay/Trellis Bay area and spent Tuesday zigzagging westward, looking everywhere for *Payback*. Hunter and his crew investigated all the harbors on the south side of Tortola then rechecked the small islands on the other side of the channel. After scouting Norman, the trawler passed north through the cut by Soper's Hole and cruised Cane Garden Bay before heading west toward Jost Van Dyke.

They inspected the boats at Sandy Key and Sandy Spit before looking into the first two harbors on Jost Van Dyke as the sun approached the western horizon. *Moby Dick* motored in and out of Little Harbour, but there were only two catamarans there this evening. The middle bay had a small village and a fairly big bar with a sign saying Foxy's but *Payback* wasn't there either. Right before dark, the trawler pulled into White Bay, the farthest west of the three harbors on Jost Van Dyke.

"Where in the hell is that damned sailboat? We checked both sides of Tortola and all these dinky islands, too. They have to be way off the regular BVI chart somewhere," said Hunter. He thought he'd better let the crew come ashore with him to keep them distracted for awhile. Hunter took Garcia and Sanchez in to the Soggy Dollar Bar and surprised them by buying a nice dinner and drinks. The white bartender recommended the flying fish sandwiches and Painkillers.

"This is where the Painkiller was invented. We only use Pusser's British Navy Rum in our secret recipe, and we put a little nutmeg on the top."

"You don't say? Hey, have you been working here all day?" asked Hunter.

"Since ten o'clock this morning."

"I'm looking for my friends on a sailboat named *Payback*. Seen them in here today?"

"Not today. One of those fancy, small cruise ships stopped in this afternoon and let a hundred passengers loose on this beach so most of the regular yachts stayed away. I had to explain to each and every rich tourist that it's called the Soggy Dollar Bar because there's no dinghy dock. See the anchorage is narrow and most yachties just swim in since their boats are anchored so close to the beach. So then we hang their money up on the line here to dry. The tourists weren't my kind of boaters today, but at least they tipped well."

"You can leave some money here to buy them a drink in advance if you think they're coming tomorrow. Of course, if you want to be sure to meet somebody on Jost Van Dyke, all you have to do is go sit at Foxy's Bar over the hill there," said the bartender, pointing east. "Every crew in this part of the Caribbean goes there eventually. All the sailors show up in the afternoons to hear Foxy do his act—except for two days from now. That's when they'll sail to Tortola to be at Bomba's for the full-moon party." The man pointed out the two bars' locations on the wall map.

"Thanks, bud. We might go there tomorrow night. Say, can I walk to Foxy's from here?"

"Sure, but you can catch a taxi if you don't want to walk. You can even use your tender if the weather's not too bad."

"I might just do that tomorrow. Say, if *Payback* comes in here while we're gone to Foxy's, don't tell them I'm looking for them. It's kind of a surprise."

*   *   *   *

On Wednesday morning, *Payback*'s crew got up early and set sail for Jost Van Dyke, an island more than twenty miles to the southwest of their starting point in Anegada. The trip was an uneventful run downwind taking four leisurely hours. On the way, Doug showed his new crew member where the emergency equipment was and had her practice a man overboard drill. Cassie had to pretend both brothers fell in the water, mark the spot by throwing out the horseshoe buoy, lower the sails, and then turn the boat around to pretend to pick them up.

"Pretty good, Cassie," said Nate, when she finished. "I had to do it on my first day with Doug and I think you did it faster."

"To end the lesson, I want to show you two new sailboat sailors something you'll always remember." Doug reached into a cockpit locker and produced a coconut he'd apparently stowed earlier. When the vessel was sailing at full speed again, he dropped the coconut over the side. "Pretend it's you with your head barely above water. Try to keep an eye on it." Looking backward from the low height of the sailboat's seats, they lost sight of the floating coconut in the five-foot waves within a very short time.

"Wow, it disappeared mighty quickly," said Cassie.

"Yeah, and think how fast we'd lose sight of you at night," warned Doug.

Cassie thought back on how she'd gotten away from Hunter. The motorboat's deck was higher, but fortunately it'd happened at night with a lot of distractions. Before reaching Jost Van Dyke, they anchored in the lee of a tiny islet named Sandy Spit and ate a casual lunch. Cassie felt a return of her earlier nervousness when she saw the large number of boats in the general area. After being way out at Anegada, *Payback* was on the tourist circuit again. She was relieved to see no sign of *Moby Dick*.

"What do you think of my little spit of sand? Isn't it exactly like those cartoons of people shipwrecked on a small hump of land with a couple of palm trees? I think I see five coconut palms on Sandy Spit."

"It's truly beautiful, Doug."

"You know, it looks so peaceful today, but I was almost hit by a waterspout here once. My aunt, sister, and mother made up my crew that week. I called it 'The Estrogen Cruise.' Anyway, I had to get the anchor up and zip over to Little Harbour on Jost to take shelter."

"Isn't a waterspout a tornado on the water?" asked Nate.

"Exactly right, Mr. Wizard. It's not quite as bad since the water it sucks up slows it a bit, but it's plenty dangerous. I saw the thing coming a couple miles away, off to the north there. They don't last long, though. It died out before it got to Jost Van Dyke, but it sure was scary at the time."

Following lunch, they swam ashore and walked around the miniature paradise in less than five minutes. They had a quick snorkel on the compact but lush reef off the southern shore. Doug pointed out and named the various wildlife. Cassie learned that, compared to Anegada, this reef had more sponges, sea fans, and other soft coral. Schools of dark blue tang swam beneath them. She saw Nate dive deep and poked a small Hawksbill turtle sleeping in the sand. The indignant turtle blinked and sped off to deeper water.

"That was fun. Where to now?" Cassie asked when they climbed back aboard *Payback*. She was hoping Doug would pick somewhere secluded again. On the other hand, counting her time on Dead Chest, it was six days since she'd gotten away from Hunter. Surely, he'd sold the coke and moved on by now.

Maybe tonight she'd ask Doug to drop her on St. John or St. Thomas in the next couple of days. At least those nearby islands were in U.S. territory. Cassie didn't feel anxious to get home, though. It was weird, but *Payback* felt like her home now.

She liked Nate and could tell he was physically attracted to her. Cassie absolutely felt comfortable with Doug, but didn't think she liked him the way she'd feel toward an uncle or older brother. She also felt grateful to Doug, but there was something more there. She was fond of him, and it was growing, but she didn't want to think too much about it yet. Besides, she didn't know if Doug actually liked her or was merely happy to have another young student in his little tour group.

"We're not going much farther," said Doug. "We'll motor around the headland and into Little Harbour to pick up a mooring. Then we can reserve a table at Harris's restaurant for supper. They have great local food and what I've found to be the best piña coladas in the world. When you want a lobster, the cook wades into the water to pull lobsters out of the holding cage with her bare hands for you. These don't have the big claws like Maine lobsters but they're sharp and spiky. She knows exactly how to grab them.

"Before supper, we can take the dinghy or a taxi west to Great Harbour where there's a little village and the famous Foxy's Tamarind Bar. You can even do some food shopping to get what you'd like to eat, Cassie, instead of the crap I brought along," offered Doug.

"I'm not fussy. What you guys stocked is okay. Although, we do need some more eggs and milk."

"We'd better check our beer supply, too," said Nate.

Doug got them underway, and *Payback* was soon moored in the easternmost of Jost Van Dyke's three bays. They went in to Harris's, paid for the mooring, and enjoyed the famous piña coladas.

"Nate, you should've seen this place during the end-of-the-century party. All of the action was over to the west in Great Harbour, of course. Every year, on what the locals call Olde Year's Eve, any boat able to make it here shows up and lands its crew, by dinghy, on the beach in front of Foxy's bar. Usually, around five thousand people show up on an island with a population of fewer than 400 souls. Heck, they didn't get electricity and a paved road until the '90s."

"My kind of place."

"Anyway, for the millennium, there were more than 15,000 people partying on a half-mile of beach—including lots of celebrities on their private yachts. Special ferries brought more people in from Tortola and St. Thomas. The bay was so crowded with boats I swear you could walk from one deck to another to get from the sea to the shore. They even had the U.S. Coast Guard here in the BVI to try to help with traffic control. It was a crazy scene. People were dancing naked up on the roofs of the bars, and drunks were passed out right in the middle of the only road. The taxis had to drive around them."

"Sounds like the ultimate party," said Cassie.

"Oh yeah! The *New York Times* listed the coolest places to be on the whole planet for New Year's Eve, and tiny Jost Van Dyke here came in third, behind Trafalgar Square and Times Square. Of course, they had their usual urban bias. This was absolutely the best place to be.

"Just getting here was awful, though. I had a bad experience with a makeshift motorboat ferry service based in Cane Garden Bay on Tortola. We left *Payback* safely over there and bought round-trip tickets to the party on Jost. Unfortunately, half of their little speedboats broke down, and several of the stupid teenagers who were supposed to drive wandered off to party instead of working. It took us two hours of waiting to get a ride over here, and then we were stranded on Jost by those sons-of-bitches, even though we'd paid in advance like hundreds of others.

"I finally bribed a guy from Jost to give us a ride back to Tortola at four in the morning. All the boat drivers insisted on going at top speed bouncing over the waves. Two local men died that night when they fell out of similar speedboats returning to St. Thomas.

"It was one hell of a party. Heck, I'm still proud I was at Foxy's for the historic event, even with all the hassles. I've got the special t-shirt to prove it, too! Would you believe a guy who missed the party offered me 200 bucks for the shirt later?"

"Did you sell him the shirt?" asked Nate.

"Shit, no. I earned it and he didn't. It always gripes me when people wear shirts with logos of schools they never went to or names of places they've never been. It's just not kosher.

"Anyway, the next year I still didn't want to risk *Payback* in the mess over in Great Harbour. So when I was down here again in the summer, I paid in advance for a December 31st mooring over in Little Harbour. When the day came, the poor lady from Harris's Place who'd taken my money attached a bunch of milk jugs marked 'reserved' all over one buoy, but she still had to chase off six other pushy skippers before I showed up. One even tried to pretend to be me. We finally claimed our buoy, ate at her restaurant, then taxied in to Foxy's for the party, and walked two miles back around the comatose bodies before dawn. So I always stop by to thank her for guarding that mooring ball."

Finishing their drinks, they piled into the dinghy at Harris's dock, saluted the mighty *Payback* when they passed her, and exited the bay. It took twenty minutes to cruise over to Great Harbour. The goats on the hillside looked startled to see people passing so close by in a noisy rubber boat.

"I wouldn't attempt this if there were any real waves or wind today," said Doug. "Not without a much bigger outboard. You'd still get plenty wet, though."

They pulled up to Foxy's dock and took snapshots of each other relaxing in the hammock by the bar's sign on the beach.

"Wait," said Cassie, "I don't want a picture."

"Come on, you look fine," said Nate.

"Well, okay, but let me put on my hat and sunglasses first."

"Are you hiding from your fan club?"

"My hair's a mess."

"Smile at least, will you?" said Nate before he took her picture.

They drank the special Foxy's Lager beer and Foxy's Firewater rum. Foxy himself came out in the late afternoon with his guitar and told jokes and sang his comedy songs.

"This guy is hilarious!" said Nate. "I loved his joke about the island dog and the song about how white people should be called 'colored' because they're the ones turning gray, red, green, etc. He's right! Black people are always black and don't change colors when they're sick or sunburned and stuff. We're the strangely colored ones."

"Yeah, he gets away with all this non-PC stuff we'd never get away with, Nate. He and his wife have a regular business empire now. Foxy even sponsors a annual wooden boat regatta here. Not bad for somebody who started by serving drinks to yachties at a bar made by laying a board across two barrels, huh?"

Cassie went off to the restroom in the back. She removed her hat and sunglasses and looked in the mirror. She felt paranoid worrying about being recognized as the same woman in that newspaper article. When she walked out of the ladies room, she was startled by a rustling in the bushes. Cassie cried out and jumped back as a brown weasel-like animal ran past her.

Nate and Doug heard Cassie's yell, dropped their drinks, and ran to her.

"What's wrong? Are you okay?" asked Nate.

"I'm okay. Just jumpy, I guess. A brown animal scared me to death and ran across the road. It was real low to the ground like a fast dachshund or something."

"It was probably an Indian mongoose," said Doug. "The sugar-cane planters brought them over in the early days to control rats. Unfortunately, they also kill a lot of native birds and lizards. They're pests here now. They won't attack you, though."

"Sorry, guys. Go back to your beer. Maybe I'll go do the grocery shopping now. How close is the store?"

"It's only two blocks. Walk west along the dirt road past the pier, and then behind the restaurant right where the road turns left and climbs the hill. Do you want us to go with you?"

"No, you just relax. I can walk two blocks." She thought she needed to stop worrying so much. She hadn't seen Hunter, or *Moby Dick*, for days. Cassie walked west paralleling the beach. She passed the police station, the school, a graveyard, and the church. Soon Cassie spotted the last establishment in town. It had a sign directing her to go around the far side to enter the small attached grocery in the rear. She turned right onto the side street.

The bushes on the roadside abruptly parted and a hairy, brown hand clamped down over Cassie's mouth. She was dragged backward, and then felt something hard and heavy smash into the side of her head. Her view narrowed and narrowed until she could only see her dragging feet making lines in the dirt before everything went black.

CHAPTER 12

▼

JOST VAN DYKE

For the apprentice pirates on *Moby Dick*, the day started at anchor off the Soggy Dollar Bar. The crew got up late that Wednesday morning and nursed their hangovers.

"Painkillers, my ass," groaned Sanchez. "Do we have any goddamn aspirin?"

"A little hair of the dog will set you right," said Hunter passing the bottle of rum. "Let's go hang at Foxy's bar, and I'll buy you another drink. We'll leave *Moby Dick* here in White Bay and dinghy in. I'm tired of chasing all over the BVI after that whore anyway. If we stake out this famous bar, then she's supposed to come to us. If she doesn't show up in a couple of days, we'll go looking again."

They took the dinghy over and left some rope and blankets in it while they went ashore. Hunter hid the dinghy in the mangroves near the ferry dock at the other end of the harbor from Foxy's. Hunter picked a secluded table where he could keep an eye on the road and the bar's dinghy dock. They had lunch, drank some more, and waited. After several false alarms, they looked up to see a dinghy with two men and a woman pulling in.

"Bingo!" said Hunter. He threw some money on the table, left the bar, and hid his group behind a beached rowboat nearby to keep an eye on *Payback*'s crew. They watched as Cassie and her companions drank and laughed during Foxy Caldwell's show. Later, they saw Cassie go off by herself. Garcia circled around to intercept her. She was only using the restroom, though, and there were too many people close by. The three novice pirates didn't understand why she gave a little shriek when she left the restroom or why the two men rushed to her aid. They watched *Payback*'s crew settle down, and finally, saw Cassie walk off alone.

"Sanchez, you stay here and keep an eye on the two solid citizens. Garcia, keep moving west along the beach, and I'll run ahead on the back street. Go!"

They crouched in a perfect ambush spot. Cassie turned off the main road and was finally all alone. Garcia grabbed her and put his large hand over her mouth while Hunter came up with a rock and artfully applied it to her temple.

"Got her!" said Hunter triumphantly.

*   *   *   *

Doug and Nate kept drinking at Foxy's, waiting for Cassie to return from her shopping trip.

"Shouldn't she be here by now?" Nate finally asked.

"Yeah, you'd think so. Maybe she bought too many groceries, and she needs us to help carry them back," said Doug. "We might as well walk over there and take a look."

The brothers took fresh beers with them and strolled west down the dirt main street. Doug pointed out the places where he'd seen the wilder celebrations during past New Year's Eve parties. There was no one in the attached grocery store behind Rudy's restaurant. Doug had to call for the clerk to come back from her bartending duties in the front of the building. The woman told them no one at all had been trying to buy groceries for the last hour or so.

"So she hasn't even been here yet? What's she doing?" asked Nate.

"Maybe she stopped in one of those gift shops on the way."

Doug led the way as they retraced their steps and poked into the half dozen establishments in the little village. They even checked the church, school, and police station before returning to Foxy's bar.

"Where the heck could she be?"

"Doug, what if she got back to the bar after looking in some gift shop and found we were gone? We might've passed her when we went straight to the grocery store. She'll figure we returned to Little Harbour without her."

"But why would she think that if our dinghy's still here?"

"Come on, Doug. I see a dozen essentially identical gray, rubber dinghies on the dock now. You're the only one who's memorized the decal number or the look of the outboard or something. I can't tell them apart yet. She sure wouldn't know the difference between ours and the other ones, either. Plus, maybe she bought a bunch of stuff that needs to stay cold."

"You're probably right. I bet she's pissed off right now, thinking we forgot and left her. Or she thinks we might've told her to take a taxi back, but thinks she misheard us. Let's run the dinghy over to Little Harbour, and I bet we'll find her at the restaurant or the boat."

The brothers zipped back to *Payback* at full speed in the lightly loaded dinghy. The wind had increased, and a chop was building up. The sun went down behind them as they raced east. When they returned to Little Harbour Doug was confounded not to see Cassie on the sloop or at the restaurant.

"Where the hell can she be?" asked Nate.

"I don't know. Let's leave the dinghy at the restaurant dock and get a taxi. We'll start from this end of the island and go back through the village at Great Harbour and all the way to White Bay at the far end. Shit, this whole place is only three miles long with one lousy road. There's no way we'll miss her."

"Sounds like a plan."

The brothers hopped in a jeep taxi with open benches in the back. Doug had the driver take them to the restaurant at the far eastern end of the road first, and then worked their way west while calling for Cassie. In Great Harbour, they stopped at every shop again, even checking the restrooms. The taxi went up and over the little hill to White Bay, where they stopped to check Ivan's campground and bar. There were a few campers who had taken a ferry to get to paradise, but no one had seen Cassie.

Finally, the road petered out at the Soggy Dollar Bar. The evening-shift bartender hadn't seen anyone like her, and he verified she hadn't checked into the small hotel behind the bar.

"I'm stumped now," said Doug.

"Maybe she got sick of us and took off with someone else. She wasn't leaving much behind on our boat, and she had the money you loaned her. It's not like we know anything about her anyway. Hey, we better check *Payback* and see if she stole anything!"

"Oh, come on. I have trouble believing that. She liked us, and we liked her. Cassie's got to be in trouble again," said Doug. "Hey, what if that Hunter guy's still around and kidnapped her? We have to find her and help her!"

"Take it easy, Doug. I know you think you finally have a chance to be the knight in shining armor rescuing the beautiful princess, but you never know with women. Cassie might not want to be rescued. I bet she's with somebody, and it could well be him. Maybe she saw him and they reconciled or something. He's probably been running all over the BVI worried about her after she jumped overboard.

"Trust me. I've had a lot of experience with females and they're totally unpredictable. Even a lot of women who leave because they're abused by their boyfriends soon return to those assholes. They think they can change the jerks. She probably thinks we're too old for her anyway."

"Okay, you might be right, but I hope you're not. I know one thing for sure."

"What's that, Sir Lancelot?"

"I know it's time we ignore what she said before regarding not going to the police. She could be in trouble, and we have to do the right thing for her—just in case."

The brothers got in the taxi and went back to town. The official Jost Van Dyke outpost of the BVI government was the only substantial two-story building. It was covered in white stucco, with a shaded veranda on each level. They marched up to the front door, but found it locked with a note on the door: CLOSED FOR DINNER. BACK LATER.

"What time later? It doesn't say shit," said Nate.

"You need Winston?" asked the taxi driver.

"Is he the policeman on duty?" asked Doug.

"Yah mon. Constable Winston Malone. He be here soon. He eat at Abe's most every night."

"Abe's is at the east end, past Harris's. Damn, we were there only an hour ago. We might as well wait right here until he returns," said Doug. He paid the driver, but the driver stayed, not wanting to miss the only excitement in town. "I'm telling you, I bet the guy's abducted her and she's in trouble again. She wouldn't leave without thanking us."

Nate shrugged and walked over to a nearby bar. It was painted a gaudy pink and purple with a bush outside decorated with beer bottles strung like Christmas ornaments. He strolled back holding three cold Carib beers. The happy driver took one and thanked him. Doug wasn't in the mood for any more alcohol, so Nate forced himself to work on two at once.

Finally, a white SUV pulled up and the constable stepped out. He was a tall, thin man with an impeccable uniform. He put on his cap and adjusted it firmly before unlocking the door and walking in. The constable didn't acknowledge Doug and Nate until he got behind the white counter and faced them. The taxi driver moved up to the front door and cocked his head to listen in on the conversation.

"How may I assist you gentlemen?"

"One of my crew is missing and I think she's been kidnapped," Doug blurted out.

"Slow down, sir. First, what is the name of your vessel?"

"It's *Payback*. She's an American-registered sailboat."

"Would it be the white sloop I saw over at Little Harbour, between Abe's and Harris's?"

"That's the one. I'm Doug Thompson and this is my brother Nate. The missing woman is Cassandra MacDuff."

"Go slowly, and tell me the facts from the beginning please."

Doug told the constable everything, while Nate chimed in on various details. The constable laboriously wrote the information on a white form. After they finished, the officer asked them to come back in a half hour to give him time to call Tortola and run it all through the police computer. Doug was impressed when Constable Malone stated he would be able to use databases from the American and British Commonwealth sources.

"That's great. I hope it doesn't take them too long, though. We'll be right next door if you get anything early. We have to find this Hunter guy right away. He probably left not long ago. I bet you could still catch him tonight," said Doug.

"Remain calm and wait outside, sir. I will call for you."

Doug was impatient, but knew better than to complain. The brothers exited through the doorway as the taxi driver quickly stepped aside. They sat at the bar and drank rum and Cokes to keep the bartender happy while they discussed their theories to explain Cassie's disappearance.

An hour later, the constable allowed them back in the station. He stood up and looked at them sternly. "You two have done some drinking today, haven't you?"

"I guess so, bud-roe...I mean, officer." said Nate. "We were drinking a little at Harris's, then we went to Foxy's, then a little more at the bar here. We probably sweated it all out by now, though. We can hold our liquor."

"Yes, I see."

"What about Cassie? What did you find?" asked Doug.

"Yes, let us discuss your young lady. First, there is no record of a Miss Cassandra MacDuff living in San Diego. Additionally, we found no Hunter Lamar in the immigration records of the BVI or the USVI. Miss MacDuff does not show up in those records either. It appears there are no such people anywhere near the territory.

"There are indeed several vessels named *Wet Dream* in the U.S. Coast Guard records, but none is owned by anyone named Hunter or Lamar. Additionally, no such boat with that unfortunate name matches the size and color you gave; nor has such a vessel officially entered the Virgin Islands. On the other hand, you two have trespassed on government land and should have made an immediate report if your story in regards to rescuing a woman on Dead Chest was true."

"Of course our story is true. You should check again." Doug protested.

"My checking work is done, sir. I have spent enough time checking to know you are wasting my time. Finally, when I was at Little Harbour, I happened to take note your vessel was not flying the proper host country flag, thereby disrespecting Her Majesty's government."

"I had one! Somebody must've stolen it."

"This is bullshit! We're the ones trying to help. This isn't about us," added Nate, swaying a little.

"Oh, but it is about you now. And I'll thank you to watch your tongue. I should arrest you both for filing a false police report. Instead, you two are hereby notified of your official reclassification as undesirables for purposes of immigration. Your permission to visit the British Virgin Islands is therefore rescinded. You have forty-eight hours to sober up, provision your sailboat, and leave our territorial waters. Failure to comply may result in arrest, substantial fines, impoundment of your vessel, and possible imprisonment."

"Oh, come on!" said Doug.

"Furthermore, on an unofficial basis, I am going to notify my colleagues in the other police forces on our computer network for the entire Caribbean basin not to believe one word you two troublemakers say relating to this matter. I will be doing them a considerable favor. You are dismissed. Now get out of my office!"

Doug and Nate knew any further argument was futile and left to taxi back to Little Harbour. They picked up the cold suppers the restaurant had kept for them and returned to *Payback*.

"I told you Cassie wasn't telling us something," said Nate.

"I can't believe she'd lie to us. She seemed like such a nice girl."

"Yeah, but she isn't a girl. She's a beautiful woman, and I can tell you about those females. You damn sure can't trust them. They're used to getting everything they want, and they don't care who they have to walk all over to get it."

"Maybe you're right, Nate. I just hope she's okay."

✳   ✳   ✳   ✳

After the recapture of their former shipmate, Garcia got the blankets from the dinghy and tied up Cassie in a long bundle. Hunter's plan had been for them to carry her over the small hill and head west to White Bay. He'd told Sanchez he would leave the dinghy for Sanchez to use to follow the two men from *Payback* and report back.

The combination of the steep hill, stony ground, and steamy heat proved too much, however, and they soon gave up on the idea of carrying her. Fortunately for them, the dinghy was over at the same end of the bay where they caught Cassie. So Hunter quickly carried the unconscious girl across the deserted road and dumped her in the dinghy. He and Garcia pushed off into the harbor.

"Should we go tell Sanchez we are taking the little boat now?" said Garcia. Beads of sweat rolled down his nose and dropped off the end like a drip coffeemaker.

"Screw him. He'll figure it out. I'll leave you with the girl and come back for him."

They made it to White Bay and loaded their "cargo" aboard without incident. Hunter tied Cassie up in the cabin, checked to be sure her breathing was regular, and returned to town to find Sanchez.

"There you are," said Sanchez. "I guess you got her, but I thought I was supposed to keep the dinghy. It is getting dark, and I was starting to worry. What took you so long?"

"Hey, the wind is kicking up now, and it's a long way. We got her, but it was too hard to carry her up the hill so Garcia and I used the dinghy. Are you still keeping an eye on those two sailor boys?" asked Hunter.

"No, they left. I watched them sit at Foxy's for awhile, and then they walked to the end of the road and looked in the grocery store. Then they went into every single bar and souvenir shop before they returned to Foxy's. They sat there talking and waving their arms about something for a few minutes before they got up and left in their dinghy. So I went to get in our dinghy to follow them, but it was gone, was it not?"

"Which direction did they go?"

"I do not know. I lost sight of their dinghy with all those anchored yachts blocking the view. If you had left me the little boat I could have followed the sailors."

"Give me a break, Sanchez. I just told you why we borrowed it. Shit, they could be heading over to where the girl is. Okay, Foxy's is in the middle of the island. If they went out of this harbor and then turned right, they'd be heading west to *Moby Dick* in White Bay. Except I just came from there, and I didn't see them pass me. If they came out of here and turned left instead, they'd be going over to the first bay, Little Harbour, or maybe farther."

"I told you I did not see which way they turned."

"Maybe she's told them the name of our boat by now," said Hunter. "I can't figure what, if anything, she's actually told them because they didn't act worried when they saw us go by them or anchor near them back on Virgin Gorda. Shit, I don't know what's going on with her and those dumb guys. Come on, get in, and let's go."

Hunter ran the dinghy west to White Bay and found *Moby Dick* secure, with no sign of Doug and his crewman around. *Maybe I should've changed the trawler's name*, he thought, *but it was a lot easier to merely change the ownership records. Maxwell would've charged a lot more to hack into all the computer databases recording the name. If he changed the yacht's name, he probably would then have to change all the hull identification numbers stamped in various places on the boat, too. Screw it.*

"Are we going to look for them now?" said Sanchez.

Hunter thought awhile and said, "No, let's just leave and hide somewhere until we can question Cassie and find out what the hell's going on. It's too busy around here. What if those assholes went to the police? We can find their boat again when we're good and ready. Pull up the anchor and let's get underway."

Hunter studied the chart while Garcia took *Moby Dick* south of the bay.

"Okay, now where?" asked Garcia.

"I think I found a good place. Turn west. We're going to hide for awhile behind an island called Big Tobago. It's at the far western end of the BVI and way off the tourist circuit. It's uninhabited and looks like it has a spot where a boat could anchor to get out of this easterly wind."

"I thought Tobago was the place to the south, near Trinidad, where we started," said Sanchez.

"Yes, it is," said Garcia. "But, there are a lot of duplicate names in the West Indies. People did not check with each other when they were coming up with all these names. Big Tobago and Little Tobago are here, in the BVI, Tobago Island is next to Trinidad, and there are five little keys in the Grenadines called the Tobago Cays. Then there is a Saba Rock here, and there is a Dutch island named Saba south of St. Martin. My Dominican Republic is Latino, but there is also an English-speaking nation called Dominica. Then the *loco* French named every other old volcano Soufriere. I will not even list all the Spanish duplicate names. You should know those already, *amigo.*"

"Yeah, well, I never traveled the Caribbean as much as you. Man, I never heard you talk so much on this whole trip! Excuse me for asking."

"Would you ladies just shut up and keep an eye peeled for somebody following us? There's Big Tobago ahead."

CHAPTER 13

▼

BIG TOBAGO

The morning after Cassie disappeared, Doug got up and completed his usual boat preparation. Without her, though, all the excitement of another day of cruising was gone. He still had Nate, so he was essentially where he was before they'd rescued Cassie. He suddenly realized she'd entered his life only three days ago. She was basically a casual acquaintance. He'd had plenty of fun before she arrived on the scene, and he should be looking forward to a few weeks more with Nate.

Still, it wasn't the same somehow. Quickly, she'd filled a big empty spot, and now she'd apparently abandoned him. He stopped his departure preparations, wrapped an arm around the mast, and silently stared south toward the open water. A young goat cried out on the hillside. It sounded alarmingly like a human baby.

"Morning, Cap'n Ahab," said Nate. "Looking for sperm whales?"

"Sorry, I didn't hear you. No, there aren't any whales this time of year. Once, though, a crazy dolphin came in here and circled *Payback* for twenty minutes. My kids jumped in the water and chased him round and round the boat until they were exhausted. I don't know why the dolphin chose to play with us."

"So now you've gone from the chosen one to *persona non grata*. Don't take it too hard, bro'. I've been thrown out of lots of places."

"Well, we still have one more night in the BVI. There's time to take you to the last couple of places I was planning to show you. Let's have some real fun before we take off. You realize what tonight is?"

"Umm, Thursday night?"

"Right, but it's also the full moon. The Bomba Shack will be throwing their infamous full-moon party tonight. It's the wildest party in the Caribbean. You get a couple of thousand people spilling into the street sometimes. Believe it or not, street vendors sell little cups of those magic mushrooms, and Bomba brews mushroom tea. Those 'shrooms are actually legal here. People get totally crazy."

"I'm not eating anything that grows in cow pies. I don't care how happy it makes you. Hey, Doug. Is this the bar made from driftwood and beach trash I read about?"

"The very same."

"Sounds like a good sendoff for our last night in the BVI."

"First, we can do a snorkeling stop at a small island on the way. Then we'll moor *Payback* in Cane Garden Bay on Tortola and do some grocery shopping. Then I want to take a taxi to the highest part of Tortola for pictures, and maybe hit town, too. We can taxi over to Bomba's after supper."

"Let's do it!"

Doug's mood brightened. Not bothering with the sails, he soon got underway and motored the short distance to Sandy Cay. Anchoring close in, the brothers jumped off *Payback* and snorkeled straight in to the beach rather than hassle with the dinghy. Unlike its smaller cousin, Sandy Spit, the island of Sandy Cay was a botanical park, donated by the Rockefellers, and it boasted a circular nature trail. The eastern end of the trail was on the top of a rocky cliff with large waves breaking at the base. From the high vantage point, Doug looked at passing boats and wondered if Cassie was aboard one and how she was doing.

After leaving Sandy Cay, *Payback* sailed on a windward course to Tortola and moored in Cane Garden Bay. The crew marveled at the bay's long beach of white sand and the fringe of coconut palms lining the entire length. Handfuls of shops and beach bars nested beneath palms with a paved road running behind. Behind the road, the land rose more than 1,500 feet like an incredibly steep jungle-covered wall.

The brothers went ashore and walked along the beach to the pink building housing a motel, grocery, restaurant and beach bar all in one. Doug paid the mooring fee, and they picked up needed ice and groceries. Nate helped him carry it all back to the dinghy. He opted to wait at Quito's Gazebo bar while Doug ran it out to *Payback*. Doug returned with the week's accumulated garbage in two black trash bags, and they carried the bags south to the green dumpster.

"There's an old rum distillery a little farther down the road. Want to stop and see it?" asked Doug.

"Nah, let's go on to the top of the mountain while's it's still clear."

"You got it."

There were five identical minivan taxis already waiting near the two pay phones. Doug negotiated a fare for a short tour climbing the mountain to Sky World, down to Road Town, west to Soper's Hole, and back to Cane Garden Bay. The driver was pleased to have paying passengers all afternoon. They memorized his license tag number so they'd find him again after each shopping stop.

Going up the mountain involved navigating steep switchbacks and blind spots, with barely enough room for one car to pass the occasional donkey or goat. The driver honked when he approached each dangerous section to alert unseen oncoming vehicles. He stopped once, on a forty-five-degree slope, to exchange greetings with a friend drinking at a roadside bar. The makeshift bar was a shack with a corrugated metal roof. Patrons sat on two folding chairs placed on the road's pavement.

"Whoa, it's a damn good thing they don't have snow and ice here. You'd slide backwards all the way down to the ocean."

"Yeah, I wouldn't want to try this in a Wisconsin winter," agreed Doug. "Speaking of temperature, did you notice how it's cooled off as we go up the mountain? There's a ten-degree difference from top to bottom. The plants change, too. There's more rain to support growth here."

"Did you see the big bull wandering along the side road a mile back?"

"Sure did. The cattle just run in Road Town where there's a stretch of flat, four-lane road. Everybody drives fast there and they can really smack into a cow. Messes up the car and the cow—big time."

"Like watching out for moose in Montana, I guess," said Nate.

"On my first trip here, I was in a taxi at night, and we had to swerve to avoid a big bull just west of downtown. We barely avoided hitting a tree. Anyway, I asked the driver where the bull was going at eleven o'clock at night. Know what he told me?" asked Doug.

"Okay, I'll bite."

"That bull going to see his girlfren,' mon!"

"Sounds like a reasonable place for a bull to be going in the middle of the night," said Nate, keeping a straight face.

"You're no fun," complained Doug.

Right before the brothers reached the summit, they passed an elementary school on the left. It was recess and the children wearing school uniforms sported big smiles as they played in the fenced schoolyard.

"See them, Nate? Compare those smiles to the expressions on a bunch of adults walking on the Chicago sidewalks at lunch hour. What happens to us all to take away the smiles?"

"Life happens, bro'. We learn it's mostly work and boredom and pain. We learn to feel guilty for taking time off for fun. We learn life's short, and finally realize we're not some special exception to the rule. We learn that fifty years after we're gone, no one will give a shit we were even around."

"Boy, you're so damn cheery today. You know, I think it's time for us to self-medicate again." The cab stopped at the summit and they walked into Skyworld's bar and ordered some strong frozen drinks. The driver had a soft drink on Doug's tab. They checked out the gift shop, and admired the restaurant tables all set with tablecloths and china for the evening.

With frosty drinks in hand, the brothers walked up the stairs to the flat roof. There was a gorgeous 360-degree view of all the Virgins, looking like emeralds laid out for display on a jeweler's dark blue cloth. The clear sky even allowed views of St. Croix and Anegada at opposite far edges of the horizon. A coin-operated set of binoculars was available to get closer views of the boats carving white wakes between dots of land. Doug pointed out the islands they'd visited as Nate looked all around the horizon.

"Wow, this is genuinely awesome, Doug. Forget all the crap I was spouting before. You've really brought a smile to my face today. See, this is what I'm talking about. You have to find time in your life for things like this. Thanks again for letting me ride along."

"You're welcome. I get a kick from showing it to people who can appreciate it." Doug's smile faded when he thought about Cassie missing his tour today. He would've enjoyed showing it all to her, too. He put a quarter in the binocular machine and made a half-hearted effort to scan the vessels for a sight of her. Soon, his time ran out, and shutters clicked down across the lenses.

The brothers retraced their steps through the restaurant, collected their driver, and set off down the other side of the mountain to Road Town. On the way, Doug noted the horse track and the various charter-boat operations. The driver parked near the new waterfront handicraft marketplace. The brothers browsed through the booths and crossed the street to Pusser's Pub. After a medium pizza, they shopped along the narrow, back streets. Doug stopped into Sunny Caribee to say hello to the owner and buy some spices for *Payback*'s galley.

"Hey, Doug Thompson! Where have you been lately?" The store owner shook Doug's hand.

"Took me awhile to get the boat redone, but I'm finally sailing again. This is my brother, Nate." The two men nodded at each other.

"Okay, don't be such a stranger."

Doug considered telling the man this might be his last time in the BVI for awhile due to the trouble with the police, but figured the story would be too long and sound too far-fetched.

When they finished with the capital city, the driver took them west along the southern shore of Tortola all the way to Soper's Hole. The narrow bay was full of yachts. A refreshing easterly breeze blew strongly through the gap between Frenchman's Cay and Tortola proper, rippling the harbor water.

The brothers strolled along the boardwalk and stopped in all the brightly colored establishments. A palm tree was growing right through the pink roof of the dive shop. Next door, the local Pusser's branch had a circular, open-air bar, complete with brass rails and carved mermaids. Nate bought a couple of cold Blackbeard Ales for the road. The sailors found their patient driver by the newsstand and started the trip back north to Cane Garden Bay.

Doug pointed out the various bays and restaurants on the up and down ride along the hilly coast. When they got to Cappoon's Bay, he alerted Nate right before they passed by Bomba's Surfside Shack.

"That's it?"

"Yeah, there's the place we're partying tonight. Didn't you see Bomba's big Cadillac with the cartoon drawings of mushrooms on it?" said Doug.

"That's him, huh? Hell, the place is only a sand floor with old boards nailed across a few poles supporting half a roof. It's like the 'forts' we used to build in the woods when we were ten years old. He's got graffiti all over and junk nailed everywhere. It looks like one big wave would wash it away."

"Don't worry; Bomba has a sign up saying a hurricane only makes The Shack stronger. He simply adds on all the new stuff blowing ashore."

The taxi let them out at the top of the dock, and they returned to the boat for supper.

"I guess we don't need to dress up for tonight, do we?" laughed Nate.

*   *   *   *

Cassie awoke slowly on Thursday morning, and felt the dried blood under her hair when she moved her head against the pillow. She found she couldn't move her arm to check her scalp since her hands were tied behind her back. Another rope pulled her hands to her tied ankles. Cassie tried to remember what happened. She was going into the grocery store when someone or something hit her on the side of her head. Suddenly her brain registered what her eyes were telling her. She was back on *Moby Dick*. Hunter had caught her.

Cassie screamed frantically. She thrashed around on the bunk and pulled so hard the ropes rubbed her wrists and ankles raw. Cassie quickly tired and realized her panic wasn't helping. She had to think fast, and physically escape or somehow talk her way out of trouble again.

"Finally awake and noisy, huh? It's about time. There's no way to make a sleeper walk the plank, but now we can have some real fun," said Hunter as he walked into the cabin.

Cassie thought she'd better try to convince him her absence was only an accident. She wondered if the knife was still under the mattress.

"Hunter, I think somebody hit me in the head. I almost drowned before, baby. Why did you leave me in the water? I looked all over for you."

"You've been looking for me? Is that right? We've been all over the BVI looking for you, liar. We hung around shitty little islands like Peter and Dead Chest for three days looking for your sweet ass."

"No, baby. You have to believe me. I came up from my cabin that night to see what was going on, then the boat tilted, and I fell off. I tried to swim to you, but you kept going, and I lost you. It was dark, and I was swept out to sea. I held on to a boat fender for two days, and then these nice guys came along and picked me up. I've been looking for you ever since."

"That's your story, huh? What happened to the load of coke then?"

"I don't know. Did something happen to it?" asked Cassie.

"You're goddamn right something happened to it! The canister and ropes all disappeared at the same time you did. Somebody has it now and you know who it is."

"I don't know anything about it, Hunter. I didn't do anything to your cocaine."

"If you were looking for me, why didn't you call me on the radio?"

Cassie hesitated a second and said, "I didn't think you'd want me to do that. I thought it might attract the cops."

Hunter paused. "Shit, you could've used first names or something."

"I didn't think of doing it. I'm not as smart as you are, baby."

"How about your swimsuit?"

"What about my swimsuit?"

"Where is it?"

She didn't know why he would ask. She couldn't say she was alone and hiding on Dead Chest when she lost half of it. Cassie thought maybe she'd shade the truth. "I still have the bottoms, but the top blew off when it was drying on the rail of the sailboat."

Hunter silently stroked his chin. "So far, I still don't know if you're telling me the truth or not, but I'm damn sure going to find out. Okay, who rescued you and what's the name of their boat?"

Cassie tried to take some time to think. She had to protect Doug and Nate. She owed them her best effort. But she worried about how much Hunter might already know.

"Hurry up, bitch! Tell me the names right now!"

"Sure, baby, I was only trying to remember the boat's name. I think it's called the *Marilyn*, and it's from Miami. The two guys are Richard and Earl. I didn't get their last names."

"Bullshit! Now I'm positive you're full of it," Hunter shouted and grabbed Cassie roughly. Her injured head hit the bulkhead as Hunter carried her from the cabin. She screamed in pain, and was heard all over the vessel.

"Now she is finally going to get it," Sanchez said to Garcia, and they both smiled.

Hunter carried Cassie to the top deck and untied her. The two Latinos helped him hold her down. She screamed and kicked and was able to nail Garcia right in the solar plexus. He fell back briefly, but the other two held her tight and started pulling her clothes off. Cassie yelled and screamed for help. She tried to curl into a ball so they couldn't get at her. She remembered Hunter's threat from the night Leo was killed, to rape and skin her, and she was sure he was going to carry out his promise.

Garcia returned to the fight, and the drug pirates were finally able to strip and tie her. Hunter looped the line from the deck crane around Cassie's feet and hoisted her into the air. Instead of lifting the dinghy, the cargo boom was now being used to lift Cassie upside down and dangle her over the water.

"First we need to wash all the blood and dirt off of you, don't we?" Hunter laughed and lowered her into the seawater. He kept her there for a full minute then raised her. Cassie gasped for air and screamed again.

"Scream all you want. Nobody can hear you. No one can even see us off behind Big Tobago like this. Oh no! It looks like I missed a spot." Hunter lowered her into the water again and watched her struggle before cranking her up to his level again.

Cassie struggled for air. When she recovered her voice and wits, she tried the surprised and innocent approach again. "Why are you doing this to me? I thought you liked me. Please, Hunter. I'm yours, baby. Don't do this to me!"

"You're such a goddamn liar," said Hunter. He whipped out his semiautomatic pistol, pulled the slide back to chamber a round, and knelt to hold it to her head. "I should shoot you right now and get it over with, but it'd be too easy for you."

"Stop it, Hunter. I'm telling you everything." Cassie thought he wouldn't actually kill her yet. He still wanted to know something. She needed to figure what she'd give him.

Hunter pulled the gun away from her head and stood up. He started moving the gun barrel all over her tanned body. He moved the Beretta in circles around her sensitive areas and began poking her violently with the gun. Sanchez and Garcia watched with amused looks.

"Stop it. You're hurting me!"

"What? Don't you like that? I thought all you demanding bitches liked something real hard. Is it hard enough for you? Is it?" Hunter slapped and slashed with the tip of the barrel. The blade of the front sight scratched her and drew blood.

"Oh, my goodness, now you're bleeding a little. I'm afraid the sharks are going to smell it and come running. Come here, you two, and help me," ordered Hunter. They took Cassie down from the crane and tied four docking lines to her wrists and ankles. Hunter dragged her to the bow of the boat.

"What are you doing? Stop it right now, and let's talk this out," said Cassie.

"You going to tell me more lies?"

"I already told you everything! Please stop," pleaded Cassie.

"I guess we're going to have to keelhaul you, just like in the old pirate days. They used to throw mutineers over the bow and drag them under the barnacled keel of the ship back to the stern. Most didn't survive." With that, Hunter pushed her over the bow pulpit. The crew took the two lines on each side and dragged her, face up, slowly under the trawler.

Cassie was able to take one deep breath before she hit the water. As she dragged aft, her stomach was scratched by the damaged area where *Moby Dick* had hit the reef in Savannah Bay. From there back, the hull was smoother. She thought she'd make the whole length of the boat at this pace without running out of air. She wiggled to avoid the propeller blades. Near the stern, the men stopped dragging her and she felt the rising need to breathe.

Cassie started to freak out and strained against the ropes trying to pull herself up one side to no avail. She recovered her wits and realized she would merely use her oxygen faster. She had to hang on until she could breathe again. Cassie couldn't afford to panic and let water into her lungs. When she felt her lungs would burst, they finally pulled her backwards and to the surface. Cassie choked and spit water. She pulled the sweet air into her lungs, and flailed around trying to swim despite the tangle of ropes.

"Bleeding a little more I see. Still not enough for these shy sharks, though," Hunter hoisted her again using the crane boom and the lines tied to her legs. When he swung her aboard, he pulled on the ropes to expose the ankles and slowly drew his knife.

Cassie screamed when she saw the knife. She had to tell him something, anything, to save her life. Somehow he knew she was still holding back. What was the last thing she'd told him before he grabbed her off the bunk? The names—that's what he knows and how he knew she was telling lies. If she did tell him about Doug and Nate, though, she'd have to find a reason so he'd keep her alive to help him. Otherwise, he'd feel free to eliminate her.

Fooling him regarding her supposed attraction to him wasn't working by itself anymore. The only other thing he wanted was the drugs. That's it. She'd have to become the key for him to recover the drugs.

Hunter abruptly pinched the skin on her right ankle and pulled it toward him. In a heartbeat, he slashed with the razor-sharp knife and cut off the quarter-sized patch of flesh containing her tiny flower and heart tattoo. Cassie screamed and sobbed. New blood joined existing flows down her leg and torso. Tears rolled across her forehead and dripped to the deck.

"Never liked tattoos on women. Only makes them look cheap. Did you know the classic pirates didn't have tattoos? The stupid idea only came in later, after the whalers visited the South Pacific. Now, are you going to tell me the truth, or do I have to cut off this bigger, uglier, barbed wire tattoo on your other ankle?"

"Okay, you win Hunter! I'll tell you everything. I swear." Cassie strained to see his face even though she was still upside down. She had to see if he would buy the pieces of the truth she was now going to feed him.

"Damn straight you will. What's the name of the sailboat?"

"It's *Payback*."

"Who's onboard?"

"Doug Thompson owns the boat, and Nate, his younger brother, is riding along."

Hunter nodded at Garcia, and the Dominican wrote down Nate's name.

"So far, so good. Keep going. What happened to the coke?" asked Hunter.

"They've got it on their boat. I didn't want to tell you this before, baby, because I didn't want you to get hurt. Both of these guys are rough, and Nate was in the Navy Seals. They're tough as nails, Hunter. You wouldn't want to mess with these men. I thought if I told you they're only a couple of cruising sailors, you'd leave them out of it. You'd figure the coke was lost in the ocean. Then we'd just go back to Venezuela, and you'd try this drug run again. I never should've tried, but at least I saved the coke for you, baby."

"What the hell are you talking about? More lies?"

"No, you have to believe me. When I fell off the back of the boat, I saw the canister floating because it was all tangled up with ropes and a couple of those inflated rubber fender things. The drum was starting to come loose and sink again so I tied it to one of the fenders and to my leg. Your drug package barely floated. It made it hard for me to swim, but I kept the canister with me hoping you'd return.

"I thought you would be so happy and proud of me. I held on to the other fender and floated for two whole nights. The tide pushed me out to sea, then back closer to where I'd see the islands, and then out again. I was so scared, Hunter! I prayed you'd find me. But those other guys found me first."

"You wanted to save the coke for yourself, I bet," said Hunter. "When they found you, I reckon your main concern was making sure you still got a big share for yourself. You probably screwed both of those pencil dicks to make sure!"

"No, Hunter," Cassie pleaded. She was doing her best to keep her head under the circumstance, but she was fighting back tears and the urge to close her eyes and scream. She hated having to play along with this savage, and especially despised having to lie about Doug and Nate, who had been so good to her.

"They both really liked me," she continued, "but I was only playing along until I'd find you again. I didn't do anything physical with them, honey. In fact, I slept straight through the first couple of days after swimming for forty-eight hours. I almost died out there. When I finally woke up, we were way north at the top of Virgin Gorda. They decided to keep sailing around like nothing happened for a couple of days so they wouldn't look suspicious.

"Baby, I looked for you near Saba Rock, then at Anegada, and again on Jost Van Dyke. I kept sneaking off on my own to find you, like I was doing when you grabbed me. Just leave them alone, Hunter. They said they've got guns, too. If you take me back to Vegas, I can get you some more money, a lot of money, and we can start over, baby."

"What did you say about me and how I got this boat?"

"Nothing, Hunter. I told them my boyfriend was a drug smuggler, but his boat hit a rock and sank. I said I was the only one who survived. They haven't been looking for you at all." Cassie hoped she'd mixed enough truth in along with the lies so he'd believe this second story of hers. In her lies, she had people acting exactly like he'd act so Hunter would buy it.

"You're probably still bullshitting me. I'm not about to leave those assholes alone anyway. I knew one name already. They don't scare me," Hunter said.

He stepped away from Cassie and walked around the side of the deck, muttering loud enough that she heard. "I'll slit those assholes' throats even if they didn't steal the coke. She's all mine, and no rag-hanging sons of bitches are going to take what's mine. They talked to her, and now they'll have to pay the price. Whoever this Doug is, and whoever the other guy is, they'll both wish they'd never laid eyes on what's mine."

Cassie thought she'd now confirmed what she'd suspected. Hunter had already known some names anyway, and he wouldn't leave Doug and Nate alone. She called his name and he stepped back around toward her. "I'm telling you the truth, baby. Get me down from here so I can put a bandage on my ankle. Then I'll help you find the brothers. Trust me. I can sweet-talk those guys into telling me where their sailboat is now and if the coke is still aboard. You have to get me back pretty quick or they'll be too suspicious.

"I'll say I got lost and chew them out for not finding me on Dead Chest. I'll say I had to catch a ride with another boat. Just get me aboard *Payback*, and then you can follow us. I'll keep you informed on the radio and tell you where they're going so you don't lose them. You know I can help you if you let me, baby."

*   *   *   *

Hunter considered her offer. She was telling the truth regarding the names so she might be coming clean on everything else now, too. He recalled he'd actually seen *Payback* and her crew at Peter. If what she said was true, she must have been in her bunk recuperating at the time, and then again in Savannah Bay on Virgin Gorda. Both of those times, *Payback*'s crew had seen him and *Moby Dick*, but they hadn't shown any concern at all. It was another point making him think she was finally telling the truth.

At Virgin Gorda, he'd seen her swimsuit drying on the *Payback*'s lifelines. The top could've fallen off earlier, near where they'd picked her up. It could've easily drifted to Salt Island. She hadn't claimed she still had the top.

If *Payback* had been way off in Anegada, it'd explain why he couldn't find the sailboat a couple of days ago. He actually could use Cassie's help spotting the sailors and being his spy on their yacht. He wanted it all to be true because she was still the one woman he wanted.

Even so, Hunter had to test her one more time. It was also essential to lock her in as part of his crew of corsairs so she could never double-cross him. Hunter put the knife on her other ankle tattoo and made an initial tiny cut. Cassie screamed again.

"Okay, now tell me the whole truth this time or I'll cut this bigger tattoo off."

"Stop it! You're hurting me! It was the truth! That's all I know. You can go ahead and kill me now, but I don't know anything else. Jesus, I want to help you!"

"Hey, you *hombres* want to pork this bitch now?" Hunter called over his shoulder. "I'm fixing to skin her alive right quick."

"Don't! I told you everything!" Cassie was desperate, but she knew she couldn't afford to change her story now.

"No way, man," said Garcia. "You got her all messy and bloody now. You should have screwed her first before you got all *loco* on her. What is wrong with you, anyway? Do you ever get horny?"

"Shut up, dick-breath! There's nothing wrong with me. I'd play hide the sausage with her right now if I didn't have to look at your ugly faces while I was doing her. Okay, look, I guess we believe her, but we need some insurance this time. Sanchez, go get the video camera." Hunter lowered Cassie down to the deck and untied her. He threw his handkerchief at her and she tied it around the wound on her right ankle. Cassie started getting dressed.

"You won't regret this, Hunter. I'll help you out, I swear."

"You're going to swear to something else so I'm sure you're truly with us," he said.

Sanchez came back topside with the camera, and Hunter had him focus it on Cassie. She finished dressing. Hunter posed her so the camera wouldn't see the lump on her head or the blood on her ankles and thighs. He told Cassie what to say and made her rehearse it a couple of times. She was hesitant, but he reminded her of what would happen if she didn't cooperate. Eventually, they had a clean tape of Cassie confessing to murdering Leo in order to steal his boat and his money.

"There, that should do it. Now if you ever think about running away you can damn well stop and think again, because I'll forward this video to the cops. You're with us now, and you're in it up to your neck."

"Don't worry, baby. I'm on your side. Come on. Let's go find Doug and Nate before they get too worried. Where do you think they'd be, Hunter?"

*   *   *   *

Cassie desperately needed to rejoin the two brothers. She felt Doug and Nate could help her escape if anybody could.

Cassie knew the islands were only a line of pinpricks in a vast wilderness of ocean. Doug would know how to hide out in the trackless sea. The fake confession didn't bother her; the police wanted her anyway. Getting away from Hunter was her first goal. Cassie was sorry she got the brothers involved with these drug pirates, but she had no choice. She and Leo hadn't asked to be hijacked, either.

"I've got a damn good idea where they'll be tonight," said Hunter. "The bartender at the Soggy Dollar told me all these rich yachties will be on Tortola for a big party at a bar called Bomba's. You go below, clean yourself up, and stay there. You two raise anchor and get us going. I'm getting a beer and something to eat."

CHAPTER 14

▼

TORTOLA

Moby Dick left Big Tobago and cruised east along the southern coast of Jost Van Dyke. Hunter and his crew looked for *Payback* in the island's harbors, then at Sandy Spit, and finally at Sandy Key. After striking out, Hunter checked the chart and told Cassie that Soper's Hole was the closest harbor to Bomba's Bar on Tortola. He explained the Soper's Hole harbor was a couple of miles south of the bar's Cappoon Bay location. Cappoon Bay had no sheltered anchorage. The alternate harbor, Cane Garden Bay, lay a greater distance off to the north of Bomba's.

"Who decorated this place? I ain't seen so many fruity colors anywhere outside of Key West." Hunter said when the shops and tourist boutiques of Soper's appeared. A dozen buildings painted in flamboyant pastels and uniformly topped by pink roofs, lined the waterfront. "Cassie, you get over to that Ample Hamper store on the left and get us some groceries before the place closes. You guys go with her and don't let her out of your sight."

Garcia and Sanchez brought her back to the trawler afterwards. Cassie made supper and tried to reestablish her dumb "gun moll" persona. It was unreal to be cooking and serving meals to three men who had tortured her so recently. It didn't appear to bother them in the least. Her ankle hurt where the tiny tattoo had been sliced off, but she realized her wounds were only superficial. Cassie knew she'd been lucky. The two crewmen could easily kill her without remorse. It'd simply be normal business as far as they were concerned.

Hunter was a different story. He was flat-out crazy, and by now she realized he had some kind of sexual problem. Hunter's emotional involvement with her made him extremely dangerous and unpredictable. If she got away again, she'd have to make sure she was gone for good. She wouldn't be able to fool him twice.

"Clean this crap up! We've got to get ashore, and get a taxi over to this Bomba Shack place before those two clowns show," ordered Hunter. "And make yourself look pretty. Remember, you're the bait, bitch."

The street in front of Bomba's was already crowded when Hunter and his crew arrived. Copycat vendors, unrelated to Bomba, sold drinks and trinkets along the roadside north and south of The Shack. During this monthly party, Bomba's operation temporarily spread inland across the road to include a make-shift restaurant and gift shop. A weak psychedelic mushroom tea was brewing in a large drum behind the plywood gift shop.

The Shack looked like a chicken coop that had barely survived a Kansas tornado. License plates, lingerie, fishnets, and bumper stickers covered the walls and ceiling. The place was packed with locals and yachties dancing to live "jump-up" music while trying not to spill the contents of their plastic cups. A large notice warned of dire consequences for using video cameras in The Shack.

Hunter grabbed Cassie by the hand and entered the bar. He sneered at the hand-lettered sign proclaiming free Bomba Punch for ladies who took off their panties and sacrificed them for immediate stapling to the ceiling. Other signs declared Bomba a divine gift to women and offered a free t-shirt if they sat naked on his lap for pictures.

"This guy's got a hell of an ego. The tourist chicks probably love it, though. Gives them a feeling of flirting with danger in the tropics. They don't know what danger is. I got your danger right here, baby," Hunter said while grabbing his crotch.

Garcia and Sanchez ignored Hunter and studied the fading official pictures of past t-shirt winners stapled to the random rough planks acting as the wall. A white reflective sign from somewhere to the far north proclaimed: "Parking for St. Mary's Convent ONLY."

"Where is St. Mary's?" asked Garcia.

"How should I know?" said Hunter. "Wiseass kids probably steal stuff and bring it down here to nail to the walls so they can show off to their punk friends."

Hunter explained his plan and divided his troops by keeping the reliable Garcia to the south of Bomba's and taking Sanchez with him to block the northern road exit. Garcia was standing on the seawall, along the road, where he could signal Hunter if *Payback* crew was sighted. Hunter and Sanchez sat on a fence rail where they could see Garcia and simultaneously scan the crowd. Sanchez would be the runner and messenger. When Hunter was satisfied with their location, he released Cassie to troll for Doug and Nate.

"Don't screw this up, Cassie. It's your last chance. Get hold of those wimps and sweet-talk them into telling you where their boat is. Find out if the coke is still there or if they sold it already. When you learn something, say you need to go to the bathroom and come tell me what the hell's going on. I may send Sanchez to break into their sailboat and steal the coke while they're still here. Maybe he can bust up their yacht at the same time so we can take care of those two when and where we want.

"Once we get the coke, we can probably finish this whole thing tonight. There's no need for you to go to their boat. We can dispose of those two clowns in the dark, once we get them away from this crowd. You get me the info and I'll decide. Remember, I'll be watching you all the time, and we're blocking both ends. Don't even think about taking off."

Cassie nodded and started circulating. She didn't see the brothers, but plenty of other men saw her and tried to talk to her. She said little or nothing in response and kept moving. Cassie considered how she might leave the party and slip away without Hunter noticing or following. The surf was rough and there weren't any yachts anchored off the rocky beach so swimming was not a good option. Hunter and his thugs could quickly intercept her if she tried to run inland up the steep hillside across the road. They had guns, and escape was apparently impossible.

She wasn't sure how Doug and Nate would be able to help her. Maybe she'd warn the brothers so they'd run to the police while she created a diversion. She decided to suggest that idea to Doug; see what he thought. Assuming he ever showed.

An hour later, Cassie spotted Doug and Nate. They had beers in their hands and looked ready to party. Here goes nothing she thought. Cassie moved in closer where she could talk to them while keeping their backs turned to Hunter. She didn't want Hunter to see their shocked faces when the brothers heard the truth.

"Cassie!" shouted Nate, "Where've you been?"

"You okay?" asked Doug.

Cassie gave them both a hug then pulled away. Keeping her back to the beach, she said, "Thank God you're here, but we're all in big trouble. Keep looking at me and don't look around because we're being watched by three armed men. Smile no matter what. Listen, I'm so damn sorry I got you guys involved in this.

Please forgive me." Cassie started to cry, but forced herself to stop and keep a smile plastered on her face.

"What trouble? Are you hurt?" asked Doug.

"Yeah, they knocked me out when they caught me by the grocery store yesterday. Then they hurt me off and on all morning."

"What did they do?" asked Doug

"They half-drowned me and cut me, but I'm still pretty much okay." Cassie stopped when she noticed Nate searching the crowd. "Nate, I mean it. Just smile and look at me or the ocean. Don't look around."

"Sorry."

"Okay, listen. I didn't actually lie to you guys, but I didn't tell you the whole truth, either."

"Yeah, we kind of found that out when we went to the cops yesterday, and they told us our information was total bullshit," said Nate with a frown.

"I'm so sorry. I didn't want to tell you everything at first because I didn't know who to trust. Later, I didn't want you two involved for your own good."

"Forget all that now, and just tell us what's going on," said Doug. "You can start with your real name." They looked pissed, and she could tell that they were struggling to keep fake smiles plastered on their faces.

"It truly is Cassie, but my last name is Spencer. MacDuff is my middle name. I did the same thing with Hunter. His last name is Schoenholz, and he's a drug pirate who thinks I should learn to like him. I had to pretend to go along so I'd survive. The shit-head murdered my friend, Leo, and stole his boat. It's Hunter's wet dream alright, but the trawler's real name is *Moby Dick*." She stared at them, hoping they'd believe her, all the while flipping her hair and balancing from heel to heel so that Hunter would think she was putting the moves on them.

"Hey, I've seen that stinkpot a couple of times this week!" said Doug.

"Yeah, they've been following you whenever they could. Anyway, they hijacked Leo's motorboat, and used it to tow a load of cocaine here from Venezuela. Hunter has a couple of crooks named Garcia and Sanchez helping him."

"No shit?" marveled Nate. "Pirates of the Caribbean? For real?"

"Plenty real and plenty bad. As soon as we got to the BVI, they either hit something or something came untied near Dead Chest, and they lost their load of coke in the ocean. I jumped overboard in all the confusion, swam to Dead Chest, and hid until you found me. They think I know what happened to the cocaine."

"You actually know where it is?" asked Doug.

"No, I don't. It's probably at the bottom of the ocean, but they didn't want to hear it. They were going to kill me, Doug. They tortured me until I finally made up something. I had to tell them you've got it on your boat. I'm sorry, but the only way I could save my life was to say you guys found the drugs."

"Shit! Now they're going to be after us, too," said Nate.

"I'm sorry. It was the only thing I could do. It didn't matter anyway. They'd already decided to go after you simply because you rescued me. They think you know too much. I tried telling Hunter I didn't talk to you about anything, but he won't believe me."

"So why are they letting you run around loose now?" asked Doug.

"I'm supposed to get cozy with you and find out where *Payback* is. Then I pretend to go to the restroom and run over to report. Hunter will send one of his men to your boat to get the drugs back. Then I was hoping I could distract them somehow so you two could escape and tell the police the real story."

"It's no use. The cops throughout the Caribbean have been told to ignore us—even on the U.S.-owned islands. We need to decide whether to fight or flee," said Doug.

"What if I tell Hunter I lied about you two having the drugs?" asked Cassie.

"No, it's too risky. He won't believe you and he'll hurt you because you aren't playing along properly. If he actually did believe you, he'd simply take you somewhere and shoot you now because you aren't useful anymore. Either way, he'll try to kill us all tonight, while he thinks he has us trapped here. It won't work," said Doug.

"You're right, Doug. You should also know I probably can't go to the police, either. They found Leo's body off Grenada, and they want me for questioning, since I was the last one seen with him. Hunter even forced me to make a false confession on video saying I killed Leo. He said he'd give it to the cops if I run away.

"But you can't fight them, Doug. They've got guns and you're outnumbered. Damn! This didn't work at all." She crossed her arms tightly so she wouldn't tremble and tried to hold back the moisture accumulating in the corners of her eyes. Maybe a quick death would be more preferable if she could get the brothers out of this mess at the same time.

Cassie made up her mind to act and said, "Look, I'll lie about where your boat is so Hunter will send Sanchez off to look. It'll only leave two pirates and they'll be separated. Then I'll try to get a gun away from one, and you two can run along the road past him while he's distracted."

"The first part's good," said Nate. "Then it's three against two, or even three against one. But we can't let you try anything by yourself."

"What if I walk to the shore and start swimming into sea? They might be distracted enough for you guys to get away."

"Also too dangerous. Forget it. We're not leaving you here with them. Just calm down while we think of a way out of this," said Doug.

"But it's my problem. You guys don't owe me anything. Hell, I owe you. I'd be dead by now if you hadn't found me on that stinking little island."

Doug turned to his brother. "Nate, do you remember what you said when we found Cassie, and she asked if she could stay until she was sure Hunter wasn't chasing her anymore?"

Nate paused and said, "Yeah. I said, 'Absolutely.'"

Doug turned to Cassie and said, "We kind of thought you dumped us last night. I guess we were wrong," said Doug. "You think she's lied to us, Nate?"

"Guess not. She didn't tell us everything, and she misled us some, but she didn't technically lie…"

Cassie interrupted, "I didn't tell you everything then because I didn't want you guys to get involved and get hurt. I still don't."

Doug ignored Cassie's protest and readdressed his brother, "Okay then. She didn't lie so we have to live by what we told her. I also remember I told Cassie she was a part of our crew, and she was welcome to stay with us. A promise is a promise, Nate."

"You got it, brother. A promise is a promise. Also, I'm getting tired of being pushed around by everybody in this world, and these three baby buccaneers piss me off the most. We need to stick it to these bastards." Nate had obviously made up his mind. Cassie was back as part of the crew, and he was ready to fight.

"Would you two stop trying to be so goddamn noble? This is real life. Those are real pirates, and they're mean as rattlesnakes. Get out of here, and sail off somewhere safe," she said, making one last try to save them from ending up like Leo.

"Yes, we're leaving, but you're coming with us, and they're not going to stop us," said Doug. "Now, tell me exactly what these guys look like and where they are."

Cassie knew she might be fooling herself, but she suddenly felt stronger and safer. For the first time, she'd cleared her conscience and told the sailors everything, yet they were still willing to help her. Maybe Doug actually could get her out of this. For the first time since Leo died, she thought she could fully trust and rely on someone.

Cassie described the three criminals. The brothers took turns scanning the crowd and noting the enemy, while keeping their heads moving casually. They continued to sip their drinks and occasionally laugh at jokes no one actually told.

"Okay, I saw them. Why does Sanchez have a video camera aimed at us?" asked Doug.

"They want to get pictures of you and Nate to be sure who you are. It's not just a video; it takes digital pictures, too."

"All right. First thing we do is improve our odds by having Hunter send one guy off on a wild goose chase. Cassie, where's their trawler now?"

"On a mooring ball in Soper's Hole," she said. "I'm not sure where Soper's is from here."

Doug smiled and said, "Don't worry. I know the BVI harbors quite well. They're to the south of us. Go and tell Hunter *Payback* is docked at Nanny Cay. It's the next harbor, on the south side, right after Soper's. Hunter should figure that it's close enough to be worth sending Sanchez there now and get a report back while we're still here partying."

"Shouldn't we tell her where our boat actually is located in case she gets away before we do? We could meet her there," said Nate.

"No, don't tell me *Payback*'s location! What if he keeps me, but you two still get away? He'd make me tell him. I don't want to know where *Payback* is yet."

"Don't worry, Cassie. We won't leave you with him," Doug said.

Cassie gave them both a kiss for luck. She walked toward the restroom, but then changed her direction towards Hunter. She checked to see that Nate and Doug turned away so it'd look like they didn't notice her maneuvering. Cassie noticed that Doug smiled at a group of five young local men who had no compunction about checking out Cassie's derriere as she walked away.

✳   ✳   ✳   ✳

Doug turned to Nate, "Believe it or not, I think I've got a plan, but maybe I should let you run this instead. You have the military experience, and you've probably gotten yourself out of shit like this before." He told Nate the details of his plan to involve the five young men to create a distraction.

"No, Doug. You're doing fine. I've slipped out of plenty of bars before, but you're the skipper, and you know these islands. I'm only the baby brother," laughed Nate. "All kidding aside, I like your plan, but you may be sorry later if you don't go all the way and kill one of those pricks if you get the chance. We both have our sailors' pocketknives. They say, 'Never leave a live enemy behind you.'"

"Maybe you're right, but I'll be happy just to get us out of here tonight and leave the BVI. There's a big ocean all around us, and we may never have to see these three assholes again."

The brothers walked over to the five locals. Doug commented, "Good looking girl, isn't she?"

The young men nodded. Most looked a little embarrassed to have been caught looking at Cassie so intently. They turned away to resume watching the dancers, but Doug stepped into their conversation huddle and gave his best smile.

"Hi, I'm Doug Robins. Her name's Cassie Schiffer. You might've heard of her. She's a famous model. Of course, she doesn't have all the makeup and fancy clothes on tonight. I'm her business manager. Nate here is a photographer with *Sports Illustrated* magazine."

"How ya doin'? Yeah, I take pictures of beautiful women all over the world. Tough job, but somebody's got to do it," said Nate, smiling and playing along. He shook hands with the men.

"We just got in from L.A. today and heard about the big party. Say, would any of you gentlemen know a good secluded beach around here where we could take some test photos of Cassie tomorrow? It needs to be private. We might be setting up some of the nude shots, so we can't have any kids around."

The men all started talking at once. Each tried to impress Doug with a different beach locale while simultaneously assuring him they were completely available to be hired as a guide.

"Whoa, guys! I'll have to do this one at a time. Hey, Nate, would you get our new friends some drinks while they tell me where these good beaches are?"

"Sure thing!"

Doug nodded and continued to discuss the merits of sand textures and morning light at various BVI beaches. When Nate came back, he was carrying a tray of shots of Jack Iron, the 151-proof island rum. They toasted their new friends and talked animatedly while waiting for Cassie's return.

"Excuse me a minute. Business calls," said Doug when he saw Cassie approach.

"Hunter bought it," said Cassie. "He sent Sanchez off in a taxi and told him to break into your boat. Sanchez was told to bring back the blow and leave the other weights and canister behind. I'm supposed to keep you happy and make sure you stay here until Sanchez returns. Doug, I hope you realize we're all screwed when Sanchez returns empty-handed!"

"Yeah, I know. I'm hoping we won't be here when it happens. Did Hunter keep the camera?"

"He did. He's using the telephoto feature to watch us right now. Don't look at him."

"I won't. Okay, stay here. Those five young men are going to look you over. Smile at the locals, but look pissed off soon after and play along. Act like a model. Play with your hair or something. I told them you're here on a photo shoot for a magazine's swimsuit edition."

"What? I'm a mess! Look at me."

"You look good to me," said Doug.

Cassie blushed. "How's that baloney going to help anything, anyway?"

"Trust me. I said Hunter's a rival photographer who's ruining our photo shoot and their new jobs assisting us."

"Okay, but I sure hope you know what you're doing."

"Me, too," said Doug when he returned to Nate and the men.

"How is she?" asked Nate loudly.

"Oh, she's mad as hell now. There's a photographer from another magazine over on the fence taking videos of her. Can you believe it? See him over there? She went over to ask him to stop, but he ignored her. He was very rude to her. He's going to ruin our surprise issue if those videos hit the news. It's just too bad," said Doug, shaking his head.

The Tortolan men spotted Hunter, looked over at Cassie, and, fortified by the strong rum, loudly expressed their sympathy and outrage. The apparent leader pointed out Bomba didn't allow videos in the Shack. Apparently, it didn't matter to them that Cassie wasn't actually standing on Bomba's property or that they weren't employees.

"That mon gots no call be making videos at The Shack. We going to humbug he camera," offered the leader.

"It's awfully nice of you fine young men to volunteer, but I wouldn't want you to get hurt," said Doug.

"No problem, mon. He be the one that be hurtin,'" said the leader, and he marched off with his squad of four recruits.

Doug motioned Cassie over and said, "Get ready to go. This is going to work. When they get close to Hunter, we'll crouch down and move north through the crowd. We've got to move quickly before Garcia sees Hunter's in trouble and reinforces him."

Doug saw Hunter get off the fence rail and focus on the approaching men, thereby ignoring Doug and Cassie. Doug got down below eye level and moved through the thickening crowd. He held Cassie's hand and pulled her along. Nate acted as rear guard as they moved northward on the edge of the crowded road.

Doug risked a brief glance toward Hunter and was pleased to see the local men standing in a tight circle around the ersatz pirate. *Payback*'s crew swept past Hunter's position to the thin edge of the crowd. The three straightened and ran north on the road to the waiting taxicabs.

Doug looked back and noticed Garcia was off his seawall perch and wading through the crowd, apparently trying to come to Hunter's assistance. Doug made it to a cab and jumped in the front seat while Nate and Cassie piled in the back.

"Cane Garden Bay! Get us there fast and there's an extra twenty bucks in it for you."

"No problem, mon."

*   *   *   *   *

Hunter remembered what he was supposed to be doing and tried to look around the black men to keep an eye on Cassie and the two sailors. He gave up and addressed the tall man blocking his view, "Hey there, Stretch. I'm trying to take pictures here. Do you mind?"

"My name Duppy. Can't be taking no video at The Shack," said the local. He grabbed Hunter's wrist and twisted it until the camcorder dropped out.

"Hey! Watch it! You don't know who the hell you're messing with!" shouted Hunter. Unfortunately, the camera had been in his right hand. Hunter awkwardly reached for his gun with his left. One of the other watching men quickly grabbed Hunter and painfully twisted his left arm behind his back. Another pushed him to the ground. Then all four of them sat on Hunter while the leader smashed the camcorder against the fence post over and over until the pieces rained down.

"Look at that. You gots a bad camera there."

"Get off me, you bunch of dumb-shit coconuts!" Hunter's choice of words resulted in a number of painful punches and kicks. The increasing pain convinced him to shut up.

Garcia pushed through the last of the intervening crowd and approached the prone Hunter. Garcia pulled his Beretta and held it discretely along his leg, but where the men could still see it.

"Enough, *muchachos*. Back off now and return to your party."

"Yah, we done here anyway. Guess this bad mon need he bodyguard," said the leader as he and his men walked off with a casual air. They didn't completely turn their backs on Garcia, though, and their eyes stayed focused on the gun until they melted into the crowd.

"Why were they angry at you? Are you hurt bad, Hunter?"

"I'll live," said Hunter when he rose slowly and painfully to his feet. "If I could find those island idiots in this crowd, I'd stab every one of them in the ass. They broke our camera. They got sand in their panties about videos around here, for some reason. Go on and block the south side again while we wait for Sanchez."

"Hey, where is the girl?" asked Garcia.

"Shit, I don't see her or those two sailors now! Come on, let's get in there." Hunter grabbed Garcia's arm, and they pushed through the crowd to where they last saw Cassie.

"She is gone again," admitted Garcia after a fruitless search.

"That tears it. She's dead! Cassie and those two dickheads are goddamn dead! They must've snuck out when I was fighting off all those big gangsters. Maybe they hired those pricks to gang up on me. I could've taken two or three, even without my gun, but it was five to one."

"Sure, sure, *El Jefe*. So what do we do now?"

"We're screwed! We've got to wait for Sanchez to return and that gives those pussies more of a head start on us." Hunter spit on the road and walked over to the south entrance to wait for Sanchez. He cursed and paced while he waited.

Sanchez returned surprisingly early. "I kept the taxi waiting while I checked the docks. Their boat was not even there."

"Figures," said Hunter. "I should give the tape to the cops now, but I'd rather take care of her myself. Cassie lied to me to get rid of you, Sanchez, and then the three cowards snuck out while five huge, local gang members hassled me. The sailors tricked us to get past me on the north road. That means the stinking sailboat's in a harbor to the north, but still on Tortola. Reckon the rag-hanger has to be at Cane Garden Bay."

"It makes sense. Get a taxi and we will go there!" said Sanchez.

"No, they'll already be on their boat and leaving by the time we make it. We'll be stuck waving goodbye with our dicks from the goddamn beach if we follow. What we do is get back to *Moby Dick* and intercept them on the water. We're going to chase the bitch and her boy toys all the way to the South Pole if we have to.

"To make it worth your while, I'm upping your share of my coke profit to twenty-five percent each. Another $5,000 bonus goes to the one who catches her alive. Okay? Let's go!"

The chase had begun.

CHAPTER 15

▼

ST. JOHN

Payback slipped out in the last of the moonlight through the unlit exit channel of Cane Garden Bay. A thick cloud cover blew in from the east and soon darkened the choppy water. Wind and waves built steadily as the sailboat fled the sheltering lee, or windbreak, of the mountains behind the bay.

Doug left the sails down to make *Payback* more difficult to see. Though the inky darkness was becoming more complete by the minute, he thought it was still too risky to raise a couple of large white sails. Running on the engine, while a little noisy, would allow quick turns and maneuvers. There were some tight channels to get through before *Payback* reached the open sea in any direction. Doug knew night sailing near land was dangerous, and he felt nervous in leaving his BVI comfort zone behind to sail new waters in total darkness. But it had to be done.

"Okay, keep all the lights off now. I don't know if Hunter will try to take his boat out to look for us with tonight being this pitch-black, but let's not take chances. Cassie, do you think he'll chase us now or wait for daylight?"

"Oh yeah, he'll come looking, no matter what. I guarantee it. So where can we run?"

"Okay, we've probably got a good head start on him, and we need to capitalize on it. We've got to get far away from the normal tourist areas. I want to be over the horizon before dawn in case he's looking from a hill or has more friends around here watching. Cassie, did you ever tell Hunter we visited Anegada?"

"I'm sorry, Doug, but I think I did. Damn, did I cause another problem?"

"No, don't worry. It might've been a good place to double back to, but now we shouldn't use it. I want to find somewhere isolated, though."

"Where else could we go?" asked Nate.

"There's not much else to the north. However, if we can slip past *Moby Dick* while it's still dark, we could squeeze through Pillsbury Sound, between St. John and St. Thomas. Afterwards, we're clear and in the open Caribbean. Then we could sail to the south, maybe to St. Croix. It's twice as far away as Anegada. I think St. Croix's our new goal."

"Are we going to be able to pull this off in the dark, bro'?"

"We're going to try, but it means going past a lot of unseen rocks and cays. I think the only way to reach St. Croix is to cross over to the U.S. side first. If I try to go southeast, exiting through BVI waters instead, I'll have to go right past Soper's Hole—where *Moby Dick* is. On the other hand, if we go southwest to get out through the U.S. side, we'd be at least a few miles farther outside of Soper's. Besides, there's an extensive system of lighthouses and lighted buoys in U.S. waters."

"Maybe Hunter would be worried about crossing into U.S. territory. They're probably still looking for him because he stole a shrimp boat in Florida," said Cassie.

"Pirating the shrimper was before he hijacked *Moby Dick*, huh? Boy, this psycho gets around," said Doug. "Yeah, maybe he'd have second thoughts. He might think we'll run to the cops in the USVI. He doesn't know the BVI police already told the American authorities to ignore us, and he doesn't know Cassie's still a suspect. Besides, he figures we've hung around the BVI for a week so maybe he thinks we'll stay here like he has."

"Yeah, Doug, cutting through those close-in U.S. islands and then south to St. Croix sounds good to me. He won't think to follow us there. Then maybe we can get our bearings and head out of the Virgins completely," said Nate.

"What can I do, Doug?" asked Cassie.

"Would you bring up the USVI chart and the small flashlight with the red lens from the navigation table?"

"Sure," said Cassie. Doug watched as she felt her way to the companionway hatch and went below.

"Doug, you'd better go ahead and tell me where you keep the gun you mentioned a few days ago," said Nate. "The shit could hit the fan around here pretty damn soon."

"Yeah, we've got a little time to talk yet, but there's no harm in being ready I guess. You know, I never thought I'd actually need a gun. Sobers you up right quick, doesn't it?"

"You got that right. I hope this girl's worth it."

Doug was surprised Nate apparently still had some resentment and suspicion regarding Cassie. Nate was slightly closer to her in age and had a history of "skirt-chasing" whether single, married, or separated, yet hadn't tried turning on the charm for Cassie. Unlike his brother, Doug had no doubts about Cassie. He wished he had time to hold her and comfort her right now. Even if he could find the time and privacy, though, how would she respond? After all she'd been through? Nate was wrong to worry. Cassie was worth it, and she was worth the wait.

"I'm betting she is," said Doug. "It's too late to worry now. We're stuck in it up past our eyeballs anyway, Nate. You're right about getting armed and ready, though. Go below and pull up the deck floorboard in front of the entrance to my cabin. There's a package in the bilge you can bring up."

"Okay, I'll get it. I'll close the curtains and only use one cabin light. Man, I can't see any stars at all now."

"Hey, Nate?

"Yeah?"

"You up for this?"

"Yeah, I never had to actually shoot at anybody before, but I think I can do it. Had some target practice in boot camp, but nothing like the jarhead Marines got. You know what's funny? In civilian life, the school guidance and human resource weenies were always telling me I scored highly impatient or hostile on their tests. I think they dressed it up and called it 'spontaneous' and 'action-oriented' or some such dog squeeze. So maybe I'm the right guy for this after all. Maybe I'm impulsive and hostile enough to take on these assholes. How about you Doug?"

"You never know until the time comes, but I think I can make myself do almost anything if I have to. It's almost as if I've been waiting all my life for something like this to happen—to confront some physical threat, and see if I can handle it. You know what I mean, Nate? It makes you feel more alive somehow. You have to realize this might be the last thing we ever do, though."

"Yeah, I know, but what a way to go—fighting scurvy pirates on the high seas!" said Nate with a chuckle.

"Now you're talking! I can't see you drooling on your lap in the old folks home anyway."

"Oh, eat me! Now you're getting too philosophical and maudlin. I personally plan on living forever in the same physical perfection you see before you today." Doug laughed.

Cassie brought up the chart and shielded the flashlight's dim, red glow with her hand while Doug checked their position. He saw *Payback*'s current general southwest course would be fine until they hit U.S. waters. Then he ran his finger straight south to a point where the yacht would approach the lighted buoys of Johnson Reef, near the coast of St. John. The chart gave the distinguishing characteristics of the different navigational lights so boaters could tell them apart. Checking the GPS, he made a small course adjustment to port to follow the new plan. Nate returned topside and laid a long package on the cockpit seats.

"Okay," said Doug. "Everybody keep a sharp lookout for the trawler. Later we'll need to use our ears, too. Tell me anything you see or hear. In another half hour, start looking for lights on our port bow. I'm hoping to see a yellow light flashing every three seconds and a green light flashing on a four-second interval. They'll show us the location of Johnson's Reef. Afterward, we'll turn the motor off and sail on through, slowly and quietly."

"Then we might be able to hear something besides this diesel," said Nate.

"Right, and I'll especially want you to listen for waves hitting rocks or a beach. After we pass the reef, we'll have to locate and slowly curve around these nasty rocks called the Durloe Cays. We do that until we see a white flashing light on a separate set of rocks named the Two Brothers. Maybe from there I can cruise straight out of Pillsbury Sound and set a clear course to St. Croix. Keep awake and keep aware."

"Aye, you got it, Captain Courageous." Nate was still wisecracking, but his tone had turned dead sober.

"I'll do my best. Hey, rocks called the Two Brothers, huh? There's some kind of omen." Cassie choked up and struggled to continue, "I want to sincerely thank you guys. I can't believe I got away again. Most people would've left me there."

"Sure, most sane people would," said Nate. "But you're dealing with the crazy Thompson brothers here."

"Yeah, and we haven't gotten completely away yet. *Moby Dick* is probably on the water by now, hunting for us," said Doug, motioning toward the port side.

"Anyway, thanks again. Let's see if I can make some edible sandwiches in the dark," said Cassie as she started below.

*   *   *   *

Cassie knew she was scared, but determined to push through it. She thought about how lucky she was to still be alive and have the brothers stubbornly risking their lives to put more miles between Hunter and her. There was something special about the brothers, especially Doug. He even brought out the best in Nate.

Doug wasn't anything like the men she'd known all her life. Most would buy her a drink and try to convince her how unique or special they were. They had an inherent need to tell her something about themselves that they thought would impress her or make a connection with her. Many struggled hard to come up with a tie to her hometown by telling her they knew someone important in San Diego she might know. Why did that make a difference?

Or they'd tell her how they'd gotten close to a celebrity once. Others would brag about their important job or their sport or hobby. The more direct ones told her how much money they made. Were they trying to impress her or themselves?

Cassie thought maybe she was being too harsh. It wasn't only men who acted this way. She realized almost everyone she knew seemed eager to find their own way to convince themselves and others that they were different and special. Why? Did it make them think they'd never get sick or die?

Look at me! No, look at me over here. I'm different! I traveled to Hawaii and three foreign countries. I live in the best neighborhood in Peoria. I have a cousin in Florence, Wisconsin who once worked for Madonna. So what? I own a Corvette. I collect ceramic penguins. Check me out! I firmly believe nothing bad will ever happen to me because I'm special. I'm not like the others.

Cassie didn't see much of that with Doug. He was a comfortable realist and didn't appear to need the admiration of others. Well, whether the skipper would approve or not, Cassie admired him for it and decided she had to try one more thing to keep Hunter away from him. And she had to be alone at the navigation table to do it.

*   *   *   *

Hunter and his men hurried back to Soper's Hole, got aboard *Moby Dick*, and quickly put to sea. Hunter figured *Payback* had an hour's head start on him. In addition, *Payback* had started another full hour north of him merely by being at Cane Garden Bay. If *Payback* planned on sailing north, and had a good wind for additional speed, it would take *Moby Dick* hours to catch up. However, if Cassie escaped to the south, she and her rescuers would have to pass Soper's Hole on their way. They'd either come directly past on an intra-BVI course, or a few miles offshore if they were headed for the USVI. Either way, heading south would cut her lead to thirty minutes or so—less if the vessel had to slow for some tricky navigation in the dark.

Hunter rounded Steele Point, using the residential house lights to see where the land ended, then turned west. Clear of the harbor, he ran the throttle up to full power, plowing though the waves to quickly locate his quarry. He'd reach a decision point soon as to whether to search south or north.

"Keep the radio on channel 16, and set the radar on its longest range," ordered Hunter.

"It is already set up," responded Garcia. "You should keep checking the GPS against the chart. This is an old GPS unit so it is probably not super accurate. *Mierda*, it is so dark tonight I can not even see to piss. You sure you do not want to turn on our lights so some big tanker does not hit us?"

"No, I want you jackasses to keep your night vision sharp. A sailboat's deck is low in the water and will be awfully damn hard to see in any case."

Moby Dick cruised west, away from Tortola, for another twenty minutes before Hunter started getting impatient. "We didn't pass them earlier and even if they're heading for to Anegada again, or even west toward Puerto Rico. I don't know."

"Hey, I have an idea. Shut off the engine!" said Sanchez.

"Why?"

"So we can listen for the sailboat. Maybe they took their sails down to make it harder for us to see. Perhaps they are using an engine. We should have been listening every ten minutes or so."

"That's the smartest damn thing you've come up this whole trip," admitted Hunter as he shut the diesel down. All three listened intently, but heard nothing but waves slapping against the hull.

"Oh, well. It's still a good idea. We need to listen every ten minutes from now on," said Hunter.

"What a good idea," mumbled Sanchez, sarcastically.

"If these damn clouds would clear off, we'd have their asses cold with this full moon tonight." Hunter listened a little more. Still nothing. Hunter moved to start the engine again when he suddenly heard a faint female voice.

"Hunter?" said the whispery voice.

"Who said that?"

"It is coming from the radio!" Sanchez said. Hunter picked up the mike and keyed it.

"Is that you, bitch? If it's you, get off of channel 16. I'll meet you on 68."

"Okay," she said. There was a pause when they both switched channels away from the calling channel that had too many listeners.

"It's me on 68. You there, you skanky whore? Don't use any names! And use the word 'over' when you stop flappin' your gums so I can talk. Over."

"I'm here. Listen to me. We won't go to the police if you go away and leave us alone. We don't have your damn drugs. Uh, over."

"Jesus Christ!" shouted Hunter, "Don't say drugs on a radio, you stupid blonde bimbo. I don't know what you're talking about anyway. I only lost a canister with chains and stuff in it. Got it? Over."

"Okay, whatever. Listen, I lied to you about the other guys having your canister. I never even saw it come off. Your stuff's probably still on the bottom where you lost it. Over."

"No, it isn't! We hired a bunch of divers and looked. Over"

"Then go look again. Maybe it moved around. Anyway, these are just regular sailors, and they don't have it. Leave us alone and go back to Venezuela before we change our minds and turn you in. Over."

"Screw you sideways, bitch! You ain't gonna report me because I got a tape saying you did it. I reckon I don't believe anything coming out of your goddamn mouth anymore. The only thing it's good for is shoving things in. We're coming to get you, and the best thing you can do now is tell me where you are. Then I promise I'll take care of you quickly and painlessly. Otherwise, you're going to spend days and days wishing you were dead. You're gonna beg me to finish it. You got me? You call me on channel 16 when you're ready to give it up. Out."

"Yeah? Well, eat shit and die, you limp-dicked, short, redneck, assho…"

Hunter turned off the radio. "I'll make her so goddamn sorry!"

"Do we have any radio direction finder equipment in case she calls again?" asked Sanchez.

"No, we don't have those gizmos, but us being able to hear her clearly probably means she's not more than eight or nine miles away. Also, it means there ain't a high island between us yet. Garcia, we're far enough from the land now, so see what the radar shows."

"It is still hard to tell. Besides Tortola and St. John, there are all these little islands cluttering the screen, and a lot of boats anchored at Cane Garden and Jost Van Dyke, too."

"Jesus, get out of the way, and let me look. I used to watch the radar screen for the owner when I was working on the shrimper. What you've got to do is watch what's actually moving on the screen. See this, you worthless dingdong? There're only two dots changing their positions on each sweep. This big puppy right ahead of us is heading toward St. John or St. Thomas. This other sucker is north of us, and looks like it's going off to Puerto Rico or someplace farther west."

"So which one is the sailboat?" asked Sanchez.

"It's got to be this joker running to Puerto Rico. The other one makes too big a blip on the screen. He must be a freighter or something. A sailboat only makes a weak return on the screen. The radar reflects off its metal masts and shit, but the rest of a sailboat is mostly fiberglass and rides too low in the water. So it's this smaller one. Okay, let's go get them. I'll make that bitch watch when I skin her little friends like alligators." Hunter advanced the throttle, and *Moby Dick* steamed off in hot pursuit.

CHAPTER 16

▼

ST. CROIX

"You okay down there, Cassie?"

"I'm fine, Doug. I'll be right up with the sandwiches."

"I thought I heard voices."

"It was somebody on the VHF radio."

"Please turn it off. We've got to listen for waves against the rocks pretty soon."

"Yeah, we're 'rigged for silent running,' like on my old submarine," added Nate.

Cassie came topside with the food, and the brothers wolfed down her sandwiches with some sodas. She noticed Nate had unwrapped his long bundle on the cockpit seat. She was surprised Doug actually did have a weapon to defend *Payback*; but, at the same time, the sight of the gun brought home the seriousness of the situation. It reminded Cassie her attempt to get Hunter to abandon the chase had failed, and there was now a very good chance of *Payback*'s crew being captured or killed before the night was over.

"Hey, what do you think of this baby?" said Nate cradling the menacing firearm.

"Frankly, it's a very scary-looking gun you own, Doug," Cassie said softly.

"Yeah, that's the point. I wanted something that looked so mean I'd never have to use it. It's a Remington Marine Model 12-gauge magnum. As the saying goes, though, its bark is worse than its bite. Underneath all these macho add-ons, it's a simple a pump-action shotgun. You still have to manually pump it after each shot to put the next shell in. Basically, it's only good for close range work—especially with this short barrel. It's rustproof for marine duty, though, and perfect for a boat. The shells are kind of old. I should've replaced them by now."

"Don't disparage your shotgun too much. It'll make one hell of a big hole in some slime bucket. Looks like you've customized that gun and tricked it out a lot, too," said Nate.

"Yeah, I put on a saddle-shell holder, a barrel-heat shield, a folding stock, an Israeli-style sling, a laser-dot pointer, and pistol grips. Here, go ahead and load it."

"Pretty jazzy. Hey, what's this other thing I found in your bundle? It's just a shiny cylinder with a hole in the breach. Is it a replacement part or something?"

"Cassie, please hand me the emergency flare gun, and I'll show Nate how the other cylinder works. Thanks. These were marketed in the '70s as a 'cutlass stopper.' When you go to an island where they impound your regular gun during your stay, you might still be able to keep this since the customs inspector will think it's only a parachute flare casing or something." Doug unscrewed the back end of the cylinder and inserted a small, .410 shotgun shell. Then he opened the breach of *Payback*'s orange flare gun and inserted the cylinder.

"See? Now I've turned the flare gun into a one-shot firearm for emergency defense. It takes a small shotgun shell or a .45 caliber pistol bullet. I generally put in a slug shell, which is a one-piece lead bullet, instead of a shell full of shot pellets. A .410 is normally a dove-hunting gun. The little birdshot pellets in a shotgun shell this small would be ineffective against an intruder unless at really close range so I use a slug instead.

"Now the other gun, the 12-gauge magnum, will take a large shotgun shell with forty substantial pellets, giving you a good spread pattern, with each pellet still being individually lethal. It'll hold six shells in the magazine and one in the chamber. I've got a box of #4 buckshot shells for the shotgun and five slugs for the cutlass stopper. After that, folks, I'm afraid we're down to three regular flares, and some sharp knives."

"Can one of you two Rambos tell me what '12-gauge' means? I've always wondered. And what's the next biggest size, a '13-gauge'?"

"Sure, I can explain it," Doug offered. "If you made a lead ball snugly fitting into the barrel of my 12-gauge, it'd take twelve such balls to weigh a pound. So if they made a 13-gauge, it'd be a smaller gun because it'd take thirteen balls, instead of twelve bigger balls to make a pound. In reality, the next bigger gun available after a 12-guage is a 10-gauge. The two common smaller shotguns are a 20-gauge and then the .410."

"Okay, I guess I've got it, but what does magnum mean? And don't tell me it's a handsome P.I. from Hawaii."

"Good question, Cassie. A magnum shell is longer than a standard shell. So it packs more lead and more gunpowder. You just need a longer chamber within the gun to load the magnum shell. Normally, a magnum firearm can shoot both regular or magnum shells, but a standard gauge can only shoot the regular-length shells."

"Hey, gun guru. I've got one for you. Why isn't a .410 measured in gauges if it's a shotgun, too?" asked Nate.

"I've always wondered myself. I guess when the barrel size got small enough; they went back to calibers, or fractions of an inch. A .410 is 410/1,000ths of an inch in barrel diameter."

"Cassie, what do they have over on *Moby Dick* in the way of weapons?" asked Nate.

"Hunter bragged he had three nines and three AKs, whatever that means."

"Oh, shit! I bet they've got plenty of ammo, too," said Doug.

"I don't know for sure. Can Hunter's guns beat your nasty looking shotgun?" asked Cassie.

"Probably. See, the nines are probably 9 millimeter, semiautomatic pistols," explained Nate. "They're also short-range weapons for close-in work. Doug's fancy shotgun would be my choice, one-on-one, but they have three handguns, shooting one bullet with each trigger pull, without pumping or cocking or anything. That's what semiautomatic means. They can also reload quickly by changing magazines. It's a lot of firepower."

"What about the AKs?"

"There's where we're going to be hurting," said Nate. "The AKs are fully-automatic assault rifles. The AK initials stand for *avtomat*, or automatic, and Kalashnikov, from Mikhail Kalashnikov, the Soviet designer who produced the 1947 model, although some argue he stole ideas from an earlier Nazi design. Anyway, an AK's got a much longer range than our shotgun, and, since it's an automatic, it'll spit out a stream of bullets as long as the trigger's held down until the magazine empties.

"They're simple and not made for sharpshooting, but easy to maintain, and they rarely jam. The rounds are 7.62mm bullets that'll chew up our sailboat in a hurry. Also, the AK's got a rifled barrel, with twisting grooves inside, and is more accurate than our smooth-bore shotgun."

"So they've got machine guns?" asked Cassie. She'd been reassured by the solid 'chunk-click' sound of Nate loading the big shotgun, but now her anxiety returned.

"Not really," continued Nate. "I know I'm nit-picking, but a machine gun technically refers only to a large, belt-fed weapon taking a crew to service. You know, like in the movies, where one guy is feeding in a belt of bullets from a box, and the other guy is sweeping this heavy gun on a tripod back and forth. A machine gun is usually too heavy to fire from the shoulder. Instead, you'd use a true assault rifle for attacking on the run. Both types are fully automatic, so they spit bullets as long as you depress the trigger. An assault rifle, such as an AK-47, is a lighter gun, kind of like the old 'Tommy guns' the gangsters used in Prohibition days, except an assault rifle uses full-size rifle bullets instead of the shorter pistol bullets a submachine gun or Tommy gun uses. The Soviets and Chinese stamped out millions of AKs and flooded the world with them."

"You know your stuff, Nate," admitted Doug. "Don't you just hate it when reporters or writers who don't know shit regarding guns or military hardware write a lot of crap about firearms? Like some cub reporter calling all handguns 'revolvers' or acting like a semiautomatic deer rifle is some kind of nasty 'assault weapon.' Give me a break."

"Yeah, you're right about the media's recent ignorance, Doug. I see it all the time. Like calling an M16 a machine gun, or calling any warship a 'battleship,' even if it's only a destroyer or frigate," added Nate. "Or confusing birdshot with buckshot. Can't they read up a little or hire a veteran who can locate his ass with both hands?"

"Okay guys, it's all very interesting with the ignorant press and all, but shouldn't we be staying quiet and listening? We're still running for our lives here. Remember?"

"It'll be hard to hear much until we turn the engine off, but you're right, Cassie. I see the flashing buoy light now. So it's time to get serious," said Doug. He adjusted the course to pass the Johnson's Reef buoys close on *Payback*'s port side.

"What can we do to help?" asked Nate.

"Leave the guns here and get ready to act like you're a pair of submarine sonarmen on Nate's old sub."

"Sonarwoman!" insisted Cassie, smiling in the dim glow from the red flashlight.

"Hey, subs are the last ships in 'this man's navy' that still don't allow women."

"Whatever you say, Nate. Anyway, in five minutes, I'm going to change course again and try to thread our way through the passage between Lovango Cay to starboard and the Durloe Cays to port. Once we're through there, we can sail quietly on a straight course. When I turn the motor off, we'll unfurl a small piece of the jib and drift through. Moving silently is worth the risk in showing a little bit of white sail. What you two can do is go to the bow and listen for the sound of waves hitting those rocky shores. If the waves on one side sound closer than the other, somebody can run back here and tell me. Don't yell, okay?"

"Aye, aye, Skipper," said Cassie. Nate and she went up and got into position.

✳   ✳   ✳   ✳

Doug adjusted his course and started to run the gantlet. He hoped this was going to work. Doug knew he had to appear more confident to his crew than he actually was. The skipper always has to have a plan, whether it's worth a damn or not.

Doug killed the engine, and unfurled half of the jib. The GPS supplied a latitude and longitude that helped him plot an approximate position on the chart, but he was worried the old unit wasn't accurate enough to rely on in this narrow channel. Everything was quiet and inky black. It was peaceful on the surface, yet he knew several boats had ripped their bottoms and sank in this same area over the years. Running slowly at a couple of knots, there was only a slight gurgling sound from the wake and faint greenish phosphorescence from the disturbed plankton behind them. The lookouts at the bow focused forward and weren't distracted by the wake or occasional chart light from the stern.

"Doug," whispered Cassie. She touched his arm to alert him to her presence.

"Jeez, I didn't even see you coming aft. Hear anything yet?"

"No, but Nate sent me to tell you we're up there listening, and everything's fine. He thought you might be getting jumpy by now."

"Yeah, he knows me too well," laughed Doug. "Give him my thanks, and tell him to stay awake."

"Will do," Cassie said and left him. Doug watched as she moved forward again. Despite the tension of the situation, Doug sensed his arm was still pleasantly warm where Cassie had touched it. He tried to put her out of his mind for the moment as he checked his position yet again.

Another few minutes went by. This time, Doug heard Cassie's footsteps on the side deck when she hurried aft. "What is it?" he asked.

"We think we hear waves hitting rocks on the port side! Nate says try turning to starboard ten degrees."

"Thanks Cassie. Go on back."

The next time, it was Nate who came aft to say they now heard waves equidistantly from both sides. Doug was satisfied and stayed on his new course. Nate was still working his way forward when Cassie suddenly broke the silence.

"Turn to port! I see a greenish-white line of surf hitting the rocks on the right."

Doug immediately turned twenty degrees to the left.

"I see the rocks now, too!" Doug said in a stage whisper. Nervously, he watched as the white line of spray receded on the stern quarter. In another couple of minutes he was relieved to see the flashing lights from the Two Brothers. The light on Steven Cay also became visible to the south since the Durloe Cays were no longer blocking the applicable line of sight. Doug started the engine, and the two "sonarmen" returned aft.

"We're past the hard part, now. Nate, you can come aft and furl the jib. Cassie, please keep a good lookout behind us to see if anybody followed us through there."

In another hour, *Payback* was safely past the last of the keys and rocks surrounding St. Thomas. Once in the open Caribbean, Doug set a course under full sail for St. Croix. Cassie went below to take her turn to sleep while Doug and Nate stayed on watch. When dawn broke, Nate took his turn below. Around ten in the morning, Nate and Cassie finally convinced Doug they could handle it without him, and it was his turn to rest.

"Okay, but wake me up if the wind strengthens or changes direction."

"Hell, Doug, you'll probably wake up in a panic if you hear a butterfly fart in our general direction. Relax. We got it," Nate assured him.

$$* \qquad * \qquad * \qquad *$$

When the expectant pirates finally chased down the smaller radar contact, Hunter wound up shining his spotlight into the startled faces of two native men on a wooden boat working the Barracuda Banks fishing grounds. Realizing he'd pursued the wrong vessel, Hunter disgustedly decided to return to their hidden anchorage at Big Tobago and give it a rest for the night.

"You lost them again," said Sanchez.

"So I lost the bitch for a little while. Big hairy deal! I thought sure the smaller moving blip was *Payback*. Maybe those chicken-shits stayed in harbor somewhere. I don't see you creating any brilliant plans, lately. I have to do all the thinking, don't I?" said Hunter.

"Hey, I was the one thinking to stop and listen for a motor."

"Screw it. Y'all get some rest now, and then we'll go see Maxwell over on Virgin Gorda this afternoon. We don't have any new pictures, but we have both of the brothers' names this time. Maxwell can use the names to access their recent driver's license photos. Using Garcia's contacts, he'll spread those names and pictures across the Caribbean for us. Somebody will eventually see those clowns. Okay, Sanchez? Hey, Garcia, can you stand first watch while we sleep?"

"No."

"No?"

"No. I have been awake all night, too. No one is going to bother in this deserted place."

"Jesus H. Christ! All right, I give up on you beaners for now. Get some sleep and eat. We'll get back on their trail soon, and you both need to be sharp."

✳   ✳   ✳   ✳

Doug rolled out of his berth at one o'clock in the afternoon. He smelled the grilled cheese and ham sandwiches Cassie was making. The earlier adrenaline had worn off, and he felt ravenous after his rest.

"See, Doug. We didn't drown you in your sleep after all," said Nate.

"Heck, I'm impressed Cassie made lunch with the boat moving like it is," said Doug.

"No problem, if you don't count half of it falling on the deck first. Just kidding. Grilled cheese is easy to make. You want a beer, too?" she asked.

"I better not. I'm still a little sleepy, and we've got a couple of hours to go. You two should get another nap before we get in." Doug scanned the horizon, and was happy to see they were still alone. The thick clouds had blown off to the west, leaving a sky of Carolina blue. *Payback* was making six knots with five-foot waves hitting aft of the beam.

Doug noted the depth sounder didn't appear to be working, but then he remembered this route took him over one of the deepest parts of the Caribbean. The little transponder wasn't going to penetrate more than 10,000 feet of ocean, bounce a signal off the bottom, and give him a measurement. They were truly sailing the deep blue sea.

Flying fish, mistaking the boat for a giant predator, shot out of the water ahead and glided above the sea for dozens of yards before knifing into the side of a wave. St. John had disappeared astern, but the green hills of St. Croix were now visible ahead. It was a gorgeous day for sailing, and *Payback*'s crew was free to enjoy it.

"Looks like we gave them the slip," said Nate.

"Yep." Doug didn't want to speculate on how long it would last. He sensed the others also wanted to simply savor their new mood and not discuss Hunter for now.

"I think I'll hit the sack after all," said Cassie.

"Me, too," Nate chimed in.

"Okay, folks. Thanks for your help. I'll probably call you when we're ready to anchor." Cassie paused and glanced back at Doug, but didn't say anything as she went below. Nate skipped his usual wisecracks, solemnly clasped Doug's forearm, and looked him in the eye. They all knew how close they'd come to not seeing this beautiful day.

Doug took the helm and sailed onward for Christiansted Harbor. In the late afternoon, he raised Fort Louise Augusta on his left. Doug piloted *Payback* along the curving line of buoys and anchored between Protestant Cay and the Christiansted docks. The mustard-colored walls of the historic Danish capital complex beckoned visitors ashore, but Doug only made a quick dinghy trip to U.S. Customs and Immigration before the office closed.

He left Cassie and Nate still sleeping soundly aboard while he took in the passports and ship's papers. He wrote his crew a note in case they awoke while he was gone. Doug left Cassie's name off the crew list and wished he could've skipped checking in all together. It was too risky, though, even in what the Cruzans, or residents of St. Croix, called "America's easternmost territory."

When his brother woke up, Doug took the shotgun sling off his shoulder and passed it over to Nate before going below to get some more time in his bunk. The crew took it easy resting and eating and staying aboard. The brothers stayed low in the cockpit and traded watches into the evening and through the night.

By the morning, the whole crew was rested enough to be getting a case of shore fever. Doug nervously looked around the anchorage, but saw nothing more dangerous than an unusually high number of unseaworthy, derelict boats taking up precious harbor space. He'd seen the same wrecks on his last trip to St. Croix and met their inhabitants in the dockside bars. Being a runaway alcoholic camped out on a wreck didn't qualify one as a cruising sailor or even a boater in his book.

"I'm sorry Doug, but we've got to get ashore to do some shopping," said Cassie. "I'm glad you kept my stuff from before, but we all need some supplies again. Besides, I'd like to stretch my legs a little. Maybe we could even walk past those colonial buildings. I've never been here before. When did America take over this island anyway?"

"We bought the Danish Virgin Islands for $25 million during World War I when we were worried the Germans would take over Denmark's colonies and put a naval base here."

"Doesn't seem like much money now. Let's go be tourists again and forget Hunter Schoenholz."

✳   ✳   ✳   ✳

Cassie was putting on a good show for their benefit, but couldn't get Hunter's threats out of her head yet. She definitely didn't want to tell the brothers of her radio conversation with Hunter. At best, they would think she was naïve. At worst, they might think she was keeping secrets again. From here on, she resolved she'd be open about everything and let Doug get them to safety. She was starting to see him as rising to the occasion. He might truly be able to pull it off—with her help, of course.

"I could stay with the boat," offered Nate. "If I see *Moby Dick* coming in I'll give two blasts on the compressed air foghorn, and you can come running. Go ahead and enjoy yourselves."

"Okay. I kind of wanted us to keep a low profile here, but I guess it'll be all right. I only want to stay one more night, though. Hunter's got a lot of islands to check in the northern group, and it'll take him more than a couple of days. Then he'd have to be real lucky to figure we went south and ended up here. I guess we're pretty safe today. Tomorrow morning we'll do a longer hop and get much farther away."

"Where to, Doug?" asked Cassie.

"I figure St. Martin will work. It's two days off to the east. Also, St. Martin's an international open port, without big customs or immigration hassles. Maybe we can start working on getting you a passport. The Dutch own the southern half of the island and the French run the other half. Good restaurants, shopping, casinos, and beaches there, too."

Doug and Cassie went ashore and brought back the supplies. In the afternoon, the three all felt more relaxed and even considered taking a taxi trip together to see Whim Greathouse, one of the restored plantation houses from the Danish colonial period. They decided to play it safe, however, and only took another turn visiting the boutiques and tourist sites around the harbor while Nate stayed aboard. Doug took his Swarovski binoculars with him wherever he went. Cassie noticed he stopped frequently to scan the horizon for arriving motor yachts. At Doug's request, Cassie hid the single-shot improved flare gun in her big bag and took it along.

"Isn't this illegal to bring ashore?" asked Cassie.

"We can't afford to worry about what's legal anymore," said Doug.

"I guess you're right."

✳   ✳   ✳   ✳

Doug and Cassie made it back in time for dinner. After supper, Doug noticed Nate started pacing on the side decks. He couldn't walk far, between the cockpit and the bow, but he was definitely pacing.

"Hey bro, you got ants in your pants tonight?"

"I've been sitting here on an anchored boat for more than twenty-four hours now. I was just thinking I should go get some more shore leave before we do another couple of days of sailing. You think those bastards will try to come in here after dark?" asked Nate.

"No, I guess not. They probably won't even think to check St. Croix for another couple of days anyway. We'll be long gone by then. It's your turn. If you want to go ashore tonight, go ahead, but be discrete. Don't talk about the boat, and use a fake name if you have to give one, okay? There's a small chance we'll have to leave you behind if Hunter finds us here."

"Sure, Doug. No problem. I think I'll go check out the new casino on the east end. I heard their commercial on the FM radio. If you guys are gone when I return, I'll figure you had to take off. If that happens, I'll go to the Frederiksted pier, on the west end according to the chart, and try to rendezvous with *Payback* at daybreak tomorrow. If you guys don't sail in to pick me up, then I'll check there every morning afterwards until you do."

"Good plan, Nate. Go ahead and cure your case of shore fever. See if you can find me a bottle of Cruzan Single Barrel rum on your way back, bro'. Cassie, do you want to go with him?"

"No, I feel safer on the boat for now," she said.

Nate waited until it was dark. As he told Doug later, he had a good night at the casino slurping free drinks, playing craps, and actually winning a couple of hundred dollars. No one confronted him and he caught a taxi to return to the harbor in the wee hours of the morning. He unsteadily walked down the dock and successfully located the correct dinghy. Nate used the oars to row back to avoid waking the other two up, but found them still awake, sitting very close, drinking wine, and apparently enjoying a long conversation. When they noticed Nate's arrival, Doug and Cassie looked a little embarrassed and moved farther apart on the cockpit bench.

"I'm not interrupting anything, am I?"

"Oh, no. We're getting ready to hit the sack anyway," said Doug with a red face. "I mean, you know, ready to get some sleep. We should all get some sleep. I don't think anybody will bother us tonight, here in the harbor. We've got a long trip tomorrow."

"I agree. Goodnight guys!" Cassie called and turned to go below.

"I guess she felt safer being snuggled up to you, right bro'?"

Doug gave Nate a sheepish grin and followed Cassie down the steps. He went straight to his cabin and undressed, but had trouble sleeping. Doug considered how much had happened in such a short time. Here he was risking his boat, his brother, and his life to save an attractive woman he hardly knew. He wondered if he should reject his new feelings for Cassie as invalid due to his on-the-mend rebound status. Was he able to tell the difference? Where do real feelings come from anyway—if not from real events? Screw it. Doug liked her and he liked feeling like he was doing something that mattered again. It was that simple, and it was valid enough.

CHAPTER 17

▼

ST. MARTIN

Moby Dick rocked slightly when Maxwell stepped off the Virgin Gorda marina pier and jumped aboard.

"Who's there?" demanded Hunter, emerging from the cabin wearing only the t-shirt he'd been sleeping in. Holding his Beretta behind his back, Hunter squinted into the early morning sun. He tried to make out the form standing on the aft deck.

"Just me, mon. You know, Maxwell! Go ahead, mon. Get some pants on 'fore you shock all the fine ladies roun' here this mornin.' I finally got some news for you."

Hunter returned to his cabin. Dressing quickly, he shouted for Garcia and Sanchez to wake up and join him, and then went topside to see Maxwell.

"Okay, Maxwell, drop the comedy act. Tell me your news."

It was good. After waiting a couple of days for any word on *Payback*, Maxwell reported a doorman and a cocktail waitress at a casino on St. Croix had independently spotted a man matching Nate's description last night. Garcia's network included scouts in the casinos, and they'd done their job. Maxwell had received the call this morning. *Payback* was in St. Croix.

"Good work! Call them back. Tell our friends to get a guy with a speedboat to watch the damn sailors. When we get there, we'll call in on the VHF. Have him use fake names." Hunter paused for a moment. "Use the *Sarah* for him, the *Joy Anne* for us, and the *Elizabeth* instead of *Payback*."

"Those are boring names, Hunter. Why not Beavis, Butthead, and Bart or something cool?"

"Shows how much you know. Most boats have girls' names. Otherwise the wives get pissed at their husbands for spending so much money on a big toy. Also, we want regular boring names so people don't pay attention and listen in. Besides, those honeys were my three favorite bartenders at the Caribee Key in Florida. If I need more names, I'll use Erica, Dallas, Katy, or Ashley from the Tree Steakhouse. I could also use Diane, Ryan, Kay, or Linda. Or maybe CJ, Kim, India, April, Paula, Laura, Jacqueline, Julie, or Nannette from Caribbee Key. Or maybe sweet Melissa from Atlantic Beach. I know a lot of girls."

"Yah, mon. That a lot o' ladies. You must really like the ladies."

"Damn straight!" Hunter asserted loudly.

Hunter paid Maxwell, adding funds to be forwarded to the Cruzan with the speedboat. *Moby Dick* got underway quickly, exiting past the jetties, and then turning south to leave Sir Francis Drake Channel via the Round Rock Passage. Hunter throttled up to full speed, set the autopilot, and brought the AKs to the pilothouse.

"You know, this trawler is made to go long and slow, exactly like me with the ladies," snickered Sanchez. "You burn a lot of fuel pushing it like this."

"Don't worry about it. St. Croix is only forty miles away. Get the guns cleaned while we're waiting."

Moby Dick made steady progress in the clear weather. The British Virgin Islands sank into the ocean behind the trawler, with the tips of the mountains the last to go. Before the northern group completely vanished, Hunter was able to make out what looked like three new islands to the south. More used to the flat terrain of Florida, Hunter was expecting one big piece of land, and thought he was lost for a minute. A very confused Hunter frantically rechecked the chart, finally relaxing when he realized he was seeing three sets of hills on the single twenty-six-mile-wide island of St. Croix.

"Okay, the island's rising from the sea," Hunter said.

"What are you talking about?" asked Sanchez.

"Never mind, I'm just talking to myself."

An hour later, the full shoreline had risen over the horizon. "Garcia, start calling on the VHF," ordered Hunter.

"*Sarah, Sarah, Sarah.* This is *Joy Anne* calling *Sarah*. Do you copy? Over."

They waited, but heard only static. Garcia adjusted the squelch control knob and tried again. "Come in *Sarah*. This is *Joy Anne* calling *Sarah*."

"Try again every fifteen minutes," said Hunter.

"Okay. The radio is working because I can hear some other boats talking."

"Yeah, we're probably too far away yet."

With St. Croix eight miles south, they finally made contact with their man and switched to a less public channel. The hired lookout told them the *Elizabeth* had already left port two hours before.

"Shit! Did you see which way they went?" demanded Hunter. "Over."

"Yeah. I followed the yacht until they cleared the reef. Then they put their sails up. I followed them another half hour until I was sure. They kept a steady course of 120 degrees, doing five knots. Over."

"Magnetic or true? Over." asked Hunter knowing there was a fifteen-degree difference in these waters.

"Magnetic. Over."

"Good enough. Thanks for your help, chief. *Joy Anne* out." Hunter checked the charts, and then turned to his crew, "We'll get the bitch now. Their steady course shows me they're heading for St. Eustatius, way off in the Dutch Leewards. It's a long way at only five knots. We'll turn southeast to intercept the sailboat in three hours before they get too far off. I'll plot it out."

Following Hunter's calculation of where *Payback* currently was and where she'd be later, Garcia made a course change to port to intercept. Hunter unconsciously licked his lips. It'd be so sweet if he could catch Cassie alive, at least for a few hours. He'd try some things on her he'd never done to a woman before. Hunter couldn't stop checking the radar screen and using the binoculars, even though he knew *Payback* was too far away to show up.

The crew settled into the chase. Sanchez stayed useful by cleaning the guns and preparing lunch. The three men were in as good a mood as they'd ever been without being completely drunk. *No one will interfere with us way out here. We'll put an end to this hide-and-seek crap, and then have our coke back before supper,* thought Hunter.

"Will we see something soon?" asked Garcia, after a couple of hours passed.

"Yeah, pretty soon. I figured it just right. We're right on their tail, I bet. It's too hazy now. That's the problem. I can only see a couple of miles in this shit." Hunter lowered the Bushnell binoculars and looked at the radar screen again. "Yee-haw! We got something on radar boys!" A large blip lit up the top edge of the screen. Hunter used the binoculars, looking again in the indicated direction, but saw nothing.

Garcia smiled, adjusting the course for a better intercept. Suddenly, his smile disappeared. "Wait, this is the exact same kind of big blip we saw west of Tortola the night they got away. You said it was a freighter before. *Que pasa?*"

Hunter stared at the screen then did some fast mental calculations. "It's them. It has to be. They're right where they should be, only doing five knots. This isn't a shipping lane. It has to be *Payback*."

"Then it was also them three nights ago, when you had us chase the wrong boat," said Garcia.

"Wait, I got it. This pussy, Doug, must be a safety nut. I bet he's got one of those fancy radar reflector/repeaters that enhance any signal to make it look like he's a big ship. Then other boats pay more attention and stay the hell out of your way. What I can't figure is whether he forgets to turn it off when he's being chased, or leaves it on so it'll fool us. I tell you what. The shit-bird can only fool me once! It's definitely him. We'll get him now."

"Don't be so sure you'll catch him today," said Sanchez with a smirk.

"Why the hell not?" asked Hunter.

"Because you are running very low on fuel! Like I told you before, you burn a lot of diesel driving this boat over eight knots all the damn time. We have never bothered to fill it since we stole this trawler. Look at this range graph I found in a drawer. At eight knots, you are running the engine at 1,900 rpm and burning four gallons an hour. At six knots, you only run at 1,300 rpm and burn 1.5 gallons an hour."

"So what? We'll catch him then steal his fuel. We can take him in tow and sell the sailboat later. Even a rag-hanging sailboat has a small diesel and some fuel."

"Maybe they'll have enough for us, but maybe they won't," warned Sanchez. "Or maybe the wind will pick up and they'll go even faster and lose us. I don't feel like being adrift here until I die of thirst or the Coast Guard stops to arrest us."

"Shit on a stick! It's always one thing or another. Why can't I ever just catch that whore, slice her up, and get on with my life? It's not goddamn fair." Hunter cursed a blue streak, but finally settled down to work out their situation with the fuel graph, the chart, and the calculator. With Sanchez's help, he "walked" the sharp-pointed dividers across the chart and determined *Moby Dick* could chase *Payback* at full speed only for another hour. Then they'd have to turn around to limp back toward St. Croix at their most economical pace.

"Or we could chase them longer if we slowed our boat now," said Sanchez. "Maybe the wind will slack off even more. They are heading close to the wind so it must not be easy for sailing."

"Yeah, I know. I still don't understand how those dumb sailboats can even go to windward. But the wind might pick up or change direction, too. We need to nab those wimps while we can. Let's go full speed as usual, and then see what happens."

Garcia grunted in apparent disapproval, but kept his speed and course. The minutes ticked by. Sanchez provided a running countdown on how many gallons of fuel were left while Hunter kept the binoculars focused on the horizon ahead. Every few minutes Hunter checked the radar screen to reassure his crew *Moby Dick* was gaining on *Payback*. The haze blew away as the afternoon passed. After forty-five minutes, Hunter stiffened like a bird dog pointing at a pheasant.

"I see the boat! I see the very top of the mast with a little bit of the sails."

"Where?" asked Sanchez and Garcia, simultaneously.

"Off the port bow. Garcia, alter course another five degrees port so we can cut 'em off."

Sanchez borrowed the binoculars. "Yes, I see a sailboat, but only when the waves raise us both at the same time. *Payback* is still far off—maybe six miles or more. We are not going to catch her in only fifteen minutes!"

"Screw you. We're going to get those cunts right now."

"Can they see us yet?" asked Garcia.

"No way. They're taller than we are so we can see the top of their rig, but they can't see us unless that Cassie bitch is straddling the top of the mast and looking aft."

The last quarter hour ticked by. Sanchez announced it was time to turn back to refuel. Hunter ignored him, keeping his attention fixed forward. The wind picked up a bit. The crew could see *Moby Dick* was still overtaking *Payback* on the radar screen, but at a slower and slower rate.

"Sanchez is right. This is not going to work," said Garcia.

"Y'all sound like a couple of old twats. Keep going."

Abruptly, the engine coughed then missed a beat before recovering.

"*Madre de Dios!*" said Garcia as he throttled down and turned the wheel. "Enough! There might be nothing but sludge in the bottom of this fuel tank. Sanchez is right. We have got to go back to fill up."

"Of course, I am right. Look, Hunter, don't worry. We can go get fueled up then return here at full speed. They have got a long way to go, and we know where they are going anyway. They have followed the same course ever since they left St. Croix. We will have them by morning," assured Sanchez.

"Goddamn sailboats!" said Hunter, hitting the horn in a long blast of frustration. He went below to sulk and drink while *Moby Dick* slowly limped toward port.

*   *   *   *

"Did you hear something?" asked Cassie.

"No," said Doug. "My ears are getting old, though." He was showing Nate the St. Martin/Sint Maarten chart at the navigation table. "I'll come up. So what did it sound like?"

"Like a car horn, but very faint."

"I don't see anything," said Doug, after scanning the horizon with the binoculars. "Sounds carry a long way over water, though."

"It could've been a sea bird, I guess."

"Okay, keep a good lookout. You're doing great. We'll take over in a couple of hours and tack the boat. This wind's picked up some. I'm hoping it'll veer more to the south by then. Call us if you notice anything else."

"Okay. When will we get to St. Martin?"

"We'll sail through the night to get there in the middle of the day, tomorrow," said Doug. "Visibility is sure better now. Believe it or not, that haze we had earlier today was probably dust blown all the way from the Sahara in Africa. It happens all the time here."

The brothers came topside early and surprised Cassie with some hot food. Doug also brought up a chart then showed her how they were sailing on a 120-degree course, as if they were going to St. Eustatius, even though their true destination, St. Martin, lay further to the north. The wind was against them, so they had to reach port by doing at least two tacks.

It was time to switch over to the other tack, and put the wind on the sloop's "right shoulder." Doug turned the wheel. *Payback* passed her bow through the wind before heeling over on her port side. Doug steadied the boat onto the new course, which was at a right angle to her prior course. Nate trimmed the port jib sheet. *Payback* accelerated again and was soon speeding along on a course of thirty degrees magnetic, leaving her old position line far astern.

*   *   *   *

Moby Dick's engine died three miles east of St. Croix. The motor yacht turned broadside to the waves then continued drifting very slowly west by south with the wind and current.

"See, I told you so," said Sanchez.

"Bite my crank!" exclaimed the red-faced skipper. He got on the radio hoping to contact "*Sarah*" to help him, but the Cruzan had long since gone to bed. Hunter finally got a twenty-four-hour marine towing service to come out with enough fuel to get them to the marina where he filled the trawler. It cost more of his time and remaining cash than he wanted to use up, putting him in a worse mood.

On the way back to sea, Hunter hurried and cut corners around the harbor buoys.

"Watch out or you will run us aground again," warned Sanchez.

Hunter snorted, but adjusted his course to return to the channel. In a few more minutes they reached the open sea and sped along *Payback*'s prior course.

By morning, *Moby Dick* reached the patch of ocean Hunter calculated *Payback* would have reached. While steaming in expanding circles, the crew used radar and binoculars to search furiously, but the sloop simply wasn't there.

"Maybe he was in a hurry and turned on his engine, too. It would give their boat a couple more knots on top of the five knots they were averaging," offered Sanchez.

"Maybe, but sailboats don't usually waste their limited fuel when they're out in the middle of nowhere and already have a good wind. I should've run those suckers down when we had a chance instead of letting you two worry so much about the fuel. Okay, we'll keep searching farther along their prior course. Maybe they caught a big favorable wind or something." Hunter steered the trawler onward all the way to St. Eustatius without seeing *Payback*. He circled the island and two of its neighbors, but found nothing.

"We should've seen them before they even got to land. This is the farthest they could possibly be," said Hunter.

"They must have changed course to the north or south after we left," said Sanchez.

"But why the hell would they do that? They were on the open sea, with no reefs or islands to dodge. They didn't know we were right behind or even in this area. So why'd they change course?" He pulled his knife, stabbing it over and over into the boat's varnished woodwork.

"It looks like we lost them again," added Garcia, needlessly.

"Goddamn it! In the last four days, we've lost that bitch due to a gang of natives, a false radar image, us running out of fuel, and now, some kind of crazy course change. This *Payback* is one lucky mother. Her luck can't last forever, though. I'll find her and kill every one of those assholes!" shouted Hunter.

＊   ＊   ＊   ＊

On cosmopolitan St. Martin, *Payback*'s crew let their guard down even further. They felt a long way off from the BVI and their prior problems. Leaving *Payback* at anchor off busy Philipsburg, they rented a car to tour both sides of the divided island. They shopped at the open-air market in the French capital of Marigot then ate lobster at an outstanding French restaurant in the town of Grand Case. Returning along the eastern shore, the crew stopped for a look at famous Orient Bay beach.

"Man, this place looks as crowded as Miami Beach," said Nate.

Tourists packed the numerous beach bars and restaurants for hundreds of yards to the north and the south. Each establishment apparently selected a uniform color to mark its territory. The bar Doug was frequenting had blue flags all along the shore. Dozens of matching blue lounge chairs were arranged in rows on the beach sand in front. The restaurant to the south had a pink theme while the one to the north favored green. Beach boys took drink orders in English, French, and Dutch while renting chairs or umbrellas. Other tanned young men solicited customers for parasailing, jet skis, and rides on banana-shaped towed inflatables.

"It's probably more like the Riviera," said Doug noting more than half the women sunbathing topless. A young, semi-nude woman in a white thong expertly zoomed past the beach on a windsurfer with a transparent sail.

"That one should paint her port boob red and the starboard one green for use as navigation lights," said Nate.

Cassie couldn't stifle her laugh.

Looking seaward, Doug noted the two small islets, Green Cay and Isle Pinel, which framed the harbor entrance. Coconut palms waved above the metal roofs. The smell of suntan lotion competed with the smell of food sizzling on a dozen grills.

"Hey, Doug, what's going on over there at the far right?" asked Cassie looking south past a small breakwater of jumbled rocks. "Everybody is totally naked."

"Yeah, you've spotted the nude beach resort. You can walk over there and look as long as you don't take pictures."

"Heck, we don't need to. They're taking long walks past our beach then back anyway. Look at those three coming this way! Man, are those the best they have?"

Doug chuckled, "You're right Nate. Most of them would look better with their clothes on."

"They should pay me to go there to lounge around nude, just to upgrade the average."

"You wish! I'll pay you to spare us and fetch three piña coladas instead," said Doug, as he moved to claim three lounge chairs.

They relaxed and enjoyed the scene for an hour until Cassie reminded the brothers of the need to visit the stores in Philipsburg before they closed. Cassie and Nate filled the trunk of the rental car with groceries and beverages. St. Martin boasts the best prices on booze in the hemisphere, so the crew took full advantage of it. The dinghy was so heavily loaded Doug had to motor very slowly while they happily splashed through the harbor to the sailboat.

While Doug returned the rental car, Cassie cooked a great steak dinner on the barbecue grill. The three followed up with cigars and glasses of Drambuie all around. They felt a long way away from Tortola and their close calls in the BVI. It was as if those events never occurred.

"I still don't like these things," said Cassie after a few exploratory puffs on a cigar. "No, by the way, I don't want to hear what Freud said. Hey, Nate? Are you going to one of the casinos in Philipsburg tonight? I know you like your gambling."

"Sure, I'll go."

"I'll come, too. We'll make a night of it," said Doug.

"I used to work in a casino in Vegas. I want to see how these little island casinos run things. Let's all go. Don't take any money we can't afford to lose, though. We'll lose it in the end, for sure. I saw it happen a million times."

The crew did enjoy their night of entertainment, but true to Cassie's prediction, their luck didn't hold. They were up and down several times until the law of averages caught up with them, as it eventually does. They each lost a couple of hundred dollars, with Doug losing the most, mainly because Cassie was playing with his money. Doug noticed one particular stickman at the craps table kept looking up, studying the three sailors. He didn't know what to make of it, but finally figured the guy was merely admiring Cassie's good looks.

✳   ✳   ✳   ✳

The next morning, Doug sat in the cockpit with Cassie as they enjoyed the sights and sounds of the city harbor coming to life. A laughing gull, apparently hoping for some breakfast scraps, perched on the dinghy and cocked its head to study the couple. Church bells rang in the distance. Cassie stretched across the cockpit seat like a contented cat and smiled at Doug.

"I feel nervous trying to get a new passport. Maybe we should wait awhile."

"They'd probably believe you, Cassie. Given enough time, we'd convince them of the whole thing. Maybe the consular office here won't know anything regarding the Grenada report. They probably spend lots of their time handling lost passports for tourists anyway and won't think anything of it. You know, I suppose we could eventually sneak in to put you ashore on the U.S. mainland somewhere or you could simply walk in from Mexico like everybody else apparently does."

"No, I wouldn't ask you to go out of your way. I'm worried Hunter's guys will have contacts everywhere, and I don't want to be noticed. I just want to disappear until it all cools off. I don't really trust cops, either. Eventually, I guess I could buy some fake ID pretty easily to get in to the States. Assuming I even want to go back. It's been great cruising around with you and Nate. You don't realize how good it is."

"It's been nice getting to know you, too. You kind of fit right in, like you've been here with me all along." Doug reddened and frowned. He wanted to go further along those lines, but didn't know what to say so he changed the subject. "Anyway, you've got another day to figure whether you feel it's safe enough to surface. I finally remembered it's a local holiday. The offices are closed."

"You're right. I recall somebody at the casino saying today was St. Somebody's birthday, and she'd have to get up early for church."

Nate appeared topside, rubbing his forehead. "You mean those bells aren't just from my hangover?"

The crew relaxed and determined to have a rest day. They cleaned up the boat and then took their dirty clothes into a coin laundry near the airport. After the laundry was done, they decided to have some lunch before getting a taxi back to Philipsburg.

Nate pointed out an obsolete airplane painted Heineken green with the beer's logo on the tail. It was now permanently installed on the side of the road that overlooked Simpson Bay, and served as a restaurant in its retirement.

"That's really cool!" Nate said. Let's eat there. Damn, I wish I had a camera on me."

The meal was good, and the crew looked through the aircraft's little windows at the yachts in the bay as they waited for the check. Doug nursed the rest of his Heineken "greenie" while listening to the locals conversing in three languages. He was startled when Cassie suddenly jumped out of her seat and pressed her face to the converted airliner's window.

"What do you see?"

"Oh, no! It can't be! Not again!"

"What's wrong?" asked Doug, trying to get a glimpse himself.

"*Moby Dick*'s here! They're checking all the boats, looking for us!"

"Shit!" said Nate.

Doug threw some money on the table, grabbed Cassie's hand, and hustled from of the plane. Nate flagged a taxi, which then sped back to the harbor. Tourists gaped when the crew jumped from the taxi and sprinted for the dinghy dock.

"Come on, we've got to get *Payback* out of sight before they make it from Simpson Bay to Philipsburg. It's only three miles from there to here. They must be working from west to east or they'd have spotted our boat already."

Doug ran the dinghy at full speed through the harbor, cut the outboard at the last second, and jumped aboard. He immediately started *Payback*'s engine while Cassie finished securing the dinghy then unlocked the hatch. Nate ran to *Payback*'s windlass and started hauling up the anchor chain while Doug motored to position *Payback* above the heavy plow-shaped anchor.

Doug advanced the throttle as soon as Nate signaled the anchor was clear of the bottom. Nate had to finish raising the anchor while it was being pushed aft by the water pressure from the vessel's increasing speed. The crew ignored the resulting smudges and scratches in the side of the bow. Instead, three pairs of eyes intently scanned the western headland. At any second, *Moby Dick* could appear to turn into the harbor.

Racing for the southeastern exit at Point Blanche, Doug was able to push the sloop above six knots in the flat waters of the harbor. The waves slowed the sailboat when he passed the empty cruise ship mooring buoys at the outer edge of the harbor. *Payback* pushed her bow into the short square chop. A shudder went through the hull at each collision. Spray erupted in geysers on both sides of the bow to drench the foredeck.

"If we can just get around this point, we'll be able to turn then head northeast. They won't be able to see us when they're dicking around in Philipsburg checking all the boats," shouted Doug.

"Too late! I see them now!" yelled Nate from his perch on the safety rail around the mast.

"Those bastards!"

"Doug, I don't think they spotted us yet! They're turning north to go into the harbor."

Doug slowed, hoping to make *Payback* look more like an innocent sailboat casually leaving harbor. Nate helped him get the dinghy aboard and secured across the cabin top. Not towing the dinghy would eliminate a half-knot of drag when they sped up again. Doug turned *Payback* slightly to put the wind on the bow, and then he set the autopilot.

"Nate, pull the jib out on the starboard side, Cassie, uncleat the furler line. Feed him some slack double quick. We should take advantage of this slowdown to raise the sails. There's not a lot of wind here today, but it'll help some."

Doug left the wheel and pulled the mainsheet off the primary starboard winch. Then he jumped to his left, freeing the main halyard. He hauled in the line manually as swiftly as he could until the mainsail was halfway aloft and he needed the winch's mechanical assistance. Throwing three loops around the shiny winch drum, he slammed in the handle and cranked so fast his arm muscles throbbed in protest. The mainsail rose quickly to the top of the mast. Doug slammed the rope clutch shut. With both sails hoisted and flapping, Doug hurried back to the wheel to resume a western course to clear the point.

"Shit! They noticed it's us! They're turning to follow now," warned Nate.

"Oh, my God!" said Cassie.

"Damnation!" Doug gave up on looking innocent and shoved the throttle fully forward. "Okay, I have to forget trying to tack around the side of St. Martin. I was hoping to hide on the northeast side. Then we could've slipped away to Anguilla and south to St. Bart's later. Screw it! We're going to have to run to the southeast now instead." Doug moved to adjust the sheets.

"Why?" asked Cassie. Her voice quavered.

"Because it'll put us on a broad reach, so we'll be on our fastest point of sail. Even with adding the engine, though, Hunter will still be faster than we are in this shitty wind. Unless things change, I figure we've got forty-five minutes before they catch up. We can't go back toward the harbor, but there's no place to beach the boat out here along these cliffs. The only thing we can do is get some sea room to run for it."

"Or we could surprise these wannabe buccaneers and turn to go right for them," said Nate. "I bet if I nailed Hunter with your shotgun, those other two would back off."

"Maybe, Nate. But they might be ready for us, and they have way more firepower. Let's try getting away first."

"We have to get away," said Cassie. "You don't know what that monster will do to me if he catches me again. I'm trusting you, Doug. You got us clear last time and you can do it again. Just tell me how I can help. I'll do anything. I mean it."

"Pray for more wind, and bring all the guns topside."

CHAPTER 18

▼

ST. BARTHELEMY

The crew of *Payback* had a lot of time to contemplate the coming fight. It was as if they were sailors in a slowly developing eighteenth-century sea battle. The resemblance wasn't lost on Doug. Both brothers had read a lot of "wooden ships and iron men" seafaring fiction when they were growing up.

"Do you think he'll fire a shot across our bow and then ask us to strike our colors?" said Doug.

"Oh, absolutely! Then we'll offer our swords, but Hunter will return them to us to signify his respect for our honorable conduct in the battle," responded Nate in kind.

"We might as well beat to quarters and clear for action, Midshipman Thompson."

"Jesus! How can you guys joke about all this? We're probably going to be dead in a half hour!"

"We know, Cassie," said Nate gently. "It helps to laugh, though. Ever hear of grim battlefield humor? Trust me; we're as scared as you are."

"That's for sure. Hey, speaking of our colors, do you see the bastard's still flying the courtesy flag for the BVI? We're not even in British waters anymore. You know, he's probably the one who stole ours. Now that truly pisses me off!"

"So now you're finally pissed off, huh? Hunter had better watch out. Oh, well, damn the torpedoes. Full speed ahead! Don't give up the ship! I've only begun to fight!" said Cassie with a half-smile. "Okay, I'm in the spirit now, but come on, what the hell are we going to do?"

Doug pointed. "See those dark clouds off the port bow?"

"Way off there?"

"Right. We have to get under those clouds quickly. It's already starting to rain. Later, it'll be a real tropical frog-strangler. Maybe we'll lose *Moby Dick* in the rain. He won't be able to see us if we can get a few yards into a real downpour."

"Are we going to make it there before they catch us?" asked Nate.

Doug looked astern at the oncoming enemy. *Moby Dick* was gaining on them slowly, but inexorably. "No. Not without a fight." Nate nodded. Looking away, Cassie bit her lip.

"Could we try calling for help again?" she asked.

"Sure," said Nate. "I don't think anybody's going to believe us, though." He got on the radio and transmitted a Mayday distress message, identifying his vessel and warning they were being chased by pirates. Two other boats came up on channel 16. Wanting to join in the fun, their skippers claimed they were being chased by mermaids and King Neptune, respectively. Nate tried again, insisting he was serious. They were getting a little far for the VHF to reach, but finally he got an official reply.

"*Le bateau Payback*, this is St. Martin Port Authority. We have heard of you from the Tortola *gendarmes* and we do not have the time for the joking. Clear this channel. *Allez-vous!*"

"It was worth a try, Nate. Maybe you should have said druggies instead of pirates, but I don't think it would have made a difference. I think we're on our own. Here's the way I see it happening; you two tell me if I'm wrong. Hunter has greater speed and longer-range weapons. If he's smart enough to realize his advantages, he'll stay just out of our range and shoot us up. However, I'll bet he's an arrogant bully not expecting anybody to shoot back at him. We need to lure him in close and then unleash everything we have while he's in range. Cassie, would you guess he's boiling mad and way out of control by now?"

"Oh, definitely. He's steaming. Hunter's determined and vicious. You don't ever want to underestimate him, but he's an overconfident psycho. You're right about that. He'll be angry and ready to charge in like a bull by now."

"Okay, that's what I thought. We'll keep the autopilot on and stay down. When he comes close, we'll drop three of our eight lifejackets over the weather rail and hide below. It'll slow him down if he investigates. Even after he sees the lifejackets are empty, it might make him wonder if we jumped overboard. Then we wait for him to catch up. Let him take the first shot.

"When he finally starts shooting, we'll lie on the cabin floor, below the waterline. We'll play possum for more time to get closer to the rain. The bad guys will come in closer to investigate. Then when they're close enough, we surprise them. Nate's our best shot so he pops up with the little gun through the forward hatch to get their attention. I move aft into the cockpit, empty the shotgun at the bad guys, and adjust our course as needed. Cassie lies flat in a stern cabin so she can get the engine between her and Hunter's boat for safety. Okay?"

"Good plan, bro'. We might even nail one or two of the pirates. The survivors will think twice before attacking us again."

"No," Cassie complained. "I'm not doing it your way. I'm not hiding to gain some temporary safety. I want to fight, too. This is my fight. I got you guys into this."

"It's our problem now. It's not your fault, Cassie. You didn't ask for pirates to pick Leo's yacht as their target," said Doug.

"I know, but I have to fight him this time. I insist. I refuse to be the little woman to be protected at all costs. If you don't let me fight, I promise I'll do something more dangerous. Maybe, I'll dance around on the deck as a distracting target while you shoot at him."

"Don't do that. We're trying to convince him *Payback* is abandoned so he comes in close."

"Well, let me shoot something at him then. I need to do it, Doug. Please!"

"Okay, you win. You can stay in the forward cabin with Nate. Take the flares. They can be lethal at close range, and they might start a fire or something. After Nate takes his shot, he'll come back down, pull the 'cutlass stopper' cylinder out of the flare gun, and hand the gun to you. Then you load a flare in, jump up, and shoot while Nate unscrews and reloads his cylinder. Aim a little high, Cassie, since it doesn't have the velocity of a regular gun. Then Nate takes his turn again. Better?"

"Much better. I want the biggest knife, too. When they come aboard, I'm going to stab the little bastard right in his guts and twist, if it's the last thing I do."

Nate whistled softly and responded in a low voice, "Remind me never to seriously aggravate this woman."

Doug laid out everything they needed and filled a couple of buckets with water in case of fire. He unpacked the yacht's repair kit and opened its package of soft, wooden plugs. The plugs were cone-shaped and designed to be hammered into holes in the hull to stop leaks. Doug found the handle for the manual bilge pump. When everything was done, the crew sat topside. Doug silently studied the clouds ahead, the knotmeter, and the oncoming trawler.

✳ ✳ ✳ ✳

Feeling immensely satisfied, Hunter cradled his assault rifle in his arms. If those stupid sailors kept going to casinos, he'd keep getting their location handed to him. He didn't think there'd be a need for finding *Payback* again, though. He had her now. Hunter stood on the small bowsprit, leaning as far forward as he could.

While the chase had taken longer than he expected, the distance to *Payback* was still closing steadily. The tanks were filled with 900 gallons of fuel for the John Deere-based Lugger diesel chugging hard on all six cylinders. Sanchez was at the rail right behind while the stoic Garcia piloted *Moby Dick* from the wheelhouse. Cassie would pay for fooling them. There wasn't anyone in sight to interfere this time. Hunter preparing to trigger off a burst to see if *Payback* was in range yet, felt Sanchez tap his shoulder.

"Look! Three lifejackets in the water! Maybe they jumped overboard."

"I don't see anybody, but maybe they're hiding under those floating jackets, hoping we'll chase an empty boat on autopilot," Hunter theorized. "Garcia! Slow down so we can check these out."

As they approached the lifejackets, Hunter scanned the water, but didn't see any swimmers. Sanchez used the boathook to bring the jackets aboard. Hunter sprayed a full clip into the water. He enjoyed the deafening noise and the silvery trails the 7.62mm bullets cut through the water. The pirates waited, looked all around the trawler, but saw no one surface.

"If that skank and her sailor boys were down there, they're dead now. Let's get after the yacht. Hey, Garcia, when we catch up, move us up on their port side so I can see their whole boat without the stupid sails blocking my view."

✳ ✳ ✳ ✳

Doug watched Nate cautiously raise his head to peek over the transom and use the binoculars.

"Did they fall for it?" asked Doug.

"Sure did. At least they stopped and picked up the lifejackets. Shot a mess of bullets into the water. I bet they scared the fish to death."

"Good. Made them lose almost ten minutes, too. Like waving a red flag in front of a bull!" Doug glanced at their knotmeter and lost some of his smugness. While *Payback's* small diesel engine was still throbbing along at its maximum rpm, the boat's speed had dropped significantly. Apparently there was a patch of calmer wind in advance of the rain. The sails weren't helping to the extent they had previously. Doug made a small course adjustment to starboard to intercept the rain patch as soon as possible, but he knew *Moby Dick* would still catch his vessel if things didn't change. The sea battle would take place in an empty patch of ocean south of St. Martin and due west of St. Barthelemy, also known as St. Bart's.

The crew went below and lay flat on the deck sole with their heads on pillows. The brothers made small talk about people they'd known when they were kids. The conversation kept their minds off the situation. They tried to draw Cassie into the exchange, but she appeared uninterested in talking.

Suddenly, a shaft of light appeared in the hull above the galley sink. Stuffing exploded from the settee cushion on the other side of the vessel. A split second later, they heard the deep crack of Hunter's AK-47. A short burst ripped through the air following the initial shot.

Cassie let out a shrill cry before covering her mouth with her hand. She hugged her pillow tighter, drew her knees up to her chin, apparently trying to make herself smaller. Nate moved in a crouch to the forward cabin while Doug risked a look though the overhead hatch.

"Stay down! Not yet, Nate. They're still too far off. I see three bullet holes high in the mainsail, but only this one in the hull."

"So much for the old shot across the bow, huh?" noted Nate.

"Everybody, take it easy. I've read shooting a fully automatic's harder than people think. The recoil kicks the barrel up and to the right. Also, it's going to be tough for anybody to shoot accurately with the boats rolling in these waves. I won't even bother using the laser dot for the shotgun. Try to ignore their firing, take your time, and aim carefully. Stay out of sight whenever possible."

"For what we are about to receive, may we be truly grateful," said Nate, solemnly pronouncing the facetious prayer of the old man-of-war sailor before receiving an enemy's full broadside.

"If you stick your tongue in your cheek any harder, baby brother, you're going to lose a tooth."

Another burst of shots rang out. The crew heard rounds ping and chip at *Payback's* spreaders and mast. The primal human fight-or-flight instinct screamed to run somewhere or return fire, but they stayed flat under the table in the main cabin, simply waiting. A third burst hit, much lower this time. Some rounds hit the engine compartment, the VHF radio, the handheld GPS, and tore splinters from the navigation table. One of the splinters pierced Doug's left bicep.

"Doug, you're hurt!" gasped Cassie, as blood spread down his shirtsleeve.

"Only a splinter of wood. Stay down! Let the pirates get closer. Goddamn them! I'll make those pricks pay for messing up my beautiful boat."

Cassie crawled to the medical kit and grabbed the antiseptic and a bandage. She cut away Doug's shirtsleeve, dressed his wound, and gave him a warm kiss on the lips before crawling back to her spot under the table. "I worry more about you than your yacht!"

"Thanks. I guess it's all self-defense now, isn't it? As if it mattered!" Doug waited, but no more shots came. What was Hunter waiting for? Doug noted the few bullet holes he could see were above the water line. A couple of them were shipping water, though, when waves slapped the hull.

Doug finally heard the distinct engine noise as the trawler moved along *Payback*'s port side. Then he noticed the sound decrease as the motorboat slowed to match *Payback*'s speed. Doug stood up, risking a look out the galley porthole.

"There they are. Twenty yards off to port. Even though we're still moving right along, they'll think it's because we left the autopilot on. They're probably wondering if we're still alive or even here. Okay, I figure they're in range for the shotgun now. If we let these guys get any closer, they'll be shooting downwards at an angle, instead of horizontally. They'll sink us for sure then. We can't let them even start shooting holes below the waterline."

Doug put his eye against the porthole and attempted to view the sea ahead. Before stepping away, he took one last, wistful look at the curtain of rain now directly ahead, but still not close enough to cloak *Payback*. Doug grabbed the shotgun and positioned himself at the bottom of the companionway ladder, looking up and aft to the cockpit.

"When I say 'go,' you guys shoot at the two bunched on their bow. I'll fire at their engine then at the guy on the wheel."

Nate moved to the forward cabin, knelt on the mattress, and unlocked the hatch. He held the cocked flare gun in his right hand. The silvery tube of the cutlass stopper stuck out strangely from the front of the barrel of the stubby orange flare gun. Cassie stood inside the forward cabin, a bit aft of Nate.

"Ready?" asked Doug.

"Ready!" said Nate.

"Wait!" cried Cassie. "I want to say something first. It might sound corny, but no matter what happens, I want you to know you two will always be my heroes. I love you guys. I mean it." She paused and took a deep breath. Her face then took on a hard, determined look as she called, "Ready!"

"I love you, too—both of you," responded Doug.

"Yeah, yeah. Me, too," said Nate. "Now can we please stop the touchy-feely hug-fest? Let's try to shoot these jerk-offs before it's too late, huh?"

Doug nodded, and gave a thumbs-up sign. "Okay. One, two, three, go!"

Exploding out of the forward hatch, Nate held the modified flare gun with both hands. He squeezed the trigger while Sanchez and Hunter were frozen in surprise.

The .410 slug loudly ricocheted off the big anchor stowed below Hunter's feet. It was a remarkable shot for a makeshift gun with both boats moving. Hunter returned fire, but he was startled, and his bullets only stitched a line in the sea forward of *Payback*'s bow.

Doug's big-bore shotgun roared with a deep-throated boom soon after Nate popped back down like a prairie dog into a hole. A large ellipse of vertical splashes erupted from the sea, slightly short of *Moby Dick*'s side. Sanchez returned fire, his military experience with the AK showing, skillfully "walking" his burst across the waves then into the side of *Payback*. Garcia reached through the window of the trawler's wheelhouse, firing away with his handgun. Meanwhile, Doug pumped another shell into the chamber and aimed higher.

✳   ✳   ✳   ✳

Cassie flinched when she heard the shots. She knelt on the bunk and accepted the flare gun from Nate after he emptied it and opened the breach for her. The gun was hinged right behind the barrel, like an old British Webley revolver. The flare slipped from her jittery fingers, but she retrieved it immediately off the mattress. She inserted the flare into the open breach then snapped the gun closed.

Cassie popped her head and shoulders out of the hatch to aim the flare gun. She pulled the trigger. Nothing happed. She suddenly remembered it had a single-action trigger and she thumbed the hammer back as Doug had instructed. Cassie heard Doug's shotgun roar again. Two chattering Kalashnikovs sent bullets whistling over her head while she aimed again and pulled the single-action trigger.

The flare flew in a shallow arc across the waves, trailing red sparks all the way to *Moby Dick*. What happened in a second felt like minutes as Cassie stayed up to watch instead of ducking down immediately the way she was instructed. The flare was headed right for Hunter. He stood transfixed, staring at the incoming missile while it flew toward him then passed directly between his legs. Cassie shook her fist and screamed, "I hope that burned your little cock off!"

Nate reached up, grabbed Cassie by the back of the neck, and jerked her down into the illusory shelter of the boat interior.

"What are you, some kind of Amazon warrior queen? Stay down until it's your turn. This fiberglass hull won't stop a bullet, but at least they won't know exactly where you are."

He took the gun from her hand and inserted his reloaded cylinder. Nate took his time, carefully taking another shot. This time it clipped Sanchez's left ear. Blood sprayed from Sanchez. It got into Hunter's eye, ruining his concentration. Sanchez yelled and clapped his hand to the side of his head. Hunter had had enough of firing while being so exposed. Both pirates dropped to prone positions on the deck before continuing to fire. Hunter was aware enough to reflect that it wasn't so damn easy when his victims could fight back. Things were not supposed to go this way for him. Not him.

Cassie was shocked by the noise, smoke, and debris filling the sailboat's interior. Incoming bullets occasionally slammed through the hull and into equipment. Holes appeared and splinters flew while she struggled to reload after Nate ducked again.

*   *   *   *

Back on the opposite end of the vessel, Doug's second shell had slammed buckshot into the engine compartment of *Moby Dick*. He was disappointed not to see a satisfyingly cinematic explosion or fire. He quickly pumped another round into the chamber. Doug switched his target. This time, the gun boomed and the window of the trawler's wheelhouse shattered.

Garcia jerked as two pellets cut grooves across his fleshy, lower back. He pulled away from the wheel, allowing *Moby Dick* to turn sharply to port, moving in a half-circle. Sanchez and Hunter changed magazines and fired, but their new shots all missed when the trawler heeled, turning her bow away from *Payback*.

Payback continued pushing to the south toward the promised refuge of the rainstorm. Cassie popped up, but Doug noticed she didn't have a clean shot anymore. At the stern, however, Doug could still bring his gun to bear. He furiously pumped three more shots toward *Moby Dick*. Buckshot peppered the trawler's white hull. More acrid cordite fumes drifted over *Payback*.

*   *   *   *

Seeing the distance widen, Hunter forgot any earlier concern for his own safety. He jumped up off the foredeck and ran along the starboard side to the aft corner of the trawler's top deck, where he could still get a shot. Exposed and leaning against the double rail, he carefully aimed toward Doug.

Across the watery gap, Hunter saw Doug plant his feet and take a snap shot at *Moby Dick*'s stern rail. The expanding cone of buckshot streaked through the air and tore a bloody chunk from Hunter's right calf, knocking him to the deck before he could get his own shot off.

Sanchez had stopped at the pilothouse to check on Garcia when Hunter screamed and fell. Sanchez ran aft to get Hunter behind cover. Meanwhile, with no one at the controls, *Moby Dick* raced off to the north.

"This hurts like a mother!" groaned Hunter. "Where did those pansies learn to shoot like that? They must have heavy firepower aboard."

"No, I looked carefully. I only counted one sawed-off pump, a flare gun, and some kind of homemade, one-shot zip gun," replied Sanchez. "All we have to do is stand off a couple of hundred meters and fill their boat full of lead. They will not be able to touch us. They got lucky because we were too damn close. You should not have come in close as soon as you did."

"Yeah, well I didn't hear you come up with any of this crap earlier, did I? We didn't even think they actually had any guns. Just get me down to the galley so I can tie something on this leg."

Sanchez supported Hunter limping below, trailing blood across the deck.

"How far away are they?" yelled Hunter from below.

"Only a couple of kilometers. We will catch them again soon. I am on it," responded Garcia.

"*Mierda*! They disappeared into the rain," said Sanchez.

"Can you see 'em on radar?" asked Hunter.

"*Sí*. The rain makes it fuzzy, but they stand right out, just like before," said Garcia. He adjusted his course slightly to follow the sailboat into the curtain of rain.

*   *   *   *

With the large raindrops suddenly drumming loudly on the overhead, Cassie and Nate joined Doug topside. They danced and whooped in the downpour as they watched *Moby Dick* disappear from view. Water plastered their hair and washed away Cassie's tears of joy.

"We sure showed those dirt-bags! Don't mess with the mighty *Payback*," yelled Nate. "*Payback* is one bad motherfu…!"

"Nate! Shut your mouth," scolded Doug.

"Oops. Sorry, Cassie. I was just talking about *Payback*," said Nate.

"Damn right. It's okay. I don't mind. Hey, we must've wasted at least one or two! Right, Doug?"

"I don't know about that. I think I wounded Hunter at least. I saw him fall on his face right at the end. You guys did a great job. Watch out for *Payback*. You bite us and we bite back. Maybe they'll give up and leave us alone now," Doug said, catching their infectious optimism.

Nate came to his senses first. "Maybe not. As soon as this rain stops they could be right here on top of us again. They won't make the same mistake twice. If they've got any brains, they'll sit off a little farther this time then hose us with those AKs. We literally need to disappear."

"Yeah, we need to sneak out of here silently now." Doug reached over and cut the engine. "I'm surprised our engine hasn't blown up after all this time at maximum revs." Doug jibed the sloop to change course to starboard so the enemy couldn't simply follow their prior course to find the sailboat.

The crew stopped their celebrating and listened closely. A few minutes later, they heard the ominous sound of the trawler's diesel approaching.

"Doesn't it sound like they're coming from directly behind us?" asked Doug.

"Yeah, they changed course, too," said Nate. "They must've made a lucky guess."

"Okay, then we'll turn the other way." Doug jibed the boat to port and then tightened the sheets to tack to the east. He plugged the coordinates for St. Bart's into the GPS then set the autopilot. "We'll lose them now." Doug sat and listened for *Moby Dick*.

"Hey, Doug?" said Cassie after a few more minutes.

"What?"

"I think they turned now, too! I hear them behind on the left now, but coming straight at us!"

"Her ears are younger and sharper than mine. I can't tell yet," said Nate.

A tense few seconds passed. The feeling of victory vanished, replaced by near panic.

"Shit! She's right. It's like they can see us right through all this rain. They turn when we turn." Doug eased the sheets and turned the sloop south. Soon, all three crewmembers heard the motorboat relentlessly moving south to intercept them again.

"How can they do that? Oh, damn! I know how. I'm such a stupid idiot!" yelled Doug as he ran below to the electrical switchboard above the damaged navigation table. He flicked a black switch off, ran back up, and turned *Payback* east for St. Bart's. "That should do it."

"What should do it? And why, specifically, are you an idiot this time?" asked Nate.

"Radar! They must have radar! We don't, but I had the reflector/transponder set up so ships would see us on their radar and not run us over. Like a moron, I left the fancy gizmo on during this whole cruise. *Moby Dick* was getting a big return signal bouncing off of it. If they're close enough, they could track us through any weather. I just turned it off.

"Now, without the usual aluminum spars, we ought to be damn near invisible on radar. We should've dropped right off their screens. Those scumbags will be checking fuses then pounding on the screen wondering what the hell just happened."

The next five minutes proved Doug right. The jittery crew heard *Moby Dick* go on by—following their prior course to the south while *Payback* sailed silently away to the east. The heavy rain continued. The crew made emergency repairs as best they could and pumped the bilge dry. Hours later, they emerged from the rain into the sun, and nervously looked around. The trendy French island of St. Bart's was directly ahead. *Moby Dick* was nowhere to be seen.

"They can't have been following us on radar all the way from Tortola," said Nate. "They would've attacked a lot sooner. I bet they lost us somehow then found us again."

"Yeah, but with all these islands, it's hard to believe they simply got lucky and found us this quickly," added Doug.

Cassie chimed in, "Someone must've seen us and contacted them. Garcia is connected in a big syndicate of some kind based in the Dominican Republic. They probably have a whole network of small-time crooks all over the place."

Nate added, "Especially up in these northern islands, close to Puerto Rico and the Dominican Republic."

"I bet you're both right. From now on, we have to stay away from bars, casinos, airports, and even towns if we can. It'll start getting dark soon. We need a place to stop to carefully check for damage to the boat. Instead of pulling into Gustavia, St. Bart's main town, I'll anchor us in Anse de Colombier. It's uninhabited and way off at the northwest tip of the island. There isn't even a road to the bay."

"Sounds like just the place," said Nate, as he put his feet up on the seats.

Payback sailed to the entrance of the bay. The crew furled the jib. Doug started the engine then turned into the wind. As they were taking the mainsail down, a shrill alarm sounded.

"What's that noise?" asked Cassie.

"It's the engine temperature alarm," said Doug looking at the gauge on the port side. "I'll have to shut the motor off and sail in."

They hoisted the mainsail again and went in the old-fashioned way. The wind was favorable, and the anchor set well in the sand and weed bottom. Nate went below to inspect the engine.

"Fan belt's shot—literally shot. It must've been hanging on by a thread right when we went into the rainstorm. There's some other damage, too—including shot up engine mounts. The whole thing could vibrate loose at any time. You're going to need some parts and time in the boatyard, Doug."

"Yeah, but we're not going to be able to get repairs anytime soon. The other problem is the engine charges the batteries. We have two sets of batteries. The engine battery bank starts the diesel and the so-called 'house' batteries run everything else. The engine batteries are isolated so we need to keep it that way for an emergency engine start. I don't have a manual starter. We could probably still run the engine for a few minutes before it overheats and seizes up.

"The house batteries have a lot of different loads on them. They'll probably be drained sometime tomorrow. We're going to have to do everything without modern conveniences or electronics for a while, until we're sure we actually lost this guy."

"If we ever lose him," added Cassie.

CHAPTER 19

▼

BARBUDA

Payback's crew slept fitfully. One person constantly kept watch with both guns fully loaded and ready. Even though off duty, Doug came topside several times during the night and scanned the moonlit harbor for any new arrivals. The first light of dawn found all three sailors awake and talking softly. Cassie started working on an early breakfast. "Can I still light the stove, Doug?"

"Sure. It runs on propane. The only electricity it uses is a trickle to open a safety valve in the line and show an indicator light. See if the valve still works. Otherwise, I'll bypass it."

"So you said the batteries only charge from an alternator off the engine?" asked Nate.

"Right. Like on a car. We don't have any solar panels or wind generators. I guess they're something I should add someday…if we make it. We've already lost our VHF radio and back-up GPS to gunfire. Now, we're going to lose our hard-wired GPS, lights, knotmeter, depth sounder, and our water pressure. I've got an emergency foot pump at the sink, but we've got less than a hundred gallons of fresh water left. The water maker runs off electricity, too. So take it easy on the stuff.

"Unfortunately, we're not going to be able to sail off to disappear across any oceans, folks. Without the GPS or a sextant and some lessons, I'm going to have to island-hop up or down the chain. I'd be nervous losing sight of land for too long unless we absolutely have to. I guess I should've been more prepared to drop back a hundred years and do it all without electronics."

"Doug, did you know about the big compass by the wheel? It got hit by a bullet yesterday, too," said Cassie.

"Yeah, I know. The binnacle compass is gone. All we've got now is a handheld compass for taking coastal navigation sightings. However, with the little compass, the charts, plus the fact I've been to most of these islands before, we should be okay for a week or so, if we don't push our luck going out too far. We've got enough food I guess."

"Hell, there's enough beer and booze, too. We'll be great on our own!" joked Nate.

"The weather looks okay, although hurricane season starts in a few days."

"The only weather I'm worried about is when it rains bullets like yesterday," said Cassie.

"You got that right, sister," said Nate.

"Okay, we need someplace better than this to hide so we can fix up the boat. St. Bart's is far too busy for us to remain undiscovered for long, even in this isolated bay. Let me ask you two a test question: where's Barbuda?"

"Isn't it the British island, in the middle of the Atlantic, way off the coast of North Carolina? You know the place they wear those knee socks with short pants and play golf all the time," said Cassie.

"Good try, but no. You mean Bermuda. How about you, Nate?"

"It must be the island with good surfing and Mount Gay rum. You know, it's way down island, but farther east than the others."

"Another excellent guess, but no. You mean Barbados. We have a family friend there, by the way. I'll tell you about him later. Anyway, I'm quite pleased with the results of my little test. If you two don't know anything about Barbuda, maybe Hunter won't be aware of it either."

"So where the heck is it?" asked Nate.

"It's sixty miles to the southwest. The island's flat with some nice, pink beaches, but very few people. It's surrounded by a maze of thick coral reefs, and very tricky to get in to. There's a frigate bird sanctuary, a lot of shipwrecks, but not much else. Just the way I like it. So, let's raise the sails and scram before anybody else wakes up."

The crew hoisted the main while still at anchor. The sail kept *Payback* pointed into the wind while Doug and Nate manually hauled in the anchor. Then Doug had Cassie push the boom to one side. *Payback* gathered sternway while Doug turned the wheel like backing up a car. The yacht obediently pivoted sideways across the breeze. The inside of the mainsail filled with wind, commencing forward motion.

Having moved silently out of the harbor without the engine or anchor windlass, *Payback* turned north to clear Point Columbier. Doug unfurled the jib. The sailboat accelerated past three rocky islets then turned southwest after clearing Isle Toc Vers. The skipper laid a course straight for Barbuda from there. The crew took turns steering, since they could no longer use the electric autopilot.

During the trip, the three discussed what they should do after completing the minor repairs.

"We can either follow the Antilles chain north all the way to Florida or we could go down island toward South America," said Doug. "You two need to tell me your preference and why you feel that way. Look I can go either way, but I've got to get this vessel at least six degrees south or eight degrees farther north in latitude as soon as possible. It means going down island to Trinidad or back north to the States."

"You need a change in latitude to give you a change in attitude, big brother?"

"I may have a shitty attitude either way. See, we're only a few days away from the start of hurricane season, so I have to get *Payback* out of the hurricane belt. If I don't, I void my insurance policy. Too much of my retirement money is tied up in this boat. I can't afford to lose it. Besides, it's my home now. I refuse to lose it to Hunter and those other ass-wipes. That's why I can't simply dock her and then fly to the States.

"Plus, even if Nate and I could use our passports to reach the mainland, we'd have to leave Cassie and the sailboat here. Eventually, Hunter would find *Payback* and sink her from spite. I'd lose my investment and my home."

"Not to mention what he'd do to me, huh?" said Cassie, pushing her lips into a pretend pout. She moved closer to Doug to change the bandage on his splinter wound.

"Come on, give me a break. I was coming to that part, too. Anyway, I have to sail to one end of the Caribbean or the other. It's closer to go down island, plus we can avoid Garcia's home territory that way. But remember, some of the so-called 'authorities' down island are worse than Hunter with his dinky crew of pirates. We'd definitely be on our own. Again, though, I can go either direction. Your turn, Nate."

"Wait a second, bro'. Tell me about this family friend in Barbados, first. The one you mentioned earlier."

"Oh, right. You remember Mr. Laird Froehlke, from Stevens Point, Wisconsin?"

"Sure. Dad knew him before the man went off to Washington. He was a member of our congregation in Stevens Point."

"Right. He was Secretary of the Army for a while. Anyway, I read he's been appointed as the new U.S. ambassador in Barbados. It's our only full-fledged embassy in the Caribbean. I figure we might be able to get there right after he takes over. Maybe we'd get in to see him before he's influenced by the police reports on Cassie and us. I bet he'd believe us if we talked to him in person first. Then we'd get some protection. Maybe get Cassie cleared, too."

"You're shitting me! This is definitely good."

"I wouldn't shit you, baby brother. You're my favorite turd."

"Har-dee-har-har-har. You're so funny; I forgot to laugh. Anyway, before I was so rudely interrupted, I was going to say it's great the guy's going to be there because my vote was to head down island anyway. Look, nobody wants another gun battle at sea. We'd get creamed this time. But I'll be damned if I'll fly home just to have you lose your yacht and risk Cassie getting hurt by that wacko. If we keep a low profile, we ought to be able to get into Trinidad or Barbados. Down island is where I've got to go in any case, and I'm not letting three lousy junior pirates stop me."

"I remember you asked about Trinidad before, Nate. Why do you have to go to there specifically?" Doug asked.

"Got a job offer waiting. An old shipmate of mine is an engineer at the new desalinization plant. He travels around the world now, setting up one of these plants every two or three years. He's got enough pull to get me a managerial position at the plant before he moves on to Kuwait. The catch is I have to physically get there to officially apply for the job.

"After flying to Tortola to hitch a ride on *Payback*, I'm basically broke. I didn't want to tell you before. I'd have to borrow money to travel home to Wisconsin, and I'm not doing it. Not with my tail between my legs. Not this time. I'd lose my rights with the girls."

"You mean like visitation or joint custody rights or something?" said Cassie.

"The judge gave me sixty days to show I had a decent job or I lose my visitation rights with my daughters. I only have a couple of weeks left. This is my last chance." Nate paused, and then said, "I don't want to sway your vote too much, though, Cassie. Doug said he'd steer either way. I'm sure he'd help me find something fast in Florida. We promised to take you where you want to go. You tell us. It's your call."

"It's okay, Nate. I'm voting with you anyway, so don't worry. I want to head down island, too. You see, when Leo took me to Trinidad, he introduced me to the right banker who taught me about tax-free, anonymous bank accounts. I left fifty grand in a numbered account there. It's all the money I have now. I used a fake name, but I need to actually show up so I can duplicate my signature to withdraw it. I worked too hard to save it, and I'm not going to run away and forget it. Once I get my money back I can repay Doug and go anywhere to start over."

"Okay, it's settled. We're repairing my boat as best we can then heading south. You've got my word on it." Doug hugged Cassie and shook Nate's hand. Nate went below for a bottle of rum and three shot glasses. When he returned, Doug was holding Cassie's hand as they sat closely together on the bench seat.

"I propose we drink a cup of grog on it to seal the deal," said Nate. "But we need a proper Limey toast from the old days of the sailing navy."

"I know one," interrupted Doug. "Here's to our wives and sweethearts—may they never meet." Both Cassie and Nate laughed. "How about 'Here's to swimmin' with bowlegged women'?"

"No, not those, you seafaring old horn-dog." Nate raised his glass and loudly toasted, "Confusion to the enemy."

"Confusion to the enemy." they echoed.

*   *   *   *

Hunter was quite confused as he looked out the porthole at busy Philipsburg harbor on the Dutch "Sint Maarten" side of St. Martin. The drug runners were still going over what went wrong yesterday in the battle with *Payback*.

"We must've shot off their radar reflector. They aren't smart enough to purposely mislead us with it at Tortola and St. Croix, then, all of a sudden, turn it off in a rainstorm. It's got to be bad luck."

"Maybe so, *Jefe*, but how are we going to find the sailboat now?" asked Sanchez.

"Ain't any use moving for a couple of days unless we know exactly where they are. Maybe they'll backtrack here. They might've had some kind of unfinished business on this island when we chased them off. Maybe they found a buyer for the cocaine. Don't sweat it. As soon as they show their faces in a casino or even a town, somebody will spot those wimps and then report in. Sanchez, what you can do is go find the guy at the casino here who turned them in. Find out if he heard the bitch and her boys talking about going anywhere else."

"Okay, Hunter. I want to get off this plastic bathtub for awhile anyway."

"Don't stay too long, though. We might get word then need to get going right away. Garcia, you go find a yacht-repair place on shore."

"Why? We have no big problems we can not fix by ourselves," said Garcia.

"Yeah, I know, but I just had a category-five brainstorm. We shot up *Payback* pretty good. They must've been hurt a lot worse than we were. I bet they're going to need to get that piece of crap rag-hanging sailboat fixed somewhere. They might even have to get hauled from the water to make repairs."

"Hey, they have such a place here on San Martin. It is right over near the restaurant," said Garcia pointing.

"I know! I'm limping around like a cripple, but I'm not friggin' blind, am I? If they come here again, they're plain stupid. But we're all set in case they're as dumb as you. Go to the repair shop then ask where the next big boatyard to the southeast is. Leave Maxwell's number in case *Payback* comes back to St. Martin later. I don't think they will, though. Every time we find these clowns, they're heading south or east. I reckon that's where they're going next."

His crew went ashore while Hunter rigged a wooden splint and strapped it to his heel and right leg to keep pressure off the wound when he walked. Sanchez returned to report the casino employee knew nothing more. Garcia asked around and brought back solid information. Apparently, very few islands had marine cranes, wheeled sling lifts, or dry dock facilities. The next place with such equipment was Antigua. Most facilities there were located at an anchorage named English Harbour.

"Okay, if they don't come in by tomorrow night, we'll go to Antigua. We'll sit inside English Harbour every night," said Hunter looking at the chart. "Every morning we'll check all the sailboats in that harbor. Then scout any other harbor around Antigua. One day soon those dildos will show up to get hauled out and repaired. Then they won't even be in the water so they can't run away. We'll have them for sure."

"Hey, I like your new wooden leg, Hunter. Now all you need is an eye patch and a parrot," teased Sanchez.

"Blow me! Just shut up and finish painting over those holes from the buckshot. We don't need people asking questions."

✶   ✶   ✶   ✶

Fortunately, the sun was behind *Payback* for the final approach to the anchorage. There was enough light left for Cassie to help Doug carefully avoid the shallow coral reefs as he closed in on the west side of Barbuda. He said his polarized sunglasses were a great help in seeing past the glare on the water's surface. Doug piloted *Payback* in very slowly and cautiously under reduced sail. Cassie stood at the bow pointing to any threatening coral heads she saw while Doug altered course to avoid the danger spots. They made it in without incident and anchored behind Tucson Rock, immediately south of the thick mangroves of the bird sanctuary.

"I wouldn't want to try that again on a cloudy day," said Doug when he finally relaxed. "I couldn't even see the island until we were only four miles off. You know, Barbuda has caused more than two hundred shipwrecks. It's almost as bad as Anegada. We don't need to add one more."

Cassie thought the scene was marvelous. The coral around the anchorage teemed with colorful fish. The neon-green male stoplight parrotfish, with their red-black mates, searched for food in the sand the anchor chain disturbed. Ahead was a pinkish beach with a thin, red line of shells and coral debris marking the level of high tide. The beach stretched for ten miles with no sign of humans in any direction. Behind the beach was a thin strip of land fronting a wide, shallow bay called Codrington Lagoon.

With the binoculars, Cassie could barely discern some buildings comprising a tiny village on the opposite shore of the lagoon. Doug had done it again. She felt safe here. Hunter wouldn't be able to find his way in without local help, while *Payback*'s crew would be able to see another boat coming from miles away. No one would try to navigate the dangerous reefs at night. She could relax for a little while at least.

"Do we have to check in anywhere?" Nate asked.

"Technically, we should've gone to Antigua first to check in since Barbuda is associated with them to make a two-island country. I don't think anyone will bother us, though. Only a few hundred people are on the island, plus most yachts anchor on the southern shore. They avoid this area due to occasional northerly swells. Also, it's off-season, so the big resort is closed."

"Doug, are those huge, black birds perching on the mangroves the frigate birds?" asked Cassie.

"Sure are. Those and the ones with the long, swept-back wings doing circles overhead. The females have a white head, but the adult males are basically black except when they blow up those bright red inflatable pouches in their necks."

"Why do they do that?"

"To attract the females. Don't you feel attracted?" laughed Doug. "The male sits on a nesting territory, inflates his pouch, throws his head back, spreads his wings, and calls to the females while he vibrates his wings. They're great flyers, but nasty birds. Basically, they harass other sea birds like fighter planes attacking a bomber until the victims drop the fish they caught. Then the frigates steal the victims' food. They even steal sticks from other birds' nests to build their own. Ornithologists call them klepto-parasites, regular pirates of the air. Hunter would love them."

*   *   *   *

Doug looked over at Cassie and felt a swelling pride when she smiled at him. He'd kept her safe so far and was trying to live up to his promises. He had a cause and a purpose again. It made him feel alive. He'd been thinking a lot about her lately—more like sexy daydreams than actual thinking.

For once, they all slept soundly through the night without having to take turns for sentry duty. In the morning, the crew commenced needed repair work on *Payback*. The bullet holes in the hull were patched, sanded, and painted to look almost as good as new. Doug climbed the mast in a bosun's chair to check on damage to the rigging. The shrouds and spreaders looked okay and he thought the mast would hold if it wasn't strained too much. There was nothing he could do to repair the carbon fiber "stick," at least with the materials he had on hand anyway.

Payback sustained considerable new strafing "damage" from the birds overhead, but it was easy to clean. The sailors never saw another person, and were fairly sure no one, in turn, saw them. By the second morning, they were rested and ready to move on.

"Doug, it's damn good we didn't have anything requiring a boatlift to fix, but you know if we'd just get into a boatyard, a few big bolts plus a new fan belt might put this engine right. We might need the maneuvering ability or extra speed."

"Yeah, I know, Nate. It's technically an oil pump belt instead of a fan belt, but I agree. This is no time to have a busted motor. Spare belts were on my shopping list to get before we left Tortola, but we left in too big of a hurry. I probably wouldn't have thought to stock those special bolts. The next place down island we can find Beneteau yacht parts will be at a chandlery, or boating supplies store, I know in English Harbour on Antigua."

"Antigua's the island you mentioned that has all the people, right? Wouldn't it be dangerous to show up there in broad daylight?" asked Cassie.

"Yes, it would." Doug scratched his unshaven chin. "Hey, you gave me a new idea. What if we don't go during the day? Antigua's fairly easy to get in and out of at night. What if we do what I'd call 'after-hours shopping' tonight? We'd leave the parts store more than enough cash to cover it, of course."

After some discussion, the other two agreed it was worth the risk. The crew took turns napping to stay fresh for the night's work, and then left in the late afternoon. *Payback* carefully cleared the reefs and turned south for Antigua.

CHAPTER 20

▼

ANTIGUA

Doug routed *Payback* as far from land as he could to avoid being seen. He kept the mountaintops in sight for navigation, and then came in closer after dark. The lights of the main town and the radio mast on 1,400-foot Booby Peak helped him triangulate his position.

After reaching Antigua's midpoint, Doug adjusted his course to curve around the island to reach the southern coast. He knew he had to be careful to ensure *Payback* was genuinely entering English Harbour instead of the similar Falmouth Harbour. Falmouth was immediately west of the smaller English Harbour. They both cut deeply into Antigua. The harbors were so close that they were separated by a mere 250 yards of land at one point.

"This should work. We need to get in and out of there before dawn, though," warned Doug.

Cassie and Nate furled the jib to minimize any noise in case they had to tack going in. Tacking under mainsail alone was not as fast or efficient, but it was easy and quiet. Doug turned *Payback* north then tried to find the channel between two steep headlands he could barely make out ahead. Heading in on a north by northeast course, he suddenly reversed course to start back south.

"Damn! No harm done, I guess."

"Why did you turn around?" asked Cassie.

"I saw two green range-marker lights at the far end of the harbor."

"So?"

"So the color means it's Falmouth Harbour according to the chart. I screwed up. I've never come in here at night, but at least I know exactly where we are now. We need the next harbor a mile to the east. That's where we'll find the store with the Beneteau parts. The store's on the shore of the outer part of English Harbour, near the Galleon Beach Club."

"What else is there, bro'?"

"English Harbour twists a couple of times and goes way in. The inner harbor is more sheltered. There's a marina equipped with a slipway, cranes, and mobile boat hoists. You'll find a bunch of tourist shops and bars, too, because of Nelson's Dockyard. We'll probably anchor farther back in where it's calmer and then take the dinghy to the outer harbor on our scavenging raid."

"What's Nelson's Dockyard?" asked Cassie.

"Wait, Doug. I know this one," said Nate. "It's a restored British naval base from the eighteenth century. The Limeys based most of their Caribbean fleet here on Antigua. In those days, sugar was king. These islands were more important than the American Colonies. Admiral Nelson was in command here before the French Revolution. Can you believe he was only twenty-eight?"

"Yeah, now it's all restored. You've been doing your reading, Nate. They have sail lofts, warehouses, fortifications, workshops, and a couple of new restaurants for the tourists. We'll drop the anchor right behind the dockyard so no one in the outer harbor can spot us."

The three soon found the proper entrance, and then worked the yacht past the parts store into the harbor. The southeast wind weakened when they sailed farther in toward the northern end of the harbor, but they made it to Doug's desired spot behind Nelson's. There were some other boats around, but it was very late. Even the seagoing drunks had gone to sleep. The water was a flat, slate gray.

The brothers put the dinghy in the water and mounted the outboard on the transom. "We're only going to use the oars to go back out to the chandlery. We can motor on the last part of the return trip," said Doug in a whisper.

Doug slowly rowed the dinghy south a half mile to the outer harbor. A waning three-quarter moon provided plenty of light. After clearing Fort Berkely Point, the crew got a clear view of the shop on the eastern shore. A big motor yacht had recently come in and was in the process of anchoring offshore of the exact chandlery having the parts *Payback* needed.

Doug stopped rowing to give them a better look. "Of all the bad friggin' luck!" said Nate. "Now we'll have to sit here awhile until those tourist stinkpotters finish and go to sleep."

"Jesus, Mary, and Joseph!" exclaimed Cassie as her face turned white as the moon above.

"Shhh! They'll hear us. What's wrong now?" asked Doug.

"Don't you guys recognize that motorboat? It's *Moby Dick*!"

"Oh, shit!" said Doug. "You're right."

They backed off quickly then moved close to shore and retreated toward the dockyard. Doug was rowing and biting his lip. He noticed Nate had a death grip on the unused throttle stick of the outboard. The sailors could still see the stern of the trawler, but fortunately no one was standing there looking at the dinghy in return. Staying close to the beach so they wouldn't stand out, Doug labored to regain the cover of the dockyard. Nate started the outboard and swiftly returned them to *Payback*.

"Do you think they saw us, Doug?" asked Cassie.

"No, but unless they're all asleep, they'll sure as shit see this sloop when we go back to sea. We'll have to tack back and forth right past them to exit the harbor. What the hell are those psycho pirates doing here, anyway? I know it's a good, sheltered anchorage, but why are they even in Antigua? Why tonight? How could that redneck peckerwood figure we're going to be here?"

"Maybe it's just plain bad luck," said Nate softly. "They probably don't know we're here, too. Or maybe they need some fancy repair work on the trawler."

"Damn. There goes our chance of getting those Beneteau bolts and belts we needed," said Doug. "More importantly, how the heck are we going to get out now?

The crew talked urgently in low tones and advanced various theories why Hunter was here and whether he knew *Payback* was trapped in the harbor behind him. There was some hope it was all simply coincidence, and the pirates would leave in the morning, but the consensus was Hunter would check the harbor at first light. Even if he didn't, some paid spy might see *Payback* struggling to exit, later in the morning, and radio *Moby Dick*. Doug felt sure no one had reported their position in Barbuda or saw them coming to Antigua in the dark.

"Okay, maybe he just got lucky. English Harbour, plus Falmouth Harbour next door, are the usual yacht anchorages and repair centers. So this is the logical place to come. Like you said, maybe Hunter needs repairs or maybe he was checking all the islands one by one and happened to pick this one at the worst time."

"Even so, we can't stay here, Doug. We have to leave tonight. We'll be sitting ducks in the morning. I vote we run for it in an hour or two. Those crooks on *Moby Dick* might be drunk or sleepy and careless by then. If they see us, we shoot our way out before disappearing into the darkness. This whole thing is a cluster. It's totally FUBAR."

"Foo-bar?" asked Cassie.

"Uh, Nate's using a military acronym. Let's just say it means 'fouled up beyond all recognition,' if you get my drift. Yes, we could try fighting our way out, but I think we need to save that as a last resort. You have to figure they'll be on alert and much more cautious this time. Besides there's not much wind, but too much moonlight now. If they see us leave, they'll chase us down faster than a hungry barracuda."

"Maybe we could ditch the boat and run for it. Just for a while, Doug. You know, hide in the hills or go to the police station or something," offered Cassie.

"Yeah, hiding's an option, but they'd find us on this island eventually. We already know what unhelpful stuffed shirts the cops have been," said Doug.

"You're saying we can't go ashore, but we can't go to sea. So what are we going to do, glue wings on *Payback* and fly her out of here?" said Cassie.

Doug paused and stared at a cluttered boatyard ashore. "Wait a minute. You just gave me an idea!" Doug leaned over, grabbed Cassie's head, and gave her a big, wet smooch on the forehead.

"What? We're going to sprout wings and fly away? Have you lost it?" said Nate.

The smiling Doug explained his new plan. The whole crew discussed Doug's idea together, fine tuning it. They scouted the target area with binoculars and noted the difficulties. Roles were assigned. The mission was set. It was doable, if nothing significant went wrong. The three concluded their deliberations quickly and prepared for action.

Nate and Doug hauled in the anchor. Fortunately, it didn't catch on one of the huge naval chains littering the harbor bottom from centuries past. Cassie jumped into the dinghy and started the outboard. She ran the inflatable boat alongside the sailboat. Nate tied the dink to the port cleats to act like a miniature tugboat so it could push the larger sailboat. Cassie locked the throttle stick in place and put the outboard in gear. With the dinghy pushing softly, *Payback* slowly moved ahead. Cassie stayed in the dink while Doug manned the sloop's helm, steering toward the north end of English Harbour.

"I need some hot dogs for bait. We got any left?" asked Nate.

"Sure, they're at the bottom of the fridge, next to the cheese," responded Cassie. "I had to cook them so they'd keep longer."

"Cooked should still work." Nate went below, returning with the hot dogs, two lengths of thin line, a flat-head screwdriver, a small bag, a flashlight, and a boat cushion. Doug prepared a message, sealed an envelope, and handed it to Nate.

Doug steered, closely skimming the end of the dock at Nicholson Yacht Charters. Nate jumped from *Payback* to the dock. Cassie slowed the engine on her jury-rigged tugboat. The yacht circled slowly in the inner bay, near the mangroves, while Nate launched his mission ashore.

After running up the pier, Nate turned left and, approached the fence around the neighboring property, Poundisford Boatyard. He needed to move from the unguarded Nicholson property into the fenced Poundisford yard. As they'd seen with the binoculars, there was one spot where the boatyard's office building almost touched the fence. The thin space between the building and the boundary fence was stuffed with marine junk, including an old rowboat propped vertically against the building.

Nate stood on the top of the fence while he braced one hand against the turquoise building's wall. With his other hand, he reached over to pry open a frosted-glass bathroom window with the flat-head screwdriver. Nate grabbed his bag and tossed it into the darkened bathroom beyond. Nate held his breath, but no alarm sounded. He stretched out and put his arms inside the window.

A large, furious guard dog suddenly rounded the corner of the building. The boatyard guardian had matted black fur and large, yellow teeth. The fierce animal looked like some kind of island mix of Doberman, Irish Setter, and yellow-eyed werewolf. The dog leaped high up onto the rowboat before falling back. Snapping and snarling, the dog launched itself again and again, trying to climb the smooth fiberglass rowboat attempting to sink its jaws into various parts of Nate's anatomy. The dog's claws rattled and scarred the boat's hull.

Nate kicked and squirmed, hurrying to squeeze through the small window. The dog leaped, snapping his teeth close to Nate's heels. Nate turned and spoke before closing the window behind him. "Ha! You just can't do it, can you, you flea-bitten junkyard mutt," Nate taunted. "Now meet me out front and I'll give you a treat for trying."

Using the flashlight, Nate quickly located the manager's office. He heard the dog still throwing itself at the bathroom window. Nate left Doug's envelope on the manager's desk. There was a labeled board full of keys on the wall of the office. He grabbed the keys off the hook labeled "front gate" and moved to the retail room in the front of the building, facing the harbor.

The dog, apparently hearing the movement of his tormentor, stopped jumping and raced around to the front door. Nate placed the hot dogs on the floor a few feet from the outward-opening front door. As he turned toward the front door, a barking second dog ran out of a backroom and grabbed the cuff of Nate's pants.

Nate jumped and turned to face his new assailant. He raised his flashlight and prepared to defend himself. Nate looked down. "Jesus! You're just a little ankle-biter! You about gave me a heart attack. What are you, the manager's pet?" Nate freed the cloth of his pants then carefully picked up the tiny, yipping dog and shut it inside the small office.

When no further canine guardians appeared, Nate moved to the front door of the building. He unlocked the door from the inside and tied his first line around the doorknob. Nate carefully pushed open the door a crack while keeping a tight grip on the line. He slipped the boat cushion between the door and the jamb so the door couldn't completely close and latch prematurely. He had already tied the second light line to the strap of the boat cushion.

Nate kept the front door nearly closed by constantly pulling on the first line, forcing the door against the cushion, but not letting it close. He then unlocked a front window over a desk to the left of the door. Nate moved the window sash up an inch. It rose smoothly. The large, black dog could see the hot dogs through the crack. It could smell them as well as the intruder.

The snarling animal was fixated on trying to force open the door with its paws and snout. Nate had to pull hard on the line to keep the door tightly against the cushion, leaving an inch of space the pawing dog was trying to widen. The guard dog started barking loudly again. A neighborhood mutt a block away added a few barks of its own.

Nate spoke to the big dog while he worked. "Sorry, doggy. You can't bark at the door all night and I can't stay here. I got the keys and I left Doug's money and apology letter. Besides, you're waking everybody up. Now cooperate with the plan and you can spend the night indoors like your baby brother. See, I loosen the door and pull the cushion out. Then you rush in to eat the hot dogs. I pull the door shut behind you and vamoose out the window before you bite my ass. Then we can borrow some equipment outside without you bothering us. Got it?"

Nate crouched in the shadows on top of the desk. Taking a deep breath, he loosened the line to the door by a couple of feet and jerked the cushion away from the door. Nate dropped the boat cushion line and opened the window.

The angry dog rocketed into the building, but instead of eating the food, began searching for the noisy intruder. Nate swiftly pulled the door shut with the first line and dropped the line to the now securely closed and latched door. He dove out the window then slammed it closed behind him. Spotting Nate, the snapping dog jumped on the desk and hurled itself at the window. Fortunately, the window held.

"I gotcha! Thumbs and a brain beat sharp teeth again! You're a better guard dog than I thought. I figured you'd eat the food first and give me more time to use the window. Now, please eat the nice treat I brought you, be quiet, and go to sleep in there like a good doggy. And tell your baby brother not to piss on Doug's envelope."

The trapped guard dog barked at Nate, ran to the door, and unsuccessfully pawed the round doorknob before returning to the window. The dog growled and bared its fangs again, but the noise coming through the window was greatly muted.

Nate walked to the waterfront and signaled the waiting yacht with his flashlight. He then unlocked the boatyard's front gates, opened them wide, and moved to the pier to meet his crewmates.

Using their little tugboat, Doug and Cassie backed the sailboat into the big slip between two concrete piers. A mobile boat hoist, manufactured by the Travelift Company, towered above the sloop like a giant alien spider. It was made of blue steel girders with rubber tires on each of the four legs. The vessel floated in the U-shaped slip the boatyard utilized to pull yachts from the water and move them onto cradles or blocks. The big hoist was sitting there, with its slings in the water, ready to haul out the next customer in the morning. It had a keyless, push-button starter.

"Good work. We expected that dog, but he sure sounded pissed at you. Did you have trouble, Nate?" asked Doug.

"He seriously wanted to tear off the family jewels. But no, I handled him. The big surprise was the second dog on the inside. It scared the shit out of me."

"Oh, no! We didn't see him with the binoculars earlier. Are you hurt?" asked Cassie.

"Nah, it was more like a big rat rather than a real dog. Just the right size for drop-kicking."

"You didn't really kick a cute little dog, did you?" demanded Cassie.

"No, you know me better than that. I just pulled it off my leg and locked it in the office. It's fine. Let's go get that crane."

The Travelift hoist started easily, but the sailors lost precious time learning to operate the controls and adjusting the slings. It took a couple of tries to position the mast to where it would clear the front beam. They'd finally succeeded in lifting *Payback* when Doug stopped the hoist.

"It was rising evenly. Why did you stop?" asked Nate.

"I forgot the damn dinghy, guys! It's still tied to the bow cleat. We can't drag it behind us down the pavement. We've got to get it back on deck first. I must be losing it," said Doug, shaking his head.

Cassie guided the dinghy and pushed it into place on the foredeck after the men hoisted it out of the water using the spinnaker halyard. The crew finished raising *Payback* into the crane's embrace. Doug used the control box wired with a long tether to the Travelift to carefully roll the box crane off the finger piers and onto the shore. Water dripped off the boat's keel, leaving a wet trail behind.

The huge machine motored slowly, exiting the front gate with *Payback* swaying underneath like a baby possum clinging to its mother's belly. Doug walked alongside as he steered the hoist along the street. He headed overland to the northwest. Nate closed the boatyard gate from outside once the yacht had exited.

"How long is this going to take?" asked Cassie.

"A little more than an hour," said Doug after doing some mental calculations.

"Shit, I might as well take a nap like I'm in a Winnebago RV or something. I thought you said the other harbor was less than a quarter mile away across this isthmus," said Nate.

"It is. There's a marina on the shore of Falmouth Harbour only a little farther on the left. The problem is this baby only moves at seventy-five feet per minute in high gear. My regular repairman on Tortola told me when I watched him move *Payback* once. I think it comes to slightly less than one mile an hour. Cross your fingers and hope nobody wakes and sees us."

After another forty-five minutes the three were nearing their destination and feeling optimistic. Without warning, a rattletrap car in gray-primer paint sped around a curve, heading straight for the Travelift. The cone of light from the headlights startled Doug. He raised his hand to shield his eyes. Spotting the blue behemoth on the road, the car's driver braked hard and moved off to the shoulder.

Doug politely nodded at the five men staring out of the windows of the large sedan as the automobile slowly passed him. Marijuana smoke drifted from the car's interior while Cassie and Nate smiled down from *Payback*'s deck. Cassie waved, and one of the men waved back. Finally, the car returned to the road and continued on to the south.

"They didn't look like the police to me," laughed Cassie.

"You guys did a good job," laughed Doug. "Keep acting like we reposition boats like this every night. I'm worried they'll tell somebody else eventually, though."

"They looked pretty stoned," said Nate. "Nobody will believe them with all the ganja smoke pouring out of their car. That thing looked like it was held together with pure Bondo. Those guys might not even believe themselves."

"Could even make that bunch swear off the weed. Okay, I'm making this thing roll as fast as I can. Nate, you might want to take the bolt cutters from the tool box and run ahead to open the other boatyard's gate."

"Okay, I'm on it."

Nate went on to clear the way. When the Travelift rolled in, he had some bad news for his crewmates.

"You're not going to like this, but this marina doesn't have one of these hoists, and I don't see another one anywhere else in this harbor."

"So what's the problem? We've already got one," said Cassie. "Sorry, that was obvious, wasn't it?"

"Shit! I know there's another one at Jolly Harbour, but it's way too far. This blue monster can't roll up any big hills to get there anyway."

"I figured it couldn't," said Nate. "There's a real wide concrete boat ramp here, though. It might work."

"Okay. See, Cassie, the problem is we need a place to roll this machine out on two short piers above deep water and then drop *Payback* into the narrower space between the sides. If they had their own hoist here, then they'd have a special slip for lowering boats back into the water. Even with a single big shipping pier, we can't merely roll to the end and dump *Payback* onto the concrete. The vessel doesn't swing forward from the Travelift machine. It only hoists vertically or drops straight down."

"Yeah, I got it now. So what are we going to do? We have to hurry! It'll be light soon."

"I guess we'll have a look at the boat ramp Nate found. We could try to run this blue baby straight into the water to see if it'll go deep enough to float us off without jamming *Payback* against the crane's framework. Even if it works, though, I hate to do it that way as it'll probably mess up the hoist or our vessel. If the water's not deep enough we might be able to kedge ourselves off. That means we'd use the dinghy to take an anchor deeper and then try to drag our sloop out of the shallows. We have to try something pretty damn quick." Even in the cooler tropical night, Doug had sweat beading up on his face.

The crew rolled *Payback* into the marina and shut the gate. Now they'd look like early-bird boatyard workers, at least until the real staff came in or somebody showed up and missed the Travelift back at the other boatyard at English Harbour.

Doug studied the boat ramp. He walked onto a beached landing craft-type vessel to see how deep the water was right off the shore. There were actually two of the flat-bottomed, ramp-bowed amphibious crafts fifteen feet apart. Additionally, a small fishing vessel had its nose on the far end of the concrete boat ramp. The rest of the wide, gently sloping apron was empty. There was plenty of room to run the Travelift down into the water.

"Those two landing boats look like something from a World War II movie," said Cassie. "I expect a platoon of marines to charge out and hit the beach. Are the landing craft government surplus or something, Doug?"

"Probably not. Amphibious craft are pretty common around the islands. Businesses need them to take cars or trucks to the smaller islands or to harbors with no road access. I see vessels like these all over the Caribbean. They're pretty useful." Doug paused and squinted at the boat ramp. "In fact, they're going to be very useful for us right now."

"How so?" asked Nate.

"Take a look. I bet we could drive both sides of the hoist right onto those two boats. They're spaced just right and their ramps are already open. *Payback* would probably dangle right between them, and then we could drop her and go."

"You might be right, Doug. Looks a little tight, though. Hey, Cassie. You better climb off the sailboat in case Doug makes a mess of this."

"Gee, thanks for all your trust and confidence."

Doug carefully lined up the hoist so each set of two legs would run onto one of the big landing craft. He took a deep breath and let the Travelift run down the concrete ramp at top speed. The front wheels bounced a little when they hit the metal loading ramps. *Payback* jumped in the slings and swayed dangerously. The sailboat's port side swayed into one landing craft, creating a loud boom. A large rust-colored scratch marred the fiberglass side of the yacht, but the hull didn't crack or dent.

"We should've rigged some fenders," said Nate.

"We'll remember those details if we ever do this again," laughed Cassie.

Doug turned the crane's wheels to better center the dangling sloop. Then he drove the hoist as far to the back of the landing crafts as it would go. The grounded ramps creaked and groaned. Their sterns squatted farther down into the water. The Travelift's momentum and shifting weight was enough to move the two vessels backward into the harbor another foot. Their bows were still securely grounded, though, when everything settled.

The crew slowly lowered *Payback*. Doug released the front sling first. When he released the aft sling, the stern of the yacht splashed into the water and pushed the sailboat ahead a small distance. The boat freely rocked side to side before stabilizing.

"We did it!" shouted Cassie. "It's floating!"

"She swims! That's what they'd say in the days of iron men and wooden ships," said the smiling Doug. He patted Nate on the back.

"Yeah, I think the part where Doug shoved the landing boats backward a little bit was what did it. The water's barely deep enough now. Man, I hope the tide's not going to fall much more."

Doug quickly put the dinghy into the water using the Travelift to help raise it off the deck. Nate got in the dinghy this time and prepared to tow the sloop straight to open water.

"I hope they don't have too much trouble getting this big, blue baby back where it belongs," said Doug. "It really saved us."

"They'll talk about it for years," said Cassie. "Come on, let's go! We're not saved yet."

Using the dinghy, Nate pulled the sailboat out against the southerly wind while Doug raised the mainsail. Nate then tied the dinghy to the stern cleat and jumped aboard. Silently sneaking past Procter's Point, *Payback* sailed east, hugging the shore so *Moby Dick* would have no chance of spotting the vessel from the other harbor. After Antigua was lost in the darkness astern, they turned south into the waves.

Having flown over the land, *Payback* was now free as a bird and cruising down island once again.

▼

CHAPTER 21

MONTSERRAT

Wailing police sirens woke Sanchez and Hunter before Garcia hurried below to warn them something very strange was happening. Garcia said he had been on an uneventful watch for the last four hours, until he heard three police cars racing to the harbor. When the pirate crew nervously gathered on deck, they were astonished to see a fireboat and a police launch race past *Moby Dick,* heading for the inner harbor. The Antiguan authorities on the boats paid no attention to the trawler anchored in the outer part of English Harbour.

"We should get the hell out of here," said Garcia.

"I know, but we wanted to check this harbor first then circle the island. I still think those sailors will come in here," said Hunter. "My guess is something's going on ashore, but it's got nothing to do with us. Sanchez, you take the dinghy in to find out what the hell's going on. Keep an eye peeled for those pricks from *Payback.*"

"Why me? Why not you?"

"You're a good talker, and I damn sure can't go limping around Antigua on this homemade peg leg. I might attract some attention from the cops, don't you think? Jesus, did your hairy mother squirt out any human children?"

"Do not talk about my blessed mother, *gringo*! I warn you."

"Okay, okay. She was a saint. Get going."

Sanchez was gone so long Hunter worried that he'd been picked up by the police. Finally, the dinghy returned from the inner harbor. Sanchez had overheard the whole story from the boatyard workers.

"They say someone broke into the building, but did not steal anything from the office. A little dog was in the manager's office. The big outside guard dog was asleep on the floor inside the building. No one knows how the dog got in," said Sanchez with a shrug.

The big news Sanchez brought back was the theft of the huge mobile boat hoist. It was found, loaded on two landing craft as if they were pontoons, on the shore of neighboring Falmouth Harbour. The police were trying to figure out if it was a prank or if someone was trying to steal the big Travelift via the landing transport vessels.

"Here is the part you are going to enjoy most," continued Sanchez.

"So tell us already!"

"At first, the *policía* thought the landing craft were used to take the hoist back to the other harbor by sea. One worker told them a different story, though. He said his brother came home at four in the morning saying he saw the blue machine driving right on the street with a yacht in the slings. The brother smokes *mucho marihuana*, though, so this man did not believe him. Here's the best news."

"So hurry and tell us! You're enjoying dragging out some damn surprise."

"The best part is the brother swears the moving boat was a big white sloop with a pretty blond woman and two older guys. He said she waved at him."

"Jesus H. Christ! It's the cooze and her two dummies. I told you they'd come in here to get fixed up!"

"But that *maricon* Douglas beat us here," said Garcia.

"We must've come in afterwards and trapped them," said Hunter. "I wonder if they had time to make their repairs. They probably saw us here last night then figured a way to haul ass using the boat hoist."

"You have to admire those sailors," said Sanchez. "It took *huevos* and some brains to do what they did."

"Screw those cowards. If they've grown any balls lately I'm going to slice them off. *Payback*'s only gained a few hours on us. We'll catch her for sure." Hunter stopped to consult the chart. "That sailing piece of pond scum has been moving south all along. The next couple of islands are Montserrat to the southwest and Guadeloupe straight south, but farther on."

"Or they could fool us and go back north," offered Sanchez.

"No, if they did, it'd only be for a day or so to try to screw with our heads. The girlie and her two boyfriends want to go down island for some reason. I can feel it."

"Nobody goes to Montserrat anymore," said Garcia. "It has a volcano that blew up in 1995. It covered all the villages on the south end with ash. Three-fourths of the population moved away. The mountain blows up whenever it wants, man. The *policía* tell boats to stay ten miles offshore. We should go to Guadeloupe instead."

"No, goddamn it! We're going to Montserrat because it's what I'd do if I was in their shoes. They're not the only ones with smarts and gonads."

✳   ✳   ✳   ✳

Southwest of Antigua, the crew of *Payback* was trying to avoid spilling their breakfast on the deck as the vessel rode steep waves from the port quarter.

"Do you think they'll discover we were in Antigua?" asked Cassie.

"We have to assume the worst," said Nate. "Maybe the boatyard has security cameras or something. We should've covered *Payback*'s name and worn some masks so they don't figure out it was us."

"There wasn't time to consider stuff like that. We got lucky back there. We were like a rabbit running out of his exit hole while the hounds watched the front entrance," said Doug.

"Oh no, now you've done it!" said Nate.

"Done what?"

"You ruined our luck! It's bad luck to mention that animal aboard a boat. All sailors know it. You can't say that animal's name. It's like an actor mentioning the play *Macbeth* in a theater."

"What animal? You mean a rabbit?"

"Man, did you have to say it twice?" Nate protested.

"I never heard that one," said Cassie, joining in. "I heard killing an albatross was bad luck, though."

"Yeah, there's a real bad move," agreed Nate. "Also, leaving port on a Friday, painting a boat red, whistling, changing a vessel's name, or having a priest or a woman on board. On the other hand, a pregnant woman's good luck, and a woman exposing her boobs at the bow can calm a storm. It's why a lot of ships had bare-breasted figureheads."

Cassie laughed. "Sorry, boys. I'm not pregnant, and there's no storm, so I'm plain bad luck tonight. No more free shows included."

"What a load of horseshit, bro'." said Doug. You don't honestly believe all that baloney, do you? Especially when you're not even religious, for Christ's sake. Aren't you being a little hypocritical?"

"I'm not so sure," muttered Nate. "One's supernatural and the other stuff is, uh, traditional superstition for sailors. Properly based on hundreds of years of sailors' drunken stories, I might add!" He paused a moment and grumbled, "Okay, you win, it's all crap."

"Oh, good! So I don't have to hurry to get pregnant today. What a relief," chuckled Cassie.

Doug struggled to get that particular image out of his brain so he could focus on the tricky navigation. He failed. Doug pictured Cassie trying very hard to get pregnant. She'd be on the cushioned V-berth in his cabin with her long legs propped up and her feet resting on the port cabinet and starboard head door. He'd stand between her soft, smooth thighs since the mattress was exactly the right height above the cabin sole. The boat would be moving gently and rhythmi-cally. Nate had even joked that you get every third stroke "free" on a boat. Doug would lean over to kiss her firm breasts as she stroked his hair. He'd put his tongue on her erect nipple...

"Doug? Doug!"

Doug snapped out of it. "What?"

"You're way off course, dude! The jib's luffing like wash on the clothesline flapping in the breeze."

"Sorry. I was thinking about something." Doug's face turned red.

"There's a welcome change," laughed Nate. "Anyway, like I was saying, whether it's superstition or legitimate religion, it always boils down to one thing."

"What's that?" asked Cassie.

"Solid fact versus blind faith—it's always the issue," said Nate.

"Okay, enough already. I know for a fact we'd better find a solid hiding place to rest today, and I have blind faith in Montserrat," chuckled Doug. "We can't get any rest in this weather until we find some sheltered harbor." He told Cassie and Nate of the sleeping volcano above the island's abandoned capital city of Ply-mouth.

The sea turned rougher as the day progressed so the crew wouldn't get a chance for a good sleep below until they found shelter somewhere. They were fatigued after being awake since leaving Barbuda. All agreed it'd be worth the risk to have a deserted harbor for the coming evening. Doug adjusted the course, and *Payback* struggled onward.

Eight hours later, they dropped anchor in three fathoms of water south of Plymouth's old city dock. The scene ashore on Montserrat looked like something out of a science fiction movie—a town in the aftermath of a nuclear war. The roofs not already destroyed by falling rocks were covered with inches of gray, volcanic ash. The gritty pumice settled into knee-deep drifts in the streets and piled up against the buildings. Wind-cleared areas exposed a layer of dried gray mud from older hardened ash flows. A few lean birds flew over the buildings, but nothing else moved in the ruined town.

"This is way too spooky," said Nate. "It's like a documentary show I saw on the Roman city of Pompeii."

"Right," said Doug. "Mt. Vesuvius erupted, though on a much larger scale, the same way the Soufriere Hills volcano did here."

"How many people died on Montserrat?" asked Cassie.

"I think it was only nine or ten in the original eruption, but another couple of dozen in 1997. The volcanic dome blew twice more last year. It smokes and spews out a lot of ash, but when it really erupts you get nasty pyroclastic flows, which is an avalanche of superheated air and ash rolling down the mountains. The flows occur when the column of smoke and ash above the volcano becomes so full of heavy rock and ash that it collapses and speeds down the mountain at sixty miles an hour. That can happen quickly here. Unlike Hawaii, the ash and heat are the real dangers in an explosive Caribbean eruption. The rare lava flows come later. It's been quiet for awhile, though," said Doug.

The three looked at the volcano a few miles to the east. The volcano looked sleepy and innocent today.

"At least the water is calm here, Doug. I want to take the first watch, though. I don't feel sleepy yet. I want to keep my eye on that damn mountain. Get some rest, bro'. I'll wake you at suppertime."

"Thanks, Nate. Odds are we'll be fine, but keep a weather eye on it. Keep a lookout for other boats, too. Although I doubt if anyone else is desperate enough to risk coming in here."

*   *   *   *

Doug and Cassie went to their cabins. Nate let the two sleep through the rest of the afternoon until dusk. He kept busy cleaning the boat. It was the noise of his brush scrubbing the deck that eventually woke Cassie. She came topside to see Nate finishing up, using the mop and a bucket of seawater.

"I see you're a true swabbie after all," she teased.

"Yes ma'am! Keeping *Payback* shipshape and Bristol fashion. Sleep okay?"

"Pretty good. Can I help?"

"Sure. Use the brush over there. Don't wake Doug, though. He needs his sleep."

"Yeah, it must be rough on him. He always has to sound cheerful and not let this get to him. Doug has to figure it all out and act like he knows exactly what to do even though he must be as worried as we are."

"Yep. It's what a skipper does. He's changed a lot lately. I've never seen him get violent before, but he sure was blasting away at Hunter when he had to. So were you!"

"Yeah, well, they asked for it. They shot first anyway."

"They deserved what they got and then some," agreed Nate.

"I hope all this trouble doesn't change you or Doug too much."

"It shouldn't. I can tell you Doug definitely used to enjoy his sailing and his boat before, but it was only a pleasant pastime. Then *Payback* became his life and his home. With all this shit happening, he's had to get completely serious about everything. It's a real burden. First, his wife dies, and then he's got goddamned for-real pirates chasing *Payback*. You wait and see, though. When this is all over, you'll see Doug back to his usual light-hearted self."

"Oh, I'm sure you're right. He's got a load of responsibility on him. Do you think he's still broken up over losing his wife," said Cassie.

"No more than normal. He's come out of that finally. Of course, he'll still be a tight-assed square compared to me," laughed Nate. "He always acts like some kind of true gentleman. Hell, I think he was born in a white shirt and tie."

"I read a book on the effects of birth order. The first-born is typically more conventional and responsible."

"That's right. So *I* should be the wild, swashbuckling sea captain, not *him*."

"Nate, I want you to know I'm sorry I dragged you into this. Trust me, I never wanted you guys involved. I wish it didn't happen this way."

"Yeah, I know. I wasn't too sure about you at the start, but you're okay. It's not your fault. We'll be fine in a few days."

"Thanks." Cassie continued scrubbing. "Man, how did the sailboat get so dirty all of a sudden?"

"It's the ash from the volcano I think. It must be constantly blowing around."

"It feels like I got some in my mouth, too. My teeth feel gritty."

"Yeah, mine too. I'm telling you, Cassie, I don't like this place at all. I know the odds are we won't have a problem, and hiding here is the smart thing to do, but it doesn't feel right. Wish we had a radio to check if there's a recent alert or watch or something on this damn volcano. I don't want to be superstitious, but, believe it or not, I sense the mountain is brooding. It's pissed off because we're here defying it. Like it's watching and waiting to nail us. I don't need the rest all that badly. We could move out to sea right away. I bet we could take watches and sleep off-watch as the weather improves. I wish we'd just leave." Nate gazed at the dark slopes leading to the caldera.

Cassie followed Nate's eyes in staring at the mountain. Something looked strange. Was the dark shadow near the crater rim getting larger? No, it was swelling upward and moving down the mountain at the same time! Nate would get his wish; they weren't going to be able to stay here after all. They had to leave immediately. "Nate, look! It's spitting out something and it's coming this way!"

A low rumble reached them. It vibrated the boat. The gray cloud was boiling up over the rim and growing amazingly fast. There was already a smell of sulfur in the air.

"Doug, wake up! All hands on deck! The volcano's blowing up or erupting or something!" shouted Nate.

Cassie continued watching. She noticed a white motorboat with only the bow showing past the distant beach. A wreck from a prior eruption? No, the boat was moving and was now completely visible. It'd been half hidden by a point of land before. "Oh, damn. When it rains it pours," said Cassie in a soft, resigned voice. "Look off there, north of town. It's almost funny in a way. I tell you, Nate, there is a God, but for some reason, he hates my guts."

"What the hell are you talking about?" Nate yelled back as he struggled to raise the mainsail.

"Hunter's here, too!"

✱   ✱   ✱   ✱

Doug, wearing only a pair of shorts, burst out of the forward hatch. He looked at the mountain then quickly scanned the horizon to see what Cassie's last comment referenced. Doug spotted a familiar trawler rounding Bransby Point a couple of miles to the north—*Moby Dick*. He spun around and refocused on the huge cloud boiling down the mountain less than three miles to the west.

Tightness seized Doug's gut and clenched his teeth as adrenalin flooded his bloodstream. The muscles of his arms and legs tensed. It was the same instant, breathless cramp a speeding driver feels when he looks in the rearview mirror at a police car racing up with its flashers on. Doug forced himself to take a breath and calculated his best option.

Nate asked, "What do we do, Doug? We've got double trouble!" Nate finished hoisting the main and slammed the rope clutch shut.

"Ignore the pirates! We have to get to sea fast! Nate, go cut the snubber line. Slash the securing line in the anchor locker, too. Let the anchor chain just dump into the ocean. Then raise the jib. Cassie, ease the mainsheet then take the helm. Move!"

Nate severed the lines with his yellow-handled, Gerber diving knife. The chain rattled out, and the end disappeared into the water. With one sail up, and free of the anchor's restraint, *Payback* started moving southwest.

Doug scrambled aft. He flipped the activator switch while pressing the engine starter button. Nothing happened. "Come on, baby! You've got to have at least three starts left in your battery." Doug pressed and held the button again. The diesel coughed and spit a puff of black smoke. The motor roared to life. Doug slammed the throttle forward to full speed. He glanced aft at the cloud of ash nearing the abandoned town of Plymouth. Wind filled the jib.

"Turn more to the south, Cassie!" ordered Doug. "We'll never be able to simply outrun it now. That stuff could fry us up to a mile offshore. We need to move along the shore and get out of its path instead."

"How the hell are we going to do that? The cloud's going to blow down this whole area," said Nate.

"Look, there's a ridge there," said Doug, pointing to the topography above the town. "It's going to channel the cloud surge I hope. Maybe it'll stay north of us if we can move slightly more to the south, away from town."

Tense moments passed. The boat strained under both engine and sails to push through the sea to safety. The temperature alarm sounded its shrill warning, but Doug left the engine going. He took over the steering while watching the temperature needle until it moved far into the gauge's red zone.

Ash and rocks blew right down George Street and exploded over the town dock. The cloud pushed over the sea like an avalanche of dirty snow. Most of its force went straight offshore, but the pyroclastic surge billowed out to both sides when it reached the level ocean. The crew of *Payback* looked back in horror at the roiling wall in the air that was pushing to the south, chasing the sailboat.

Doug saw the oncoming cloud slowing and thinning slightly, but realized *Payback* wasn't going to totally escape the hot ash. The air stank of sulfur. His eyes were burning and it was harder to breathe. Doug used the end of the starboard jib sheet to tie the wheel in position. The crew hustled below. They crowded into the forward cabin then hurriedly secured the hatches and portholes.

The boat suddenly heeled sharply then sped off more to port as a strong hot gust slammed into the vessel. Daylight coming through the hatch faded away while the crew felt a blast of heat through the fiberglass hull like someone had turned off the lights and pointed a giant hair dryer at *Payback*. Cassie screamed and held on to Doug. Nate grabbed the bed sheet off Doug's berth and threw it over their heads. The crew labored to catch enough air.

An eddy from the superheated ash cloud caught *Payback,* punished her, and then spit her out to the side. The yacht quickly righted and rocked side to side, still pushing ahead. The rest of the surge flow puffed up in huge clouds astern of the sailboat. Seeing his vessel suddenly in clear air, Doug rushed to the cockpit, shut down the sputtering engine, and then hopped around in pain as he retreated below. The small chunks of pumice on the deck were far too hot for his bare feet.

"Get some shoes on! I'll get the bucket!" Nate pushed Doug aside and grabbed the mop bucket. Using the attached line to dip the bucket over the side, Nate frantically worked to wash the thin layer of hot ash off the deck and hardware before it could damage anything. Cassie untied the wheel to resume course directly away from the lingering cloud. Before going below, Doug helped Cassie pull the neck of her t-shirt over her mouth. He worried as she struggled, between coughs, to breathe through the thin cotton. Tears streamed from her irritated eyes.

Doug shoved his feet into his Sperry topsiders and climbed through the forward hatch. His first fear was that the sails would be gone—leaving *Payback* with no means of propulsion. He looked up with relief to see the "canvas" looked fine. The constant rippling and shaking of the sail's vertical surfaces saved the white fabric from any lengthy contact with the hot ash.

"We must've gotten hit by the extreme fringe of the cloud only for a second or two," marveled Doug. The weight of ash on the sea was already smoothing the waves. "It's a miracle we made it through the eruption alive and basically undamaged."

"Thank God! Hey, where's Hunter? I hope the bastard fried or choked to death!" said Cassie.

"I can't see him," said Nate, looking north. "There's still too much ash in the air."

"Then he can't see us either," said Doug. "He's on the other side of the ash cloud. We have to figure he was too far north to get hit, though. This wasn't a full eruption. The safe thing is to act like he's still alive and hunting for us. By the time he goes far offshore, skirting the cloud, it'll be too dark for him to see us. I want to be well away from here by then anyway."

"Yeah, the whole mountain could blow anytime," added Nate. "Doug, I couldn't get any sleep around here even if twenty scientists guaranteed me it'd be dormant until the Cubs win the World Series. I've had enough of Montserrat. Let's get the hell out of here!

"You got it."

CHAPTER 22

▼

GUADELOUPE

Payback sailed south to clear the lower tip of Montserrat by at least ten miles before turning northeast to cruise into the open Atlantic. The crew finished washing ash off the boat and wolfed down sandwiches for dinner.

"I hate sailing at night without the GPS telling me exactly where I am," said Doug. "We should be okay, though. There's a big gap in the chain of islands from here to north of Guadeloupe. We'll sail right through before daybreak without much danger of hitting anything."

Doug paused before admitting, "I don't know where to go afterwards. I've gone to the wrong place twice. I've lost my touch, I guess. Maybe you two should tell me how to proceed from here on out. Perhaps we need a pure democracy here instead of a captain."

"Bullshit, Doug!" Nate protested. "You're the best skipper we could ever have. Things just happen. You can't put all the blame on yourself."

"Nate's right," said Cassie. "Stop that kind of talk right now. We never would've escaped from Bomba's or Antigua if it wasn't for you. You're the one who was right about luring Hunter in close during the gunfight. The pirates never found us on Barbuda, either. We've simply had some bad luck lately."

"Oh, sure. Bad luck like the Spanish Armada or Titanic had," grumbled Doug.

"Come on," said Nate. "Belay that crap, skipper. You might be an old poop as a big brother, but you're the best captain I've ever seen. Shit, I hated Montserrat, but the volcano saved us from Hunter. I never would've thought to abandon the anchor to save time like you did either. You even predicted the way the ash cloud would go. You saved our lives, Doug. You're still captain, and that's final!"

"Well, thanks. You two may be sorry later, though. Today sort of blew my confidence. Those bastards on *Moby Dick* are getting better and better at finding us. They're getting into my head somehow. The pricks are figuring out exactly where I'm going to go next. We need to do something totally unexpected this time."

"Like what?" asked Cassie. "You're the captain. You decide where we're going next."

"Okay, then I decide we go nowhere."

"Nowhere?" said Nate.

"Right. Let's not go to any particular island for a while. Let's get way the hell off into the Atlantic and sit there for a while, before moving south again. It should fake out those impatient assholes."

"Sounds like a plan to me," said Cassie. "What do you think, Nate?"

"Sure, I'm game. Let's drive those *Moby Dick*-ers crazy, really get their panties in a bunch."

✳   ✳   ✳   ✳

Five days after escaping from Montserrat, the crew of *Moby Dick* stagnated in the harbor of Roseau, Dominica. Hunter knew they'd all become seriously stir-crazy from inactivity. He was forced to let his crew wander ashore during the day to keep them occupied and out of his hair. While ashore, Garcia and Sanchez were supposed to visit all the alternate harbors and casually ask the locals to let Hunter know if their "friends" on *Payback* appeared anywhere.

Garcia and Sanchez both took advantage of their new freedom to drink heavily and keep increasingly late hours. When the two finally returned to the boat, they were in no shape to stand proper night watches. Hunter had to set an alarm clock to get up and personally check the harbor a couple of times a night. Such was the extent of their limited watch-keeping lately.

Five days earlier, on Montserrat, *Moby Dick* completely escaped the ash cloud, but not the random rain of rocks ejected by the volcano. A baseball-size chunk of air-cooled lava smashed a hole in the Portuguese bridge, the protective walled walkway in front of the pilothouse. Another rock smashed a window in the main cabin then continued on to destroy the controls for the air conditioning. The crew had loved their air conditioning. Now the men were forced to sleep on deck when it got too warm below.

The trawler had warily circled Montserrat a distance. The drug pirates never saw *Payback* or any wreckage. After a day, they proceeded south, searching Guadeloupe, Marie Galante, Dominica, and Martinique, then back to Dominica. The sailboat had vanished. Hunter was now forced to sit waiting in Dominica, nervously twitching like a cat trying to watch four mouse-holes at once.

"Hey, Hunter, why not steal another boat?" asked Garcia. "We need a faster one with working air conditioning."

"No, I like this boat. It's a little slow, but we don't have to stop on every damn island to fill the tanks. It's strong and never quits—just like me."

"What a bunch of *loco* shit," said Sanchez. "I think we should go back to Martinique. I liked the women there. Why did you turn around and take us north to Dominica?"

"No friggin' way! I didn't like Martinique. It felt wrong. Remember St. Pierre, or whatever that town's name was, still sitting there all tore up? That Mt. Pelée volcano could be fixing to blow again at any time. It's too much like Montserrat. Martinique made me crazy like a blue crab caught in a bucket.

"Besides, Dominica's a good spot right in the middle of this whole mess of islands. We can move anywhere in the chain from here when somebody finally sees those pansies and calls Maxwell. Plus, the natives speak English here. I don't like those French islands like Martinique. Their English sucks."

"Jesus! Hunter, you are such a redneck *gringo*. The people on Martinique would definitely think your French sucks, if you even had any. We should go to some Spanish-speaking island. Then Garcia and I would get laid every damn night.

"Do you not know there is a boiling hot lake in the hills right here on Dominica? There must be a big volcano underneath this island, too. No place in the Windward Island group is safe from volcanoes," said Sanchez.

"I don't care. We're staying put until the sailors show up on 'St. Somewhere.' I'm tired of chasing my tail."

＊　　　＊　　　＊　　　＊

After leaving Montserrat, *Payback* spent five days in the open Atlantic as Doug had planned, but didn't make the progress he'd hoped for. On the second day, when Doug figured he was west of Dominica heading south, the wind died. Flat out died. The residual swell rocked the boat from side-to-side, causing an irritating noise when the flapping sails and boom constantly came to a hard stop on each side of the boat. The futile repetitive movement drove the crew nuts until Doug finally gave up and dropped the sails.

The swells died and the calm sea eventually flattened into a blue mirror. He tried to make the best of it by going swimming in the placid ocean, but soon climbed back aboard. The persistent thought of unknown creatures swimming unseen in the great depths beneath him was simply too uncomfortable.

Day after day, the crew sat broiling in the tropical sun. If *Moby Dick* discovered them in their helpless condition, Hunter would have an easy victory.

One morning, after five days of dead calm and a glassy sea, Doug awoke and went topside to scan the horizon. Once again, there was no wind, nor other vessels. Nate greeted him with a mumble and went below to get his breakfast while Doug took over as lookout. Cassie had taken the first night watch and was still asleep. Doug realized that the members of the crew were all sleeping more yet acting increasingly tired and surly. He noted Nate and Cassie were snapping at each other as well as second-guessing his every action or decision. Doug was having trouble keeping his little group from falling apart in this frustrating weather.

"Shit!" exclaimed Nate from the galley below.

"Now what's wrong?" asked Doug.

"You're out of water!"

"Sorry. There's still some juice, sodas, and beer." Doug noted that Nate said "You're out" rather than "We're out." Yesterday, Cassie had told Doug a lot of "his" food needed to be thrown overboard because "his" refrigerator had become hot inside. *Funny how it was all "mine" only when things were going wrong*, Doug thought. *Why am I always sorry, anyway? I didn't ask for all this to happen. Where's the goddamn wind?*

Cassie came up from her cabin and wordlessly plunked down wearily on the cockpit bench opposite Doug. She coated herself with sunscreen while Nate told her about the water situation. He sucked down a warm beer with his breakfast.

"Hey, Doug? You figure this damn sailboat of yours is still technically moving due to the rotation of the earth or continental drift or something?" Nate asked.

"Real funny. Come on, this is working fine, guys. We still have some beverages. We're not in danger of dying of thirst yet. Sure, we wanted to make southerly progress, but we've hidden here successfully for five days. Hell's bells, isn't that what we wanted to do? Remember? We decided to go into the open ocean to hide. Maybe Hunter quit and went home."

"Not likely," murmured Cassie.

"Okay, as soon as we can sail somewhere, we'll go in to get some fresh food and water. You've got to admit this is way better than the other extreme—trying to stay out here in the teeth of a storm. We'll be fine." Regardless of his assurances to his crew, he was obsessing about the water supply. He wanted to go below immediately to count the beverages. He couldn't do it because he didn't want to frighten the others. Doug thought he'd check it later, and then work out some sort of rationing system if genuinely required.

He wished he knew exactly where *Payback* was. He couldn't see any land. The hand compass showed his direction, but Doug was confident of little else. His dead reckoning put *Payback* somewhere east of Dominica. At best, they were east of Martinique. Either way, they'd be safely clear of the two islands' rocky windward shores. Doug couldn't be sure, though. The prevailing ocean currents could've swept *Payback* back to the northwest while she'd been becalmed. It didn't matter, he realized, because he couldn't do a damn thing about their position anyway.

Even so, it would be nice to know something more. Doug didn't have a sextant, but he thought he might be able to measure the angle of the sun at noon with a protractor attached to a pencil. Maybe he'd manufacture a crude astrolabe, the ancient instrument predating the sextant. Then he'd see if the angle was changing daily so he could figure if *Payback* was drifting north or south.

It still won't work, he realized. *This is summer in the tropics, and the sun shines down steeply. So what if the angle, at a set time, did change from day to day? What did it prove? How would he know if the change was from the normal seasonal progression or from the yacht moving? He needed a book of sight reduction tables and some knowledge of the procedure. Screw it.*

"Want to play cards again?" asked Doug

"No, thanks," said Cassie.

"Nope," said Nate.

"Chess?"

"Screw it."

"Backgammon?"

"Nah."

The three sat around reading dog-eared paperbacks or merely staring out to sea. Any conversation tended toward monosyllables. Doug finally lowered the swim ladder and determinedly swam for a good five minutes before the usual mental images of large, toothy fish spiraling up from the deep brought him aboard.

Doug toweled off then stretched out on the starboard cockpit bench with his feet pointing aft. He'd go below soon to take a beverage count under the guise of fixing lunch for the crew. If they were in real danger of running out, he'd try signaling their distress tonight by shooting off the remaining flares or building a big fire in the barbecue grill. It was time to rejoin the world. How did sailors in the old days live with weather like this—sometimes for weeks on end while eating salt beef and boiled peas? A pure sailing vessel could circumnavigate the world without a drop of fuel, but couldn't navigate at all without wind.

As Doug lay flat, looking at the rigging above, he noticed the small U.S. flag on the backstay hanging limply. It flopped over to the right, to the left, and to the right again. *It's only the swell,* he thought. *Wait a minute. There aren't any damn waves left.* He sat and glanced at the flag again. Now it was actually waving and standing out a bit from the rigging. Doug checked the water around the boat. Yes! There were small ripples and cat's paws disturbing the surface. Even better, a line of clouds was peeking up over the eastern horizon.

"Wind!"

The crew looked around and felt a breeze cool their smiling faces. It wasn't much yet, but it was enough. They quickly hoisted the sails. Doug took the helm to steer directly west. The wind freshened. Soon *Payback* was reaching what Doug guessed was six knots or better.

"Avast, me hearties! We sail for the Spanish Main!" joked Nate.

Cassie and Nate talked and laughed while they kept a sharp watch over both sides of the bow. It was amazing how fast morale improved when the boat was moving along swiftly again.

"Where are we going? Down island again?" asked Cassie.

"Eventually, but we'll head straight west for awhile until we identify the nearest land. Frankly, I don't know exactly where we are. We need to pinpoint our position before we turn south. We're also going to have to risk stopping for water somewhere soon. Fresh food would be nice, too. I don't want to stay long or show our faces in a big town, though."

Payback sailed westward in good weather for hours without sighting land or another vessel. Doug began to worry he'd ended up passing right through a gap in the chain of Lesser Antilles generally oriented from north to south. Maybe *Payback* was already on the west side of the Leeward Islands, lost in the vast Caribbean Sea. If that happened, the crew would eventually stagger ashore somewhere in Central America, assuming they all survived the trip.

No, it couldn't be. He'd noticed sea birds flying west for home each of the last five evenings so the islands must still be to their west. The yacht couldn't have drifted very far through a gap overnight. *Payback* couldn't have traveled so far west that the line of islands was already over the horizon to the east of the boat. Not in a dead calm. Even so, Doug illogically looked astern as if something would suddenly be visible back where he'd recently been. Realizing that was stupid, Doug turned and faced forward again. He'd spot something soon.

Nate and Cassie took turns using the binoculars. It was Cassie who finally sighted land, although she wasn't sure of it at first.

"Hey, I spotted something! See the white stick? There, off the starboard bow," she said, pointing.

"Yeah, I see it, too," said Nate, taking his turn using the optics.

"What is it? The mast of a ship or something?" she asked.

"It's too thick for a mast. Let me have the binoculars please." Doug struggled to focus on the tall image while the boat rolled in a slow, corkscrew fashion. "I think it's a lighthouse!" He changed course to put it dead ahead.

"Can you tell which one?" asked Cassie.

"No. In the dark, I could check the rotation speed and flash pattern against the chart, but can't tell a thing now. There won't be anybody running it to ask. They're all automated now."

When *Payback* moved closer, Doug could see two small, flat islands with the lighthouse on the near tip of the bigger one. There were brown patches of coral surrounding the pair of uninhabited keys. It looked like a great snorkeling spot.

Doug approached the isles cautiously under reduced sail. He now saw a much larger island in the haze to the northwest. As *Payback* neared the pair of small islands, the crew noticed a large open-decked catamaran with a boisterous crowd of snorkelers leaving the vessel to get in the water and enjoy the reef. One man remained aboard. The French tricolor flag flew from the excursion boat's stern. Doug turned to pass alongside within shouting distance, but offshore to clear the snorkelers.

"Ahoy! *Bonjour!*"

"*Bonjour, monsieur!*" replied the captain of the day charter boat. "*Parlez-vous français? Je ne parle pas anglais.*"

"Oh, great," said Doug, trying to remember his rusty French. "The guy doesn't speak English. Maybe we're off Martinique somewhere. Cassie, I don't suppose you speak fluent French? I damn sure know Nate doesn't."

"Back off," said Nate. "I can French kiss, and I can swear or order beers in five languages. That's all any sailor needs."

Cassie laughed. "No, you're on your own on this one, Doug," she said.

"Uh, *quel est le nom de cet endroit?*" Doug called to the captain hoping the Frenchman would understand his poor accent as he tried to ask the name of the place.

"*Iles de la Petite Terre,*" said the captain, pointing at the adjacent two little islands. Then he pointed toward the larger island behind him and said, "*Il y a Guadeloupe.*"

"*Merci,*" called Doug, waving goodbye.

"So are we lost, Captain Cousteau?" asked Nate.

"No. At least I know exactly where we are. However, we didn't make as much progress down island as I'd hoped. The current must've swept us back north a bit when we were becalmed. We're right off the eastern tip of Guadeloupe. The next big island to the south is Dominica, then Martinique.

"I think we can make the leeward coast of Dominica tonight. It's another small, independent island nation. We're smarter to go there than risk checking in with the French authorities on Guadeloupe. There's a quiet place I know on Dominica where we can sneak in without a problem. We'll make a quick stop for water and a good meal if anything's still open."

Payback ate up the miles quickly as she sailed between Guadeloupe and Marie Galante. The vessel rounded the northern tip of Dominica, returning to the sheltered Caribbean side of the island chain. Doug turned south and sailed halfway down the west coast of the island. Using town or radio mast lights to navigate, he brought the yacht into a small, isolated anchorage off the Castaways Beach Hotel. Fortunately, *Payback* was the only boat there. Nate pulled the storm anchor out of the cockpit locker. He rigged it on the bow to replace their abandoned primary anchor. Doug grabbed the star-shaped key wrench for the water tank access then locked up the boat.

All three went ashore and made it inside the hotel well before the restaurant closed for the evening. Cassie laughed when they all noticed her newly acquired awkward gait on land—the land rocked gently even as she stood still. Nate teased Cassie regarding her bowlegged seaman's walk.

"Not very lady-like," he said. "Have you been riding your horse today?"

"She's been a real sailor for weeks so she's acquired authentic sea legs," added Doug.

Glancing down at her shapely limbs, Cassie said, "Oh, they're sea legs alright. I wish I could check into the hotel and sit in a bubble bath and shave these legs properly."

"Sorry, Cassie. It's risky enough to stop and eat. We can't push it by trying to check in," said Doug.

"I know. At least, I've still got Nate's *Payback* crew cap to cover this filthy head of hair."

Doug arranged for a hotel employee to go out with the water tender motorboat to fill the sailboat's tanks. The man took the wrench to access the water tank fill cap on *Payback*'s deck. The small-capacity tender had to make two trips. Without the electric watermaker operating, Doug needed to get the maximum number of gallons possible stowed aboard *Payback*. He paid for ice to be placed in the cooler he'd left on deck. The attendant also sold him a white plastic barrel previously used to store rainwater collected off the restaurant's roof. Doug rinsed it, filled the drum with water from the hose, and rolled it aboard the dinghy to take back later.

Nate and Cassie went straight for the bar to luxuriate in their first frozen drink in a long time. When Doug finished paying for the water, he found his crew in conversation with a red-haired man on an adjacent stool.

"Doug, this guy's originally from Streator, Illinois!" said Nate. "Now he owns a grocery store just south of here."

"Yep, in a little village named St. Joseph. I also run tours to see the Carib Indian settlement, the springs, and the waterfalls. Everybody here runs two or three operations to make a living. My name's John."

"Pleased to meet you," said Doug, shaking John's hand. "You own a store, huh? Well, I'm very pleased to meet you. In fact, I have a proposition for you. I know it's late, but I'd like to pay for your dinner if you'd join us. Then I'd be happy to pay you a twenty percent premium over sticker price if you'd drive back and bring us some canned goods and other provisions from your store. Unfortunately, we need to leave very early in the morning."

"I think it's doable. You folks can stay here and relax. I'll reopen the store tonight then drive the stuff over. Are you going to join your friends in Roseau in the morning?"

"What friends?" asked Doug.

"Your friends on *Moby Dick*. They've been here asking around for *Payback*. A couple of Latinos. I couldn't help but notice the lady's cap said *Payback*."

Cassie's eye's widened. She put her hand on the offending cap immediately.

"Oh, right! Those guys!" said Doug, recovering quickly. "Yeah, we're looking for them, too. We met them on Antigua. Don't tell anybody else, though. We'd like to surprise our buddies."

"Sure, no sweat."

Distracted by news of the pirate's proximity, the crew had a nervous dinner with John. Before she sat down, Cassie apologized and left for the ladies room.

When she came out her hair was combed and only the brim of the cap was sticking out of her bag.

With Doug dictating, John wrote a list of supplies *Payback* needed. Unfortunately, his little grocery store didn't carry boating equipment of any kind. The best he could do was offer a full case of flashlights, with plenty of batteries and candles. After dinner, John left to get their gear. The crew retreated to the dinghy dock to wait for him.

"Sorry about the cap."

"It's not your fault. I didn't think about it either," said Doug.

"Don't sweat it, Cassie," added Nate. "A bunch of people saw us, and those guys probably gave our descriptions, too. They would've eventually found out we came ashore here."

"Yeah, but for once, we know where the bad guys are, but they probably don't know we're on Dominica yet. Maybe we can use that knowledge to our advantage and take the offensive this time," said Doug.

"Now you're talking, Captain Nemo. I've always been in favor of sticking it to them if we got a chance. Let's go kick some drug-pirate ass. It's time for some serious payback!"

CHAPTER 23

▼

DOMINICA

Payback's crew sailed steadily south along the coast of Dominica and prepared their vessel for war.

"Congratulations, young Master Luke, I'm glad to see you've finally come over to the dark side," joked Nate in a low voice. "All right then, let's step it up. Let's kill these piss-poor pirates. I mean it. They'll be sleeping off another night on the town by the time we get there. I bet we can easily board them and cut their dirty throats."

"Whoa, hold on there, Darth Vader," said Doug. "We need to do a full reconnaissance first. If they're on guard, we'll turn around and run on down island. We'll probably get a good head start before the druggies hear we were ever on Dominica. Maybe we can make it all the way to Trinidad before they find us again."

"Yeah, but maybe not, and I'm sick of running. I don't like leaving an enemy behind us. The generals always say the best defense is a good offense."

"I agree, but I don't want to get us all killed. Remember, Nate. The pirates are better armed and more experienced at this kind of thing. We're amateurs."

"Okay, Captain Blood. Let's say we check it out then find those counterfeit corsairs are all dead drunk or asleep. What do you want to do then, Doug?"

"I'm thinking more along the lines of a hit-and-run sneak attack. Maybe we can do something to slow or sink *Moby Dick* so Hunter can't chase us for quite awhile. We don't need to actually kill anybody or take undue risks. What do you think, Cassie?"

"As much as I personally want to see Hunter burning in Hell tonight, I think Doug's right. We're not able to face them one-on-one, but I'm willing to take some risks to hurt those bastards. If we only keep running, they'll eventually catch us. We should take this opportunity."

"There's a good wind tonight, plus it's cloudy," said Doug. "We should be able to hit that stinkpot hard and get away in the dark. I'm a little worried about reversing or maneuvering within Roseau's harbor, but I have an idea for some extra propulsion."

"Okay, you two win," said Nate. "As someone once said, 'Discretion is the better part of valor,' and all the usual hogwash. Someday, though, you're going to agree with my direct approach, Doug. You're going to get mad enough to want to kill those assholes in any way possible, fair fight or not."

"I'm getting there, believe me. What I'm thinking for tonight is to ram them, then toss firebombs on the deck to keep the bastards' heads down while we sail off and watch them sink." Doug explained his full plan of attack to his crew. They set to work with a vengeance. Following Doug's recipe, Cassie mixed dinghy gasoline with powdered detergent and poured it into empty beer bottles. Instead of using rags, she took the tampons she bought on Virgin Gorda and jammed them into the bottles' necks for fuses.

"Great idea!" laughed Doug. "Now I wish we had some Styrofoam to melt."

"Why?"

"To get the recipe closer to napalm."

"I love the smell of napalm in the evening," chuckled Nate.

"Jesus, Doug. How do you know all this stuff? I thought you were a banker or something," said Cassie.

"I read a lot. It's kind of a Walter Mitty thing."

"Who?"

"A character with a fantasy secret life. From an old story by James Thurber. Old like me, I guess. Forget it."

Nate loaded the two guns. He took the .410 and Doug took the shotgun. Then the brothers labored to strap the anchor to two teak-deck gratings joined in a V-shape. They lowered the rough construction over the bow and tied it in position so the anchor flukes were spread over the gratings. The wooden gratings lay against the hull thereby allowing the anchor shank to point straight forward, barely below the waterline.

"Damnation!" said Doug. "This isn't good enough."

"Why not?" asked Nate. "It looks good."

"It doesn't stick out far enough. The top of our bow slants too far forward, and it'll hit their hull first, before this anchor shank. See my plan is to ram them below the waterline. We can't risk taking all the impact on the tip of our bow."

Doug considered what other materials he had to artificially lengthen their ram, but drew a blank. He couldn't sacrifice the boom, but he didn't have a spinnaker or whisker pole. While he was thinking, he helped Nate reinforce the front edge of the bow with locker doors and the legs from the settee table. The brothers tied the spinnaker halyard near the bow and tensioned it. The halyard might support the mast in case the wire forestay snapped from the collision.

"I got it!" said Doug.

"Use the propeller shaft?"

"No. Darn good guess, though, Nate. It'd work and it hasn't been much use to us lately. But I figure we've got two starts left on the engine battery, so we'll still get a few minutes from the engine, shaft, and screw. We'll need it tonight, in fact. Plus, it'd take a lot of work to get the prop off anyway."

"So what's your new answer?"

"Let's try the emergency tiller, the big angled pipe that fits over the top of the rudderstock post if the wheel steering breaks. It's long and made of thick steel. It's the perfect shape to stick in that stinkpot and sink her."

After securely lashing the tiller alongside the anchor shank, Doug moved to the stern to lower the swim ladder. Nate manhandled the outboard motor off of the dinghy and into position while Doug secured it to the ladder. The outboard, strapped to the stern, would act as a makeshift second engine with its small propeller sufficiently underwater. He furled the jib to clear the foredeck for action. *Payback* was ready for battle.

As he approached the harbor, Doug rehearsed his crew. "Cassie, I'd really like you to stay below. You can watch for leaks after we hit."

"No way! I insist on being part of this attack. I need to hurt those boys big-time. I was fine during the last fight. Remember?"

"I don't know about fine. A little berserk, maybe. Okay, you win. You can go forward with Nate. Take the boathook. This butane lighter, too."

Doug smirked when he realized he was preparing to attack an enemy vessel by using fire bombs and ramming—the exact methods and naval tactics the ancient Greeks used against Xerxes and the Persians 2,500 years ago.

Payback hugged the shore as she moved south into the harbor. Doug was pleased to see a large cruise ship anchored slightly north of the primary boat anchorage. He ran his smaller vessel alongside the ship then sailed a little past the giant's stern to take a look. After a quick glance at the anchored boats, he spun the wheel to hide behind the big ship again.

On his second peek, Doug spotted *Moby Dick*. On the third surveillance, *Payback* stayed out in clear view longer so Doug could use the binoculars to scan the trawler. The lights were off with no one visible on the deck of the trawler. A couple of night owls sharing a bottle of champagne peered down curiously from the high railing of the cruise ship.

"Okay, here goes nothing! We're going in, folks. Remember to brace and hold on to something right before we ram the bastards. Then throw the Molotov cocktails, really hard so they smash! Then, Nate, you put a shot below her waterline. I'll do the same with the shotgun. If we're still close enough, hit them again with the firebombs to keep their ugly heads down when we pull out. I'll try to cover you if Cassie has to use the boathook to fend off. Everybody ready?"

Nate gave him a thumbs-up. Cassie ran back to surprise Doug with a hug and a lingering kiss before returning to her position on the starboard bow.

"Hey, where's my kiss?" asked Nate. Cassie punched him in the arm then gave him an exaggerated big, wet kiss on the cheek.

"Wow!" said Nate, raising his eyebrows.

*   *   *   *

Cassie's expression turned dead serious again as she faced forward and prepared. She stopped and wondered what the hell she thought she was doing. At any second, a stream of bullets could reach out from *Moby Dick* to cut her friends down. It was surreal standing on the bow of boat ready to smash and burn her enemies. She was an ex-cocktail waitress from Las Vegas, not a heroine in an action movie. Yet she was eager to do this—eager to strike at the men who'd tortured and degraded her. She was taking the law into her own hands, but it had to be done.

*   *   *   *

Doug put the sloop on a close reach across the wind. He planned to ram *Moby Dick* midship on its port side. The wind was increasing, giving *Payback* good speed on her silent approach. As he got closer, Doug was pleased to see no sentry keeping watch. He reached behind and started the outboard engine now attached to *Payback*. The yacht accelerated slightly.

With less than a minute to go, Doug pressed the start button for *Payback*'s diesel. It turned over, but didn't fire. He pressed again to no effect. The trawler loomed ahead. The engine had to start immediately or it he'd have to circle around to make another pass. More likely, somebody would awaken from all the noise and begin shooting. Doug swore, pressed a third time, and held it. The diesel started.

Doug ran the throttle full ahead. He could sense the boat going faster. Would there be time to build enough speed? It was too late to abort. *Moby Dick* was so close Doug couldn't miss colliding with the trawler even if he wanted. Doug struggled to keep the bow aimed straight at the motorboat's side to ensure *Payback* wouldn't glance off. At the last second, a gust of wind pushed *Payback*'s bow a little to the right, slightly aft of *Moby Dick*'s center.

"Hang on!" yelled Doug, gripping the helm with white knuckles.

The boats collided with a tremendous shock. The makeshift ram punched through the trawler's hull, just aft of the port beam, then ripped upward like a zipper when *Payback*'s momentum pushed the sailboat's bow higher than the motorboat's rail. *Moby Dick* rolled to starboard, recovered a little, and then stayed at an angle. The two boats stuck together like two antler-locked bull elk.

Doug saw Nate and Cassie lose their footing in the crash, but recover quickly. When the bow stopped moving, Cassie lit the gas-soaked fuses of two bottles. She swiftly handed Nate one. They simultaneously smashed the flaming bombs onto the enemy's deck. Nate aimed the modified flare gun to his left and sent a slug punching through the waterline of the trawler.

After Doug heard the shot, he moved the throttle through neutral into reverse. He quickly turned, moved to the outboard, and shifted it into reverse as well. The sailboat lurched backward then stopped. The boats stubbornly stuck together. Leaning over the transom to operate the outboard, Doug struggled to avoid falling overboard when the boat jerked to a stop.

Now what? He needed to cover Nate and Cassie. Climbing back into the cockpit, Doug grabbed the shotgun with his right hand then triggered a shot off at *Moby Dick*. Nothing happened. He pumped a second shell into the chamber, aimed, and pulled the trigger again. He heard a slight fizzing sound. The shells were duds! He realized the rounds were too old and had been soaked by seawater too many times. Doug silently cursed, knowing he should've checked the ammunition earlier.

Doug had no time to check to see if any of the remaining shells were good. He threw the shotgun to the deck and grabbed the wheel. *Why wasn't his sailboat pulling away from Moby Dick?* The ram was solidly stuck. It wouldn't come loose

Maybe it was because the vessels collided at a slight angle instead of straight on like he wanted. He had to get *Payback* loose somehow.

Cassie and Nate lit their second salvo of firebombs. Together, they threw the Molotov cocktails over at *Moby Dick*, trying to hit the hatches this time. The detergent helped the flaming mix stick to everything it touched. Flames and smoke erupted all over the trawler's weather decks.

✳   ✳   ✳   ✳

The initial crash violently shook the drug pirates, as if someone had noisily thrown them into the nearest hard surface. Garcia was supposed to be on watch, but was drunk and asleep on the forward deck, near the port bulwark. He hadn't been visible to Doug earlier. The first set of Molotov cocktails splashed burning gasoline on Garcia's ankles and shoes. Garcia tried to beat out the flames with his hands. Now his hands were burning and bubbling. He was in the process of sitting when the second barrage came in, setting his entire upper body on fire.

✳   ✳   ✳   ✳

Cassie was startled and horrified by the apparition appearing without warning on the foredeck of the trawler. A man with flames covering his head and torso rose screaming and staggered around the deck. He was burning so intensely Cassie couldn't tell who he was. The shrieking torch finally staggered to *Moby Dick*'s rail and toppled into the sea.

"Fend off, Cassie! We're stuck! Push us off or cut off the ram lashings!" Doug shouted. Cassie shouted her acknowledgement. She joined Nate on the starboard bow. Using the boathook, they grunted and shoved, but weren't able to disengage the two boats. Cassie realized the other two pirates would soon be on deck to blow away their victims at close range. She frantically kicked and shoved at *Moby Dick*'s hull. Cassie glanced over to see Hunter's head emerge from a deck hatch. He looked dazed and wild-eyed. She saw him poke his rifle through the hatch and start to climb out, but searing heat and flames apparently drove him back. Cassie cried out to Doug, resulting in Hunter firing through the open hatch, in her direction. The AK spat a stream of bullets high over the heads of *Payback*'s crew.

*   *   *   *

Hearing the rapid-fire weapon cut loose at close range, Doug ducked and despaired. He couldn't get *Payback* off of *Moby Dick*. He knew there wouldn't be enough time to cut or untie the myriad lines and cables firmly attaching the ram to the bow before the remaining two pirates could shoot the sailors. He had to figure out something quickly.

Payback had initially "T-boned" the motorboat at a right angle. Now, however, the wind was pushing the sailboat's stern around until the sides of the two vessels touched. The makeshift ram groaned as it bent. Reinforcing materials broke off and dropped into the sea.

Doug saw what was happening. *Moby Dick* was anchored so she had been pointing straight into the wind. *Payback* had come charging in at a right angle with the wind on the port side and the mainsail set over the starboard side. Currently she was stuck to the motorboat with the wind pushing on the side of the sailboat, spinning *Payback* counterclockwise to lay parallel with the trawler. The bent ram still held the vessels together. The flapping sails pointed uselessly into the wind.

Doug realized he could harness the wind to help the motors pull his yacht away, releasing the ram. He jumped up on the port side and pulled the boom across the cabin top. He grabbed a central section of the main sheet and looped it around the midship cleat to assist his effort. Soon the mainsail hung out over the port side of the vessel. It was backwinded, with the force of the wind pushing hard on the forward side of the sail.

The engine temperature alarm went off, adding to the bedlam. Bullets whistled overhead. Doug ignored it all. He pulled hard on the boom to catch the wind. Crouching low, Cassie and Nate strained to separate the two boats. The outboard plus the main engine thrashed the water astern. All the forces combined to focus on the ram and fiberglass hull around the collision site. There was cracking and wrenching from the bow as the trawler's hull flexed and tore. *Payback* jerked backward, freeing her from *Moby Dick*'s grasp.

Cassie and Nate fell to the deck as the sailboat lurched aft. Doug let go of the boom, released the mainsheet, and raced to turn off the overheated diesel engine. The boom returned to the center line of the boat. The wind and the little outboard continued to take the vessel downwind, stern first.

As the sailboat backed away, clearing *Moby Dick*, Doug turned the wheel to lay his yacht across the wind. He shifted the outboard into forward gear, and then hauled in on the mainsheet. *Payback* sailed forward, exiting the harbor. Doug noticed the same two party animals staring at Payback as she passed the giant ship.

One pointed with a champagne bottle and yelled, "Hey! Why did you do that?" He turned to his companion and slurred, "Melissa, did you see that? The sailboat just rammed and firebombed the motorboat."

Doug smiled and shouted back, "They stole my favorite anchoring spot!"

"Jesus, Melissa. They sure play rough down here."

Nate and Cassie cleared the wreckage from the bow. They were able to save the anchor, but the other gear was twisted and ruined.

All three stood in the cockpit, let their heart-rates slow, and gazed back at the flames on *Moby Dick* until the trawler was blocked from view by the hull of the cruise ship.

"Man, we totally messed them up!" crowed Nate. "They're probably swimming ashore crying for their mamas."

"Yeah, but we could've lost everything. I didn't think we'd ever get loose again. I cut it way too damn close for comfort. It's too bad those two drunks saw us," said Doug.

"Who will believe them? You did great Doug, but let's never try ramming again," agreed Cassie.

*   *   *   *

Sitting silently, Cassie realized that the whole skirmish only lasted a few minutes, but seemed to unroll in her mind in slow motion over and over. She couldn't get the image of the screaming burning man out of her mind. Cassie hadn't planned on anyone getting hurt tonight, but the pirates deserved it after what they'd done to her and Leo. It was exactly what she'd wanted to accomplish, yet she was still shocked at the reality of violence at close range. She figured the brothers were equally shaken, but didn't want to discuss it. Cassie knew she couldn't—at least not yet.

*   *   *   *

Sanchez was the last to wake after the collision. Sleeping in the port midship cabin put him closest to the collision site. The crash had slammed his head against the bulkhead, knocking him out. He woke up on the cabin floor with a stream of water splashing his face. The water was gushing through a single .410 shell hole in the side of the boat.

Sanchez stuffed a portion of a blanket into the bullet hole, slowing the leak. He staggered into the passageway only to have Hunter, carrying a fire extinguisher, push him aside.

"Grab the other extinguisher and follow me!" ordered Hunter.

The two went out through the starboard wheelhouse door and advanced on the flames. The men soon extinguished the fire, as it had not spread below. In the end, *Moby Dick* only sustained some cosmetic damage from the firebombs.

"Where is Garcia?" asked Sanchez.

"Yeah, where the hell is he? I didn't see that bastard helping us. Find him."

They searched the boat, but failed to discover Garcia.

"Maybe he swam for shore. Let's worry about him later. Come on, we've got to see if we're sinking then see what the hell we can do about it."

Hunter and Sanchez inspected the damage at the collision site. There were gouges and cracks in the side with a jagged hole that extended below the waterline. Diesel fuel was gushing through the rip and spreading over the water's surface on the port side. The two men entered the engine room, but saw nothing amiss.

"Why is there no water pouring into the engine room?" said Sanchez. "We should be sinking, no?"

Hunter checked inside and out twice more. He consulted a diagram of the boat's layout posted inside the engine room door before he finally realized what was going on. "Those pussies rammed us, but they only punctured our built-in port diesel tank. The ram didn't get all the way inside. Ha! That whore and her two pimps probably think they sank us, but all they did was cause a big fuel spill. The tree-huggers of the world will be pissed, but we're okay. All we have to do is close off the valves to the tank and then plug it, or let it fill with seawater. We still have two other tanks and plenty of fuel. I'll isolate the tank while you get the anchor up."

"We are not staying here to repair all the damage?"

"Are you nuts, Sanchez? We damn well woke this whole island with gunshots. Can't you see the boat's spreading hundreds of gallons of diesel all around? You want to stay here, pay a shit-load of fines, and answer questions? Not me, *hombre*! We're leaving right this minute so we can nab those stupid sailors before they get too far. Nothing is going to stop me this time! Do you hear me? Nothing!"

Sanchez started the engine then went forward to operate the anchor windlass. Using the tethered remote control, he pulled a few feet of the chain in, but immediately stopped when the screaming started. That's how they found Garcia, desperately holding on to the chain using his blackened palms and three remaining fingers.

CHAPTER 24

▼

MARTINIQUE

Moby Dick churned south leaving a frothy white wake on the warm, dark water. Hunter stood at the wheel restlessly searching the darkness through the binoculars. Every couple of minutes, he'd use the small searchlight mounted overhead to sweep the waves. He figured *Payback* was ahead, innocently sailing south to pass along the leeward side of Martinique. Sanchez was below, futilely trying to comfort Garcia.

"Can't you do something to keep him quiet?" growled Hunter. "I can't concentrate with all his goddamn groaning and screaming."

"What can I do?" Sanchez had come to the wheelhouse rather than let Garcia overhear him. "He is a mess. Everything is burned from the waist up. His ankles, too. I put wet towels all over except for his mouth and nose. He is in real bad pain."

"Well, give him a bottle of booze plus every drug we've got. He's driving me nuts."

"He needs to go to a hospital, Hunter. Maybe they could save him."

"We ain't got time. Even if we dropped him off somewhere, they couldn't fix him around here. These little islands don't have hospitals that good. Doesn't matter, 'cause he's a goner anyway. Don't feel too sorry for him, either. It's his own damn fault. Garcia was supposed to be on watch when we got hit. I bet he was sleeping on the job again. He screwed us all. You should be mad at him. So just shut him up!"

"Man, you are one hard-ass *yanqui* son-of-a-bitch, you know that?"

"Did you just call me a Yankee?"

"You are a *norteamericano,* are you not? So you are a *yanqui.*"

"The hell I am! I'm from the Deep South. I'm a natural-born Reb, not no goddamn Yankee. Stop worrying so much about Garcia. Shit, you see me crying to go to a hospital so I can get my leg fixed proper? It still hurts every damn day. I bet you want somebody to check out your ear, too. But first we catch those slippery sailors and get our cocaine back. Then we can all go to a doc."

Sanchez shook his head, and went below.

*   *   *   *

Given the success of *Payback*'s risky attack, Doug was confident he'd be safe enough tonight. The main danger at present was being run down by a freighter in the Martinique passage. Accordingly, he'd taped two flashlights with colored lenses to the bow—red to port and green to starboard—and one clear white light to the stern. A red lens cover had been included on one of the grocery store flashlights, but Doug had to cut off a piece of a cellophane food wrapper to create the green color. If he heard any vessel come close in the wee hours of the morning, he planned to shine another light directly on the sails. The lights would indicate *Payback* was under sail and entitled to right of way. At least that's how it was supposed to work if anyone on the big ships was actually paying attention. Doug wished he still had electricity so he could use the radar repeater again. The GPS and knotmeter would have been nice to have, too.

The weather was good for once—not great, but good. Doug reckoned *Payback* might be making five knots as he steered her south. He intended to sail along the Caribbean side of Martinique. *In this weather, three sailors could trade watches around the clock,* Doug thought, *by keeping two crewmembers awake in rotation to keep sailing. With luck, Payback would make Trinidad in a few days.*

Nate came on deck with cold sodas and hot food for both men. He sat with his feet on the cockpit bench and leaned back on the cabin bulkhead. The younger brother tore into his food; he only stopped occasionally to throw crumbs over the side. Facing aft, Nate watched the crumbs disappear in the wake behind the boat.

"Thanks, Nate. Fresh food with actual cold sodas, This is great! That first stop on Dominica was well worth it."

"Yeah, but tomorrow I'm using the rest of the ice on the beer. I'm not wasting anymore on mere sodas."

"Can't blame you. Say, how's Cassie doing?"

"She was going to try to sleep. I bet she won't, though. We're all still pretty tense."

"You got that right."

"I didn't think we'd ever get *Payback* unplugged from *Moby Dick*. Maybe I should've thrown a bucket of cold water on the bow to get them loose."

"Why would you do that?"

"Heck, it worked when our old dog would hump the neighbor's poodle."

"Good one, Nate."

"Hey, Doug?"

"What?"

"You know if we could see how far these crumbs went behind us in a certain amount of seconds, we'd probably be able to figure how fast we're going."

"Yeah, it'd work if you could measure the distance behind us. But I can usually make a good guess based on the sound of the wake or the way the boat moves and reacts. You know. From sailing her all these times. It would be useful, though, to make an actual log tomorrow."

"What kind of log are you talking about?"

"In the old days, they'd take a piece of wood and tie a long thin line to it. The line had knots tied in it at measured intervals. One sailor would call time with a watch and another sailor would toss the chip log overboard and count how many knots slipped through his fingers before the first man said to stop."

"No shit? Is that where the term comes from? So the knots in the rope would correspond to actual nautical miles per hour of speed?"

"Yep. With a nautical mile being equal to one minute of longitude at the equator. I bet we could make a chip log if we need one. We should make a lead line to toss out and measure depth, too."

They sat in silence, enjoying the night for another few minutes. Nate kept observing aft. "Hey, Doug?"

"Speak directly into the oracle, baby brother."

"I just noticed there's a weird lighthouse back on Dominica?"

"You mean the one on Scott's Head at the southwest tip?"

"No, I see that one. There's another one. It flashes around every couple of minutes or so with no pattern. Sometimes it's pointed this way for a long time and sometimes only for a second."

"There's no such lighthouse on Dominica I know of."

"Sure there is. Take a look."

Doug turned to the sea behind them. Soon he noticed Nate's mysterious light.

"Shit, shit, shit!"

"What's wrong?"

"That's no lighthouse! It's a boat's searchlight. It must be *Moby Dick* looking for us!"

Nate watched the pattern of the light. "Goddamn it, you're right. Those bastards are getting close, too. How did they survive the big hole we poked in their stinkpot? I put a bullet through that trawler's waterline, too."

"Either they plugged the holes somehow, or we must not have punched all the way through. It never ends with those bastards!"

*   *   *   *

Cassie heard the commotion and abandoned her attempt to sleep. Her eyes widened when the brothers told her what was happening.

"Turn off the flashlights! Hunter will see those," she said.

"It's too late," said Doug, "He's close enough to see us now, even at night."

"Hey guys, the light's steady and pointing in our direction," reported Nate. "You got any more tricks in those deep pockets of yours, Captain Kangaroo?"

"Hell, I don't know. I need time to think. Start the outboard again. It'll give us a bit more speed." Doug changed course to put *Payback* on a broad reach, the fastest point of sail. Cassie trimmed the sails under Doug's supervision to match the new course. Their pursuer matched their turn, but wasn't catching up quite as quickly as before.

"Shouldn't I turn our lights off? Maybe it'll get misty or rain or something," she asked.

"No, don't turn off the lights yet. I've got an idea. It's a very old trick, but it might work if we can get a little farther away from him first. We have to slow him down somehow, if only for a few minutes."

"How're we going to do that?" said Nate.

"Wait a sec. I've got an additional, but more modern idea for temporarily slowing *Moby Dick*. Cassie, could you describe Hunter's drug canister?"

"It used to be our raft container. You know, white and round like a small oil drum."

"I was hoping you'd say that. Did it appear anything like our new white rain barrel I've tied to the mast?"

Cassie contemplated the barrel and said, "I guess so. Ours was a little smaller, though. Also, it opened across the middle like a clam."

"Close enough. Any markings on your raft canister?"

Cassie closed her eyes to try to remember. She pictured Leo showing her all the emergency equipment. Cassie remembered Hunter rigging the canister and boasting how smart he was. Competing emotions fogged the picture as she recalled the recent past. Here she was in great danger yet again. She had to remember. It was important for some reason only Doug knew. She thought of Doug in order to stay calm with the sense of warmth and trust he brought her.

"I've got it! There were black letters saying 'CAPACITY SIX PERSONS' with a second line saying 'MOBY DICK.'"

"Great!" Doug ran below and fetched a roll of electrical tape, a wrench, and a small, blinking light designed to be used on a lifejacket. "Put those words on the water barrel using this black tape then attach the strobe light. Let half of the water out then plug the barrel again. Then tape a wrench to the opposite side of the letters so the barrel floats face up. Tell me when you're ready to drop it overboard. Got all that?"

"Okay, I guess."

"Nate, go get another three flashlights from the grocery box. Tie two of them to the bow of the dinghy. Then make a raft from two fenders, and put another flashlight on the raft. Aim that light backwards. Make a bridle on the stern of the dinghy, and tie the fender raft to the bridle. Let out forty feet of line so the fender raft trails straight behind the dinghy. Got all that?"

"Aye, aye, Captain Drake! Good thing we bought the whole case of flashlights. I bet I know what you're doing. I think I saw this in a movie once."

"Yeah, well it was in several naval history books before any movie. This trick probably hasn't been used in 200 years. I only hope *Moby Dick*'s motley crew doesn't know about it."

"Not unless it was in a comic book or a porn movie."

＊   ＊   ＊   ＊

Doug marveled at Nate's good spirits. The excitement of danger always made Nate optimistic. Nate seemed to live for risky situations. Doug wished he could react the same way. *Payback* had been caught again. The whole crew could be fish food in Davy Jones' locker in another half hour. Doug fervently hoped there was a God. If so, maybe the crew would awake in Fiddler's Green, the mythical paradise for sailors' departed souls.

"The timing is everything, Nate. If the crooks go for the bait, that's when we do the switch. The dirt-bags will be focused on the drum. I'll fire a flare at them to mess up their night vision, too."

"Good idea. Try to hit the bastards for fun if the flare will carry that far."

"Cassie can steer," Doug continued, "while you and I shift the outboard back to the dinghy. You turn on the fender raft light right when I extinguish the real stern light. Then Cassie can go forward to switch off the bow lights at your signal. Tie the outboard's tiller straight ahead and don't run the motor too fast."

"No sweat. I got it."

The crew was ready in ten minutes. *Moby Dick* was approaching AK-47 range when Cassie rolled the barrel over the side. Doug sounded a long blast with the compressed air horn to put Hunter on notice that something unusual was happening.

*   *   *   *

"Did you hear something?" asked Sanchez, coming up to the wheelhouse.

"Sounded like a horn from the sailboat. The slut and her sailor boys must've finally noticed us. Maybe they're hoping somebody will hear them. Shit, there's nobody around here in the middle of the night. This slaughter will be over right quick."

"Why did the sailors leave their boat lights on?"

"Those assholes thought they sunk us. They're acting like the idiot tourists they are again. It's too late to bother turning lights off, though. I could easily follow their wake this close. Hell, I can even hear their noisy outboard going. They must be trying to use it as a little pusher motor or something. I bet we shot out their main engine."

"Hunter, there is a blinking light in the water behind the sailboat! It looks like *Payback* dropped something. Watch out this time! It could be a bomb. Slow down and do not hit it."

Hunter slowed *Moby Dick* when he got closer and moved cautiously to the side of the object with the attached strobe light. Hunter knew *Payback* was becoming increasingly distant, but the vessel still had her lights on. He could catch the yacht anytime.

Hunter circled the area warily. Sanchez swiveled the small searchlight and illuminated a white barrel.

"I think it is our canister! The woman must be trying to give it back to us. Hey, Garcia? Can you hear me? We are recovering the coca. Hang on, *amigo*. You are going to be wealthy. Then we will get you to a hospital. You see the drum, Hunter?"

Hunter tried to steady the binoculars. "Sure do! I can read it. It says '*Moby Dick*.' Go get the boat hook. See, I told you the sailors still had the stuff."

A red flare arced across the sky then hissed in the water forward of *Moby Dick*.

"*Caramba*, that hurts my eyes! Why did they shoot a flare?"

"Maybe the pussies are still calling for help or maybe they wanted to make sure we see the canister. It won't help them, though. If those chicken-shits think I'm going to let them go on their merry way after all this, they'd better think again. Just because they gave me the coke doesn't mean I ain't going to waste them all anyway."

Hunter lost more precious minutes maneuvering so Sanchez could reach the canister. Off to the south, the lights of the sailboat flickered. *Payback* appeared to change course to move straight downwind. Hunter guessed the yacht was trying to go a little faster. No matter, their lights were still on and he'd be after the vessel soon.

"Oh, shit! You are not going to like this, *Jefe*."

"Now what?"

"The sailors tricked us again. It is only a white barrel full of water. The letters are made with black tape. There is no coke! *Nada*!"

Hunter frantically scanned the darkened horizon. *Where's* Payback? Hunter thought. *I can't see her anymore.* Then the next wave raised *Moby Dick* higher allowing Hunter to catch a glimpse of the running lights. "There they are! The bastards were stalling for time, but we'll get 'em."

Hunter took out his knife then stabbed the labeled plastic barrel several times to ensure it would sink. He didn't want anybody reporting an apparent life raft canister with his boat's name on it. Hunter then advanced the throttle and spun the wheel around to chase the distant lights. The pursuit would take another hour and a half.

Hunter was puzzled by the actions of the boat ahead. At times, the lights receded away from him in a straight line. Just when it seemed his prey was getting away, it appeared *Payback* would change course and lose the advantage she had. These changes corresponded with a change in the wind or waves. *Maybe this Doug guy is not such a hotshot sailboat skipper after all*, Hunter thought. "Hey, we should rename that sailboat *Old Snake Wake* since it can't keep a straight course."

Finally, the target slowed considerably. Sanchez said, "I can not hear the outboard noise anymore. The sailors ran out of gas for their outboard engine. We have them, Hunter!"

"Yeah, but it's getting windier. The rag-hanger should still be going pretty fast. His outboard couldn't have been helping all that much. I don't get it. Let's be real careful this time. They could be laying for us somehow."

The pirates cautiously moved within range. Sanchez commenced firing from his position in the bow. The flames stabbed out into the humid night. Sanchez changed clips twice to send numerous high-power rounds tearing into the nearly stationary target. Some shots were wasted on the empty waves where the middle of the boat should have been. Nevertheless, enough rounds hit so the lights jerked around as the decoy was shot repeatedly. The bow lights went dark first, and then the false stern light died.

"Okay, enough! I think they're sinking, let's move in, but be careful. They could be playing possum again." Hunter maneuvered *Moby Dick* closer and turned on the searchlight. He expected to see bloody bodies on a half-sunk vessel. Instead, the circle of light only revealed a shredded dinghy with its partially inflated bow in the air. The empty gas tank floated above the submerged outboard motor. A single fender trailed behind.

"Goddamn, it's another stinking trick. It was just a dinghy towing something with lights. No wonder it was so fast and hard to catch. Shit on a stick!" Hunter scanned the dark horizon with the binoculars, but saw no sign of the elusive sailboat. In a fit of rage, he sent dozens of bullets from his own rifle into the wreckage. He kept shooting even after the rubber boat slipped beneath the waves.

"Oh, what a wonderful night we have had! Bravely chasing false barrels and false boats. So where are we going this time, great *capitán*?"

"Screw you, Sanchez. South, of course. Those cocksuckers are constantly moving south. We head south, and we'll see them again. I guarantee it."

"*Sí*, I thought you would say that. Personally, I have had enough fun for tonight. I am going to sleep for a while. Check on Garcia once or twice. He is very drugged, but the pain will come back."

Hunter didn't reply. Sanchez shrugged and went below.

*   *   *   *

A couple of hours later, enough sunlight reflected over the eastern horizon to illuminate the increasingly steep waves. Hunter saw the gray hump of Martinique to his left, but a frustratingly empty sea everywhere else. Sanchez slept soundly below. Hunter wished Garcia would follow his example. The gravely injured man had been moaning in pain for the last hour and it was deepening Hunter's rage. Finally he put the helm on autopilot and went below.

"How you doing, buddy?"

The muffled reply was unintelligible. Hunter searched for Garcia's handgun, found it, and slipped it under his own belt, behind his back.

"Keep it down, Garcia. You're going to wake your buddy Sanchez. Here, step outside with me. You need some fresh air. I'm taking us right to the hospital. You'll be there soon."

Hunter held Garcia and eased him over to the stern rail.

"Martinique's right over there. I know you can't see through those bandages and shit, but maybe you can smell the land. They've got a great burn unit at their hospital. Maybe they'll even fly you free to Paris, France, for treatment. Imagine that."

Hunter propped Garcia against the rail, stepped away, pulled the pistol out, and shot the man through his bandaged temple. Bits of bone, fabric, and tissue formed a red cloud briefly hovering over the water. Garcia's body slumped to the deck. Hunter rushed to place the gun in Garcia's left hand, the hand that still had a trigger finger. He returned to the wheelhouse as fast as he could, awkwardly climbing the steps on his reinforced leg.

"What was that? Garcia! Sanchez! Get out here!" shouted Hunter in mock concern. He got halfway back down to Garcia's body when Sanchez burst out of the main cabin.

"Garcia!" yelled Sanchez, running to the corpse.

"Oh no!" said Hunter. "Oh my God! I'm so sorry. I only left him alone for a couple of minutes to go check on the course. I didn't know you let him keep his gun. The pain must've been too much for him."

"I did not even think about his gun. I never thought anything like this would happen."

"Hey, Sanchez. Maybe he's better off this way. He's not feeling any pain. You know Garcia was a goner anyway. We damn sure have to catch that piece of ass this time. We'll make her pay for this! Poor Garcia."

The Latino stared hard at Hunter, but said nothing. Sanchez knelt next to Garcia's body and made the sign of the cross.

CHAPTER 25

▼

THE GRENADINES

The first rays of the rising sun illuminated *Payback* sailing at top speed to the southwest, angling away from the line of islands into the open Caribbean. The wind had picked up throughout the night. Every few minutes, Doug nervously swept the horizon with binoculars, but saw no sign of *Moby Dick*. The decoy trick had succeeded.

"Wow, how fast you think we're going, Admiral Yamamoto?" asked Nate as *Payback* surfed down the steep slope of a following wave.

"Admiral? I thought it'd be Captain Queeg or worse by this point."

"No, I promoted you after your slick trick with the dinghy last night. The bastards had us until you faked them out."

"Thanks, but I sure can't pull that one again. We don't have a dinghy or an outboard anymore. They cost a boatload of money, too! To answer your question, we're definitely hitting hull speed and more with the wind and waves both pushing hard like this. We might be hitting nine knots. Definitely faster than that damn trawler can do."

"No shit?"

"Yeah, even if those jerks knew our location, they couldn't catch us today. *Moby Dick*'s a long-range motor yacht with a full displacement hull. Given her size, she can probably do just over eight knots. Of course, that's way better than us most of the time. Hunter can do that speed all day, every day until his fuel runs out."

Doug wanted to get a few more miles over the horizon into the trackless sea before he slowed. It's funny, he thought, the last time he went this far out to sea to escape was over on the Atlantic side. The Caribbean side of the island archipelago was normally more sheltered. Yet *Payback* had been becalmed in the Atlantic, but was currently facing stormy winds. "We get screwed every time. If only we had a radio to hear the weather," Doug muttered. "Okay, let's furl a third of the jib and take one reef in the sail, Nate. There's a storm coming."

"Aye, aye, Admiral Farragut. Oops! In your case it should be Admiral Beer-a-gut."

Doug grinned. He was constantly amazed by Nate's irrepressible spirits when things got dicey. After he'd shortened sail, Doug was pleased to see the boat's motion become more comfortable and controllable even though the speed only declined slightly. The crew could rest now and Cassie went below to take a nap until lunchtime.

*   *   *   *

"So, where are we?" asked Cassie when she finally awoke.

Doug pointed out their position on the chart. Cassie moved very close and leaned over, apparently to see it better. Doug took a step away to give her room. *That was a mistake*, he thought. *Why am I so damn shy and uncomfortable with close personal contact?* He was now concerned she'd think he didn't like her.

As Cassie leaned over farther, her top hung away from her neck, giving Doug a good view at the swelling rise of her breasts. She raised her eyes from the chart and caught him looking. Doug's face reddened. Cassie smiled. Doug quickly refocused his eyes on the navigation table.

"Uh, right here, directly west of the Pitons on St. Lucia. I'm heading south now to parallel the chain of islands, but staying well offshore and out of sight."

"What are the Pitons?"

"They're twin peaks rising 2,500 feet straight up out of the ocean. You get an amazing view from a resort on the saddle between them." Doug blushed again and struggled to get back on track. "On the waterfront there's this restaurant with wonderful seafood where the host is a very eccentric Scottish nobleman. It's a wonderful island. I'd love to take you there when this mess is all over."

"I'd like that."

Doug nodded and turned away before he put his foot in his mouth again.

"So are we going to St. Lucia, Doug?" asked Nate.

"No, we might as well use this coming night and aim farther south. I don't want to arrive at a tricky spot in the dark and sink on a reef after all we've been through."

"You know another good place to hide?"

"Yeah, I guess so, Nate. You know, speaking of hiding plus St. Lucia, reminds me of an interesting historical tidbit."

"Oh no, here it comes again. Interesting and historical don't usually go together."

"Forget it then. I need to switch the jib anyway."

"Go ahead and tell me. I'm only rattling your cage, Admiral Nimitz."

"Okay. There's a very pretty harbor up north a ways, on this side of St. Lucia, called Marigot Bay. There's a sand spit peninsula with palm trees on it coming from the north side and hiding the back of the harbor. I think Hollywood filmed part of the original *Doctor Doolittle* movie there. You know the one with the talking animals?"

"You're digressing."

"Oh, right. Anyway, a British admiral was being chased by a larger French fleet. It was Admiral Rodney, I think. So he hides his fleet in Marigot Bay, behind the sand spit and has his sailors tie coconut palm fronds to the masts. The French sail right by, but don't spot the hidden ships."

"Should we change course and go there, Doug?"

"No, there's a modern marina with all kinds of boats now. We'd be the talk of the islands if we pulled the palm fronds bit. Those bastards would hear of it on the coconut telegraph in a minute. It does give me a great new idea, though."

"Now what?"

"Camouflage! If we could disguise the boat, we'd get out of this weather while hiding in plain sight."

"How are we going to do that?"

*   *   *   *

Payback turned and sailed southeast after nightfall. At first light, Doug tucked into Admiralty Bay, Bequia. He quietly anchored in the middle of a large group of sailing yachts off the town of Port Elizabeth. Bequia is the most northern of the Grenadine chain of small islands. The Grenadines are bounded by St. Vincent to the north and Grenada to the south. Bequia, like most of the Grenadines, was administered by St. Vincent, but Doug had no intention of registering with a new set of authorities.

"When the stores open, I want to do our business, and then leave here bloody quick, as the Limeys' say."

"Okay. We'll hustle, Doug. But do you see the open-air bar on the south shore, the one with giant bones making an entrance arch? Could we at least see that bar before we go?"

"Yeah, all right. Maybe we can get a water taxi to drop us off at their dock and walk through the bar on the way into town. Keep an eye peeled for boats with yellow signboards on them. You'll see all varieties of boat boys buzzing around here soon hoping for business. Strolling into town from a bar will make us look more like regular touring yachties anyway.

"That big arch is made from a whale's jawbone, by the way. The bar's called the Whaleboner. The bar stools are made from whale vertebrae. It's very unique."

"Where did the owner find all the whalebones?" asked Cassie.

"Bequia was an active whaling station in the old days," Doug continued. Nowadays, the island's authorized to take two whales annually. The local people are required to hunt the old-fashioned way, with harpoons hand-thrown from an open boat. Then they render the whale blubber over on Petite Nevis, a small uninhabited island to the south."

"Wow, I'd love to see them do all that," said Nate.

"Next trip, maybe. You can also buy whale scrimshaw here and legally import it into the U.S. A large number of the locals make their living from fishing or carving fancy model boats. Bequia's a unique place."

Doug flagged a water taxi down. The crew went ashore to the bar with the whalebone arch and walked north on the Belmont Walkway along the shore into town. They tried for anonymity with sunglasses plus hats. This time the three made sure they didn't wear anything with the name of the boat on it. Cassie split off to the supermarket while the brothers headed for the hardware store.

"I'm worried I'll run out of folding money, Nate. I've still got more than three hundred, but we might need it. I don't suppose you have any I could borrow?"

"I'll give you what I've got, but I'm about tapped out. Believe it or not, though, I saw a sign on the door saying the store takes credit cards for any purchase over fifty dollars."

"Great! I've still got credit cards."

Doug was surprised. He spent a lot more than he thought he would as the store turned out to carry a few essential boating supplies. He picked up a hand-held Magellan GPS and a Grundig shortwave radio receiver. Both devices would run on the AA batteries *Payback* still had in stock. Additionally, he found a plastic inflatable canoe designed more for kids than three adults, but it'd serve as a makeshift dinghy. The inflatable came with two paddles. Doug inquired about weapons, but was disappointed when the storeowner said guns and ammo weren't available for sale.

"Why would you need a gun on Bequia, anyway? We love yachties here," the man teased.

"Oh, no doubt about it. This is a friendly little paradise you got here. But my brother and I have to meet our sister in Kingston, Jamaica. We're sailing there to bring her supplies for her Christian mission work."

"Yeah, Kingston's a dangerous place. You're right to pack a gun there if you can get away with it. Sorry I don't carry them. Anything else you need today?"

"Yes, indeed. I'd like two buckets of cheap dark blue paint, three brushes, four rolls of masking tape, and a can of gold or yellow trim paint. We promised to help my sister paint the mission church in Kingston."

Doug paid with the credit card, and the brothers left to meet Cassie at the town dock.

"If Hunter has passed the word to be on the lookout for us, maybe he'll hear I said we're heading to Jamaica. It couldn't hurt. I hope the guy doesn't mention the paint, though."

"Mission work, huh? That's a good one. Praise the Lord!" Nate loaded the supplies into a waiting water taxi then helped Cassie when she walked up encumbered with groceries.

Exiting Admiralty Bay, *Payback* sailed close to the peninsula forming the south side of the harbor. The water was deep all the way to the rocky shore, and the crew got a close view of the eccentric architecture of the Moonhole community. This is an isolated group of vacation homes built into the rocks and cliffs. An escapist's dream, the otherworldly buildings have no glass, electricity, or right angles. The structures, built with swooping arches and large patios, appear to grow right out of the hillside.

After passing the navigation light on West Cay, *Payback* turned back to the east. She sailed silently along Bequia's southern shore, past the new airport, before turning to starboard for Petite Nevis. Doug approached the western shore of the quarter-mile long island and moved in as closely as possible before anchoring.

"Let's snorkel in from here to scout the safest route to the beach for the boat."

"Why would we want to take *Payback* closer to the shore than this, Doug?"

"Because I'm going to beach this boat, Nate. Going to lay her on her side. Then, at high tide, we'll float her off again, turn her around and lay her down on the other side. In the old days, sailors needed to do this frequently to clean their ships' bottoms. It's called careening."

"Okay, I got it. But we're not just cleaning the bottom, right? That's what the paint's for."

"You got it there, *mon frère.*"

"Would one of you secretive gentlemen mind explaining your plan to me?"

"See what Doug wants to do on this little key is ground the boat, lay fenders on the side toward land, tip the yacht over, and then paint her sides down to the waterline. We bought blue paint at the hardware store."

"I wondered what was in those tubs. Why are we taking time to do maintenance today, though?"

Doug turned to Cassie and said, "It's not maintenance. We're going to disguise the boat. With a new color, a new name, and a cheap new dink, we should be able to fool those bad boy buccaneers of yours."

"Mine? They're sure not mine!"

"You had them first," said Nate, playing along.

"Right," agreed the smiling skipper. "Anyway, they aren't real sailors so they'll have trouble distinguishing one sailboat from another. We've got a new GPS so I thought about sailing out of sight then coming back in at Trinidad. Then I wouldn't have to worry about disguising *Payback* to fool Hunter. Unfortunately, our new radio tells me we only have one day of good weather left before it gets nasty again. We're getting into the hurricane season."

"I hope it's not going to get as nasty as last night," said Cassie.

"Maybe not, but between bullet damage, the ramming shock, and strains from that last bit of weather, I can't risk losing the mast or rigging in a storm on the open sea. We have to stick close to the shelter of the islands for this last part of our voyage. Maybe this disguise will let us sail right past Hunter if we're unlucky enough to meet him again."

"Hey, Doug. Maybe we should wear disguises, too. Perhaps Cassie could dress like a man?"

"I could hardly appear any less feminine than I do now after three weeks without decent clothes or makeup!"

While Doug thought she was still plenty feminine, both brothers laughed at Cassie's displeasure before they went below to get their snorkel gear. They picked a careening spot close to the north of the ruined cement pier. The chosen location was a small gravel beach there, with a 300-foot hill rising behind it.

At the base of the pier, Petite Nevis has a natural arch or hole in the boulder where you can walk underneath or even store a dinghy. To the right, slightly south of the shortened pier, is a seasonally abandoned shed with machinery and giant iron pots for boiling the whale blubber. Farther to the right is a grove of coconut palms. Beyond the trees, Petite Nevis has a flatter plateau, sloping south from the hill into the sea. The plateau has a couple of stone terrace walls with a ruined house foundation.

The crew ran the vessel aground then set an anchor to seaward to prevent *Payback* from getting washed too far up the beach. Doug led a line from the shed through the arch below the pier. He connected it to the main halyard. After knocking off some rust, Nate and Doug were able to use the giant winch in the open shed to haul in on the line, tilting the boat over on her side.

"This works great! It's a lot easier than trying to use *Payback*'s winch."

"Yeah, I figured this one ought to be powerful enough. I saw this big mother here last time I visited. It's one of the reasons I picked Petite Nevis. Normally the islanders come here to use the winch to haul a whale's carcass from the water. You know, I saw giant white bones in the water right in front of the shed. Too many rocks to risk hauling the boat straight in that route, though, even if the bones weren't in the way."

The crew took the rest of the day to paint the port side. Doug didn't sand or prep the hull as well as he normally would, but he hoped the paint job would only need to last the three or four days required to reach Trinidad. The first side dried during the night.

In the morning, the crew floated the yacht at high tide then turned her around so they could access the starboard hull. The brothers used the big carcass winch to pull *Payback* over on her other side for completing the paint job. After the blue paint was applied and fairly dry, Doug broke out the gold paint for the transom.

"I'm glad you're along for this part, Cassie. I remember a good name I saw once, but my painting would be too sloppy for detail work like this. Painting a boat's name can't be any tougher than painting your nails, I figure."

"Sexist pig!" laughed Cassie.

"Make it say '*Sailbad the Sinner*' with a home port of Waukesha, Wisconsin. That should throw them off. Straight lines are too hard to do by hand so try artsy-fartsy cursive."

"I'm on it, baby!"

*   *   *   *

On Virgin Gorda, Maxwell had been waiting for a break when the call came through late in the morning. The contact in the States reported a certain Douglas

Thompson used his bankcard at Bequia Hardware, Inc. in the country of St. Vincent and the Grenadines, W.I. The syndicate-connected data processing supervisor at the bankcard center apologized for taking so long to report back. Normally his underworld clients demanded same-day service. The delay was due to Caribbean transactions running in the last batch.

Maxwell thanked him anyway and then made his own call to the island of Canouan, less than two dozen miles south of Bequia. Soon a young man in a yellow Rastafarian t-shirt with a picture of Haile Selassie was rowing a leaky, wooden boat across Charleston Bay to deliver a message to *Moby Dick*.

"Come on, Sanchez. Get the anchor up. We went too far. Those queers are still north of us in Bequia."

"*Muy bien*, Hunter. I do not like this island anyway. The Tamarind Bar is nice, but I find nothing else for me to do here. I miss having Garcia to talk to. You know, I had to walk way over to the post office to mail a note to my family in Venezuela this morning."

"Yeah, yeah. Work while you talk, will ya?"

"Hey, I am working! Anyway, to get to the post office, I had to walk around a donkey and two dogs sleeping right on the main street in the middle of town. Then, I thought I heard a baby crying from the graveyard on the hillside on the left. I looked up and saw it was only a herd of goats. Most of them were sleeping on the headstones. It is not proper."

"So what's your point? Did it make you jumpy or what?"

"Like I said, I do not like this place. It is too damn quiet. I have a feeling something bad will happen to us in these islands."

"Jesus H. Christ, just get going already."

Three hours later, Hunter was interviewing the white owner of the hardware store on Bequia. Hunter was pleased to hear the guy remembered and described Doug because of his failed attempt to buy firearms. He went back out to *Moby Dick* to rejoin Sanchez.

"So what did the store man say?"

"The owner didn't recall much, but he remembered the head shit-bird trying to buy guns. Said he needed them for a trip to Jamaica. He didn't get any, so it means we still have a big advantage in firepower."

"Jamaica is a long trip. We better get more fuel first."

"Hell no! Those maggots ain't going to Jamaica. They're only spreading a lie to trick us again. They're heading south. I'll bet my life on it."

Sanchez gave Hunter a hard look. "Yes, well make sure it is only *your* life this time."

On their way south, the two pirates examined a dozen white sailboats anchored in Admiralty Bay. They cruised around to the other side of Bequia and inspected two more anchored in Friendship Bay. *Payback* wasn't there either.

Hunter knew the next inhabited island to the south would be Mustique. Then he'd reach Canouan again. Hunter checked the chart and noted, after Canouan, the Grenadine group continued on to the south like a series of green paint spots from a dripping brush. The remaining principal islands would be Mayreau, Union, and Carriacou, before reaching Grenada proper. Hunter set the first leg of his course for the in-crowd's private island of Mustique, second home to Mick Jagger, Tommy Hilfiger, Raquel Welch, and the location of the famous Basil's Bar.

Heading south, *Moby Dick* cruised past the tiny uninhabited islet of Petite Nevis. Through the binoculars, Hunter saw a single blue boat, floating right off the beach, apparently making a lunch stop. It didn't look like *Payback* to him. *Moby Dick* continued on to the southeast.

*   *   *   *

"We did it!" said Doug, below with Nate cleaning paint off his hands. "A little sloppy, plus we've added a few new scratches on the keel, but she sure looks different."

"Good job, Admiral Halsey. Now we're 'sailing under false colors,' I guess. You should see Cassie. She looks different, too."

"Oh, no. What did she do?"

"She cut her hair short. She's still in her cabin messing with it."

"That's a real shame. I like longer hair on women. Shit, I was going to give her my other floppy-brimmed hat to hide her hair under."

Cassie came out to the galley. "You can lend me the big hat anyway. God, I hate short hair, but it's the biggest change I could make without finding a bottle of hair dye. I'll wear sunglasses, too. I'm damn sure not going to pretend to be a man. Maybe you two could dress like women."

"Not likely," said Nate.

Doug ran his eyes down the womanly curves of Cassie's body. He silently agreed it would be nearly impossible to disguise her gender.

"Okay, are we ready to go or not?" she demanded.

Nate and Doug hauled up the anchor. Doug charted a course of south by southwest. By late afternoon, they'd passed Mustique, Canouan, and anchored in

Salt Whistle Bay on beautiful Mayreau. A crescent of pure white beach lined with coconut palms lay within swimming distance ahead.

The island's one small resort is immediately behind the fringe of palms. Mayreau's only road comes from the resort, runs up and over the ridge, through the small village on the other side, and ends at the main anchorage of Saline Bay.

Doug considered swimming in for a cocktail or a burger. Cassie and Nate were below, changing into their swimsuits. Doug decided to stay aboard, listen to the shortwave, and relax for a while. He fixed a rum drink then watched as Cassie and Nate dived off the bow pulpit into the turquoise water and swam for shore. Beside the new "*Sailbad the Sinner,*" their current harbor sheltered a blue motor yacht and a red-hulled, tug-style motorboat from Canada.

Cassie surprised Doug when she returned only fifteen minutes later. Cassie climbed up the swim ladder and left a trail of water on the deck when she walked past him to grab her towel off the lifeline. Doug couldn't help but gaze at her shapely thighs and firm behind when she bent forward to dry off her legs.

"Tired of swimming already?"

"Yeah, I thought I'd come sit and relax for awhile. You seem comfortable for once."

"I am. I think we've actually lost them this time. The paint job should keep us safe in any case. I finally believe I can slack off and enjoy the scenery."

"This spot's absolutely gorgeous. It's like a tropical dream. Thanks for getting us this far, Doug. Few men could've done what you have. I hope you realize it."

"No, I'm not anything special. We've had our share of good luck. You two have certainly done as much as I have. Say, is Nate coming back right away, too?"

"Not for an hour or more. He stayed ashore to hit the resort's bar. Said he wanted a couple of frozen drinks and a cheeseburger for a change. Last I saw him, he was sharing a table with two lovely young ladies from Montreal."

"They must be from the red stinkpot. Nate will ignore us for a while, I bet."

"Yep. Just you and me, sailor. Mind if I have one of those drinks, too?"

"Sure! I mean, no, I don't mind." Doug scrambled to get Cassie a clean glass and fill it. The new swimsuit was great on her, he thought. The suit wasn't overtly sexy; she was.

"Thanks for the drink, Doug. Hell, I constantly need to thank you for everything. I'd be dead if it wasn't for you."

"Oh, I didn't do so much. I don't know how anybody could go through what you have while keeping her head on straight. I admire you, Cassie, I really do. You are one tough girl...er, woman, I should say."

"You can say 'girl.' I don't mind."

"I'm a lot older than you, I guess, so it slips out occasionally."

"You're not that much older, Doug. Plus, all the sailing keeps you in great shape. Anyway, I like older men. Older guys aren't so self-centered. They consider others' feelings more and know how to treat a woman."

"Yeah, I suppose you're on to something, Cassie. Young men are still trying to prove their manliness. Most guys my age have been there, done it, and bought the t-shirt. We're comfortable with who we are."

"You still don't seem comfortable around me, though. Why can't you come over here and sit next to me so we can talk? Don't you like me?" she laughed.

Doug rose and moved closer. Cassie patted his hand and held it.

"Of course I like you, Cassie. You're smart, you're beautiful, and you're courageous. What's not to like?"

"Well, thanks. I like you too, Doug. I was starting to worry since you haven't actually tried anything with me. Most guys I meet put the moves on me in ten minutes or less. I was kind of wondering if it was because of your wife."

"Uh, no, I guess I'm over losing her as much as I'll ever be. You and I haven't been together very long, and I didn't want to take advantage of you in your condition. You know, after all you've been through, I figured you might want to avoid men altogether."

"No, don't worry. I can tell a good man from a monster like Hunter. You know, the psycho never actually raped me, even though he hurt me and constantly threatened to rape me. I don't think he's capable of it. He might be impotent. Maybe it's part of his problem."

"I'd say the guy has a number of serious problems."

"Anyway, Doug, I know all the psychological bullshit, and I can see past it. You wouldn't have been taking advantage of me. Although, I think there actually is something about facing death that makes you want to enjoy life more fully. Don't people say combat soldiers only sense they're truly alive during battle, then can't handle the boring peace afterward? I bet you find a lot of frantic sex going on during a war."

"You're probably right." Doug returned Cassie's warm smile and was finally sure. He slowly leaned over to kiss her. She didn't pull away. To the contrary, she moved her hand up behind his head and held him close. Her mouth was warm and welcoming. It was strange how her face felt so warm while her wet swimsuit was so cold and clammy where it touched his skin.

He kissed her again. This time he kissed her with an aggressive urgency. Doug stroked her hair. He slowly moved his hands all over her back and thighs. She squirmed and pulled away.

"I'm sorry," Doug blurted. He moved away a bit on the bench.

"Don't be sorry. I liked it. I'm just a bit uncomfortable here where other people might be watching us."

"You're right. Let's go below." Reassured, Doug led her to the galley. He turned her around and kissed her harder than before. He pulled her closer, getting his shirt wet from her swimsuit.

"This oven rail is biting into my back," she said. "Maybe, we better move to a cabin. Just for awhile."

"Uh, sure. My cabin's bigger, but it's a little messy. I could go in to clean it first."

"You're so cute," Cassie said. She stood and took him by the hand to the forward cabin. Doug shut the door behind them and laid a dry t-shirt out on the berth. She sat on the cotton shirt and put her arms around his waist. Doug leaned into her, pushed her slowly on her back and gently kissed her neck and shoulders.

"Wait a minute," said Cassie.

"Sorry, sorry. I know this is too fast. I'll leave you alone." Doug scrambled to his feet and moved away.

"No, silly, I only want to stop a minute and take this wet suit off. It's giving me goose bumps, and it's getting you all wet." She stood and peeled off her suit, lifting her feet one at a time while holding his shoulder for balance. Then she reached into the head, grabbed a towel, and rubbed it briskly over her naked body.

Doug couldn't believe how wonderful she appeared as she stood and unselfconsciously dried off. Her breasts were perfect, like he remembered from the first day he saw her on Dead Chest Island. Her stomach was flat and her hips smooth and white. The tan line around her breasts and pelvis emphasized the normally unseen flesh she was offering him.

Cassie finished toweling off, dropped the towel on the bed, and reached out to him again. His hands firmly cupped her breasts, touching her moist, cool skin on their surface, but sensing the heat building underneath. She fumbled with his belt and succeeded in taking his pants off just as Doug fell back onto the mattress.

"I've been hoping for this for quite awhile, Cassie. I even had a dream about making love to you on this very bed."

"I've wanted you, too, Doug. I need you. I truly need you now." Cassie climbed onto the bed. Doug held her close and rolled to position her underneath him.

Suddenly, the boat moved a little as someone climbed the swim ladder. Doug raised his head in alarm and slid off the berth.

"Doug! Doug! Are you here? Cassie? Get up here, quick!" Nate yelled from the stern.

"Hold on! Just a second! Shit." Doug responded, struggling to put his pants on. He glanced back at Cassie.

"Maybe later," she said with a smile and a shrug. She stood to kiss him before letting him leave.

Doug rushed to the cockpit. Cassie followed soon after, adjusting her suit's shoulder strap as she climbed the companionway ladder.

"They're coming! They're coming here," Nate panted, worn out by his top-speed swim from shore.

"Slow down. Who's coming? *Moby Dick*?" asked Doug.

"Yeah, coming from the north. I crossed the spit of sand between our beach and the windward side. I was walking with these two girls, you know, searching for seashells."

"You can skip the girl part," said Cassie, anxious to hear the news.

"Sorry. Anyway, I looked up to the north, toward Canouan, and saw a white trawler coming here. I only stayed long enough to be sure it was *Moby Dick*, and then I ran over and swam out. They're coming fast. Should I raise anchor?"

"No, it's too late. We'd seem suspicious rushing to leave. We'll have to trust our new paint job." Doug looked aft at the sinking sun. He squinted and saw another boat, rounding the point and turning east. It was coming straight from the sun toward the harbor. "Oh shit!" Doug yelled, hitting the deck to stay out of sight. "It's them already. You two get below! Nate, get your gun ready."

"What if the pirates attack us? What do we do?" asked Cassie.

"Damn, they're coming right toward us. Cassie, you get below and be ready to crawl out through the forward hatch and swim ashore when they attack." Doug risked a peek above the gunwale. "Wait! They curved into the harbor a little, but now they're leaving."

"Didn't they see us?" asked Nate.

"Sure, they saw us. We're the only sailboat in here. The paint must've worked! They saw the blue hull, read the name on the stern, and moved on south. It's like we're invisible. This is great!"

Nate and Cassie cautiously came up on deck. The trawler had disappeared around the headland, but the motor yacht's wake was still rocking the anchored boats in the bay. The brothers smiled and slapped their palms together in a "high-five."

"I know I shouldn't worry, but I'm not totally comfortable yet. Let's climb the road to the ridge top to see where *Moby Dick*'s going," said Doug.

"I'll change out of my swimsuit. Lend me your wide-brim hat again," said Cassie."

After the crew was dressed, Doug packed his binoculars and helped Nate paddle the inflatable canoe ashore. The three climbed the steep road to the churchyard at the top of the hill. Scanning south, Doug saw *Moby Dick* turning into Saline Bay below. To see better, he moved to an overlook near the multi-colored restaurant called "Righteous and de Youths."

"Damn it, the pirates are anchoring. I expect they're spending the night here on Mayreau. We sure aren't staying then. This island's too small for us to go unnoticed for long. What if they walk over this ridge to our bay for a steak dinner and spend an hour studying our boat? They'll figure it's us after all."

"Okay, but we know where *Moby Dick* is, Doug, so why don't we attack again and blow the bad guys away this time. Shit, they're still set on killing us. Maybe you and I could sneak aboard in the middle of the night and stab those pirates to death before they get a chance to do it to us. We still have the jury-rigged gun, too. You know, we burned one man pretty badly so they only have two healthy guys. Plus, I bet they're still messed up from the first gun battle. We should just take them out and finish it."

"No way, Nate! You two men aren't leaving me to go off and do something crazy. Hunter could've hired more guys, and he might have a lookout posted all the time."

"Cassie's right. The disguise is working, if no one observes *Payback* too closely. We proved it when the pirates overlooked us at Salt Whistle Bay. I'd love to finish them off, but we don't need to risk a desperate confrontation if we can move *Payback* then sail onward tomorrow."

"But where can we go this late in the day, Doug?" asked Nate. "The wind's increasing, and you'd have to go quite a ways offshore to avoid hitting a reef at night. You said you didn't want to risk this gimpy boat in stormy weather."

"Yeah, I know, but there's a good spot in a marine park called the Tobago Cays only a couple of miles away. The Cays are five tiny islands protected by a big horseshoe-shaped reef slightly east of here. They're uninhabited and at least we'd be safe during the night until Hunter searches again in the morning. We can't risk those bastards walking over to Salt Whistle Bay for dinner tonight. We definitely need to get off Mayreau."

Cassie and Nate agreed to the new plan. They hustled back down the road and got *Payback* underway. With the sun behind him, Doug was able to maneuver through the reef to hide his vessel behind one of the cays. Just like Anegada or Barbuda, the Tobago Cays were only accessible by daylight. Doug saw it was a popular anchorage with a dozen cruising boats on their hooks. Several small bumboats scurried around trying to sell souvenirs or food to the yachties.

One of the brightly colored wooden motorboats approached soon after *Payback* anchored. It was an open rowboat with an outboard on the stern. A middle-aged black man in a gray-flecked beard smiled at Doug while holding up two wiggling spiny lobsters by their antennae.

"Hows 'bout it, skip? Fix you nice lobsta dinna right over there on that beach. Gots the charcoals and everything. Need ice? Bread? Take the trash away for you fine people?"

"No thanks. Be careful, friend. Don't bump the side of my boat, please. I don't want any paint scratched off."

"No problem, mon." The vendor reached out and pushed off the hull.

"Wait a minute. On second thought, I might have good business for you after all. You got a buddy or partner out here who could help you? It's a two-man job."

"Sure thing, skip. See that red boat? That my frien', Lambert. We neighbors over in Clifton, on Union Island. What you need?"

"Okay, here's the deal. I have a nice lady aboard who doesn't want to see her ex-husband ever again. The guy doesn't know what boat she's on, but he's been poking around wanting to pester her. It's worth good money to me if you and Lambert go sit in the water on the other side of Petite Bateau Cay to watch the boats coming in. You were ready to give it up for today until we came in anyway, right?"

The vendor nodded.

"Okay, this guy will be a short redneck with a Latino crew on a white forty-foot trawler named *Moby Dick*. He's a mean bastard so don't mess with him. If you see him coming, just get back over here quick and then give your boat to Lambert to tow away. You'll sit in our cockpit here and pretend to be the hired captain of this sailboat."

"No problem, skip."

"If anybody asks, tell them you work for the charter company, and you only have two customers from Japan aboard this week. You can quit when it gets too dark for a stranger to get his boat in here. Then you come to see me and get your money. It's worth fifty bucks and another fifty if you actually have to pretend to be the charter skipper and talk to somebody. American dollars, not just Eastern Caribbean dollars. Got it?"

The vendor readily agreed. He went off to enlist his friend, Lambert.

"I bet that hustler will tell poor old Lambert the job only pays twenty EC bucks and he'll keep the rest," laughed Nate. "Having a lookout will definitely help me relax over dinner, though. It's a good idea, Admiral Nelson, so let's break out the beer and unwind."

Doug ruefully recalled how he and Cassie were close to really "unwinding" before Nate had interrupted him. The three sailors enjoyed a nervous, but uneventful, meal while the sun set. After dark, the lookout returned to collect his money. Doug watched while both men motored off toward the south for Union Island. He was glad to see the locals weren't heading west, to Mayreau, where Hunter lurked.

Trusting to their new disguise, the sheltering reef, and the late hour, the three shipmates went to bed without worrying about setting up watches. Doug thought about seeing if Cassie would like to "sleep" in the bigger cabin tonight, but was uncomfortable pushing it with Nate aboard. Sound carried easily on a sailboat, and they'd be at their destination in a couple of days anyway. He settled for a quick kiss as he passed Cassie in the galley. Tomorrow could be a tough day. The whole crew would need their sleep.

CHAPTER 26

▼

GRENADA

In the morning, the repainted and renamed sloop slipped out through the secondary channel opening to the south. Leaving the Tobago Cays astern, Doug turned to head southeast into the open Atlantic. He wasn't comfortable tacking his tired vessel into the strong breeze and steep waves, but he wanted to move farther out from Mayreau. This way maybe *Moby Dick* back in Saline Bay wouldn't see *Payback* passing.

After two hours, Doug judged it was safe enough to make the turn to the southwest, back toward the island chain. He briefly toyed with sailing straight for Tobago Island, the northernmost of the two significant pieces of land that comprised the single nation of Trinidad and Tobago. It was too rough today to try all in one leg. If he could make it as far as St. George's Harbour, on Grenada, he'd be in a good position to sneak into Tobago tomorrow. The angle on the wind would be better, plus the sea would be calmer with the partial shelter of Trinidad and Tobago to windward.

"Why are you smiling so darn much?" asked Nate.

"I don't know. I guess I'm thinking we might make it after all."

"Yeah, but don't go whistling any show tunes or anything. Remember, renaming a boat is very bad luck. So is whistling for a wind. You can get more than you want."

"Didn't we have this discussion regarding luck already?"

"Yeah, but it can't hurt to be careful."

"Now, that's what I told you about churchgoing. It's cheap insurance, Nate."

"Your mama."

Doug laughed. He was pleased with the way things were turning out. The boat's disguise was effective. *Payback* currently had a GPS plus plenty of supplies. He only wished he'd been able to buy longer-range weapons or even new shotgun shells for the 12-gauge.

Doug thought if he was able to sneak in to the more laid-back island of Tobago tomorrow, he might not have to sail on to Trinidad proper. Once ashore, maybe Nate and Cassie could fly a local puddle-jumper over to the main island without any immigration hassles. Then he'd sail *Payback* over to Barbados single-handed, see the ambassador, and clear this all up.

The skipper smiled then consulted his new GPS. He turned to Nate.

"Hey, check this out, Mr. Grumpy. The machine says we're in perfect position, zipping along at seven knots. We're on our way! Help me tack, will you? I'm going to turn so we pass inside of Carriacou. Then we can stay on the leeward Caribbean side all the way to St. George's on Grenada."

Cassie fixed lunch after reaching sheltered water. She was amazed by the many giant rocks and small islands scattered across the sea between Carriacou and Grenada. "I don't understand how you can figure which island is which with all these dinky ones out here."

"They can get confusing. You need to constantly check and double-check to be sure you know exactly where you are. On the other hand, it's pretty deep all around here so we don't have a lot of shallow reefs to worry over. These little islands are the tops of several steep submerged mountains. Having sailed here before helps me a lot, too."

"What's the one over there?"

"On the south side of Carriacou? It's Frigate Island. Those three small rocks sticking up are the Bonaparte Rocks."

"How about the first real tall one out toward Grenada?"

"That one's 700 feet high. It's called 'Kick 'em Jenny.' South of that's Isle de Ronde, then Caille Island. Believe it or not, there're a couple dozen fishermen living on those last two. The two nasty rocks to the west of Isle de Ronde are named The Sisters. Lots of nesting birds."

"Hey, Admiral Decatur. Didn't you once tell me Grenada had an underwater volcano with that same name of Kick 'em Jenny?

"Good memory, Nate! You haven't lost all the cells in your brain to alcohol after all. I told you about the volcano right before we found a certain topless sunbather on Dead Chest Island. If I remember, you said you wanted to check out all of these volcanoes."

"Yeah, well, I changed my mind. I've had enough of volcanoes after Montserrat. That Kick 'em Jenny island over there doesn't look like it's underwater. Did it rise recently?"

"No, the active volcano is 500 feet deep and three miles southwest of Kick 'em Jenny Island. The eruption spot is actually slightly west of The Sisters and Isle de Ronde. I don't know why the locals call the volcano Kick 'em Jenny. Maybe it's all part of the same underwater mountain. It last erupted fifteen years ago. Gas and hot water boiled to the surface, the whole bit. Should be pretty safe today, though."

"I don't care," Cassie said, entering the conversation. "I agree with Nate. Let's stay miles away from any volcano."

"Okay, Cassie, you got it." Doug swung *Payback* farther offshore to curve around the hot spot before heading south to St. George's. He considered stopping in a smaller harbor on Grenada's west coast, but the radio was predicting deteriorating conditions and St. George's was the only all-weather port on the leeward side. To be invisible to any boat passing by along the coast, *Payback* could hide in the calm southern part of the lagoon.

As the sloop sailed south along the leeward side of Grenada, Cassie was the first to notice the delicious smells. "Do you two barbarians notice how nice this big island smells? It's like someone placed a huge spice rack in the middle of a flower shop."

"It's quite fragrant, isn't it? Last time I was here I took a jeep tour all over the island to see the plantations and waterfalls. Grenada's called the Isle of Spice. A large part of the world's nutmeg and mace come from here. Grenada has loads of flowers, cashews, and fruits, too. It's very pretty in the interior, assuming everything has recovered from Hurricane Ivan."

Payback arrived at the port late in the day then maneuvered to reach the inner harbor near the Grenada Yacht Services docks. Doug anchored without using the engine. *Probably impressing the other cruising boats*, he thought. *But I wish Payback was only showing off instead of crippled.*

He was grateful when the anchor dug in right away so he could avoid diving into the murky water to set it by hand. St. George's was a substantial town with a busy commercial harbor subject to various oils and pollutants from runoff or ship discharge. At least the harbor was well lit and buoyed. It had to be; vessels arrived and departed at all hours.

"Hey, Admiral Nelson. Didn't we invade this place in the early '80s? I remember something relating to Cubans building a military airport and Ronald Reagan rescuing medical students. There was even a Clint Eastwood movie made about it, right?"

"You're right. It was back in 1983. Many locals remember it well and actually appreciate the American help in reestablishing democracy.

"Man, that's unique," said Nate. "Usually we hear 'Yankee go home!' around here."

"A lot of the fighting was at Fort George, by the harbor entrance. On the hill behind us, you can see Fort Frederick. That's where the prison is."

After the boat was set up to stay for the night, Cassie fixed a great supper of grilled fish. The brothers had Drambuie and Cuban cigars in the cockpit after dinner. They all relaxed while the lights of the small city came on one by one.

"When did you get these cigars? I thought we were out."

"You were out, Doug. I got a dozen when I went shopping in Bequia. I forgot to mention it the last two nights. This is the first night we've made a real meal for a while, anyway."

For once the three sat discussing the future instead of concentrating on the latest current crisis. Doug and Cassie sat very close and lingered topside until late. No one went ashore as they hadn't checked in with customs. They considered paddling in, but it wasn't worth the risk in the heavily populated area. Nate went to bed early.

✳   ✳   ✳   ✳

Nate was the first to rise the next morning. When he got out and scanned the harbor, he dropped his soda can on the deck then scurried below.

"Wake up!"

"What is it? Can't I sleep late for once on this trip?" The wind had increased during the night. Doug had been up twice already to check if *Payback* was still securely anchored. He'd had trouble getting back to sleep due to thoughts of Cassie. He couldn't wait until the two of them would get an hour alone on the yacht.

"Open your eyes, but keep quiet. *Moby Dick*'s here! The pirates are only two boats over from us."

Doug forgot his sexy dreams. He sat bolt upright, painfully banging his head. "Not again! You've got to be kidding me! This Hunter guy's like the goddamn boogeyman in a bad horror movie. I can't kill him, and I can't get away from him. He just keeps coming and coming. Shit! We only needed one more day."

"What should we do?"

Doug immediately cut off the useless self-pity and tried to think. "Go wake Cassie, but tell her not to make any noise or show her face topside. Does *Moby Dick* have a lookout on deck?"

"I didn't see or hear anybody. They must've come in late at night. Maybe they're all still asleep."

Nate left to go wake Cassie. Doug got dressed then grabbed the flare gun loaded with the .410 cylinder and slug. He met Nate and a very nervous-looking Cassie in the main cabin. Doug took a quick peek outside to confirm it was *Moby Dick* to the north. He noted the accumulated damage of broken windows, plugged holes, and fire scars marring the once-beautiful vessel. At the present, the stinkpot was just plain ugly and menacing.

"Come on, let's finish it with these assholes," said Nate. "We can quietly paddle over, packing this gun and a couple of knives to put an end to it while the bad guys are sleeping. It's still self-defense if you ask me. Anyway, when the authorities figure out who those maggots are, they'll be overjoyed somebody finally nailed those pirates."

"Yeah, Nate, but the situation's about the same as at Mayreau. Our disguise is working fine or they would've noticed us last night. Also remember, we only have one working gun. The pirates don't know we're here so maybe we can sneak off before they know they let us slip away. Without the outboard, I can't try ramming again, especially in broad daylight. Besides, we only have one long day of sailing to reach our destination."

"But what if Hunter catches us on the way?" said Cassie. "He knows we're moving south every day."

"Plus we've never been so close since the BVI. We should attack and be done with it," said Nate.

"Okay, you two have got me thinking. I agree we should take advantage of their ignorance, but not with a direct attack. It's too dangerous.

"So what do you have in mind, Admiral?"

"Okay, let's say we get all ready to go and sail off. But then we circle around and, if the pirates still aren't up, I go over the stern with my snorkeling gear on. I could take the old dinghy anchor and chain with me. It doesn't weigh too much. Then I dive to wrap the chain around their prop and shaft. When they start the engine later today, it'll tear up their propeller, maybe even their transmission.

Hunter will think he got tangled in somebody's anchor chain overnight. We'll be long gone, of course. We won't be stuck in the side of their trawler like last time."

"I like your plan, except for one thing," said Nate.

"What's that?"

"I should do the underwater work."

"Why? You don't have to be a hero for us. I can do it."

"Yeah, I know you can do it, but you're too valuable. You can sail the boat way better than I can. So you could get Cassie to Trinidad if you have to. I'm expendable. Plus, I'm the submariner, so I should be handling underwater warfare. You're only a skimmer, a surface sailor."

"Nate's right," said Cassie. "We need you to sail the boat. I need you. I sure can't maneuver a sailboat in this tricky situation, inside a crowded harbor. Also, if this attack doesn't work, Nate can swim ashore and hide. Grenada's a big island. We need you on the boat."

"Okay, Cassie. I'll agree, under protest. Let's do this quickly before the crooks wake up. Nate, do you want to use scuba gear for this?"

"No, there's not enough time to mess with it. The trawler's screw is only a couple of feet underwater, anyway. I only need a mask and fins so I can still swim with the chain. I'll be okay."

Doug put on his dark sunglasses and a hooded foul-weather jacket to change his appearance before going topside. He hauled in the anchor and then set the mainsail as quietly as possible. He was prepared to give the killers on *Moby Dick* a friendly wave if they appeared topside and spotted him.

Cassie helped Nate get ready. Then she crouched in the cockpit with the gun, ready to cover Nate as needed. Everything was set.

"You good to go?" asked Doug.

"Yeah."

"Hey, Nate!"

"What?"

"How can you walk with that set of balls you think you have, bro'?"

"Bowlegged, like John Wayne did," said Nate with a smile.

Doug sailed toward the exit on a port reach, but then fell off and jibed the boat, coming back on a starboard reach to cross the trawler's bow. He tacked upwind to turn around again at a slower speed. Nate slipped over *Payback*'s stern when blocked from the motorboat's line of sight. Again, the skipper sailed for the exit and watched the time until he'd turn around for the pickup.

"Okay, that's five minutes outbound. I'm turning around and heading back. Another five minutes then we're picking him up whether he thinks he's done or not. Please flip the swim ladder over so he can grab it when we make our pass."

Cassie moved onto the stern platform to prepare the ladder. "Okay, it's ready," she whispered. Cassie used a rag to wipe blue and gold paint from her hands. Both Nate and she'd been climbing all over the transom. All this activity on the scoop-stern was rubbing off portions of the new paint.

Doug was relieved when he got closer and spotted his brother. Nate was hanging onto *Moby Dick*'s anchor chain with one hand while giving them a thumbs-up with the other one. As *Payback* silently approached, Nate swam out farther from the trawler's bow then reached for the sailboat's moving ladder. He snagged it and swung aboard like a Navy SEAL boarding a speeding Zodiac inflatable.

"How did it go?"

"I think I got it. I wrapped the chain around so it'd tighten and get worse when Hunter puts it in forward gear. I tried to be quiet."

"Good. Okay, let's get the hell out of here. We have to head southeast before the weather gets any worse."

$$* \qquad * \qquad * \qquad *$$

Hunter was having bad dreams again. First, kids made fun of his name and size. Then he was surrounded by five women who reached for him and begged him to satisfy them. They laughed and spit on Hunter when he failed. One of the females had Cassie's face on a totally different body.

In the middle of the dream, an incongruous vision of Marley's ghost from Dickens' *A Christmas Carol* appeared.. The phantom shook his chains at Hunter and wailed.

Hunter definitely heard chains clanking. He came to full wakefulness and sat up. *What a weird dream*, he thought. *Damn bitches! Did I actually hear chains? Was something wrong with the anchor chain?*

Hunter popped his head through the forward hatch. No, he wasn't dragging the anchor through the harbor. He checked his bearings to confirm *Moby Dick*'s position hadn't changed. Most of the boats from last night were still in place, but the neighboring blue-hulled sailboat was passing his stern and heading for the harbor exit.

There was something fishy about the blue boat, though. The choppy waves and polluted harbor water had attacked the vessel's paint job. Right above the waterline, several patches of white showed. Hunter looked hard at the stern and saw numerous smudges. More white surface was exposed along with the black letters A and Y and B. He now realized what yacht it was.

"Sanchez! Wake up, goddamn it! Get your guns! It's *Payback*, and she's getting away."

Hunter scrambled out of the forward hatch and limped aft as quickly as he could, entering the wheelhouse through the outside door. He started the engine, leaving it in neutral to prepare for raising the anchor.

Sanchez came charging up from below and pushed into the wheelhouse, colliding with Hunter. The startled Hunter quickly spun around. As Hunter turned, his elbow hit the throttle and pushed it into full reverse. Immediately a loud clanging sounded below the stern. The motorboat strained backward against its anchor. Then the clanging stopped. In was replaced by a thumping vibration.

Beneath the hull, Nate's chain, which he'd wound to tighten and tangle when the prop rotated in forward gear, had come loose when Hunter accidentally ran the engine in reverse. Even so, the flailing chain banged and bent the edges of a couple of blades on the propeller before unwinding and dropping to the harbor bottom.

"What the hell was that?"

"I don't know! Watch out! You almost knocked me down." Hunter put the throttle into neutral and the hull vibration stopped. "The devious piece of tail was right here near us all night and we didn't know it! The sailors painted their boat blue, but the paint was coming off, and I spotted them. Let's get the anchor aboard and get after those shit-birds before they get too far."

Sanchez ran the windlass. He soon signaled the anchor was aweigh. Hunter slammed the throttle fully forward. The hull vibration immediately resumed and increased in intensity. Hunter throttled back. The vibration ceased. While the trawler headed for the harbor exit, he experimented with various settings.

"Why is there such a noise, Hunter?"

"Something's all tore up. Maybe we ran into our own anchor chain when you pushed me into the controls. I can't go more than 1700 revs or the shaft vibrates like it's going to tear us a new asshole in this boat. We'll barely get seven knots out of this engine now."

"I did not push you into it. You are the one who hit the throttle arm."

"Screw you, Sanchez! Forget it. Just get ready to blast those sailors when we catch them. They don't even know I saw 'em leave."

Moby Dick moved past Fort George. Hunter turned hard to port and pointed the trawler's bow southeast to follow the coastline. He used the binoculars to peer ahead. Sure enough, *Payback* was way off at Point Saline.

"Look, Sanchez! Over by the end of the airport runway. The blue sailboat. She's changing course to disappear around the point. I'm telling you it's the girl and her two *Gilligan's Island* rejects. We'll get her this time, for sure."

In reality, Hunter worried that the wind was strong enough to make the sailboat faster than *Moby Dick*, especially with the damage the vessel had just suffered. *It doesn't matter*, he thought. *I'll chase Payback for as long as it takes.* Hunter had a hunch today was the day.

∗   ∗   ∗   ∗

Doug put *Payback* over onto a starboard tack, steering her southwest for Tobago. With the strong southerly wind, the yacht was making 7.5 knots according to the handheld GPS. He was glad he had plenty of batteries for the power-hungry device since he expected he'd be far from land during most of the day.

The whole crew kept glancing aft, checking the way they'd come. Their mood steadily improved as another half-hour passed, and they still didn't see any other boat rounding Point Saline astern.

"I bet the pirates are still sleeping it off back in St. George's."

"Maybe you're right, Cassie, but after they wake up, I bet they'll pull their shaft right out after what I did to them with the chain. That'll make Hunter's day," said Nate.

"I hope you're both right. I just want to sail over the horizon quickly. Hunter doesn't ever give up. We're going to have to drive a stake through his heart, if he's got one."

Fifteen minutes later, the skipper's fears were realized. There was *Moby Dick*, in clear sight, rounding the southern end of Grenada and pushing toward him.

"Damn, damn, damn! What can we do now?" asked Nate.

"Shit!" Doug watched the trawler for a while before making a real response. "Okay, everybody take it easy. I think you actually did damage their boat, Nate. They should be catching us if they were running at their full speed, but they're not. We're actually widening the distance at the moment. If this keeps going, we'll lose sight of us and we can change course again."

"Yeah, I must've hurt him after all. On the other hand, by attacking Hunter, we've announced our presence. Maybe we could've gotten clean away today if I hadn't insisted on attacking."

"Come on, Nate. You can't figure it that way. If he was only planning to sit there all day, he wouldn't have started his engine and damaged his prop already. He was moving out anyway. Either he had an itch to search today, or a spy, or a problem gave us away."

"What if you're both wrong?" asked Cassie. "What if he's just searching to the south as usual and saving fuel by going slower? Maybe he only sees a blue sailboat here? I bet he doesn't even know it's us."

"I hope to hell you're right, but it's time to find out." Doug turned forty-five degrees to port, putting *Payback* on a reach heading for the open Atlantic. He watched the GPS while the yacht picked up another half knot of speed. He wasn't heading straight for Tobago anymore, but he'd gain even more distance against the damaged trawler this way.

Payback's crew observed the enemy astern. Would *Moby Dick* change course and follow to the east? Tense seconds passed without words, the silence accompanied only by the sound of the sailboat cutting through the water. Cassie's face became pale.

Moby Dick's bow steadily curved to port until it pointed east. The skipper was the first to speak and admit the obvious. "That's it. They've turned to intercept our new course. They know it's us somehow. It's a pure race from here on."

"But we're still beating them, right?"

"You're right, Cassie. Notice how you can't see their full hull anymore? You can barely see the superstructure. It means we're sailing over the horizon, leaving those bastards behind." Doug hoped the situation would continue. He considered turning even more downwind to pick up more speed on a broad reach, but hated to lose every bit of his accumulated upwind progress toward Tobago.

As expected, *Payback* pulled away slowly, widening the distance from her pursuer. During a quick lunch, Cassie stood on the cabin top and declared she could no longer see *Moby Dick*.

"Yeah, but I'm not turning south for Tobago yet. You can't see them, Cassie, but I bet they can still see us. Our mast and sails rise fifty-seven feet and show up for a long way. If you climbed the mast you'd see them. Trust me, they're still following us. Give it another hour."

Unfortunately, they didn't get another hour. Soon after lunch, the wind noticeably weakened. *Payback*'s speed dropped to seven knots and then to six.

"Don't worry. The wind will come back," said Doug, but he didn't believe it. The grim faces on the other two showed they didn't buy it either. The breeze dropped further. Soon he could see the topsides of *Moby Dick* and then part of the hull. He briefly debated using the last engine start and the few minutes of run time he thought the diesel had left, but decided to save it. He wished he'd bought another small outboard engine from someone in Bequia. It would have helped a little.

"Maybe I should've listened to you, Nate, and attacked the crooks while they were sleeping."

"No, you did the logical thing, skipper."

"I'm going to change course to return toward the north end of Grenada and Kick 'em Jenny. We'll just have to give up on making Tobago or Trinidad today. Going back north will put us on a broad reach in this wind. Maybe we'll get another quarter of a knot."

"Good idea, bro'."

"Yeah, we just need a bit more time for the wind to come back," said Cassie. "I'm praying for it."

Doug knew they were merely trying to act upbeat for group morale. He knew *Payback* was in trouble, and his crew knew it, too. The wind was still decreasing. In fact, the weather was becoming altogether strange and undependable. Ahead, the sky had a weird green-yellow tinge to it. The clouds were darkening and building into an odd shape. Something unusual was happening.

"Oh my God. Look at that!" Cassie cried.

"Where?" Doug was still looking aft at *Moby Dick* and wondering how soon the enemy vessel would be in range.

"Off the port bow!"

Now he saw it: a gray funnel cloud stretched downward from a swirling cloud mass. It undulated in slow motion like a cobra dancing to a snake charmer's music. While he watched, the tail of the cloud reached out and touched the surface of the water. The funnel turned silver in color as it sucked tons of water into the sky. "Oh, shit! It's a waterspout!"

CHAPTER 27

▼

KICK 'EM JENNY

"Cassie, get your safety harness and lifejacket on! Clip on to the lifelines behind you!" ordered Doug.

"How do we dodge a waterspout?" asked Cassie.

"We're not going to try to avoid it, yet. We're going to sail right for it."

"Isn't that a bit risky?" asked Nate, raising an eyebrow.

"Absolutely, but maybe Hunter will chicken out first and turn aside. I don't know another way to lose those guys." Doug adjusted his course straight for the waterspout.

Cassie had a strange sense that this was her fault. She'd prayed for more wind, and now *Payback* faced a tornado at sea. Shaking off her misplaced guilt, she helped Nate partially furl the jib at Doug's instruction. The foresail work was accomplished from the relative safety of the cockpit. Doug wouldn't let anyone go to the mast to work on reefing the mainsail. He said it was currently too dangerous. *It was kind of funny*, she realized. *Doug says he's worried about our safety, and yet here we are, heading right for a tornado trip to the Land of Oz.*

Cassie glanced back and saw *Moby Dick* still following *Payback* straight toward the dancing funnel cloud. The situation was so incredible that she stood in frustration and yelled at Hunter, even though she knew he couldn't possibly hear her. "Are you crazy, Hunter? Goddamn you! We *have* to do this, but you don't! Nobody's chasing you, you asshole! Give it up and go away, for Christ's sake!"

Doug grabbed Cassie's arm and pulled her down. "Stay low. Things may violently fly around here pretty soon." Her eyes widened further. After his warning, an intense gust hit the sailboat, knocking *Payback* over on her side and putting the leeward rail in the water. Cassie and Nate grabbed the lifelines and hung on.

Doug struggled to the winch and quickly let out the mainsheet, releasing the direct pressure on the sail. The boat slowly righted. He pulled the boom back in to a safe angle. Cassie could sense the acceleration when the sloop surged ahead to reach maximum hull speed, still aiming straight for the waterspout.

"Look!" yelled Nate. "I think it's stopping."

Sure enough, the bottom tip of the waterspout had lifted away from the ocean's surface and was retreating into the swirling clouds. The tornado twisted and undulated as if reluctant to leave. Finally, only an area of disturbed water below the dark clouds remained—without a funnel of any kind.

The yacht turned further to port. Cassie watched as Doug skillfully maneuvered his vessel to ride the heavy winds around the edge of the area where the funnel had been. Small fish rained from the sky for a few seconds, littering the deck with stunned, flopping creatures. They'd been siphoned up by the spout then released. Cassie pushed all the slippery stowaways she could reach over the side of the boat and back into the sea.

Payback curved around the edge of the spiraling winds, which allowed the crew to utilize the twister's remnants to slingshot the yacht to the north. Finally the strong Caribbean trade wind reasserted its usual force, sweeping in east by southeast. In the constant breeze, Doug said he was again able to lay a course for the north end of Grenada to keep *Payback* on a broad reach, its fastest point of sail. Checking aft, Cassie could see the spate of extreme weather had also hindered *Moby Dick*. The trawler had fallen well behind, but was doggedly following again. Cassie thought about what it would mean to be caught alive by Hunter and prayed.

✳   ✳   ✳   ✳

The chase continued in a seesaw manner over the next couple of hours. *Moby Dick* gained on *Payback*, but then the wind would temporarily increase, giving *Payback* the advantage. Grenada was in sight on the port beam. When Doug got closer to land, he saw breakers slamming into the rocky, windward coast. Spray soared high above the shore.

"Doug, do you know anyplace we could put Cassie ashore on our way past?"

"I doubt it, Nate. We're already past the midpoint of the island, and there's no harbor on this side. Unfortunately, there are coral reefs or high cliffs from here on. Maybe she could swim in on her own if we make it as far north as Isle de Ronde, up near Kick 'em Jenny."

"Forget it! I had enough rough swimming when I was on Dead Chest. You're not dumping me overboard anywhere. I'd rather take my chances sticking with you guys."

Doug sensed the wind decrease again as the afternoon progressed. The new GPS confirmed their speed had dropped significantly. Glancing back and seeing *Moby Dick* slowly closing the distance reinforced the bad news.

Under Doug's supervision, the crew worked on lightening the boat for better speed, throwing anything unnecessary overboard: dishes, food, the stereo, the empty propane tank, and the storm anchor. The house batteries made a big splash alongside. Nate even jettisoned the sodas and beer, but kept one bottle of rum. He humored Cassie when she insisted he punch holes in the cans so they'd sink to the deep seabed and not litter the beaches. Doug decided to save the clothes, the second propane tank, and the scuba gear.

"In the old days, we'd be dumping our cannons and livestock overboard at this point. What's the bottle of rum for?" asked Doug.

"For medicinal purposes."

"Yeah, we may need it one way or another."

Doug constantly trimmed the sails while adjusting the rigging. He checked and rechecked the GPS to see if each change helped or hurt their speed. Getting the weight out of the boat had helped a bit in the light winds. The skipper struggled to set the storm jib as a makeshift staysail, using the idle spinnaker halyard to hoist it. The forward bottom corner of the sail was tied to a windward cleat. Finally, he thought he'd done everything he could; yet the trawler was still creeping up. Doug had a hunch the coming confrontation would be the final one.

Payback sailed on past the Sandy and Green islets, then split the distance between Sugar Loaf and the arched rock formation called London Bridge. The yacht cleared the north end of Grenada. Once clear of the main island, the sloop was pushed sideways by a strong tidal current. Doug adjusted the course slightly westward, adding the current to his speed instead of fighting it. Unfortunately *Moby Dick* followed his lead. He had to come up with another advantage or trick.

"Nate! You and Cassie gather all of the docking lines, spare anchoring rodes and painters. Any line you can find that's not currently in use. Take the wire life lines out of the stanchions, too."

"Okay. What are we going to do with all the rope and wire?"

"Tie fenders, cushions, locker doors, or anything that floats on the ends of each piece of line. Then drop it all, one piece at a time, over the stern. Make a floating mess behind us. Maybe one line will get sucked into the stinkpot's propeller."

The crew completed a dozen of these entangling hazards and tossed them into the wake. Several clumped up, but many stretched out menacingly across the trawler's path in the way Doug envisioned. Doug figured the obstacles wouldn't work, but they couldn't hurt either. In any case, it was good to keep the crew active and hopeful.

Doug watched when *Moby Dick* approached the minefield of floating lines and wires. The pirates were alert enough to notice the traps, slow down, and go around each one. The trawler weaved and twisted, but was soon back on course to intercept the sailboat.

"Shit, that didn't work as well as I'd hoped."

"It's okay, Doug. At least you slowed them down. Every little bit helps," said Cassie.

Doug knew he was going to have to slow *Moby Dick* considerably more than a little bit. He consulted the chart and realized he would have to jibe soon or *Payback* would be sailing directly over the hot spot of the Kick 'em Jenny underwater volcano. Over the last twenty-four hours, *Payback* had circumnavigated Grenada. She was very close to where she'd been the day before.

"Do you feel lucky?" asked Doug.

"Lucky about what?" asked Nate.

"Unless I change course, we're going to be sailing right over the top of the underwater volcano we avoided yesterday. It'll cost us a bit of our slack if I go around it. Maybe Hunter won't follow us directly across. After Montserrat, I'll bet he's a little skittish regarding any volcano."

Nate and Doug watched Cassie. She was generally the cautious one. Doug already knew what his impetuous brother's vote would be.

Cassie swallowed, looked up, and softly said, "Go for it."

Doug wiggled the wheel to create a "snake wake" hoping it would alert Hunter that he needed to make a directional decision at that point. Then he steered straight for the hot spot. As *Payback* neared the danger zone, Doug didn't see anything unusual. No smooth patch in the waves appeared. He saw no gas bubbles rising—nothing to mark the volcano.

On the cockpit bench, Cassie softly recited a prayer while Nate needlessly checked and rechecked the loaded .410. Doug glanced aft at the enemy. Was more of the trawler's starboard bow showing than the port bow? Yes! The motorboat was turning.

"The punk's chickening out!" yelled Doug. "He'll charge right at a waterspout with us, but doesn't want to mess with a sleeping volcano again. Go figure."

"I guess it would've been too much to ask to have the bastard follow us, and then have the volcano erupt right under his butt after we passed," said Nate. "It definitely would've happened if this was a damn TV movie of the week!"

Cassie smiled slightly, but asked, "Are we safely past it yet?"

"No, but another couple of minutes should do it." Doug watched as *Moby Dick* turned aside and moved around to the south edge of the volcanic area. *Payback* had gained at least five minutes. Doug decided to jibe and turn to the northeast after clearing the danger zone. It would put the wind on his starboard quarter. More importantly, it would keep the volcano between the two boats, forcing the trawler to circle farther around the outside of the hot spot before continuing the chase.

"What's going on?" asked Cassie when Doug changed course.

"We're past the volcano so you can stop holding your breath. I'm putting it directly behind me and turning to gain another five minutes. Playing 'pig in the middle' with your old boyfriend. Maybe it's 'monkey in the middle.' Hell, I don't remember. Anyway, the point is that Hunter won't want to cut the corner straight across the volcano."

"Good idea, Admiral Rickover," said Nate.

The plan was working well, and the sailboat was in the lead by more than ten minutes, nearing The Sisters rocks, when the weather completely failed them. The wind died to a whisper. *Payback* coasted to less than a knot, rocking in the waves.

"Oh, shit! Now what do we do?" asked Nate?

"Damn! I guess we start the engine and hope the wind returns."

"But if it starts, you'll only get a couple of minutes before it overheats and locks up, Doug."

"Yeah, I know."

"A couple of minutes are better than nothing," added Cassie, in an apparent attempt to stay optimistic. "The wind will come back. I just know it."

"Hey," said Doug. "I've got an idea on how we might get five minutes or more out of the engine this time. By then, it'll shake right off the mounts or blow from all the other damage anyway."

"We'll wait and worry about that when it happens," said Cassie.

"What idea? We need something quick here, bro'."

"Okay. Cassie, do you have any nylons?" asked Doug.

"Sure, I've got a pair of pantyhose I bought days ago on Virgin Gorda. Obviously I haven't had a chance to use them. Are we going out for dinner and a movie tonight, honey?" She tried to stay in good spirits, but was worrying Doug was losing it under the strain.

"I wish. Seriously, I once read you can make an emergency fan belt from a nylon stocking. You and Nate run below and try it, and then I'll see if the engine will start. Okay?"

"You got it!" said Nate, rushing below with Cassie to try Doug's idea. Doug stayed topside tweaking everything he could to help *Payback* keep ghosting along through the water.

Less than a minute later, Cassie called, "Try it! We cut off one leg and tied it as tightly as we could."

Doug crossed his fingers and hit the starter button. It whined and chugged, but didn't catch. The second push produced a surprisingly strong start. He threw the throttle into forward gear, heading for Isle de Ronde at half speed, hoping to make the repair job last.

"It's still holding!" shouted Nate. "Well, blow me down, Popeye." Nate closed the engine compartment and scurried topside with Cassie.

Doug was amazed when the engine temperature alarm was still silent after two minutes. He sensed there was now more breeze, but suspected it was only because the motor was moving the boat faster through the water.

Checking astern, Doug saw *Moby Dick* approaching The Sisters rocks. The trawler was still gaining on them, although at a slower rate. He could make out the figure of a man with a rifle limping across the foredeck to the bow. *It must be Hunter*, he thought. The man raised his rifle and fired at extreme range.

The crew heard the shots and automatically ducked below the rail.

"Oh my God!" exclaimed Cassie. "This is it, isn't it? I guess we did our best. When the end comes, remember I love you guys."

"Stop it!" ordered Doug. "I'm not giving up and I'm not letting you give up, either. We keep fighting no matter what. Maybe we can make the beach on Isle de Ronde and hide ashore. There should be a few fishermen there. They might have guns we could borrow. Shit, I don't know. I'm not letting that bastard get you, Cassie. I'll tear out his throat with my bare hands if I have to!" But Doug knew there'd be no help on the small island ahead. The drug pirates would easily hunt them down ashore and kill any innocent witnesses as well.

Bullets slapped the sea behind the vessel, but caused little concern, yet. *Payback*'s crew stayed low while gazing aloft at the sails hoping to see the 'canvas' fill with wind. They also listened anxiously to the engine, waiting for sounds of a massive failure.

More shots rang out and a loud metallic "twang" sounded immediately above the cockpit. Doug glanced up and saw a lucky shot had severed the single backstay running from the stern to the top of the mast. He frantically spun the wheel to turn the boat into the remaining wind to ease pressure on the mast. He wasn't in time. The previously weakened and now poorly supported mast snapped in two and fell forward onto the pitching deck. The boom and mainsail hung over the side while the headsails collapsed across the bow.

"Goddamn it! Cassie, you steer!" yelled Doug. "Nate, clear away wreckage with your knife. I'll get the bolt cutters." Doug raced below to get the tool needed to cut the wire stays and shrouds. Nate and he desperately slashed and severed the rigging to detach the sharp, dangling wreckage before it could smash a hole in the hull or slow the vessel further. The brothers were able to save the storm jib and tie its head to the sharp stub of the mast. They grabbed the boom with the boat hook, hauled it aboard, and secured it to the deck.

"Hurry, they're getting closer!" cried Cassie.

Doug took the helm again while Nate returned fire with the .410 slugs. Doug was again amazed at his younger brother's calm demeanor in combat. He considered advancing the throttle from half to full speed, but rejected the idea given the engine's condition.

"I know the *Dick* might be out of range. I also know I can only get off one shot a minute with this thing, but I like taking any kind of action at this point. Makes me feel better. Hell, maybe it'll keep them off balance," said Nate as he carefully fired a second shot. He quickly unscrewed the shiny barrel to reload.

Without warning, a loud vibration came from below decks. It sounded like an unbalanced washing machine was jumping around in the engine compartment. Doug heard a metallic screech then the motor gave a final thump before seizing up. Even half speed had apparently been too much. Black smoke poured from the exhaust vent, streaming aft.

"Well, that's the end of our poor, old diesel," said Doug. Nate went below to see if he needed to utilize the fire extinguisher.

The boat coasted to what appeared to be a dead stop. Doug read the GPS screen showing *Payback*'s speed. He found the yacht moving at a half knot under the jury-rigged storm jib. He noticed this time no one bothered to ask him what to do next. Doug thought his depressed crew must realize he didn't have any more tricks up his sleeve.

Doug glanced at the chart and the GPS readout. He figured he was in deep water a half mile out from the small anchorage on Isle de Ronde. Kick 'em Jenny rock loomed a mile to the northeast. The chart indicated the bottom would soon rise to sixty or seventy feet deep slightly closer to the island. The water along the rocky shore was only a dozen feet deep, but he knew they wouldn't make it that far before *Moby Dick* rammed them or shot *Payback* to pieces.

Doug looked aft at the oncoming motorboat. His view was partially blocked by The Sisters rocks, which were temporarily in the line of sight between the two boats. Disturbed seabirds took wing, wheeled, and screeched their displeasure above the rocks. *It's too bad* Payback *can't fly away like the birds on The Sisters or as she did back on Antigua,* he thought. *This time we're trapped, and there's nowhere to hide. Or maybe there is.*

"Nate, what was the last title you gave me?"

"Let's see. It was Admiral Rickover, I think. He was a real mean, little son-of-a-bitch. Smart fellow, though. I met him once when he inspected our sub."

Cassie quizzically observed the brothers. "Why are you two discussing some dead admiral at this point? More gallows humor? She began praying softly again. again.

Doug ignored Cassie and concentrated. "He was a submarine admiral, right?"

"You're right. He spearheaded the program to build the *Nautilus*, the *Skate*, and the first missile subs."

"Okay, it gave me a new idea. I'm going to turn *Payback* into a submarine and then dive it."

"What?" Cassie and Nate said simultaneously.

"Yes! I'm going to open the through-hull seacocks and sink this boat with us in it."

"Are you crazy?" demanded Cassie.

"I'd rather die fighting than commit suicide," said Nate.

"No, we'll be okay! We have two sets of scuba tanks and maybe there'll still be a couple of air pockets. Nate and I are both certified scuba divers."

"Yeah, but remember me?" asked Cassie.

"We'll buddy-breathe and share the regulators with you. You can put your norkeling mask on. We also have waterproof flashlights. If we can make it a little closer to land, the bottom will be deep enough to hide us, but shallow enough so ve can stay at least thirty minutes without getting the bends. After Hunter leaves, 'll activate the yacht-saver airbags and raise the boat. It can work!"

"Shit, what's our alternative?" said Nate. "We can get shot here, or maybe swim to shore and get shot there. I'm willing to try. How about you, Cassie?"

The brothers faced Cassie. She slowly nodded her head in assent.

Nate shouted, "Dive! Dive! Aaaaoooogah! Aaaaoooogah!"

CHAPTER 28

▼

ISLE DE RONDE

"First we have to convince those pirates *Payback*'s in distress and sinking," said Doug.

"Oh, we're in plenty of distress! That's for sure," said Cassie as another lucky shot from *Moby Dick* pinged off the swim ladder.

"The engine is still smoking. I think a flashy explosion might convince Hunter he hit us and blew up the boat. Nate, reload the flare gun with a real flare this time. Be careful, it's our last one. I'm going to lock the wheel and get the extra can of gas we had for the dinghy. I'll add the propane tank that's almost empty and tie it all on top of a seat cushion then float the mess over the side. Cassie and I will duck below the rail then you shoot the gas can before it drifts too far away."

"Okay, I got it."

Doug glanced astern at the trawler and ahead at the island. He thought the water might now be shallow enough to put *Payback* on the bottom. If he waited any longer, the motorboat would be past the visual obstruction of the rocks between the vessels and Hunter would see exactly what Doug was doing. "Ready? Set? Go!"

Doug opened the valve on the propane tank, pushed the explosive raft into the wake, and shouted, "Duck!" Nate waited a bit, steadied his aim, and fired. There was a tremendous flash of flame. Doug felt the heat on his exposed skin. The crew tumbled below, closing the main hatch behind them.

Doug cursed, thinking he should've sent Cassie below earlier in case the explosion spread shrapnel. Fortunately, none of the three was hit. "Cassie, break out the scuba gear from under my berth." He watched her while she hustled off to fetch the items. Then he opened the smoky engine compartment and disconnected the raw water intake hose. A stream of saltwater shot up, causing steam to rise from the hot engine. Satisfied, he then moved on to the heads, pulling hoses and opening valves. Soon water was pouring into the bilges and over the floorboards.

"We should open a couple of top hatches to vent the boat," said Nate.

"Good idea, *Herr U-Boot Leutnant!* But do it slowly so they don't notice you." Doug heard another shot ricochet off a winch above. The enemy was closing in on them.

The water in the sailboat was at knee level. The brothers struggled to put on the scuba tanks and regulators. Cassie grabbed her facemask then got onto the dining table to stay out of the rising water. She threw her fins over on the navigation table.

Water rose to the brother's hips. The yacht was noticeably low in the water. The sailboat had stopped rocking in the waves due to all the new ballast. Their forward progress halted as the slight wind on the storm jib was no longer able to push the sluggish sinking vessel. Doug could only hope he'd reached water shallow enough for the crew's survival.

Two bullets zinged through the cabin roof, opening new vent holes over the galley and navigation table. Cassie screamed and jumped off the table to get lower. Water rose to their chests. *Payback* sank by the stern, raising her bow in the air. The seawater ran aft to fill the stern cabins first.

"Doug, why don't we sink the sailboat and then swim away underwater?"

"We shouldn't try it, Cassie. First, our air will last longer if we sit here instead of swimming around while waiting for Hunter to leave. Secondly, there's still a heck of a westerly current running around these rocks. Until the tide changes, I'm worried we'd get swept out into the open Caribbean instead of getting ashore. Finally, I'm not giving up my boat while there's still a chance of saving her."

Doug grabbed a handhold and stood on the tilting teak sole. He tested the regulator, taking a breath of air then exhaling. Doug pulled Cassie close and helped her put on her mask. He put the regulator in her mouth. He could see her relaxing as she found she could breathe easily prior to putting her head underwater. Doug gave her the okay sign with his circled fingers. He raised his eyebrow and she responded with the same hand sign.

Water rose to their necks. Cassie kept her head in the air pocket near the overhead. She took the regulator out of her mouth to speak. "I'm okay. We'll take turns when we need it," she said. "Do I use some of Nate's air, too?"

"You got it, Cassie. We'll all share," said Nate.

Water cascaded in through the overhead hatches. Nate pulled them down and dogged them. Trapped air was still whistling out through the cowling vents. *Payback* was not designed to be completely watertight from solid water above.

The three crewmates gazed through the clear hatches at the startling scene. Water swirled over the top of the boat. Soon they were staring through several feet of water, looking up toward the mirror-like surface of the ocean. The boat slid backwards toward the bottom for a few seconds before stabilizing to sink on an even keel. Glancing through the hatches and ports, they saw the light fading and the color turning to a darker blue as they sunk deeper and deeper. Doug held Cassie's hand and fought his strong urge to get out immediately and swim to the surface.

"Hey, Captain Doug. I guess you went down with your ship after all. Man, you've got to drop all this traditional salty shit you've been pulling!"

Doug saw Cassie also smiled at Nate's wisecrack.

They kept their heads in the small pocket of trapped air in the forward starboard corner of the main cabin so they could still communicate. The churning motor and propeller noise from the trawler got louder as the enemy vessel approached the floating debris at the site of *Payback*'s disappearance. Immediately, bullets came zipping into the water toward the sinking sailboat. Viewing the scene through the hatch, Doug could see their silvery trails reaching downward until they were spent.

"I hope to hell they don't have any grenades or dynamite. Don't make any loud noise that would let them know we're still alive," said Doug, turning on two of the waterproof flashlights to light the dark cabin. He figured their dim glow wouldn't mean anything to Hunter if he saw it. Most boats had various sealed waterproof lights.

Payback was still falling deeper into the sea. Doug worried he wasn't close enough to shore or if maybe the yacht slipped backward too far while it sank. He checked the depth readout on the scuba instrument pack. It read forty-five feet, fifty feet, fifty-five feet, and was still moving. If *Payback* got much deeper, the air wouldn't last long. Worse, the crew would have trouble with nitrogen narcosis—he dreaded "bends"—when coming up after too much of a delay on the seabed. There was a jolt as the keel hit bottom. The sailboat bounced a bit, and then came to rest on its port side, pointing slightly uphill.

"That wasn't the way we used to dive on my submarine, Doug. We're going to have to send you back to sub school."

"I'll get it right next time, boss. I promise." Doug listened to his boat scraping and sliding around on the bottom as the current moved the vessel. He didn't want to say anything, but worried *Payback* was slipping deeper. There was a significant lurch. The yacht caught on something and stopped moving. The bow rose a little more, and then all motion ceased. Doug shined his flashlight on his depth gauge: sixty feet.

Cassie stood on the settee to keep her head in the shrinking air pocket. She pushed floating items out of her way. The water was colder at this depth, and the crew already felt the chill. The three of them huddled closely together to conserve body heat.

Besides muffled gunshots, they heard what sounded like large raindrops hitting the cabin top and starboard side of the hull. "What the heck are those?" Cassie asked.

"Fish noises?" said Doug.

"No, Doug. I've heard biologics through sonar headphones before. It's not that." Nate paused, cocking his head. "I know. It's raining bullets! Those idiots up there are still shooting into the water. The bullets slow and stop, then drift down onto our boat. You can hear the rounds rolling down the deck and hull, too."

"You're right. Okay, I'm going to use a portion of my tank air to go reconnect hoses and close the seacocks so we're ready to surface and pump her out later. Everybody okay for a while?" Cassie and Nate nodded. Doug submerged to prepare the boat for possible resurrection.

＊   ＊   ＊   ＊

Cassie moved closer to Nate. "While he's gone, I want you to know I really do love him."

"Yeah, I know. He's my favorite brother, too."

"You're so funny. He's your only brother. Damn, this is scary! Keep talking to me. It keeps me from thinking about this too much. Hey, did you ever go through anything like this in training at submarine school?"

"Actually, I did. The overly modern wimps have removed it since then, but there used to be a 100-foot water tower called the escape tank-training tower at the New London, Connecticut, sub school. A bunch of us had to enter a separate airlock chamber off the bottom of the tank. Then the instructors flooded the entry chamber until the water was as high as it is here. Then they opened the door to the main tank. The air pocket in our chamber was compressed by the weight of the 100 feet of water in the tower. We took a breath and swam down through a hatch into the main column of water.

"As we swam up through the silo-shaped tower to the surface, we had to constantly let out air into our escape hoods by shouting 'ho, ho, ho' while we rose. The fabric hoods just kept our head in a bubble of air with a plastic window to look out of. It wasn't like breathing from a scuba tank. If you didn't follow instructions, the compressed air would expand as you rose and rupture your lungs with an air embolism."

"Did anyone ever die trying that?"

"Yeah, the Navy lost nine men over the years there."

"Oh, great! That's not too damn comforting, Nate. Weren't you scared?"

"Nah, just the first time. Then I wanted to do it again. Cassie, it shows you how we can swim out from here with no worries. We're only sixty feet deep, according to my gauge. If we rise while breathing with the tanks or riding in this air pocket, you'll breathe normally, and you'll be fine. No sweat, Cassie. You watch and see. The bad guys will be long gone, and we'll be okay."

Cassie wasn't convinced.

$$* \qquad * \qquad * \qquad *$$

Doug resurfaced to let them know he'd closed all the hull fittings. After a while, he noticed having to take bigger and more frequent breaths. "I think this air pocket is basically used up folks. I don't know about you, but I'm breathing harder and getting a headache. We're going to have to get on the tanks from here on."

"Yeah, it's the carbon dioxide building. The headache's the first symptom," said Nate.

"Okay, I'm going to get on the tank air. Let's all try to stay calm. Breathe slowly to make it last. I'll breathe twice then give Cassie two breaths. Then she can turn to you, Nate, to get two from your tank. Signal when you're only showing 500 pounds of pressure in your tank. I'm starting with less so I'll run low first anyway. Then I'll trigger the air bags, and we'll ride this boat to the surface."

The three kept their heads under the waterline, trying to relax while they shared the air from the two scuba tanks. Their exhalations rose to expand the air pocket with more stale air. The excess bubbled out from the sunken vessel and reached the surface.

Doug heard the trawler making passes above like a destroyer hunting a sub. The spinning screw noise would strengthen then fade. After a few passes, the sound decreased. After awhile, he didn't hear *Moby Dick* at all. Doug was pleased that the drug runners had given up and left. Maybe they were returning to Grenada to hire a diver to recover the drug canister they thought was still aboard *Payback*. Even with the pirates gone, Doug thought it was better to stick with the plan and wait until the air was nearly gone to ensure *Moby Dick* was well out of sight.

The sailors waited it out, trying to stay calm. Doug consciously tried to slow his breathing and heart rate. Cassie shared the brothers' regulators. It was hard to sit passively. Without wetsuits, the whole crew was losing body heat.

As expected, Doug ran low on air first. He signaled the others to rise for a quick conversation. They stood in the stale air pocket, but unless actually speaking, kept breathing from the tanks. Doug showed them his air gauge reading 500 pounds.

"Now what, Doug? We ready to surface?" asked Nate. He replaced his mouthpiece to listen for the answer.

Doug gave his regulator to Cassie and said, "I'm going to trigger the airbags. Stay in the middle of the cabin so you don't get in the way. Cross your fingers, and hope there's enough pressure in the activator cylinders to fill the bags at this depth." Doug stopped to take a breath off his regulator before continuing. "They weren't designed for this. If the boat doesn't rise, I guess we'll swim for it. If we have to do that, remember not to hold your breath as we rise. Maybe the current has turned toward the island by now."

Nate and Cassie nodded at Doug and moved away from the side of the hull. Doug regretted sharing his worries regarding the salvage bags inflating. *A skipper should keep such doubts to himself,* he thought. He swam into the deeper port aft cabin to pull the pin, triggering the first bag.

Doug heard the satisfying sound of the hissing cylinder filling the bag. He moved on to the other cabins activating all the bags before returning to Cassie and Nate. They rose into the pocket to talk again.

"That should do it. Just breathe normally through the regulators while we rise. If you sense fullness in your chest, push air out of your lungs into the water."

"Nate told me already. He says he did it without tanks from 100 feet once."

"He's the expert." Doug heard the bags stop hissing. He was disappointed when he noticed the red sausage-shaped bags weren't as full or firm as they'd appeared in the advertising brochure. The water pressure must be squeezing the bags too much. Would they still provide enough flotation?

The boat moved a little. Was it simply the current? He grabbed a handhold inside the cabin while shifting his weight back and forth. It might be wishful thinking, but maybe he'd help rock the yacht loose from any sea bottom suction. Nate noticed what he was doing then joined in.

Doug heard a scraping sound from the grounded side of the hull. The bow rose and the forward cabin's bags puffed and grew noticeably. Then the stern came up inflating the bags more and more with the decreasing depth. The boat was rising.

There was an abrupt jolt as if *Payback* had been grabbed from behind by a giant hand and yanked backwards. The bow continued to rise until the vessel was pointed nearly vertical, as it strained to reach the shimmering surface of the sea. Furniture and equipment broke loose and violently slid to the stern. The crew grabbed for something to hold onto while sliding objects tore past or fell on them. The two brothers each reached to snag hatch handles above. Then, in spite of sounds being muffled by the water, Doug heard a high-pitched scream.

He grabbed a flashlight and swam deeper in the main cabin. He soon found the navigation table had collapsed in the starboard aft corner. Doug remembered it'd been shot up and weakened in the first gun battle off St. Martin. Without warning, flailing arms in the dark water grabbed his legs and pulled him deeper. Hands reached for his face and ripped the regulator out of his mouth.

Trying not to panic, Doug shined the light at the area of the navigation table. There was Cassie. She was trapped with her leg under the collapsed table, which was wedged against the bulkhead. Cassie's hair floated above her head as she strained to pull loose. She'd jammed Doug's regulator in her mouth. He reached over her and tried to move the furniture. It wouldn't budge. His lungs burning, Doug hit the quick release on his tank harness belt and slipped out of his scuba gear. He left it all with Cassie then swam upward to find the air pocket.

With the steep angle on the boat, the air pocket had migrated to the extreme forward corner of Doug's cabin. He pushed Nate aside and surfaced in the pocket, gasping in the stale air. Nate followed him into the pocket and quickly pushed his own regulator into Doug's mouth before speaking.

"What's wrong? Where's Cassie...and where's your tank?"

"I had to give it to her," Doug panted. "She fell when the bow rose. Everything slid down on top of her. She's trapped by a table. There's only a few minutes of air left in that tank. We've got to free her!"

"I'll go with you, Doug. Don't worry. We'll get her out." The brothers swam down to Cassie. The men shared Nate's air tank as they strained and heaved at the collapsed furniture. It was no good. With the sloop hanging vertically, they couldn't get enough purchase to sufficiently push or pull. Doug tried to smile at Cassie to reassure her, but the eyes behind the facemask were wide with fear when the brothers turned to leave.

Surfacing in the bow pocket again, Doug said, "We can't do it. She's stuck and the boat's stuck on something, too. We could swim to the surface, but she'll drown down here if we do."

"If we can't get her loose, then we have to free the boat and let it finish rising. It's the only other way. Maybe *Payback*'s caught on an old anchor chain or a rock ledge," said Nate.

"You're right. Okay, your tank has more air left so you stay with her while I go check it out. Use up both tanks. If I need help I'll swim back and get you. I'll take your big knife. If I free the boat, I'll swim to the surface. I'll meet you there."

"No way, big brother. I should do it. I'm younger and I do all the underwater work." Nate started unbuckling his scuba gear.

"There's no time to argue or switch gear. Don't let her die! If I don't make it, tell her I love her." Doug took a deep breath off Nate's regulator, snatched Nate's diving knife off his leg, and swam aft into the main cabin. Passing Cassie, he gave her a thumbs-up sign when he moved through the companionway hatch.

Doug slid the main hatch open then kicked hard with his fins to get below the boat. Once there, he moved his head from side to side, trying to see enough through the facemask to discover what was wrong. His eyes adjusted to the lower level of light, Doug saw the boat was actually clear of the bottom, but there was a strange web all over *Payback*'s rudder and propeller.

Time was running out for Doug. He moved closer and saw it was a tangled mass of old, commercial fishing net. It would take several minutes to slice through it all, but he had seconds, not minutes. He glanced deeper, following the clump of net to its source. A single, thick line was wrapped around a huge rock ten feet below. If he could get there and cut it, he'd free the vessel from the sea-bed.

Doug realized he only had enough air for one attempt to cut the attaching rope then try for the surface. If he failed to cut it, he wouldn't be able to get all the way back into the sloop to get more air from Nate's tank. Did Nate and Cassie still have any air left to share at this point? Doug made his decision, dove for the bottom, and equalized the pressure by pinching his nose and blowing air into the passages to his ears.

The marine growth encrusted on the net's attaching line made it difficult for Doug to cut. He sawed away with the knife, getting through half of it. His lung demanded air, but he kept at it. When the line had only a third of its original thickness left, the pull of the now-buoyant sailboat proved too much for the old polypropylene rope. It snapped. Doug barely avoided having his arm severed as the sharp, stretched line whipped past.

Doug kicked hard for the surface. His lungs burned from lack of oxygen, yet they now had an expanded, full sensation. Doug remembered to let a portion of the stale air out, easing the pain. He burst up through the sparkling surface of the ocean. The sailboat was rising, building speed and momentum as it ascended.

Doug's head rose high above the water due to the speed of his ascent. He fell back gasping, both for air and from the shock of what he'd just seen—*Moby Dick* was still there! The trawler was quietly anchored right over *Payback*'s supposed "grave." Hunter apparently decided to take no chances at all. Maybe he planned to have a diver come straight out to the site of the sinking.

Doug treaded water and looked around to see where *Payback* surfaced. He determined to swim to the sailboat, wherever it appeared, so he could defend his woman, his brother, and his boat. Doug still had Nate's diving knife gripped tightly in his teeth. Maybe Hunter was celebrating and wouldn't notice the approach of a lone swimmer.

*   *   *   *

The sailing yacht surfaced just seconds after Doug did, but in a more spectacular manner. The momentum of the entire 23,000 pounds of the swiftly rising sloop focused at the sharp end of the single shattered mast. The vessel came up directly under *Moby Dick*. The mast, acting as a giant spear, punched through the trawler's bottom, through the starboard head, and up into the wheelhouse.

"Jesus!" Hunter frantically jumped aside when the jagged carbon fiber mast magically sprouted from the deck and sliced open his right forearm. *Moby Dick* rose up from the force of the impact and splashed back to ride higher than before. Unearthly screams erupted below. Hunter limped down to investigate. He determined the noise was coming from the head.

"Help! *Madre de Dios*! Help me!" screamed Sanchez from inside.

Hunter pulled open the door then stood with his mouth agape at the horrifying scene. The mast had smashed the sink and skewered Sanchez's torso like a martini olive on a toothpick. Blood covered the walls, yet the impaled man was still alive and flailing about.

Hunter recovered to say, "I can't do a damn thing for you, bud. Sorry." He slammed the door shut then climbed the stairs. Abruptly, *Moby Dick* tilted over to lay its starboard side in the water. The sea poured over the rail into the trawler while Hunter desperately pulled and crawled upward.

*   *   *   *

Doug watched in astonishment when *Payback* surfaced under *Moby Dick* and fell back underwater. He suddenly realized Nate and Cassie were still submerged beneath the trawler. Doug swam toward the boats at top speed. As he approached, the weight of the motorboat tipped both boats over on their sides.

The side of *Payback* was visible above the surface, but it was still connected to the sinking *Moby Dick* like two chickens on a barbecue spit. Doug reached the sloop, scrambled over the lifelines, and moved forward.

"Cassie! Nate! Where are you?"

Just then, the waves succeeded in pushing the sailboat to the rear, away from the anchored heavy motorboat. As the vessels groaned and separated, the mast slipped out, widening the hole as the spar tore its way free. Both boats popped up to float on even keels, but very low in the water. The top of the mast was coated with blood and tissue.

Doug fell against a stanchion when the sloop rolled upright. He lost his knife over the side, but held onto the boat, and then fought his way to the main hatch. Water cascaded off the deck and poured out of the cockpit scuppers. *Payback* rose higher, while the nearby *Moby Dick* sank lower, and then rolled on its side toward the sailboat. The sinking trawler rolled over again in the waves and became wrapped inside the old net that had risen with *Payback*, snaring both vessels.

"We're down here! Help me with her!" shouted Nate from below.

Doug hurried through the waist-high water to find Nate supporting Cassie's head above the wreckage and seawater in the cabin. There was a cut on the side of her head. She was groggy, but alive. Doug was overjoyed until he remembered she remained trapped by the wreckage. She'd still drown if *Payback* sank.

Doug struggled back to the cockpit locker to find the handle for the manual bilge pump. Using the steel pipe as a crowbar, he levered the jammed table. Nate and Doug braced firmly against the bulkhead and finally pried and pulled the wreckage far enough away from Cassie's leg to free her.

Supporting Cassie between them, the brothers staggered up the ladder into the newly drained cockpit. Doug stuck the pump handle into the receptacle under the helmsman's seat and then pumped vigorously. A stream of water spurted from the side of the yacht. Pumping *Payback* dry would be a long process under the broiling tropic sun.

Nate put Cassie on the bench seat. He walked to the stern to take over from Doug. "I'll do that. The air bags are fully inflated so we'll be okay if you get us clear of that trawler. What was holding us down on the bottom anyway?"

"An old fishing net. It's still tangled around our useless propeller. The other end was snagged on the rocks. I had to cut it loose."

"Yeah, but your plan worked. We had enough air to make it to the surface, although we got banged around a bit. Looks like *Moby Dick*'s still here, though."

"Yeah, believe it or not, *Payback* came up right under the stinkpot and punctured *Moby Dick* with our broken mast. Then both boats rolled over until the stub worked loose. I'll have to jury-rig a sail using the boom for a replacement mast, I guess. Anyway, I saw the whole thing. It was amazing! The damn trawler is done for. It's definitely sinking."

"Hot damn!" said Nate. "We were a submarine dealing death from beneath the waves. I love it! You are hereby promoted to Grand Admiral Dönitz, head of all the U-boats."

"Lucky me. Remember? His side lost. Hey, how come we haven't drifted away from our 'torpedoed' victim yet? Oh, shit!" said Doug, glancing over the side. "We're still attached to the big net and the trawler has rolled over into it."

"We caught the great *Moby Dick* in a net?"

"Yes, but when the pirates go to the bottom, they'll drag us down with them!" The brothers went over the side with galley knives and swiftly sliced and hacked away their end of the net. Being sure to stay clear of the stretched web, Doug cut the last strand. The severed net rebounded to wrap more tightly around the crippled *Moby Dick* as the boats separated. The men didn't see any survivors from the trawler.

The sailors scrambled back up the swim ladder. The stationary sailboat was still very low in the water. Doug was gratified to see Cassie sitting and alert. Doug salvaged a wet lifejacket and put it on her for warmth and safety.

"Doug, look at this!" said Nate. "The big stinkpot is drifting back towards us. They must be dragging their anchor or swinging."

Doug untied the boat hook. He prepared to fend off the trawler as his crew watched. Before the two vessels' sides met, the trawler rolled over again, exposing its keel to the wind. The three sailors were shocked to see a body hanging in the netting at the waterline, and spread-eagled on the side of the white hull.

"It's Hunter!" said Cassie.

"So the psycho's finally dead," said Nate. "Time to crack open that bottle of rum I saved in the booze locker."

Hunter opened his eyes. He raised his head above the water to stare directly at Cassie. His leg with the wooden support was twisted at an unnatural angle and blood oozed from the wound in his arm. He shifted his gaze to Doug, and yelled, "See you in Hell, asshole!"

"You're going there first!" responded Doug, jabbing Hunter with the blunt tip of the boat hook. Pushed beyond mercy or moderation, Doug twisted the pole, snagging its curved arm on Hunter's clothes. Putting his weight on the boat hook to hold Hunter below the water. Doug shouted, "Why don't you just die, you bastard?"

Hunter desperately grabbed the boat hook with his good arm and tried to pull it away from Doug. Bubbles escaped from Hunter's mouth. *Moby Dick* ended the men's struggle by rolling one last time, dragging Hunter farther under the waves. The motorboat's bow rose in the air briefly before smoothly sliding down and backward. Still holding the pole like a harpoon, Doug glared fiercely at his nemesis until the trawler slipped completely beneath the waves.

EPILOGUE

▼

ATLANTIC OCEAN

The pontoon boat *Scuby Do* left Tortola loaded with a group of eager divers on a package tour. Most of the tourists were from the Cincinnati area. The vessel tied up to a park-service buoy over the R.M.S. *Rhone*. As the divers went into the water, the divemaster reminded them to stick with the group and not get lost.

One diver, a surgeon from Butler County, decided to ignore the advice. Alone, he swam past the bow of the wreck and out into the scattered debris field where divers rarely ventured. Glancing down, he spotted a white canister caught between a rock and an encrusted metal plate from the wreck.

The doctor brushed the sand aside. He saw ropes holding the clamshell container closed. He pulled on the ropes, but was unable to free the jammed container. The diver pulled his knife from its leg sheath then stuck the tip of the knife into the seam between the two halves. He twisted the knife, but the canister wouldn't crack open.

Finally, the doctor, holding the knife like a scalpel, stuck the blade fully into one end of the sealed joint then worked it all the way around, cutting the ropes, and unknowingly slitting the bags inside. The top half of the canister floated open. A white cloud mixed with the seawater and swirled away in the current. The diver grabbed at the powder, but it slipped through his fingers. And faded away like the lives of the men who so badly wanted to possess it.

*   *   *   *

Cassie Thompson held on to her husband's belt as he leaned over the lifelines. It was noon, and he was trying to "shoot" the sun with his new sextant.

"Got it!" said Doug. "This should give us a good position fix showing the boat a lot closer to the Azores. We're more than halfway to Europe at this point."

"Aren't you glad you took the course?"

"Yeah, I had to do something while the boatyard on Trinidad was fixing up poor old *Payback*. Can you believe the damn insurance company tried to say they didn't cover damage from terrorists? The money you withdrew from your account was a big help. By the way, I'm having a portion of my own funds wired from the States to a bank in London. So I'll pay you back soon."

"You don't have to pay me back, silly boy. It's all *our* money now, not mine or yours. Remember the pastor on Barbados said it was 'for richer or poorer.' Your friend, the ambassador, was there, too, so I've got a great witness. I must say a brand new passport, in my married name no less, was quite an unusual and impressive wedding gift."

"Okay, you win. How was I to know I'd end up with a wealthy wife? It was quite a surprise when we found out Leo had deposited such a generous gift for you in that bank account. Nate's girls are going to appreciate the college fund we set up for them."

"I hope he'll get to see his daughters more. At least he said his job at the desalinization plant is going well."

"You know, it was tough to leave Nate behind after all our excitement. It still seems kind of strange for the two of us to be sailing *Payback* without him."

"Nate said he'd had enough sailing to last him for quite awhile, sweetheart."

Doug smiled then went below to stow the sextant in its bin forward of the dining table. He ran his hands over the bottom of the bin, making sure the secret compartment below was still well secured. Along with his shotgun, there was a new Barrett .50-caliber sniper rifle with tremendous long-range capability hidden underneath. The Barrett was deadly accurate at more than 1,000 yards and powerful enough to shoot right through a car's engine block.

Doug came topside to rejoin his wife. "With good luck, this weather will hold so we'll make another day of great progress tomorrow."

"Don't worry. I'm positive we'll have good luck for the rest of this voyage," said Cassie, brushing back her long, silky hair.

"What makes you so positive? Didn't Nate warn us a woman is bad luck on a boat except when you display a topless woman to calm a storm?"

"Sure, sailor boy. But there's one other exception. Remember?"

Doug's brow furrowed. Then his jaw dropped. "Do you mean what I think you mean?"

"Yes, darling. I'm pregnant."

*   *   *   *

The End

978-0-595-3840:

0-595-38402-

Made in the USA
Lexington, KY
15 June 2011